W9-CND-333

CARTER CLAY

ALSO BY ELIZABETH EVANS

Locomotion

The Blue Hour

CARTER CLAY

A NOVEL BY

Elizabeth Evans

HarperFlamingo
An Imprint of HarperCollins*Publishers*

Grateful acknowledgment is made for use of the lyrics from the song "Cherish" on page 64. "Cherish" words and music by Terry Kirkman © 1965, 1966 (Renewed 1993, 1994) Beechwood Music Corp. All Rights Reserved. International Copyright Secured. Used by permission.

HarperCollins books may be purchased for educational, business, or sales promotional use. For information please write: Special Markets Department, HarperCollins Publishers, Inc., 10 East 53rd Street, New York, NY 10022.

FIRST EDITION

Designed by Alma Orenstein

Library of Congress Cataloging-in-Publication Data

Evans, Elizabeth, 1951–
Carter Clay : a novel / Elizabeth Evans. — 1st ed.
p. cm.
ISBN 0-06-019265-8
1. Vietnamese Conflict, 1961–1975—Veterans—Fiction. I. Title.
PS3555.V2152C37 1999
813'.54—dc21 98-30756

99 00 01 02 03 ❖/RRD 10 9 8 7 6 5 4 3 2 1

For Jesse and Nora,
forever and ever

Thanks to my editor, Robert Jones; my agent, Lisa Bankoff; friends Maud Casey, Robb Forman Dew, Margot Parlette, Joy Williams, and Bonnie ZoBell; Rhoda Sokal of Bridges; MacDowell Colony, Ucross Foundation, Arizona Commission on the Arts; and especially—as always—Steve Reitz.

One cannot be a man in a generalized sort of way.

—*The Faith of the Church*

Prologue

This is before the accident. No one is dead yet. Blood circulates just as it should, two ounces per pump of the heart. Watch the man who stands on this piece of Florida roadside. Watch for the scarcely visible tick in that vulnerable inch of neck just inside the open collar of his blue shirt. You know the location of that inch of neck—his neck, our necks—the spot to which hands might fly at an unexpected noise or tap on the shoulder.

The man is lost, and so he scowls a little as he stares out at the Florida grasslands and the grand steers that feed there. Aberdeen Angus. Beef cattle. Black. Hornless.

If you do not believe in accidents, if you hold everyone responsible for everything, then the events that follow will appear tidier but more hideous. God is let off the hook then, yes?—if, after all, God is to be allowed? Some sort of God? Perhaps responsible for no more than these props, this setting?

What a white, white ache of sky! Beneath it, the primary-green grasslands go to chartreuse as the man's view/our view contracts, and we move closer, closer still to the ditch at his feet. The ditch—a halvah swirl of sand and broken shells—has been quite recently ripped open by the yellow earthmoving equipment parked on its banks. Ancient monsters, dinosaurs; of course, that is what the pieces of equipment resemble, snouts down, as if the great beasts feed. But this is Florida, 1993. Any sediment on which a dinosaur might once have walked now lies buried thousands and thousands of feet beneath our man.

Joseph Alitz. Professor. Fifty-seven years old. Paleontologist at a respected southwestern institution. Dr. Alitz. Basically a good man. Joe. Caught just now in this sour moment of his life.

On his head, Joe wears a red canvas hat, its brim turned up like that on the hat of a sailor. The hat belongs to his widowed mother-in-law, Marybelle Milhause, aka M.B., who is the reason for Joe's trip to Florida. Taken together with Joe's shoulder-length hair and careful beard, M.B.'s red hat gives Joe a somewhat fantastical look. He might be the king of diamonds in the deck of cards that—just now, back at her pink stucco condominium—M.B. lays down in one of her perpetual games of solitaire. *Sip, sip, sip* go the cards as M.B. pulls a trio from the pile in her hand, gives the top card a steely inspection through the enormous designer eyeglasses that transform her otherwise human face into the mug of Jiminy Cricket.

How many miles is it to M.B.'s retirement condo from the roadside where Joe stands? Suppose Joe could calculate the distance. Would it help him find his way back?

No. Knowledge of distance is no substitute for direction. Uselessly, Joe scans the useless horizon, then glances to his left. There, just a few feet away, stand his adolescent daughter and his wife—the latter, Katherine Milhause, Joe's former student, now a paleontologist in her own right. Mother and daughter share a pair of binoculars through which they study certain large birds that weave in and out between the feet of the Angus.

Perhaps it would be better—more accurate—to say that Katherine is the reason for the Florida trip: a visit to her mother. Without doubt, Katherine is the reason for the Christian radio program that booms through the open door of the family's rental car:

"Devil's bigger than you, friends, and you all know what happens when you get in a fistfight with a fellow what's bigger than you, now, don't you? You get beat up! That's right! You get the stuffing knocked out of you, now, don't you?"

Earlier in the afternoon, after tuning the radio to this particular program, Katherine gave Joe a light punch in the shoulder and grinned. Back then, broccoli-green trees still pressed close to the road, and the rental car took the family past the occasional rickety tricks of wood and tar paper that certain Floridians had no choice but to call home. Back then, Joe had not yet admitted that the family had driven down the wrong road, and Katherine was laughing about the radio show, and saying, "One thing you have to admit about these shows, Joe; they may parade self-righteousness as humility, but at least they talk about things of consequence!" At the time, poor Joe was preoccupied with finding signs of their location and did not point out that Katherine made much ado about covering her ears whenever M.B. listened to the very same program back at the pink condominium. Poor Joe did not know then—he will never know—that when he left Arles' Mineral Springs, he took the wrong turn. Yes, at the time that the poodle-faced clerk at Arles' Mineral Springs gave Joe directions, she was mentally reviewing the contents of the patio's vending machine—which chips should she buy on her break?—and so, with no malice intended, the clerk told Joe *left* when she should have said *right*.

To clarify Joe's appearance, let us add that as he stands on the Florida roadside his present worries make him appear a worn king of diamonds. A face card once stashed in a back pocket against an emergency, then forgotten and sent through the washer, and the dryer, too.

Joe could have stopped a half an hour ago to ask directions at the occasional store or café they passed. He has known for at least that long that they travel the wrong road. But Joe is a man who prefers to solve his own problems.

Now, as he stands on the shoulder of the road—Post Road, its name, though Joe does not know this—Joe wrestles open a map purchased that morning at the Exxon station in Bradenton. The crack and explosion of crisp paper drive his wife and daughter back a step. A bright, bright yellow map. On certain panels it holds colorful graphs and drawings and photos: Ponce de Leon and the Fountain of Youth; sprays of orange blossoms; distances from here to there; portrait of the state's smiling governor who, owing to the printer's poor color-processing, appears to have just quaffed a mug of clotted blood.

Perhaps it would be more pleasant to focus on the birds that Katherine Milhause inspects through the binoculars?

"Are they some kind of vulture?" asks her daughter.

Katherine laughs kindly. Though she wears a soft bun, long skirt, silver hoops in her ears, she bears a superficial resemblance to her husband. Sinewy forearms, sun-bleached hair, skin flecked like granite (pink, ocher, white) from a working life often spent out-of-doors. "Not *vultures*, sweetie," Katherine tells the girl, "cattle egrets." Then flips open the bird book in her hand to Vultures, and explains that vultures would surely be found as handsome as eagles but for their lack of head feathers. Small, mean, an infected red; that is, indeed, how the featherless heads of the turkey vultures appear in Katherine's bird book.

"Lack of feathers protects them," Katherine explains. She and Joe are forever offering their daughter—Jersey, age twelve, long hair the color of unsalted butter—information about the natural world. Hoping that a store of such delights will inoculate her against life's ruder aspects. It may be, of course, that it is these heaps of information that have caused that slight rounding of the girl's shoulders. Or perhaps she is merely self-conscious about her height, the jutting knees and elbows of adolescence. She bites her nails. See how her poor fingertips resemble baby mice.

"Being featherless makes their heads less accommodating hosts to the parasites on carrion, you see?" Katherine explains.

Katherine cannot know, of course not, that later in the day several vultures *will* arrive in just this spot, circling down in their mossy undertakers' coats. When the ambulances finally arrive—summoned by a sobbing caller who, ironically, will find the first available telephone at Arles' Mineral Springs—a vulture identical to the one in Katherine's book will be engaged in an exploratory stroll across poor Joe's back. Distraught, the lead ambulance driver will run toward the bird and scream, "Get off, you fuck!" as the great wings rise with a horrible soft sucking flap. "*Get!*"

Now, however, the landscape is quiet. The cattle egrets feed on bugs roused by the movements of the steers. They dart so close to the ponderous hooves that Katherine calls, "Look out, birds!"—then laughs at herself.

"Did I ever tell you about playing 'Castro,' Joe?" Katherine erects a smile meant to show Joe that she does not worry over their being lost. Twice in the last twenty minutes—three times?—she has assured him in a wife's consoling tones that to be lost on an American roadway today means that one is only a short distance from being found.

"Remember the dunes I showed you in Indiana? That was Cuba." Katherine bends to pick up a shell, something turned over by the big pieces of earth moving equipment. Sand—impossibly fine, tan, silver—falls from the shell in a sugary sweep as Katherine runs her finger around its interior. "We'd run up and down the dunes for hours, pretending Castro chased us!" She smiles. "*Pelecypod*," she says, and hands the fossil shell to Jersey, who gives the thing a dutiful if slightly bored glance before sticking it in her pants pocket.

Katherine laughs. "Remember the Cuban missile crisis, Joe? They made us pray. At school, they made us put our heads down on our desks and pray."

Later—a blessing?—Jersey will remember nothing of standing on this road or the accident. She will know only that at some point during the drive she broke off her coloring of Plate 11 in *The Human Evolution Coloring Book.* Before the trip to Florida began, when the family was still at home in Arizona, Jersey's parents assigned her the completion of one plate a day. Plate 11 featured small illustrations of human, monkey, pig, chicken, and salamander at various stages between, and including, fertilized egg and full-formed adult. "Limb buds appear" was the stage at which Jersey stopped coloring, and, after the accident, every now and then, an image of Plate 11 will swim up alongside the girl to suggest that it holds some explanation—then disappear into dark unreason, like a water snake disappearing into the flick of its tail.

Though her intelligence and powers of memory have often been remarked upon during her relatively short life, Jersey will not be able to recall why she and her parents traveled on Post Road. She will forget the morning's trip to Arles' Mineral Springs—though it was, in fact, she who discovered the spa's laughable brochure (a Pleistocene mammoth smiles as it takes a drink at the Springs; a masseuse works on a client whose arms are larger at the wrist than at the elbow).

Bubulcus ibis reads the bird book now held open in Jersey's hand. Cattle egret. An Old World species. U.S. presence established in 1952 when a Mr. Richard Borden unknowingly captured the birds in footage he shot at Florida's Eagle Bay Ranch.

Joe squints at his useless map. Though he understood even before opening the thing that its scale was entirely wrong for the present problem, he had hopes. Now he looks out at the cattle once more and says in a bitter voice, "Florida's dying, only everyone's so busy filling up oranges and swimming pools with the Everglades, they hardly notice."

At this, Katherine laughs again and moves close to Joe to give him a little sideways hug. Because Joe's sentences do delight her. And because she wants him to know that, of course, of course, she sides with him against pink retirement condos built on the backs of alligators. Also, in siding with Joe on this, by extension, she sides with him against her mother, M.B., who has driven Joe to distraction since the start of this Florida visit—and, truth be told, never liked Joe anyway.

Another reason for Katherine's laughter: she hopes to diffuse whatever unpleasantness might arise from Joe's shame at their being lost.

"Look!" Noting her father's moroseness, knowing her mother's potential for being dragged into a depression by such moroseness, Jersey offers a distraction: drops down in the sand to point at the fat black bug that ever so delicately picks its way up a clump of sand. "Remember in the Everglades when we saw those orange grasshoppers? At first I thought they were something a little kid had dropped, like the prize from a Happy Meal!"

Joe and Katherine smile and nod. They adore this daughter of theirs—so much so that, on occasion, Jersey must seek shelter from the hot light of their devotion. If only, just now, Jersey were to turn away from her parents' approving smiles—if any *one* of the trio were to train that very fine pair of birding binoculars down the road—well, that might save the day. He or she would see the battered van that approaches, and how it weaves back and forth there, raising a cloud of dust as its tires skip off the asphalt and bite into the gritty shoulder.

When Jersey stands once more, Katherine rests her cheek upon the girl's silky head. Katherine closes her eyes, and says in a dreamy voice, "When I first moved to the Southwest, I thought it was like the moon. All the rocks! Then I realized that it was just—like itself, a part of the planet. And I liked the way the rocks and mountains reminded me: I live on a planet in the solar system in the Milky Way in the universe."

At this, Joe laughs. Because Katherine has reminded him of that earnest midwestern student who actually took notes when he first invited her out for cups of coffee. Happy times, those days, and because he would like Katherine to think of them, too, Joe says—using the name she long ago penned at the top of her class work—"But, Kitty, where on earth could you have imagined you lived before that?"

How Joe flushes when Katherine pivots her pained face his way! For he too has registered that his question sounded not like that of a fond and reminiscing husband but, instead, like a trick quiz got up by a parody of himself, some Professor Higgins, voice all plumed and wry.

This is not the first time that Joe Alitz has had such a moment. We all have our share of such moments. Crabbed by a failure of character, our fondness balks, and a remark that we hoped to adorn with wit, we infect instead with derision. Then comes the silence, the burning cheeks.

Joe Alitz would not want to be remembered for such a moment; of course not. Still, it is somehow sad that no one will remember the moment, or know that the last words that Joe ever spoke failed to convey anything at all of what it was he meant to say.

Part One

1

Whenever M.B. Milhause has found herself in a group in which people trade stories of their lives' most dramatic moments—such stories used to arise often in the box-cramped room where M.B. and her work chums took coffee breaks, and M.B. still hears them at the hairdresser, at the doctor's office—at such times, M.B. has always trotted out her Ferris wheel story.

In the late 1940s, M.B. told her Ferris wheel story with shivers, all the while hugging at her skinny arms. Back then, she was the youngest girl working a Marshall Field's makeup counter, and while she told her tale she shook her head back and forth, auburn pageboy whipping across her face à la Barbara Stanwyck and Bette Davis: "Oh, kid," she said, "I was *scared!*" In the fifties, her delivery became languorous—perhaps an effect of the more elegant look she took on when she married Lorne Milhause and Field gave her Elizabeth Arden. In the late sixties, M.B. cut her hair short and tried to quit smoking and ran the less chic but much larger Revlon unit. The Ferris wheel story grew zippy. In 1982, Field eased her out. That was when the story turned grim. That was when M.B. began to use the recent death of her mother as a lead-in. Sometimes, after she finished, she felt that she had tainted her mother's memory, and she had to leave the room.

Why'd I tell that old thing again? she would wonder. Really, she never felt that she got the story right. Really, at least half of the importance of the story lay in her memory of the stars that night—whirlpools of color, though surely some of the color had come from the lights of the Ferris wheel.

M.B.'s Ferris wheel story involved a night in her childhood—back when M.B. was still "Marybelle." Marybelle and her brother, Dicky, and their mother and father were finishing a tiresome visit to relatives in Miles City. On their way back to Sheridan, for miles and miles, the children watched a brightly lit Ferris wheel slip tantalizingly in and out from behind Wyoming's late-night hills and buttes. *Couldn't they stop? Please, couldn't they stop if they passed it?* Marybelle and Dicky were terrified that the Ferris wheel actually sat on a road other than the one they were driving on, or that it would be closed before they arrived; indeed, by the time their father finally pulled off onto the bumpy bit of rangeland where the thing sat, the operators—two men living out of a trailer—were about to shut down for the night.

Marybelle's mother—a tiny woman; slap of a red birthmark on one cheek—would later lament: "*We shouldn't never have got on that ride. I smelled the alcohol on that fellow's breath! What was I thinking?*" But the ride was lovely at the start—the red and blue lights, the stars, the music, the warm breath of summer air that played over Marybelle's bare legs and arms. She wanted the ride to go on and on, never end. But then, when it *did* go on and on, the fun began to drain away because, somehow, she knew that such pleasures ought not to last so long that a person began to wonder: *how long can a pleasure last before it stops being a pleasure?*

Even then, Marybelle was good at pretending, and for quite a while she acted as if she had not noticed that her mother had turned around in the gondola that the two of them shared. Eventually, however, Marybelle's mother poked her, and demanded, "What's Dad saying?" and so Marybelle had to turn and look, too.

In the gondola at her back—their faces both lurid and shadowed with lights and fear—Marybelle's father and Dicky shouted words that could not be heard over the Ferris wheel's music and machinery; still, it was clear that the pair made gestures toward the ground.

What was it?

Because of the dark, and the thick growth of sage, Marybelle and her mother required several revolutions of the machine before they spied the white socks of the Ferris wheel operator, and understood that he lay in the brush, knocked there by one of the gondolas.

"Hey!" they shouted. "Help!"

Though visible through the window of the trailer, the other operator did not hear their cries, and later, when she was grown up and told her Ferris wheel story, M.B. always said, "Who knows what would've happened if some joyriders hadn't come along and stopped?" She imagined her family going up in flames, ignited by the Ferris wheel's constant turning. She imagined them hurtling off into outer space. Or the Ferris wheel tearing away from its bonds, rolling across the hills of Wyoming, faster and faster, taking the family toward the crash of death—

None of M.B.'s versions of the Ferris wheel story mentioned how the joyriders laughed when the ride was finally brought to a stop, and Marybelle and her mother had to hustle straight to their own automobile because, in her fright, Marybelle had wet the seat of the gondola, and both her own skirt and her mother's were soggy across the back. That was M.B.'s secret; and besides, it always turned out that her audience was scarcely interested in M.B.'s role in the story. What people really wanted to know was: Did the operator die? Recover?

When she first began telling the story, M.B. answered truthfully: she did not know. She did not even remember the man's being retrieved from the brush. She remembered only her sense that she and her family had been saved from death, and that she had been embarrassed by her wet skirt. In time, however, she came to see how her audiences' needs shaped their response to her tale, and when people asked, "What about the operator?" she learned to answer, almost as if surprised, "Why, he was killed *instantly*, of course."

M.B. is now sixty-three. She cannot recall when she stopped caring about the Ferris wheel story, but she is very much aware that for the past two years she has offered it up only as a means of *not* telling anyone how, on what was to have been her and Lorne's first morning in their Palm Gate Village condominium, she had reached across to Lorne from her side of the bed and found the cold and rigid object that sent her running up and down the second-floor balcony, calling, "*Anybody! Help, please! Anybody!*"

▪ ▪ ▪

"And just think: you wouldn't have needed to be at all afraid if you'd truly been walking with the Lord back then!"

So said the smiling little organist from Vineyard Christian—no more than four days ago—when M.B. told her the Ferris wheel story. And why did M.B. tell it, then? Was there a lull in the social hall conversation?

▪ ▪ ▪

No matter.

Today, M.B. is empty of any story at all. *Oh* is the only word M.B. knows today, and here, in the silent hospital room assigned her granddaughter—what will M.B. do if the girl wakes and asks for her parents?—M.B. does not allow herself even to form the word with her lips, let alone make its sound: *oh*.

Across the hall, in that bright box of a room that houses M.B.'s daughter, Kitty, it is all tap and rattle, the whir and the suck and gurgle and murmur and the babble and the click of those well-meaning brutes (metal boxes, drip lines, lengths of black hose, plastic tube, wires) that monitor and drain and sustain what remains of Kitty since she was thrown some fifty feet and her skull slammed into the asphalt of Post Road.

Here, the relative quiet presses its hand across M.B.'s mouth. Here, each breath that comes from the gray, bandaged girl in her slab of bed—each and every breath must be heard, registered, attended to by M.B. so that the next may come. This is all that M.B. knows. Here, where the only windows are walls of glass that open onto the glare of the nurses' station, it is eternally twilight, and M.B. does not even understand that morning has come again until she sees the aide motion to her from the other side of the window.

A tiny woman with fuchsia lipstick and almost matching hair, the aide holds up a rumpled doughnut and a cardboard carton of orange juice. "Breakfast?" the aide mouths, then smiles in sympathy as she taps her wristwatch to indicate that M.B.'s fifteen-minute visit is almost up.

Morning again? *Yesterday* morning—M.B. does remember that indigestible clump of time because yesterday morning certain people led her out of this building and into the bright day and then into a smaller building where she was asked to look at the body of her son-in-law. Yes. *Yes* is what M.B. had to say. Then she walked back to the first building to listen to doctors and meet with the mortician, talk casket, plot, flowers. She could not do that now: talk. Even last night, when silver-haired Pastor Bitner of Vineyard Christian came by to speak of accepting God's will, and of her son-in-law's meeting with Jesus and Lorne and his other loved ones in heaven, *rest your mind on that, Marybelle*, even then, M.B. felt herself falling, and Pastor Bitner's sentences were no comfort, they were branches, and as M.B. fell, the branches broke against her, snap and snap, snap.

Oh! A terrible mewing rises from the girl's barred bed. The noise sends M.B. hurtling from her chair and straight toward the door. Her heart gallops in her chest. Her ears ring. And then she forces herself to begin the journey back to the nightmare bedside.

Doesn't it seem a sacrilege that her shoes bark like seals when she walks on the hospital linoleum?

"It's all right, kid." M.B.'s whisper is hoarse. "It's all right." Gingerly, she tugs at the bed's top sheet, eliminating the shadow caught in a wrinkle there. Anyone seeing the patient would imagine: not bad. A few tubes in, a few tubes out, a nasty scrape on the cheek, a broken hand. M.B., however, has been told: bad.

"Kid," she says, "sorry, kid." Because the last conversation she had with the patient was an angry one.

Jersey.

Really, M.B. scarcely knows this Jersey. When Jersey and her parents arrived at M.B.'s condominium, both M.B. and Jersey hesitated, then shook hands. *Shook hands!* But what else could M.B. do? She had seen the girl four times in her life. Baby, toddler, shy kid at Lorne's funeral, and, finally, the gangly girl of this summer's visit.

As soon as M.B. knew the trio was coming to Florida, she had bought a pot-holder loom for Jersey. As a girl, M.B. had loved making pot holders in the summer. "Oh, thanks," Jersey said when M.B. brought the loom out to the dinette, "that's nice," but Jersey did not leave off her game of chess to make a pot holder, and M.B.'s feelings were hurt and so she asked—her voice scratchy with irritation; she could hear it herself!—"But how can you play chess alone, Jersey?"

The girl had a disconcerting tendency to look M.B. straight in the eye, then glance away as if she had seen something embarrassing. "I play as well as I can for both sides," she said. Then she shrugged a shrug that was an exact replica of the lifetime of shrugs that M.B. had received from Kitty, and so maddened M.B. beyond words.

Now, however, the girl cries MEW! MEW! Her lips work back and forth, and, heart aching, M.B. presses her hand against the girl's forehead. Is there a fever? Through the mandatory gloves, M.B. cannot tell. Would there be a fever?

Once, Kitty yelled at M.B., "You never remember anything!" but she was wrong. The cries of Kitty's daughter remind M.B. of the shrill alarum of the killdeer that roam Palm Gate Village's golf course. And she first recognized those plump-bodied, spindle-legged birds on the golf course from a memory of the gravel roads of her childhood: handsome, irritating, the killdeer ran ahead of her bicycle, and cried and cried as if they did not even know how to fly; but that was a trick, M.B.'s father had said, a hoax meant to draw your attention away from the killdeer's nests.

Really, M.B. remembers many things. When the aide comes to knock on the window again, then indicates with a swivel of her head that she is setting M.B.'s doughnut and juice on the nurses' station, the carton of juice in the aide's hand reminds M.B. of the small square house picked up by the twister in *The Wizard of Oz* and dropped upon the Wicked Witch of the East.

After a last glance at her granddaughter, M.B. stands and heads for the door. Identity smeared by weariness and fear, she claps her palms to her sternum to still the sudden rattle that she assumes comes from inside herself but is in fact a cart passing by the nursing station with a clatter of glass on metal.

The balding nurse who sits at the station looks up at M.B. His smile reveals a set of silvery orthodontic appliances that take M.B. by surprise, but she manages to smile back, to work her way out of the hospital's gloves and mask and gown and shoe covers, deposit them in the correct bins; then she carries off her juice and doughnut to the outer hall.

What a start she receives from her reflection in the crash doors! Under normal circumstances, M.B. takes pride in her appearance. She upped the red in her hair before the gray became an issue. Had her "colors done" when she hit her fifties—an investment that she has always believed saved her from becoming one of the pale matrons that she and her pals at Field's called Dust Bunnies. Today, however, the bright tunic top that she was wearing when the police officer arrived at the condominium—that tunic top's bright patchwork of gold and emerald and sapphire silk is now wrinkled and rucked-up on one side in the elastic waist of her capri pants. The skin that surrounds her eyes blazes forth in queer white wrinkles, while her usually perfect cap of hair is in disarray and exposes pale scalp.

No getting around the fact that she reminds herself of a certain sick parrot that Kitty once stole from a neighbor's snowy back porch (*rescued* was the term that Kitty used).

With her fingertips, M.B. touches the deck of cards that she tucked in her tunic's left pocket back when the police officer rang the condominium doorbell. M.B. does not like callers to catch her with her cards out. Sometimes, to avoid picking up a game, she simply does not answer the door. She considered not answering the doorbell yesterday, but then she looked at the clock and saw how late it had grown. She supposed that it was Kitty at the door, returning with her family from their day's outing.

A deck of cards weighs a scant three ounces, not much at all, but after so many hours, those three extra ounces have made M.B.'s shoulder ache, and she shifts the deck from one pocket to the other to relieve the strain.

This morning, the majority of the reception area's vinyl couches—two melon, one turquoise, one a grimy yellow—are given over to the slumber of a large family of Dominicans whose beloved son/nephew/brother/grandson has been injured in a grisly motorcycle accident. The family speaks only Spanish, but M.B. is certain she knows which woman is the victim's mother: the one who is always painfully awake; the heavy-lidded one who sits on the floor, legs extended straight out before her, shoes removed, the feet of her nylon stockings now in such ruins they form a frill around her ankles. M.B. nods hello. The woman, hands resting on her thighs, raises an index finger by way of greeting.

Over by the windows, a man named Mr. Hurley weeps. M.B. has spoken to Mr. Hurley several times, and so knows about his grown sons and daughters; his office supply store in Owatanna, Minnesota; and his collie, Mr. Chips. Poor Mr. Hurley. Beneath his royal blue jogging suit, he appears to be a creature made up of wire hangers. Still, when he sees M.B., he blows his sad gray sponge of a nose, holds up a palm as if to say *Wait,* then stuffs his kerchief in the pocket of his jogging suit and steps to her side.

"Mrs. Milhause." Because so much of him remains in the intensive care unit with his wife and her embolism, Mr. Hurley's voice comes from far, far away when he asks, "Any news?"

M.B. shakes her head.

Unlike M.B., Mr. Hurley feels a need to speak, and he moves his tongue about in his mouth, searching for helpful moisture. "I pray, for your sake," he says—again, tears fill his eyes—"I pray they find the son of a bitch and give him the chair."

M.B. nods to show that she appreciates the thought; then, quickly, she retrieves the items she has stashed under the magazine table (jacket, package of Salem cigarettes with disposable lighter on top, black plastic bag containing items that someone—who?—thought to remove from the rental car and bring along to the hospital). She points toward the set of telephone booths.

"Of course," says Mr. Hurley. "Don't let me keep you."

■ ■ ■

Once inside the telephone booth, M.B. picks up the receiver, holds it to her ear, pretends to dial. She moves her lips, yes, but does not go so far as to invent sentences. Actually making sounds would frighten her too much, make her worry that someone might answer.

It is Lorne to whom M.B. would actually like to speak. Lorne would know who to call, what to say.

Joe's parents are both dead. Joe's actor brother—how will M.B. ever find him? Tom? Dave? No. Sam. Sam Alitz. M.B.'s own brother, Dick, disappeared into the army some forty years ago and never contacted the family after his return from Korea. Really, when you come right down to it, M.B. has no one she *needs* to call. When her mother died, M.B. cut all ties to Wyoming, and, truthfully, she cannot think of a soul back in Gary or Chicago to whom she would want to speak.

Might there be someone from town? From Vineyard Christian? No. The only person at Vineyard Christian that M.B. can abide is Pastor Bitner himself.

Eventually, she *will* have to telephone Palm Gate Village. People at Palm Gate Village notice an absence, and if the Today's Date calendar on M.B.'s doorknob goes unchanged for twenty-four hours, someone will call the manager and—a distressing thought—the manager will use his passkey to enter her unit, to see if she has broken a hip, slipped in the tub, kicked the bucket altogether. M.B. supposes that the person she will have to call will have to be Patsy Glickman. Patsy Glickman is a widow also. The two women met the morning M.B. discovered that Lorne was dead. It was Patsy who helped M.B. back into #335, and called 911, and waited with M.B. until the ambulance came.

Still, M.B. does not mean to tell Patsy more than this: "There's been an accident. I'm at the hospital." Not a word more—though she knows Patsy will want to drive to the hospital, immediately, with her Tupperware container of Mandelbrot, and advice about tears being good for the soul—

So M.B. cannot call Patsy yet. She is not up to that just now. Now her teeth chatter, and she must press her forehead against the back wall of the telephone booth to conceal the horror she feels overtake her features.

"Lorne," she whispers. "Please, God."

Maybe she and Lorne should have kept Kitty out of college. Maybe that would have prevented all of this. She remembers a night when Kitty was still in high school. M.B. and Lorne sat in the front room, watching the Golddiggers dance on *Dean Martin*. In came Kitty. For some reason, she had put her hair in braids. Trying to make herself look like a hippie, M.B. thought, but Kitty—bouncing around the room, grinning—Kitty waved away M.B.'s objection to the braids. She didn't want to talk about *braids*, she said. What she wanted was for M.B. and Lorne to listen to something. She waved around a book that she said proved that birds were the descendants of dinosaurs! Could she turn off the TV and read them a couple of paragraphs?

M.B. had not gone to school beyond the ninth grade. Then, as now, she tended not to believe in the possibility of things that she did not understand. Hence, she appreciated the decisive way in which Lorne said, "Keep away from the set, kid," and did not even look away from his show while the girl went on about her intention to study with the book's author.

Who turned out, of course, to be Joe Alitz. The Professor. Mr. Knows Everything Better Than You Do.

So maybe Lorne should have paid attention?

As she steps out of the hospital telephone booth, M.B. is careful not to glance Mr. Hurley's way, get caught in his sad eyes once more. *I'm going outside for a cigarette*, she will say, if he tries to stop her. *Going for a smoke. Gotta have a cigarette*.

Luckily, the buffed stainless steel doors to the elevator stand open, and she is able to step inside without ever having to look Mr. Hurley's way.

She knows this elevator now. The black scuff mark someone made on the wall to her right is something she has come to recognize. Also: that bobby pin wedged in a crack where linoleum meets door tread. Yesterday morning, she took this elevator down to the first floor before making her trip to the morgue. At the morgue, the face of her dead son-in-law was his own, yes, but no longer under his management, and that was enough to make M.B. temporarily set aside old bitterness and weep for the end of a life.

The new morning proves a harsh phosphorescence, but M.B. is able to stay in the portico's sweet honeycomb of sunbeams and shade. Thanks to the hospital's rules against cigarettes, she now encounters odors she is usually too smoke-cured to detect. Sunshine heats the landscaping gravel; this, in turn, heats the underlying dirt, whose cakelike fragrance is also released by the needles of water that hiss from black plastic emitters—one gone a little haywire, spray shooting up out of the rocks to produce a nervous rattle on the underside of a small but sturdy croton leaf.

Others have stepped outside to smoke, but M.B.—taking a seat on a brick planter—pretends not to notice: two teenage girls in identical black jumpsuits, one of them singing, pretending to hold a microphone to her lips; an administrative sort in aqua silk dress and name tag; a young mother with two small children, one wailing because she wants the mother's cola drink rather than her own orange soda.

Usually M.B. would give the young mother a sympathetic smile: *kids*. Today, however, she has only enough strength to stare at the new oncology center across the street: white, almost puffy-looking. In the *Gulf News*, fans of the oncology center's Italian architect have made a number of dubious claims for the design, but M.B. is not alone in believing the thing pure silliness, Frosty the Snowman, Pillsbury Dough Boy.

Kill me? Is that what the teenage girl is singing? Sometimes M.B. feels she has extracted every last bit of pleasure the world has to offer; all that remains is husk, the lightest crumbs, ready to shatter, and, oh, what wouldn't she give, right now, for a glass of Patsy Glickman's MD 20–20? Two glasses? To fall back into the arms of that sweet, dark wine, which sometimes feels—it *does*—like life itself flowing into her veins?

Is that fair? That the universe holds goods capable of making a human being feel so much better, yet fails to circulate a supply in the blood?

M.B.'s face goes red at the thought of what Pastor Bitner would say to such a question. *The Bible makes clear its prohibi-*

tion against strong drink and drunkenness. The wine Jesus mentions here and there would have been a watery fruit drink, more like your kid's Kool-Aid than what you'd find in today's liquor section.

Kill me?

The teenage girls spin out into the covered drive. The laughing one glances M.B.'s way and tries to keep her hand over the singer's mouth while the singer jerks her head this way and that, bits of her words escaping through the other's fingers—

Oh! M.B. shivers. Her eyes begin to tear, and she squeezes them tight as she prays: *Lord. Dear Lord. Dear Jesus. Please heed the words of your most humble servant, Marybelle Milhause, and spare the lives of Jersey and Kitty. Take me, Lord. Kill me. Right now. Take me, instead, Lord.*

It is a great disappointment, but not a shock, that upon opening her eyes M.B. finds herself still seated in front of the hospital entrance. Smoke from the cigarette in her hand continues to waft upward. The croton leaf rattles. The teenagers have disappeared, and a very large man—bearded, wearing a red bandanna—now steps out of the bitter sunlight and into the portico's shade.

But wait: M.B. stubs out her cigarette and makes fists with both hands. The points of her fingernails bite into her palms with perfect familiarity. Alive. She gives the hair at the nape of her neck a discreet yank.

Alive.

Unless pain endures even after death. Everything endures after death: the dull ring that sounds when the child drops her empty pop can, the sick-sweet smell of diesel fuel from a passing bus. No relief, ever. But wouldn't that be hell? M.B. feels certain *this* can't be heaven, but suppose she is in hell?

Hell feels just like life?

In an effort to regain her equilibrium, she forces herself to eat her pink doughnut and drink the carton of orange juice. *Calm down*, she whispers to herself. When this does not help, she tries to put the same words in the voice of Lorne—*Calm down, M.B.*—but the fact that she cannot make that voice move out of memory and into her ears is merely painful.

She lights up a second cigarette and, for occupation, begins to pull the items from the black plastic bag at her feet: Colored pencils held together by a rubber band. Hairbrush. Binoculars. An army surplus backpack, upon whose drab canvas someone has boldly drawn a maze that has as its goal the name JERSEY ALITZ. A little red book with pagodas and flowers and tiny people and boats stitched into the cloth cover, and a pattern of roses pressed into the binding: the girl's diary, M.B. realizes with a start and immediately sets the book down. Half-empty box of chocolate chip granola bars. Binocular case holding an unused postcard from a place called Arles' Mineral Springs. A book containing graphs, and drawings of noses and apes, and diagrams that explain the fertilization of the egg by the sperm—a coloring book, apparently, though its heavy paper and schoolbook illustrations and text look nothing like what M.B. remembers buying for Kitty (pulpy things whose themes were fancy-dress weddings or movies like *Oklahoma!* and *The Swiss Family Robinson*). Sometimes M.B. herself used to "color" with Kitty—though when M.B. looked up from her own careful work (opalescent watered silk one of her finest effects), often as not, she found Kitty across the room, working logic puzzles or reading some book brought home from the library.

Footfalls. This is what M.B. registers first. The footfalls come to a stop in front of her. Without raising her head, M.B. looks at their owner's enormous shoes, then sneaks a quick, upward glance: the big bearded man in the red bandanna.

Trkkh, trkkh. The man's breath labors above her. She lowers her eyes to his timber legs, then raises them to the chest broad as a sidewalk; then—frightened—she looks off to her left, her right. Where are her witnesses? The lady in the silk dress now makes her way through the hospital foyer while the young mother has herded her children across the drive—

Trkkh, trkkh. M.B. looks up again. The man shakes his head. Little chick feathers of blond hair stick out from under his red bandanna. His eyes wobble—with tears?

"I"—the man leans down. With a hand covered in gauze bandaging, he picks up the army surplus bag at M.B.'s feet and dumbly holds it out before M.B. "Where'd you get this?" he asks.

Does he take the bag for a purse? What? A wild noise escapes M.B.—a snort that would embarrass her greatly under other circumstance—then, thank heaven, like a blessing, the hospital's doors are flying open with a gassy *chunk*. One hand on his holster, a tiny gray-haired security guard hustles toward M.B. and the man in the bandanna. "Say, fella, unless you got business here," the guard calls ahead of himself, "I suggest you move along!"

M.B. does not want to hear or see what happens next, and so she stares down at the coloring book in her lap, a page labeled "Sickle-Cell Trait: Defense Against Malaria." This is a page not yet colored. Black-and-white illustrations of normal cells, sickle cells, a little map of Africa.

Only when she hears the change in sound that the big man's shoes make as he steps out from beneath the echoing portico and into the street—only then does M.B. raise her head once more.

The guard gives her a wink. "Rough-looking character!" he says. He takes a seat beside M.B. on the planter and lights up a cigarette of his own. With a laugh, he leans close to say, "Guess now us smokers know how the niggers used to feel, huh?"

M.B. glances at the street, the diminishing figure of the man in the bandanna. It has been many years since Kitty informed M.B. that, at the very least, the use of the word *nigger* branded the speaker as ignorant, *and surely you don't want to sound ignorant, Mother*? Still, when M.B. turns back, she smiles at the guard because, after all, Lorne continued to say *nigger* until the day he died; all of the men at the mills said *nigger,* and the guard only means to be friendly.

Which is not to say that M.B. wishes to talk to him, no, and to prevent further conversation, she begins slowly flipping through the coloring book.

Gardner Glazier is the security guard's name. Until quite recently, he worked in the parking lot of Southeastern Savings: days spent greeting customers, telling the occasional joke, getting tough with the jerks who had no bank business but wanted free parking while they ran to the pharmacy or met a friend for lunch. Gardner often forgets that the people he meets at the hospital are, for the most part, worried over disease and injury and death, and so he teases M.B., "You going to do some coloring, there?"

Too weary and worried to register the man's teasing, M.B. replies, "This is my granddaughter's book. I guess this is the sort of coloring books they give the smart ones, nowadays. My granddaughter—" She hesitates at an illustration of a cutaway of the human brain that is distressingly similar to the illustration shown her by the neurosurgeon now attending her daughter—corpus callosum, Broca's area, Wernicke's area—and a second illustration that depicts what occurs in the brain's various regions: Writing. A hand moving a paintbrush. A long-haired girl looking sad.

While M.B. stares at the illustrations, Gardner Glazier tries to recall a joke that someone told him about kids nowadays, but he can remember only the one about the Martians who showed up at the Welfare office. Something about aliens. *We hear you have great benefits for aliens*? Maybe he could tell the woman that one, he thinks, and sneaks a look to see if he still has her attention.

Uh-oh. The white face, the tremor of her lips remind Gardner of where he is. "Miss," he says, with genuine solicitude, and pats her arm, "you look awful pale, miss. Is there anybody I can call for you?"

M.B. shakes her head. No. And there is no one she can die for, either. No one for whom her death would do a bit of good. She stares across the street at the notorious oncology building, so white it gleams in the morning sun, and, oh, it hits her then what that marshmallow stack of a building is—it is a *joke* that she does not get, a joke that she is not meant to get, and, thus, its white walls of exclusion form the backdrop against which the shadow of her next thoughts play out:

Jesus, at least, could die for people. Jesus could exchange his life for the lives of all mankind. Jesus was *lucky!* People thought: How sad, poor Jesus, dying on the cross. But when you think about it, really, when you really think about it, Jesus was the luckiest of them all.

2

Granted, the Carter Clay encountered by M.B. outside of Memorial Hospital appeared piratical (beard, bandanna); when clean and clean-shaven, Carter Clay is a man with the face of a choirboy; so much so, in fact, that his face appears somewhat mismatched to the rest of his forty-two-year-old self.

As a boy, however, while Carter was growing up in the green, green sectors of Washington state—despite that innocent face—his height and width of bone made him appear older than his peers. More than once, while at play with classmates, Carter found himself grabbed by a passing grown-up who mistook the boy for some older roughneck pestering the little ones.

Other facts about Carter Clay: he tends to believe that the world is made up of the haves and have-nots.

Also: His hair, though thinning, remains the baby-fine blond of his youth. One large, maroon telltale capillary runs across his left nostril like a piece of fraying thread, but otherwise his skin is good. Women are attracted to his big, bearded woodsman looks, a fact of which Carter seems unaware, though it might be more accurate to say that he is impervious to such attentions. His responses to the world tend to be wary—a little congealed, or *moony*, even. He has been deaf in one ear since serving in Vietnam, which is where he also acquired the minor scars to be found on his neck and right arm, but not the five doozies that mark his back; those he acquired a little over a year ago, in a stabbing near a picnic shelter designated #6 in the city of Sarasota's own Edmund Howell Park.

More details: Only three nights ago, Carter Clay went off to a Tuesday night meeting of Alcoholics Anonymous, and, there, claimed a "chip" for his first year of sobriety. That was in tiny Sabine, Florida, in the Sunday school classroom borrowed from the Full Gospel Baptist Church. The other AA members clapped as Carter went to the front of the room. Carter smiled and flushed as he received the metallic coin from a grandmotherly former junkie named Earla R.

That Tuesday night, Carter *was* on the right road. He was continuing to practice the lessons learned at a halfway place called Recovery House. His basic honesty remained intact while a tendency toward gullibility had been pruned to a more reasonable size. He did not pretend to have entirely lost all interest in the delights and demons that lay, so cozily coiled, inside a helping of methamphetamine, grass, booze, Percodan, cocaine, and/or whatever else might be offered or sold in a bar or a car, at a baseball game, park, public john, even an espresso cart at an indoor mall whose shops featured windows only as a means of displaying more merchandise—

Still, three nights ago, at the AA meeting, Carter's cravings appeared to have shrunk to something relatively small.

Suffice it to say that Carter did not understand this appearance of diminution to be largely a feature of distance, as with a great warship that might be covered by the tip of your little finger when the vessel sits on the far horizon. However, things had improved for Carter. On the occasion of that Tuesday-night meeting of Alcoholics Anonymous, for the first time in four years, Carter had a means of transportation: a used van that he had been able to purchase, cheap, from his Recovery House counselor. He had a regular job: cook at a storefront place on Sabine's main street. The owners of the Accordion Cafe had lost a big, blond-haired nephew in Vietnam; when Recovery House called about a job for Carter, not only were they tearfully happy to give a veteran a job, they also helped Carter find a room to rent.

A nice room in a nice house belonging to a nice lady named Mrs. Dickerson. Two double-hung windows, one on the north and facing the neighbors, one on the east and looking out into Mrs. Dickerson's crust of yard and the two orange trees whose fruit was concealed by their own summertime green. Across the hall, there lived another boarder, a friendly younger man with an interest in drawing cartoons about a rat who was friends with a cat.

On top of his room's three-drawer dresser, on a bit of crochet provided by the kindly Mrs. Dickerson, Carter kept a clear bowl, round as a globe, containing a blue and red betta fish that conjured up its own phosphorescent beauty in its circular travels. Sometimes Carter did wish that he had photographs to display next to the fish. At various points in his life, he *had* possessed photographs: a childhood picture of his big sister, Cheryl Lynn, and himself by a manger scene; Instamatic photos of high school friends and friends from Vietnam. There had been a great picture from a softball picnic: Cheryl Lynn, Carter, his friend Neff Morgan, Bonnie Drabnek—the Inuit woman with whom Carter had lived once upon a time—and Bonnie's three little kids.

How all of those photographs leaked from Carter's life, he did not know. A number of the people in them were dead now. Worse, without the photographs, *all* of them seemed dead.

In lieu of photographs, a hardbound copy of *Alcoholics Anonymous* (aka *The Big Book*) sat next to the fish bowl, along with two gifts from Carter's Recovery House counselor. The first gift was an inexpensive gold picture frame that contained a blurry newspaper photo of Howell Park's Shelter #6 and the accompanying article:

> An area homeless man, Carter Thomas Clay, remains in critical condition after being stabbed in the Howell Park area. A pair of early-morning joggers found Clay near death on the park's service road. Motive for the assault has not been established, though police seek information regarding a man with whom Clay was said to have fought earlier Friday evening. Witnesses to that fight described the second man as in his forties, slender, approximately five-ten, redheaded and wearing a

black Indy 500 jacket. The second man allegedly drew a knife on Clay during the quarrel.

The homeless men who congregate at the picnic shelter at the far end of Howell Park have been a source of complaints from area residents, who charge the men are often drunk and belligerent and come into neighborhood yards to use residents' outdoor faucets and urinate. In 1992, a gunfight at the shelter resulted in fatal injuries to two men; in the past six months, police have suspected foul play in two deaths, one involving a gunshot wound, the other a drowning in the nearby canal.

"That's so you don't forget where you've been," said the Recovery House counselor, whose second gift was a copy of *Moby-Dick*. According to the counselor—a muscular former biker—*Moby-Dick* was the best book ever written. Ten pages a day, the counselor advised Carter. Anybody can read ten pages a day, right?

Carter trusted that *Moby-Dick* was a fine thing to read. If you counted the many notes at the back, *Moby-Dick* appeared as thick and full of ideas as *Alcoholics Anonymous* or the Bible. The Recovery House counselor had marked his favorite spots in *Moby-Dick* with a watermelon-bright highlighter, and the pages flashed cheerfully whenever Carter flipped through them. But Carter had never spent much time on books. Reading *Moby-Dick*, Carter was like a thirsty man who holds ice in his aching hands in hopes that, within the leaky cup formed of his fingers, the heat of his body will melt enough ice to provide him with a drink. You understand: sheer physical discomfort makes such a man give up the task over and over again.

Up until three days ago, however, Carter did a good job of following the rest of the routine that the Recovery House counselor advised: each morning, brush your teeth and make your bed. Before leaving for work, kneel and say the prayer on page 63 of *Alcoholics Anonymous*. Tuesday, Thursday, Friday, and Sunday evenings: attend the AA meetings in the basement of the Baptist church (cotton-ball lambs frolicking on Sunday school bulletin board; bad fluorescent lights; a sharp, ineradicable odor of mold that reminded Carter of Washington state and gave him a familiar and thus not entirely unpleasant sense of anxiety).

The people at AA liked Carter. He was not sullen. In fact, he was often whistling some bit of old rock and roll as he came through the back door of Full Gospel Baptist ("Stairway to Heaven," "Badge," "Light My Fire"). Carter wanted to be good. He spoke often of how he yearned for a Higher Power like the one that lit up the eyes of certain of the group's star members. He earnestly related his past failures and was even able to laugh about a number of them. It did not hurt Carter's case, of course, that he was big and pleasant to look at, if not precisely handsome; or that the story he told of how he came to AA was tinged with the glamour that can attach itself to even sordid disaster (the war, of course, and then the fact that—albeit while homeless and drunk—he had been most grievously stabbed for defending a fellow vet).

After meetings, people often asked if Carter would like to go with them to the new Village Inn out on the interstate. Carter, however, still tended to feel glassy while socializing without a leg-up from chemicals more ambitious than those found in coffee and chocolate cream pie. He did not have much to say once he had told a person where he lived, what jobs he had held (cannery work, hanging sheetrock, roofing, and house-painting); hence, he generally went straight home to Mrs. Dickerson's after meetings. Before sleep, sometimes he did open *Moby-Dick* or *Alcoholics Anonymous*. Usually, however, he lay on his bed with his Walkman and whistled along with the cassettes that one of the waitresses at the Accordion had kindly made up for him from her collection of albums from the 1960s: the Doors, Hendrix, the Who, Credence Clearwater, Steppenwolf. Carter loved to whistle. He sounded sweet as a bird, Mrs. Dickerson said. Sometimes he whistled her up the Hoagie Carmichael "Stardust" that his mother used to request.

All was relatively well, then, until two mornings ago, at which time a customer entered the Accordion Cafe and ordered a bagel.

In little Sabine, Florida—forty-five miles inland from Sarasota—people ate so few bagels that the owner of the

Accordion insisted that the help keep the café's bag of bagels frozen and thaw them in the microwave before toasting. The bagel customer of two mornings before, however, had insisted on "no nuking," and so Carter had attempted to cut the frozen bagel with a cleaver.

"I trained in Massachusetts," said the clinic doctor who subsequently put seventeen stitches into Carter's finger. "We get a lot of bagel accidents where I come from. I had a patient almost cut off two whole fingers!" The doctor gave the last stitch a tug that, despite local anaesthesia, Carter felt pass along his finger bones and right up into his elbow. Still, Carter liked the doctor, who wore a ponytail and sandals and a strip of rawhide knotted around his wrist. Carter laughed when the doctor said, "Man, you are my first *southern* victim of an encounter with a frozen bagel!"

The surprise of so much blood coming from his finger; the embarrassment of walking over to the clinic with a towel-wrapped hand held over his head; his need for the doctor to like *him* as much as he liked the doctor—all of this left Carter feeling loose, giddy. He assured the doctor that he, Carter, was no southerner either; though he did *not* explain that he had wound up living in Florida because, in 1988, at a party in Seattle, he and a couple of other men had decided to go to D.C. and visit the Wall. At the Wall, the mother of a dead Marine had invited Carter and his friends to Thanksgiving dinner at her home in St. Petersburg, Florida. That Marine's mother touched Carter's heart as she stood there in the windy cold, her gray hair blowing this way and that. *She could be my mother*, Carter thought. *If I'd died in the war and she were still alive, she could be my mother*. While the others drove back to Washington state, Carter had hitchhiked to St. Petersburg—though he never actually did make it up the steps of what turned out to be the lady's very impressive home. No. On the steps, smoking a cigarette, there had sat a skinny young woman—almost a girl—in an enormous sombrero and silver high heels. "You don't want to go in there," she said, and then she set the sombrero on the steps, and pointed to a car, and drove Carter to an even more dazzling house. She guided Carter through a side door to a group of rooms that she called her parents' "master suite," then drew a whirlpool bath for herself and Carter while they drank wine and smoked dope. That girl was cute, but her parents' bathroom—it was as large as the entire first floor of the house in which he had grown up! It had, in addition to the whirlpool, a sauna, polished wood floors, a tiled shower stall big enough for a group, two built-in hair dryers, enormous baskets of red and green towels that—with a sneering drawl—the girl explained were put out by her mother for use only at the holidays. Of course, Carter had blown all that by pissing in the girl's bed while they slept, and so he had to sneak out of the house before she woke up and saw.

"I'm a Washington boy myself." This was what Carter *did* tell the doctor stitching his hand. "I mean to go back as soon as I save up enough money. A person can still lead a decent life there, you know? Clean air? Trees?"

Head bent over his work, the doctor asked, "Were you in 'Nam?"

"Sixty-nine, seventy."

The doctor looked up, winked. He was a small man—wiry, with wiry hair. Younger than Carter, or perhaps just better preserved, less damaged. He had plenty of money, Carter supposed. He would have stayed in college while Carter was over there.

"You taking any antidepressants?"

"No."

"Francie"—the doctor stuck his hands in the pockets of his white coat and turned to the nurse—"call the Accordion Cafe and tell them we're going to give Mr. Clay, here, a shot and send him home for the rest of the afternoon."

When the nurse left the room, the doctor leaned close to whisper, "Demerol. This stuff'll make you feel so much better, if you went back to work, you might cut your whole finger off and not even know it!"

For fear his face might give him away, Carter covered his mouth with his good hand and tried to look merely curious, sociable. Which was not easy. In Carter's good ear, *Demerol* was a hymn so lovely its pure vibrations ignited and burned to ash the message that Carter carried with him from the poster in the front hall of Recovery House:

NO PAINKILLERS, DIET PILLS (or other stimulants),
SLEEP AIDS, TRANQUILIZERS, COUGH SYRUPS,
MOUTHWASH, and/or **MUSCLE RELAXANTS.**
What does *no* mean?
NO MEANS NO.

Once the smoke from his little fire cleared, Carter reflected—heart thumping—that surely, if it was normal for a doctor to prescribe a shot, it was normal to take it; and when the nurse returned with the syringe held up before her like a holy candle, and the doctor told Carter to lie back for a minute, Carter did not allow himself to think of the chip ceremony of the night before or how, while everyone else clapped, Earla R. had hugged him to her old-lady breasts—big and loose as feather pillows—and whispered, "Think," and then as she released him, "A word to the wise is sufficient."

"Man"—the ponytailed doctor raised Carter's chart to his forehead in merry farewell salute—"man, your hand may still hurt, but you ain't gonna give a damn!"

Blessings. By the time that Carter got his shirt on, and spoke with the woman handling the paperwork, and stepped out into the waiting room, he felt suffused with blessings. Best of all, he was quite certain that those blessings had nothing to do with the Demerol. They had to do with the friendly doctor and the kind nurse and the *world*. He smiled at the fish in the aquarium who wafted by the bubbling deep-sea diver and his trunk of treasure. Yes. The world gave off blessings at every moment, and Carter had simply been stupid not to have noticed this before. *This* was what the old-timers at AA spoke of! *Life* was a blessing, damn it! Life was great! People were great!

The receptionist looked up from her desk. When Carter lifted his bandaged hand in a salute that was a close copy of the salute of the doctor, she grinned and shook her head as if she knew Carter well—as if he were a familiar, lovable troublemaker.

"You take care of yourself now, Mr. Clay," she said, "and don't think you have to be bleeding all over the place to come by for a visit!"

Outside, the bright blue day blazed, but the heat did not bother Carter. Rather, it was bracing, a sweet stimulation of his cells, and so he stopped at the top of the clinic steps and breathed and felt privileged to give his attention to the world.

91°, read the digital marquee on the bank across the street. *11:38 a.m.*

He tried to whistle—"Take Five" was on his mind—but his mouth proved too dry, and so he looked down Sabine's main street, Crown Street, a quiet place, with roadway and buildings bleached pale as soda crackers in the midday sun. One block up and on the corner sat the Accordion Cafe. Closer to the clinic: Bilby's Drug, Marty's Photo Studio, a 7–11, Hasseloff's Florist—where, just then, a small boy and his mother struggled to raise an uncooperative banner of neon-orange paper.

Should he help them? Carter wondered.

He should have helped them. Helping them, he would have had to turn his back to the street. With his back to the street, he would perhaps have been missed by that desiccated creature who now tacked this way and that down Crown Street, like some old Christmas tree, needles gone, meant for the trashman but carried off, instead, by a stiff breeze.

By nature, Carter was a slow man. The Demerol made him slower. While he considered whether to offer the boy and woman help, he remained at the top of the clinic steps. While he tried to make out the message obscured by the drooping folds in the orange banner—ZEN RED OSS $99—the odd creature tacked nearer to hand, and then he stopped at the base of the stairs, and he called out, "Clay! Jesus Christ, you're not just *alive*, man, you're getting a gut on you!"

Carter looked down the steps to the little man. Something familiar about those large, pointy ears, that mossy sail of a windbreaker. Oh! Carter's heart expanded in pleasure and pity when he realized that the battered wreck before him was his old pal from Howell Park, Private Rear End, or, as Carter felt it more polite to call the man, R.E.

Half an hour before, Carter—perhaps—would have heeded his Recovery House counselor's warning: avoid buddies from your bad old days, fellow veterans or not. Now, however, Carter was all aglow with excellent pharmaceuticals, and his good sense stepped right out of the way of his much more gratifying twinges of sweet friendship and concern: *Who the hell had made such a mess of his old friend R.E.*?

"Hey, bro," Carter called—doing his best to appear unaware of R.E.'s lost teeth and skewed nose—"what you doing in Sabine?"

R.E. grinned. "I heard you were straight, man, so I came as fast as I could!"

Laughing, drifting, chubby clouds of sweetness ringing his wrists and ankles, Carter came down the steps. He had always been flattered that someone as smart as R.E. had befriended someone as uneducated as himself.

"Man"—R.E. extended his hand for a shake—"Clay, I know I fucked up, man, not coming to see you at the VA! You don't have to tell me! I did get my ass over there finally, but they'd moved you, man!" He hesitated, then said in a lower voice, "And, damn, it was probably 'cause of me—you taking my part, man—that's probably why that fuck stuck you, you know? Don't think I haven't thought about that, man. Plenty of times."

Carter rubbed his hand across his cottony mouth and grinned and tried to think of what his counselor had said once: *Carter, getting stabbed may have been the best thing that could have happened to you! Some of us have to get stabbed or shot before we get the message that it's time to get our shit together!* Just now, however, Carter could come up with only, "Hey, man, you're like a brother to me."

"Man"—R.E. looked off down the street—"I thought I'd lost track of you for good, but then I met this guy—Hayes? He said you guys had lived at some halfway house together, and he'd heard you'd landed over here." R.E. made a doubtful face, then mimicked working a spatula on a grill, giving a pancake or a burger a flip. "*Cooking*, man?"

"Hayes! Sure! From Recovery House!" Carter smiled and ran a dreamy hand back and forth across the top of his head. His muscles contained little silver streams. He imagined his heart: cool and gaily colored as those gel-filled pacifiers that dark-eyed Bonnie Drabnek used to keep on ice for her babies.

"Man, you should have let your old buddies know where you'd gone, Clay!"

Carter blinked at this reminder that he was, in fact, not supposed to be with old buddies at all. Still, he would have cut off the finger he'd just had repaired rather than have R.E. imagine that he, Carter Clay, now believed himself somehow superior to an old friend; and, just to make certain R.E. understood that this was *not* the case, Carter added a self-depreciating, "I'd hoped to be back in Washington by now, but so far I ain't saved up enough for a Port-a-Shed, let alone a cabin!"

Disappointing to Carter: R.E.'s failure to laugh at his little joke. The spring before last, Carter and R.E. had sometimes slept in a Port-a-Shed in the backyard of an Iowa couple who came to Sarasota only during the winter months. Carter had always appreciated the fact that R.E. characterized their Port-a-Shed nights as "goofing," something funny, as opposed to desperate.

"So, how about Louie and them guys, R.E.? How're they doing?"

R.E. bobbed his head up and down. Chewed his crumpled lower lip. "You haven't seen them, huh? Well, they were good, man, last time I saw them. Real good." R.E. stretched his arms out in front of himself and yawned. "It's been a while, though." He entwined his fingers. "I'm not hanging in Sarasota these days." Pushed the entwined fingers outward with a quick crack of the knuckles. "But, hey"—he motioned for Carter to follow him up the street—"come on, man. I got a present for you. You were out of it when we first visited you at the hospital in Sarasota, but I got this for you—a get-well present—before I knew they were going to move you up to the VA in Tampa."

Carter hesitated. Across the way, the woman and boy in front of the florist's shop had succeeded in hooking one end of their banner over an old flag standard. Now they tossed the banner's other end at what seemed to be sheer brick—as if they hoped the banner might just stick to the building of its own accord.

Schirmer, B. Paige, G. Names written in marker, in different handwriting, on the heels of R.E.'s mismatched running shoes.

It was not Carter's nature to speculate upon what sort of mess his old friend had got himself into, but he understood that something had happened. R.E. had been the one who shamed the rest of the Howell Park vets by doing five hundred sit-ups each day. Push-ups. Pull-ups. R.E. had been the smartest of them, and the best storyteller. Though to Carter's way of thinking, too many of R.E.'s tales involved the worst sort of details of the war (heads on spikes and dead babies and rapes, blood spouting from a bullet to the brain like water from a drinking fountain), Carter also found irresistible R.E.'s praise of the man who was a soldier as opposed to a scholar—

"Wait up!" As he drew abreast of his friend, Carter lowered his voice to say, "I really am straight, R.E."

R.E. gave Carter an appraising look. "Could have fooled me," he said, then laughed and started down an overgrown alley.

Carter knew his Recovery House counselor would say not to follow R.E.

> But all the things that God would have us do are hard for us to do—remember that—and hence, he oftener commands us than endeavors to persuade. And if we obey God, we must disobey ourselves; and it is in this disobeying ourselves, wherein the hardness of obeying God consists.

Carter had read this highlighted paragraph from page 45 of *Moby-Dick*. Also: Carter received a clear signal of warning from the alley, a jungly corridor in which Cape honeysuckle engulfed the telephone poles and wires, and large dogs barked and leaped up against a length of chain-link fence that twanged with the dogs' weight, and framed in metallic diamonds the flash of canine eyes and teeth.

Still, when R.E. disappeared through some invisible break in a tall hedge of privet, Carter felt as he had when he was a kid and he witnessed a friend's dangerous tricks: he *had* to duplicate the trick, hurl himself along, or be lost, and so he called in a low voice, "Hey, R.E. Where'd you go?"

A hand emerged from the privet to give Carter a yank. Twigs from the hedge poked and scratched Carter's face, his neck. He found himself in a shady slot between the hedge and the back of a garage the color of orange sherbet. A crammed-full Winn-Dixie shopping cart sat by the garage's back wall, and Carter was just taking this all in, when a bug—some big ball of black and buzz—caromed off his eyebrow. "Rh!" he said, and leaped to one side, setting the logs of a tumbledown woodpile to knocking one against the other.

"Quiet!" R.E. hissed. "Somebody's in the garage, man!"

R.E.'s gravity—the way he stood stock-still, wide-eyed, absolutely *furious*—struck Carter as goofy, and he had to cover his mouth and turn away.

A surprise: he recognized that stitchery on a dark fold of cloth in the Winn-Dixie cart. In the past, it was a point of honor with Carter and R.E. that they did not push carts, but Carter knew that stitchery to be part of the insignia on R.E.'s prized Yankees cap, and so he was not startled when R.E.—after first making a kid's "zip your mouth" gesture—pulled a plastic bottle from the cart and tossed the bottle to Carter.

Whose bad hand missed the catch.

"Sorry," Carter mouthed as he stooped to retrieve the bottle from the dirt. Rubbing alcohol. He knew even before he read the label. The party-time tint of the contents suggested that its cut was orange soda. Rub-a-dub. Commandant of the skid row dream, gastric distress, chills and spills. Carter had drunk rub-a-dub several times in his own hazy past but never knew R.E. to do so. Carter had always considered R.E. too smart for that. A rub-a-dub drunk was a bad trade; turning over a piece of today's misery for a bigger chunk of tomorrow's. Carter used to bracket his own rub-a-dub drunks much the way he had bracketed certain memories: his father raining kicks and blows upon the family; his mother's attempts to kill herself; the moment when Tim Kramer turned to smile at Carter and the barrel of Tim's M–16 caught the trip wire that blew him into thousands of pieces, a number of which penetrated Carter's ear (a fact so sad and shameful—the terrible intimacy of it—that Carter's reports regarding his subsequent hearing loss were purposefully vague). There was worse from the war. Coming upon a trio of men he *knew*—men he had to live with afterward—and what was left of the girl those men had raped, then finished off with a flare up the vagina—

A door slammed. "I think they went in the house," Carter whispered to R.E.

"Sh!" R.E. extracted what appeared to be a piece of bread from one of his windbreaker's enormous pockets. He poked it through the shopping cart's gridwork sides—was he saving scraps of food?—then he pointed, frowning, at the bottle of rub-a-dub, still unopened in Carter's hand. "What's with you, man?" he hissed. "You gotten too good for rub-a-dub?"

Little coins of sunshine danced through the privet and onto Carter's shoulders. He could not recall the last time that the dappling of light and shadow on his skin had felt so fine, so—full of the precise meaning that life was good. Still, R.E.'s words hurt Carter. Carter was no snob, and he never had been, and so he said, "Hey, man, when was I ever too good for anything?"

R.E. turned his head to one side, listening, then hunkered down beside the cart. "You tell me, Clay," he muttered, "you tell me." From the cart's bottom shelf, he began to yank all manner of plastic bags, shoe boxes filled with pens and pencils, packets of restaurant ketchup and wooden clothespins, egg cartons, a bundle of Post-It notes, gloves, several Wonder Bread bags filled with bundles of newspaper clippings, audiocassettes. A Tootsie's Bread bag contained three books: *The Birth of Tragedy*, *A Christmas Carol*, and *The Analects of Confucius*. Here were two packets of queen-size panty hose crushed against several small Styrofoam buckets of instant oriental noodles and something that appeared to Carter to be the pressure mechanism designed to keep a screen door from slamming.

Without looking up, R.E. handed Carter a record album that Carter recognized immediately: the Electric Prunes. "Your favorite, right?" R.E. whispered.

Carter was touched. "I told you that?"

"Ha!" R.E. made a face that looked to Carter almost like a face of disgust, but then R.E. continued in a soft rush, "'I Had Too Much to Dream Last Night'! The anthem of your salad days, man! Oriental whirligigs, crashing drums, lyrics delivered with hazardous glottal stops, drunken longing, and fury!" A fleck of spit bounced on R.E.'s tattered lip. "And you were in love with—let's see, some sweet thing with the limply lovely long blond hair of those distant days?"

"Amazing!" The name of the girl R.E. referred to eluded Carter for a moment—a lawyer's daughter. *Becky Pattschull*. He could remember entering her house for the first time. An enormous dove-gray house cantilevered over the bluffs of Fort Powden. Before he had entered that house, Carter had assumed all houses smelled like pulp from the paper mill where his own and all of his friends' fathers worked. A miracle that Becky Pattschull had gone out with Carter at all. Of course, it didn't last. Nevertheless, Carter had felt irreparably damaged by the fact that it didn't last; in an effort to give the girl a small taste of such damage, he had poured a five-pound bag of C and H sugar into the gas tank of the baby-blue Mustang coupe she received for her sixteenth birthday.

"So you want it or not, Clay?"

Carter turned the album over in his hands. Its cardboard cover gaped in a way that suggested the record within was impossibly warped. Who knew? Perhaps it was Carter's own long-lost copy of the album? While Carter had been in the service, his mother had finally managed to remove herself from the planet. As a response—in one of those drunken rages that had surely fanned Betty Carter's desire to die—Carter's father, Duncan, tossed every item from their little rental house onto the broken curb, alongside a large sign that read FREE! ALL MY WORLDLY GOODS!

In fact, not all of those goods had belonged to Duncan Clay. The heap included the family furniture, cigarette-burned and battle-scarred though it was; the rosebud dishes Betty Clay had received from her own mother and would surely have left to Cheryl Lynn; an old RCA Victor TV; the childhood dolls that Cheryl Lynn had meant to save for *her* children; a little suitcase record player and all of Carter and Cheryl Lynn's record albums.

A part of the group photo on the cover of R.E.'s album was missing—torn away by a piece of tape or a large price tag, but enough remained that Carter marveled over the appearance of the band members: swags of bangs, bad skin, absurdly skinny legs in striped trousers. And he had wanted to look like them, once upon a time!

Out of a sense of charity, Carter asked his old friend, "How much you want for it, R.E.? I mean, I don't have a record player, but—"

R.E. looked up from fiddling with the wheels of the grocery cart and made a face. "It's a *present*, man. Jesus. You want me to get down on my knees and beg you to take it? And if you're not going to drink that rub-a-dub, pass it here."

"Well, thanks, R.E. You know?" After another moment's hesitation, Carter unscrewed the cap on the rub-a-dub. An eye-watering smell. He set his tongue as a dam across the lip, tipped the bottle, pretended to drink. Maybe taking the Demerol had been stupid, but at least he was not going to *drink*.

"Now you're talking, man!" R.E. grabbed the bottle and raised it for a hit. "Okay! And, hey, you got the dough for something better than this shit, we can get properly fucked up! Have a high time while you haul me and my shit down to Solana in your van."

"Oh," Carter said. For a moment, the world looked a little too green. Things were bubbling away from him. Yes, he still held onto some notion that he should not buy alcohol, but even this notion was shrinking to a notion that he should not be *seen* buying alcohol. He needed to buy some time. He asked, "How'd you know I had a van, R.E.?"

"Hey, Clay"—R.E. grinned, revealing the unfamiliar and unnerving gaps of gum and tongue once more—"you went to Recovery House, man, not Witness Protection!"

Carter tried to laugh. "Well, it's over by the 7–11."

"All right!" R.E. began to work the shopping cart out through the hedge. "Good place to buy us a bottle, too!"

How about I just give you a ride? This was what Carter wanted to say, but how could he, without appearing to insult or deny R.E.? Well, he could not, and so he found himself taking out his wallet and handing R.E. two ten-dollar bills. "Here." He looked back into the wallet, stalling. "You go pick out what you like. I'll catch up with you in a second."

R.E. hawked and spit on the alley's hot dust but did not move, and, finally, Carter had no choice but to look up again.

"You ashamed to be seen with me and my cart?" R.E. asked with a grin. He sounded as if he were teasing, but Carter felt guilty all the same, and so he started off down the alley, saying, "Hey, I'm coming, man. I'll even wait with your damned cart while you go in and pick us out something good."

▪ ▪ ▪

In the shade of a clump of oleanders, while he waited for R.E.'s return, Carter gave the shopping cart little pushes and pulls, back and forth, as if it were a stroller that held somebody's baby.

"Hush-a-bye," he crooned. Then laughed, and crooned some more, "Something something pretty horses."

In the swirl of baseball cap and flannel shirt and plastic bags heaped on top of the cart, the Florida sunlight reflected off a disk of shiny white: the very top of the white cap on R.E.'s bottle of rub-a-dub. A little white cap with tiny grooves all around to make the cap easier for fingers to grip, turn, and remove. That cap—Carter had a notion about that cap that made him smile; that cap covered an entrance to a hidden place as large and wonderful as the cave made famous in *Ali Baba and the Forty Thieves*.

Ali Baba and the Forty Thieves was dear to the heart of Carter, who remembered, as a boy, watching on his family's new television Sal Mineo in the role of the poor woodcutter who gains entrance to the treasure cave of the Forty Thieves by learning the magical phrase "Open, Sesame." The thrill of the cave opening upon shining urns! Trunks overflowing with gold coins! King-size heaps of precious lamps! Casks of gemstones fracturing the light! (Mistaking the realities of stage sets for a failure of story, Duncan Clay had scoffed from his big vinyl chair, "What do you bet that jewelry ain't real, and they got lumber or hay bales propping all that other stuff up too?")

"Open, Sesame." Carter—now dappled gold and mauve by the sun coming through the oleanders—laughed at the funny phrase, and, really, since he had already received the Demerol from the doctor, who could hold it against him if, today, he took a sip of the rub-a-dub? And wouldn't taking a real sip of rub-a-dub correct what had been, in fact, a kind of lie told to his old buddy R.E.? If anything, Carter's affection for R.E. had grown since he had last seen the man. Okay, maybe they could not spend a lot of time together. Okay, maybe that would be unwise. But what kind of shit was he to lie to a fellow vet about something as stupid as a swig of rub-a-dub?

Carter set the fingers of his good hand around the neck of the bottle and pulled it from the folds of blankets. A noise followed the bottle's removal—a rustle, a skitter. Carter started at the sound, but then a mockingbird flew out from the nearby oleanders and Carter assumed that his lousy hearing had tricked him about the noise and its location.

▪ ▪ ▪

It was not until after Carter and R.E. roared down Post Road—drunk, drunk, drunk, the Who singing "Magic Bus"—and one wheel of Carter's van went off the berm, and then two, and R.E.'s shopping cart slammed into the wall of the van and tipped over; it was not until then that there was proof that the sound Carter had heard in the alley had indeed come from the cart: it was the sound of a pet ferret belonging to R.E.

After the cart tipped—enraged, one paw crushed—the ferret, Nietzsche, managed to scamper across the van floor and up the big body of Carter, who was, by then, too blotto and numb and busy trying to steer the van back onto the road to notice the animal until it took his earlobe between its sharp, sharp teeth.

It was the ferret that Carter was battling when the family turned up in front of his van. A nightmare of boom, and boom, boom.

3

That accident—it was blood spilled and damage done to tissue and bone and lives changed forever. Worlds of *hurt*, hurting.

But it is necessary to ask: Is there a difference in your experience of this horrible event if you proceed from *here*, rather than some later *there*, with the knowledge—still unavailable to Carter Clay—that his old friend R.E. had come to Sabine that August morning with the express intention of killing Clay? That, in fact, it was R.E. (*né* Finis Pruitt) who had done his best—one year ago—to stab Clay to death in Howell Park?

Also, consider: how much will you make of the fact that the unwillingness of Joe Alitz to ask directions placed his family in the path of a man, Carter Clay, who was unwilling to refuse the chemicals that would contribute to his driving his van into Joe Alitz's family?

Unlike R.E., neither Carter nor Joe meant to do evil, or even ill. Of course, neither could be strictly said to have been doing *his best*—if his best was something over which either man truly had control. And granting that Joe's being hit by a drunk driver as he stood, lost, on Post Road is even more fortuitous than, say, Joe's being hit by a driver to whom he had "flipped the bird." And that refusing to ask for directions falls into a different category of failings from driving while drunk.

■ ■ ■

The preceding considerations, of course, did not occur to the first motorist to happen upon the accident scene. She—having gone through a life in which, at first glance, she often mistook roadside garbage (seed bag, sweatshirt, tarp flown from a camper's roof) for injured human or pet—this time mistook actual bodies for rills of spilled industrial rags.

By then, almost half an hour had passed since Carter Clay's van hit the family.

▪ ▪ ▪

Immediately following the accident, when Carter Clay brought the van to a stop, R.E.—frantic, his plans for killing Clay falling apart before his eyes—R.E. began to scream, "Drive! Get us out of here, fool!"

But Carter Clay could not stop himself from bursting out of the door of the van, batting off the ferret as he ran back toward the bodies in the road. He screamed and flailed his arms about—

Someone else screamed, too, but then that strand of sound disappeared and there was only the thunder of radio preaching entangled with "Magic Bus"—

"Get back in the van!" R.E. yelled. "You're hurt, man! Your head's bleeding! Come on! We got to get out of here!"

R.E. had recaptured the furious Nietzsche by the time he drew even with Carter and the first victim. R.E. struggled to hold the ferret with one hand while trying to pull Carter toward the van with the other.

"He's dead, man! Come on!"

With a moan, Carter ran to the next victim. He knew such things could happen to a human being, of course—he had seen bodies transformed into trash again and again during the war—still, Post Road tipped when he looked at what he had wrought on that sunny day. His knees buckled, and he grabbed at the roof of the blue sedan where its door stood open to the backseat.

"Jo-nah was afraid to do God's bidding," clamored the sedan's radio, "now wasn't he, friends? Jo-nah tried to run from the task given him, but he could not hide!"

"Where's the other one?" Carter wailed. Boom, boom, boom. Three, he knew for certain. His knees hit the metal rim of the sedan's threshold. Horror at his deed had set the world ablaze. The sedan's backseat and its contents glowed: radiant hairbrush, lady's purse, colored pencils, army surplus knapsack with a homemade maze decorating its green canvas flap. JERSEY ALITZ: the name written in the center of that maze.

R.E. used his free hand to reach past Carter to grab the lady's purse from the spot where it sat on the car floor.

"Put that back!" Carter wailed. "We got to look—I think there's another one!"

Carter started down the bank of the ditch. Had he taken a few steps more, he would have found Jersey Alitz, who lay in a tall stand of cattails, but something struck his shoulder then—hard enough that he turned.

R.E. In one hand, R.E. held the twisting ferret; in the other, a gun with which he motioned wildly toward the van. "Move it, Clay!" he shouted—ferret dangling, purse swinging. "Get back in the van!"

Carter stared at the gun, and what he felt just then was not so much fear of the gun as anger that someone asked him to put up with greed and impatience at this nightmare moment, and the blow that Carter delivered to the jaw of the astonished R.E. pumped straight out of Carter's heart, and it made R.E. crumple, contract like a concertina.

Carter moaned and rubbed his hand and sank down on his haunches while the ferret slunk off across the road and disappeared.

For a time, then, time stopped for Carter on Post Road. To keep from seeing the woman beside him—she looked as if she had shot herself in the head with that gun that now lay between herself and R.E.—to keep from seeing her, Carter stared at the gun. A Colt .45. The gun Carter knew best in all the world, and not just because the .45 had been standard issue in Vietnam. No. Carter's father, Duncan Clay, had brought home a Colt .45 from World War II. He always kept it sandwiched between his T-shirts in his underwear drawer. "Why didn't you use my gun?" Duncan Clay had demanded of Carter's mother after her penultimate suicide attempt. "You wouldn't be whining around if you ever thought to use something that'd get the job done!"

With the tip of R.E.'s gun's barrel, Carter pulled the purse off R.E.'s arm and returned it to the backseat of the sedan.

Impossible to fit the long-barreled Colt into the pocket of his pants. There was blood on his shirt and pants, but that was his own blood, from his forehead. That blood did not matter.

The moment he finished thinking this thought, a second thought occurred to him: he should have *made* R.E. shoot him. Administer immediate justice.

"R.E." In his own ears, Carter's voice was strange, small and trembling, an echo. "Hey, buddy! Wake up!"

R.E.'s eyeballs rolled behind their lids, but the lids did not open.

Carter pulled his sticky shirt away from his chest in order to drop the big gun down the shirt's open neck. He did not hear the song that played on the van's cassette—"My Generation"—or any other noise. He looked around—for a hook to draw him up into the white-bright sky? But everything was as it was, ruined, and he saw his van hit these ruined people again (boom, boom, boom), and, then, a new terror overtook him. The woman on the ground was no longer just his victim—she was evidence, and so was the man back further down the road.

"Hey, man," he murmured as he hauled R.E. up from the ground and slung him over his shoulder and hustled toward the music-blaring van. "You're going to be okay, man," he said. And it all felt reassuringly familiar. The rescue of a downed man from the field.

Careful, careful, Carter placed R.E. upon the softest of the litter that had spilled from the shopping cart and onto the van's ribbed floor; then, with an eye on the road, he pulled a flannel shirt from the litter and wrapped it around his own bleeding head.

Once, when Carter's mother had cried over some meanness done by Carter's drunken father, father turned to son to say, "*I* only cry when I'm killing someone." Carter was nine or ten at the time. He took his father's words as instruction, as he was, no doubt, meant to do. Since the war, Carter had not cried. Now, crying, shuddering, he climbed behind the wheel of the van and he drove.

4

The universe that Jersey Alitz inhabits at the hospital is much denser than the sunlit acre that the Sabine doctor gave Carter Clay in exchange for the stitches in his hand. Jersey's dope has put her to work measuring those interesting interstices between here and there. Still, she has found a hole through which she understands that the woman who sometimes speaks is M.B., her mother's mother, her own grandmother, yes.

To whom does M.B. speak? To Jersey herself? To the silver-haired man in black who stands at the end of the bed? No matter. Jersey is shiveringly delicious. Jersey is a dish of cream being lapped up by her very own tongue, a sensation so lovely that it makes her laugh aloud.

Ah! M.B. and the man in black turn Jersey's way. Such sad faces! Yet *funny* is the word Jersey means to say to them. Because she feels exquisite, and the light is liquid pearl, and could the man in black be the silver-haired lunatic who preaches at her parents' university? St. Tom the Baptist, the student hecklers call that one. Tanned and handsome Tom, who looks as if he might officiate at a country club. Preacher Tom. Tommy Boy. And because of his silver hair, Foxy.

When Jersey says, "Structure," M.B. and the man in black bend close. It is Jersey's plan to tell them that the hair color of the man in black, like that of St. Tom, is the result of structure, not pigment. Under a microscope—Jersey has seen this—a strand of such silvery hair is crystalline as a handful of snow.

"What is it, kid?"

Jersey tries again: "Struc-ture." But the act of speech has changed. Speech, she discovers, must now be built with the solid mass of tongue, carefully detonated into echoing skull and mouth; and there is a distraction, a smell, something that reminds Jersey of one of the solvents her parents use in the field—

Up pops M.B.'s tiny wrinkled face! Like a toy that has been held under in a tub of water! Then the smell and M.B.'s face recede, and M.B. says to the man in black, "Just chatter. They got her so full of dope, she don't—*doesn't* know which end's up."

"Poodle in the noodle?" Jersey laughs as she says the silly phrase—which is, in fact, M.B.'s own phrase for someone mixed up. M.B. and the man, however, seem not to hear. They are farther away now, farther. Leaning together, they make up a slender volcanic cone along Jersey's very private, very white horizon, and she wishes she could show them how strange they look, make them come over where she is, and look back, and see themselves.

Over *here*. Please. Because Jersey is suddenly very alone over here, and the heaven in her head begins to shudder and grow and prove itself no heaven at all, no, it is a *box* that heaves with its own vile contents.

"What is it? What's happened?" she pleads, but all that she receives is M.B. and the strange man, squeezing her hands and saying, "There, there," words without meaning, *there, there,* pretenders to content—like blanks in a gun. Jersey, however, is a smart girl, and when she considers the object at which the pair points those words, *there, there,* what does she find but herself, and so she opens her mouth, and then opens it wider still and begins to scream.

5

Though the *Gulf News* does not detail the death of Joseph Alitz (full impact, hit and run), a week later the paper does run a complete article on the accident. The accompanying photograph of Joseph Alitz is drawn from the jacket of his most recent book, and Finis Pruitt—aka R.E. and/or Private Rear End—Finis Pruitt, reading the newspaper behind the Accordion Cafe, tries to imagine Joseph Alitz in front of a class. Quite erroneously, Finis Pruitt decides Alitz was a prig, the type to oh-so-dramatically remove his watch at the beginning of each lecture and set it on the corner of the desk for periodic, purse-lipped referral.

With a little clipper he carries for the purpose, Finis Pruitt cuts the article from the newspaper. Wonders, not so idly: has Carter Clay seen it?

Amazing to Finis: that he has such a piece of clearly bad shit on Clay. And frustrating: the *Gulf News* of two days before included a bit with M.B. Milhause, mother of Katherine, begging people to come forward and collect the twenty-five hundred dollars being offered for information leading to arrest and conviction of the driver.

Finis's money, for the asking! But Finis does not want Clay in prison. Finis wants Clay *dead. Kaput*. Finis wants Clay *FINIS*.

The truth: This second failure to kill Clay has left Finis ashamed of himself. And so he will be until Clay is no more.

Where he went wrong: He hesitated before shooting Clay. He did not behave like a warrior.

Perhaps it is true that it is hard to kill one's own monster. You fall in love with it a little.

Mr. Clay, a veteran of the Vietnam War, was known to suffer from depression and various addictions.

So Finis had imagined the newspaper saying after the police found Clay dead with a hole in his head: clearly a suicide.

Oh! Finis jumps as someone from the Accordion Cafe flings open the back screen door and tosses out some horrific thing, head-sized and dripping. Oh!

Iceberg gone to rot.

The screen door slams back into place. Finis holds his heart—even in private he tends toward the dramatic—and continues to excoriate himself:

I was lazy at the penultimate moment! I was too eager to entertain myself with an amusing notion: *Why not have Clay drive me to Solana before I do the deed? Yes, and there I'll suggest we stop for a time at some remote little park, where Clay shall drink until he passes out—as Clay always does when he drinks—and there I shall put the .45 in Clay's mouth, and do the deed.*

Not a pleasant prospect, the shooting, but it had to be done. He was prepared to do it, he felt certain.

Could the people in Sabine be lying when they tell Finis that they have no idea where Clay has gone? Since the accident—between nights spent under a kudzu-covered bridge—Finis has done nothing but try to find Clay again, but both times he telephoned the Accordion Cafe, he was told, *We don't know where Carter went. If you see him, tell him we miss him, OK?*

And at the AA meetings—when Finis hinted, in a voice oozing concern, that folks ought to keep an eye out for a now-missing member of their flock as he might be a little *loco en la cabeza*, folks—the members listened politely, but not one of them pressed Finis for details or offered a theory about where Clay might be.

On page 3 of the *Gulf News*, the article about the accident continues. There are two more photos: Jersey Alitz-Milhause and her mother, Katherine Milhause. In addition—clip, zip—here's a tidy illustration of the trauma that occurred to Katherine Milhause's brain after her skull slammed into the asphalt road. In the illustration—perhaps to spare the newspaper's readership—the head has been reduced to little more than an oval with a bump for a nose. Finis judges that this outline appears less that of a head than, say, a swimming pool. He may be correct, but this does not stop many readers who see the illustration from experiencing odd pluckings in their joints and guts as they pull back from the big sheets of newsprint in their hands.

■ ■ ■

It is certainly true that three weeks later, when Jersey Alitz convinces her doctors and her grandmother that it is safe for her to take a gurney ride to the room of her brain-damaged mother—a bright space, all white walls and stainless steel—the poor girl can locate nothing of her pretty mom in that smashed and bloated jack-o'-lantern she finds in the hospital's snarl of machinery: tracheostomy tube, feeding tube, heparin drip, heart monitor, oxygen meter, catheter, respirator. This creature's hands are swollen large as catcher's mitts. Even the feet at the end of the bed are strange blue roots, frozen, pointing one toward the other—

Jersey *wants* the creature to be her mother—she wants her mother—but she has not expected this. The juddering in her chest makes her fear she may be ill, and she reaches out a hand to M.B., and says an urgent, "Here."

Like Jersey, M.B. has lost a great deal of weight since the accident, an occurrence that has made Jersey look younger, M.B. older. M.B. tries to give Jersey a smile of reassurance, but what comes out is crumpled as the balled-up kerchief she holds in her hand: a grimace.

The grimace leaves Jersey feeling bereft; however, before M.B. arrived, Jersey determined a rule for herself: no tears during this visit to her mother. None. There was a period, Jersey knows, in which she screamed. Not in pain but—vigilance, an attempt to alert the heavens to what had happened and convince them that they must reverse it. Those screams—she drove them out of herself like horses from a burning barn. Still, when she was done, she found that nothing had been saved. All that remained were ashes, and herself to contemplate them.

So: no tears. And perhaps she will succeed. While the neurosurgeon, Dr. Subhas Mukhergee, explains in his mellifluous voice, "Even five years ago, chances are she would not have made it," Jersey distracts herself by imagining that she is the needle that draws the thread that forms the little blue seashells stitched into the leather of the handbag that sits in M.B.'s lap. Threads of powder blue and cerulean and royal, lighter grading into darker and back again, under and up and over, up and over.

Diffuse is the word Dr. Mukhergee uses to describe Katherine's injuries: contusions, lacerations, bleeding, cerebral cicatrix. When he moves his hands about in soft circles of expression, M.B. nods.

"We just got to remember," she says, "the Lord don't put a thing in our path we can't handle, right, doctor?"

Up and over and down goes the needle. The first shell is a conch, and the second a murex, but Jersey cannot help hearing her grandmother's words, and she protests, "Don't say that!"—a mistake, for as soon as she opens her mouth, her eyes well with tears.

Though M.B. might ignore the words of the girl, she feels wounded by the solemn nod of agreement from Dr. Mukhergee. Overexposure to death and disaster have given the doctor a patina that, in combination with his heavy-lidded eyes, his dark skin, makes M.B. regard him as a gilded and slightly dangerous god.

Jersey, on the other hand, does not know what to make of the man. Suppose he is fourth-rate, and how is she to know? Can she trust the judgment of M.B.? Back when Jersey was six or seven, Katherine—always trying to prepare for disasters—decided that the family should have a code word. With a code word, in an emergency a person unknown to Jersey could prove himself parent-approved. *Christmas tree* was the code word that Jersey selected, but no one ever had to use it. Joe or Katherine or a duly appointed friend or sitter always managed to retrieve Jersey at the swimming pool or Girl Scouts. There were no disasters until *now*, when neither Joe nor Katherine can give the code to anyone.

Dr. Mukhergee crouches beside the girl's gurney, bringing his face level with Jersey's own. "Your mother's a real fighter," he says. "You're both fighters. You're lucky."

Lucky. Dr. Mukhergee is, of course, correct in a world in which survival is considered a good, but that does not stop Jersey from turning her face from his hot breath. She does not yet understand that the others whose stories appeared in the newspapers—the victims about whom *she* used to read—they no more planned to partake in disaster than Jersey herself. Later, she will see how the way in which she once interpreted the details of other victims' stories as harbingers of their now-published disasters was a kind of mental knock on wood. (Surely the heart-shaped locket that the rape-murder victim wore in her senior class photo indicated a nature too trusting for this world?)

"Dr. Mukhergee—" She wants to ask him if she might touch her mother. Her mother's toes, perhaps. That would be some sort of consolation, she thinks. Skin to skin. Her cheek pressed hard to the sole of her mother's foot. But just as she wonders how to ask permission for this small thing—suppose her touch is explosive, all of the sustaining equipment blasts apart—a terrible darkness flickers through the white room, and Jersey cries, "Oh! Is she okay? Did the electricity go out?"

Dr. Mukhergee gives a kindly laugh. "It was just a gull flying past the window. You just saw the gull's shadow."

▪ ▪ ▪

A herring gull.

Which has nabbed a Cheeto tossed up to it by Carter Clay, who eats his lunch on a bench in the little sculpture garden below. Carter Clay has recently begun work at the hospital, as an orderly. He lives in Bradenton now, occupying the echoey unused second floor of a storefront beauty salon (lavender paint from last month's resident masseuse, the sweet stink of permanent wave solution and shampoo wafting up from below).

With clean-shaven head and face, white work clothes, and apologetic air, Carter Clay now looks very little like that bearded pirate M.B. spied beneath the hospital portico three weeks before.

The day that he shaved his head and face with those razors originally purchased for use on his veins, penance was Carter's acknowledged aim—penance and some sort of removal of self—but as soon as people on the street began to call him Mr. Clean, Kojak, and Yul, he had to admit that he had also fashioned a disguise.

6

After the accident, on the long drive back to Sabine, somehow or other Carter's grief had veered into another region, where he began to entertain what now seem to him the most absurd of thoughts: he would return to work at the Accordion Cafe, to his little room, to the friendly AA meetings at Full Gospel Baptist. There had been no witnesses to the accident. Luck was with him. After he cleaned up the front of the van in a slough, and reassembled the contents of the shopping cart—R.E.'s Colt .45 forming the hot coal at the center—he drove his comatose friend back to that alley in Sabine. There—in some other lifetime, it seemed—dogs had barked and R.E. had given Carter the Electric Prunes album. Now, the dogs stood quiet as accomplices when Carter lifted R.E., and then the unwieldy Winn-Dixie cart, from the back of the van. R.E. groaned but did not wake when Carter laid him on the pile of firewood behind the privet hedge, nor when he attached a twenty-dollar bill and a note to the buttons of R.E.'s shirt:

Sorry about your jaw, buddy. Had to take off.

It was only after Carter parked the van in back of Mrs. Dickerson's rooming house that he began to return to reality. Mrs. Dickerson was out in her yard, whisking bedsheets from the line. She looked the same as always—steel-gray bob, pastel knit pants with the stretch waist—and seeing her, Carter understood that *he* was different because of what had occurred on Post Road.

"Hey, Rambo!" Mrs. Dickerson called with a laugh. "You look like something the cat dragged in!" She was far enough across the yard to miss the way the Carter's teeth rattled while he told her his story: bumped his head while helping a friend clean out a septic tank. Mrs. Dickerson held her nose and giggled and called to him, "You better get in the tub, boy! And use some hydrogen peroxide if you got a cut!"

Though Carter was still drunk, by then the Demerol had begun to wear off. He was ashamed that he could even *feel* pain after what he had done, but there it was. Big. Throbbing. He shut himself into the green bathroom in Mrs. Dickerson's hall. While he tried to think what roads he could take to get himself out of Florida the quickest, he unwrapped R.E.'s shirt from his head and removed the now filthy bandages that the doctor had so carefully wrapped around his hand earlier that day. The doctor's gauze had retained the water from the slough, and in the logy white skin of Carter's finger, the stitches looked like a parasite that had locked onto him but good. His forehead should have been stitched, too. Had he looked into the mirror of Mrs. Dickerson's medicine cabinet, he would have seen that when he hit the windshield of the van, the skin had burst open in a fat X. His cut, swollen forehead resembled a gruesome dough—pink, clotted, slashed across its top to help it in the rising.

But Carter did not look in the mirror. Could not. Could not stop shaking. Could not even call out that he was not hungry when Mrs. Dickerson knocked on the door and said, "Supper!" Could not read the highlighted parts of *Moby-Dick*, or page 58 ("How it works") of *Alcoholics Anonymous*. Could not make room for the books' words above the battering in his head.

Boom, boom, boom.

"Carter"—it was dark when Mrs. Dickerson returned, and she kept her voice low on the other side of his door—"you need anything, dear?"

"I'm just a little under the weather, ma'am, but thanks."

Trembling, he fed his fish. Said the Serenity Prayer and the Our Father, the way they did at the AA meetings.

God forgives us everything we do, but we still have to make amends to His people. So said the AA old-timer with whom Carter had been paired by Recovery House. An ex-Marine with a trucker's cap that read Young Fart, the old-timer had volunteered to explain "working the Steps" to Carter.

"If you like, you can share your moral inventory with me," the old-timer had murmured. The two sat in the Recovery House kitchen at the time—a high-ceilinged white room, its only color coming from the many boxes of cereal on a shelf over the stove. "Since I was over there, too, you wouldn't need to feel you had to leave anything out with me. If you raped a girl, whatever—I'm pretty much shockproof." One of the younger residents, passing through the kitchen, grinned at the old-timer's cap, and the old-timer yanked the thing off and wedged it between his thigh and the seat of his chair.

Carter said he had never raped anybody, he would never rape anybody. The man nodded. "Fine."

"I wasn't some Charlie Manson. And I had a chaplain tell me—over there—he said you didn't judge people by what they done in a war. People ain't themselves in a war."

The man leaned forward. He put his hands on Carter's knees. A red band across his forehead showed where his cap had pressed into his skin. "You believe that?" he asked.

Carter had not known how to answer.

And now—in peacetime, with no excuses at all—he had probably killed two people. Maybe three—

Between the last pages of *Moby-Dick*, Carter kept the money that he had saved from work: nine one-hundred-dollar bills. He took the bills—crisp, ironed—out of the book, and inserted them in his wallet. Sat on the side of the bed. Clutched Mrs. Dickerson's chenille spread with his good hand.

The thought of Mrs. Dickerson finding out about the accident—it gave Carter a shoulder-jerking chill.

Say he called Fort Powden—his sister, or his old friend Neff Morgan. When Bonnie Drabnek and her kids had left Carter,

Neff Morgan helped Carter look for them. Neff Morgan nursed Carter through the worst drunks of those days. Both Neff and Cheryl Lynn had put up with a lot. Once, when Neff tried to stop Carter from going out on the road, Carter broke Neff's collarbone, and Neff not only forgave Carter afterward but loaned him money. Actually, Carter still owed both Cheryl Lynn *and* Neff money.

Say Carter killed himself. Or turned himself in to the police. He wouldn't need money then. He could split his nine hundred dollars between Cheryl Lynn and Neff and Mrs. Dickerson.

His father—he could not call his father. The last time he had run into Duncan—a little pit bull of a man—Duncan had walked into Rex's Bowladrome, swinging. There had been a number of occasions when, out of old fear and a sense of rank, Carter had allowed Duncan to beat him, but that last time, Carter had hit back, sent the old man sprawling into tables and chairs.

Well. Well. And, really, what would be the point of calling Duncan or Cheryl Lynn or Neff about the accident? Just to share his guilt? Bad enough that R.E. was mixed up in the mess. Why put the crap on one more person's shoulders?

Carter lay back on the bed. The former bed of Mrs. Dickerson's daughter. When he reached up to turn off the lamp, he could see on the wall the outlines of a trio of painted-over decals: Mary with her little lamb as it followed her to the school.

Even with the lamp off, the nighttime walls of the room rang with light. The crescent moon outside the window was a tear in the fabric of the sky, and Carter knew it delivered a message from a world beyond that he was not pure enough to read.

Well, sleep was impossible.

At three-thirty—clean red bandanna covering his forehead, clean gauze covering the stitches on his hand—he drove the van into the pale gravel lot across the street from the Sabine police station. Parked. Such a lot of noise that gravel made!

I'm the one, he would say. But he did not get out of the van. Could not. The pain in his head had affected his hearing, his vision. The glass in the police station door—he took it for a sheet of white paper until one of the officers, can of pop in hand, crossed behind it. Would that be the officer to whom Carter would have to tell his tale? A chubby guy. Laughing, now. Or maybe just yawning.

Is it ironic that when Carter had first arrived home from Vietnam, he considered becoming a police officer? Before he ever got around to applying to the academy, however, he went to do a roofing job and, high on THC, backed off the roof, hurt his back. Which led to an intimate relationship between himself and Percodan. Eventually, then, he concluded that the idea of being a police officer sounded like a little kid's dream; not all that far off from his childhood notion that when he grew up he would work at the pulp, like his dad.

What? Carter had once dreamed of going to a stinking slop of a job making paper bags for America's groceries so that he could come home each night, drunk, and get a little drunker and bat around a wife and kids? Of course not. In Carter's dream, the thermos and lunch box were the knight-in-armor's disguise. The knight might appear cruel at home, but every day, he saved the family from starvation; and every night, his cruelty kept from the door those dragons more vicious than himself.

After Carter returned from Vietnam, if you had asked him when he gave up the dream of working at the pulp, he would not have been able to tell you the answer. Which is not so unusual. How many people remember the abandonment of childhood dreams? However, a few years later, Carter also would not remember if the roof accident came before or after he worked up the coast at the cannery or painted houses with Jim Miner. He *would* know that he worked at the cannery when he lived with Bonnie Drabnek and her kids because, in the beginning, both he and Bonnie Drabnek worked at the cannery. In the beginning, Bonnie seemed like the answer. She reminded Carter of certain beautiful, smiling women he had seen at work on family farms in the hills of Vietnam. In the beginning, just like a regular couple, Bonnie and Carter and the kids went to picnics and softball games with other people from the cannery. Together, they rented one of the quonset huts owned by the cannery. The days seemed innocent and good—though Bonnie told him she would not marry him until he stopped drinking so much. Sometimes, she said, he scared her, and the little ones, too. He knew he screamed in his sleep now and then, but Bonnie said—she was sorry, she had to tell him—sometimes, when he passed out, she saw dead people rise out of his head. *Like steam*, was how she put it.

Then, somewhere along the way, Bonnie took up drinking. Stopped getting up in the morning. Tears ran down her cheeks at all hours of the day. She locked herself in the bathroom. *Living with Carter was poison!* she cried from behind the door. *Carter was cursed!* During the war—so the Invit part of Bonnie believed—Carter's soul had gone to the land of the dead and tasted the food there, and so become forever lost.

Carter was worried that winter night when Bonnie's aunt and uncle and a cousin drove up to the quonset hut. Bonnie had stopped taking care of the children by then, and though Carter tried to keep them fed and clean, he supposed the relatives had heard things were bad. But the relatives climbed down from their old truck as if everything were fine, this was a social call. The uncle and the cousin each carried two bottles of Jim Beam. Like bracelets, a couple of rings of summer sausage hung from the aunt's thick wrists. The aunt was supposed to be the tough member of the group, but even she did not complain about the fact that you could see your breath in the hut (there had not been money to have the gas tank filled); and soon Carter was drunk enough to feel close to all three visitors. He drew a kitchen chair up to the easy chair where the aunt sat. "Things'd be better if Bonnie would marry me," he said.

The aunt laughed and gave Carter a tap on the arm with the brush she was using to work out the snarls in Bonnie's hair. "Look at her," the aunt said. "Look at you. Why should either of you want to be with either of you?" She shook her head, but she laughed. Carter thought they were having a party until he came to, and found himself alone—the only thing left behind, except for the empty bottles of Jim Beam, and the training papers for the stray he'd recently brought home for the kids.

In the war, other people were always trying to kill him while he was trying to stay alive. What was crazy: after he got out, he often thought of killing *himself*. "I'll just have to kill myself," he would say—sometimes right out loud—because his head was full of too much bad stuff. But he did not kill himself. He didn't even try, and sometimes he had to wonder if this showed he was at heart just the coward his father always said he was.

▪ ▪ ▪

In the police station parking lot—brain racked with fear and guilt from yesterday's drugs—he watched the night sky fade to a phlegm-colored dawn that suddenly rustled its wings and turned into a parroty pink thing that gave the impression it had been dreamed up to move a human heart.

An officer came out of the station at five-fifteen. He headed straight toward the parking lot, and, for a moment. the left artery in Carter's neck did a little dance of fear. Should he bolt? Should he say, *I am the one, I am the one who—*

Blood thundered in his ears. It seemed the officer headed straight for Carter and the van, but then the officer veered right, to a little hatchback a few feet off. A man close to Carter's own age. Slender. Hispanic, Italian. He came into the Accordion for coffee, and, on Sunday mornings, sometimes showed up for breakfast with a pretty wife and two little girls.

The officer dug in his pockets for his car key. He began to sing, a song out of his own and Carter's youth:

Oh, I could say I love you, but then you'd realize
That I want you just like a thousand other guys
Who'd say they'd love you
For all the rest of their lives
When all they wanted was to—

"Cherish." Carter and his friends had made fun of "Cherish"—a "girls' song"—but Carter, like many of those friends, had secretly liked it.

The officer broke off his singing. He turned. Yes, there was another person in the lot. "Excuse my—serenade," he murmured to Carter, and climbed into the hatchback.

Carter tried to nod. *Thumpthumpthump* went his right foot against the floor of the car—as if he were a dog scratched in the wrong spot. He could remember that foot-thumping from other times: terrified, crouched in a foxhole, knee jerking up and down like a piston.

Surely it was wrong for one man to have the power to scare another man as much as the officer had scared him. Such fear made Carter angry, and his anger made him forget why he had felt afraid of the officer in the first place, and as soon as the little hatchback disappeared from sight, he started up the van.

I could kill myself. So he thought. *Administer my own justice instead of messing with those fools*.

He pulled onto Crown Street. Drove past the Accordion. Crossed over February Street, which led back to Mrs. Dickerson's, and then the street that led to the little Baptist church where he had attended so many AA meetings. But hey, he was obliged to make sure that R.E. was okay, wasn't he?

He found his way to the alley behind the tangerine garage. Parked. Stuck his head through the privet. Sweet relief. Neither friend nor cart remained in the spot.

The houses thinned as he reached the edge of Sabine. Now and again he felt like crying, but what he created was more steam than tears; heat radiated from his cheeks, forehead, and chest. For quite a while, he simply drove north on 17. Boom, boom, boom. His hand ached. His head ached. His feet prickled with the heat coming off the engine. The sun-shocked landscape left him nauseated, but it helped to focus on the landscape and his bodily pains. When he withdrew from them, he found himself shaking, staring at the woman who looked as if someone had shot her in the head—

Two children and a dog. Stepping up onto the shoulder of the highway from out of nowhere.

Carter made an exaggerated swerve to the left, then shrieked at himself, "Pay attention!"

At the next exit, he turned around. Drove south. Where to go?

When he finally turned east at Bartow, it was not a decision, just a movement of the arms; as was his subsequent turnoff in a town whose name he did not even bother to absorb.

A weedy little place. It cracked open before him like an old, dusty book. Would you suppose he had trouble finding the store that sold liquor?

An old silver trailer. Just inside the trailer's screen door, a German shepherd lay on a love seat. When Carter stopped to adjust his eyes to the trailer's dark, the animal stretched its neck long to look up at him. "Hey, there." Carter crouched to pet the handsome creature. "Hey." Had he been alone in the store, he would have sunk his face into the dog's ruff and stayed there a while.

"That's Cleopatra," called a woman working on a ladder at the back of the trailer. With her chopped and oily hair, her shorts revealing legs knotted and bruised with veins, the woman reminded Carter of Ellie, who ran the bait shop of his childhood. He found himself thinking of the clerk as the age of his mother, before it occurred to him that she might be younger than himself.

"What do you need?"

Razor blades, please, and a fifth of Smirnoff.

Just across the street from the trailer there sat a sagging place called the Turquoise Motel. Not bothering to move the van from the bit of packed earth and weeds that served as the store's parking lot, Carter rented one of the Turquoise Motel's eight rooms.

A flute of grime decorated the baseboards. The batting showed gray through the threadbare coral and turquoise quilt. Carter opened his bottle while the ancient television set warmed.

Lassie, from the 1950s. Carter's heart heaved painfully at the sight of the beautiful collie on the screen, and the sweet and melancholy whistling that played over the credits. *Lassie* was the show that had first made Carter want to learn how to whistle. His father forbade his whistling in the house, but Carter whistled up and down the alleys and streets, and he could remember how he had felt, whistling the *Lassie* song, that he and his family were actually wonderful people who had been cast under an evil spell.

After *Lassie* ended, on came the succession of old programs (*The Real McCoys*, *The Andy Griffith Show*) that the channel's Christian broadcaster believed to represent better family values than more contemporary productions.

While he drank his vodka, Carter half-listened to Sheriff Andy Taylor sing to his son a song about picking a bale of cotton and a bale of hay. Carter wished that he had kept R.E.'s gun. He could have put the .45 in his mouth, pulled the trigger, and taken care of everything. Though *not* at the Turquoise Motel. Cheryl Lynn had told him about cleaning up after their mother killed herself. It would be almost as bad to slit his wrists at the motel. Coming upon such a sight would surely hurt even a stranger.

"It's only by the grace of God that I'm here today, alive." So Carter had often said at the AA meetings at Full Gospel. In Vietnam, he could have been killed fifty times over. Drinking and drugging, he could have OD'd, or choked on his vomit, or walked out in front of a car. He had a friend at Howell Park who did that. Got drunk and stepped right into traffic.

At AA, Carter liked to tell of the doctors' amazement at his recovery from those stab wounds received at Howell Park: "By the time the lady runners found me, I'd lost so much blood, the doctors weren't sure I'd even be good for donating organs! I guess God wasn't through with me yet!"

Now, however—while Sheriff Taylor and his incompetent deputy, Barney, bickered harmlessly—it seemed to Carter that his earlier escapes from death might have been a terrible mistake, missed opportunities for avoiding yesterday's disaster.

I guess God wasn't through with me yet! Yeah, folks, God was saving my sorry ass so I could go smash up some innocent people while they stood on the side of the road!

Boom, boom, boom.

Carter lay back on the motel's saggy bed. Closed his eyes.

Had there been a third person? A kid?

The credits for *Andy Griffith* played as he crashed into the motel room john and was sick. *The Power of Prayer* was just starting when he plunged back to the bed, and before he passed out, he spent a few minutes watching. The host had skin polished to a rosy granite. He and his pretty wife drank out of fancy teacups on a fancy couch and discussed Ephesians 2:8, 9.

> For by grace are ye saved through faith; and that not of yourselves: it is the gift of God:
>
> Not of works, lest any man should boast.

The nylon stockings on the wife's legs caught black blades of light when she turned on the couch and said to the TV audience, "We hope you know Jesus loves you, friends. Whatever you've done, He loves you still, and He's just waiting for you to take Him up on His offer of eternal salvation!"

■ ■ ■

"We had a deal!"

"I don't make deals!"

Carter's neighbors at the Turquoise Motel were arguing. Two men. It was their shouting that had brought Carter around. The men were much louder than the aged preacher who now spoke on Carter's TV.

A sound of scuffling.

Something falling over with a crash.

Carter raised himself onto his elbows to call, "You okay over there?"

"Mind your own business!"

"Yeah! Fucking mind your own business, Jack!"

The two resumed their quarrel.

"What kind of lousy motherfucking shithead are you, anyway?"

"It is the blood of Christ," said the elderly preacher on the television. Ram-faced. Vaguely familiar.

In an effort to drown out his neighbors, Carter stood and raised the volume on the television: ". . . and His divine and merciful love." Quickly, he changed channels.

A nature show. Baby antelope drinking water. Delicate legs splayed outward. Big eyes. Tail flickering like flame.

"You fuck! You owe me!"

Just then the nature show's only sound came from birdsong in the distant background, and even with the volume set as high as it could go, the song could not compete with the neighbors. A fly landed on the little antelope's ear. Its buzzing gave the birdsong scale. Then the antelope twitched its ear. The fly flew away. The camera panned from the antelope through greenery to a cheetah. Carter jerked as the voice of the authoritative narrator came on, booming:

"Will the cheetah get her chance, now that the antelope has come down to the water hole to drink?"

Another reminder of his childhood, with all of its Disney segments in which beautiful animals were sent through gripping but ultimately harmless adventures.

Shocking, then, when the next frames revealed the cheetah's successful leap, the pathetic struggle of the baby antelope to free itself from the cat's jaws. Flop, went the little neck, and the antelope became—though still in possession of its sweet face—food.

The motel television's reception was apparently limited to a few channels—the Christians, the nature shows, the news—the latter now flashing a set of photographs that stopped Carter's hand, and made him scramble to lower the volume.

Three faces in a row, looking out from the screen like travelers passing by on a train. Underneath them the names: Joseph Alitz. Katherine Milhause. Jersey Alitz.

Carter turned down the volume, but not so much that he could not hear: one dead, two in critical condition in Bradenton Memorial. Boom. Boom. Boom. Said a newscaster in a grave but mellifluous voice:

> The highway patrol continues to investigate yesterday afternoon's accident. Distinguished paleontologists and professors at Arizona University Joseph Alitz and wife, Katherine Milhause, along with daughter, Jersey, were hit as they stood on a rural Manatee County road.

Shots of the accident scene.

A toll-free number for reporting information leading to the arrest of the driver.

Carter's eyes filled. Of course, he had known all along that people would want to arrest him. Still, it made him so agitated, he had to get up again and change the channel.

Carter McKay. That was the name of the ram-faced preacher. Carter McKay had been the preacher Carter's own mother had watched when Carter was a boy. "You come watch, too," Betty Clay would call to Carter and Cheryl Lynn. Betty had named Carter after the preacher, but that was a secret, and maybe Duncan would not like it, so don't tell.

Every Sunday morning, skinny Betty, hands briny from hours spent scrubbing other people's floors, perched on the edge of a kitchen chair, ready to jump up fast and turn off Carter McKay should Duncan thunder into the room. Back in those days, McKay was a handsome man and his show took place in a huge tent, and he howled while he healed the crippled, deaf, and blind. "Jesus, Jesus, cast the devil out of this soul! Jesus, heal this woman's cancerous womb! Jesus, take the darkness from this poor sinner's eyes!" A wild and exciting spectacle back in those days, when Carter McKay spoke often of how he had been a fornicator, a drinker, a liar, a thief, one of Satan's own—until he was called to the Lord.

The motel television sat on a dresser and Carter pressed up against its warm screen while he lifted the bandanna from his forehead and, using the dresser's mirror, inspected the mess now cooking beneath the cloth. Carter McKay used to talk at length about the mark of the Beast. The Beast marked his own, Carter McKay had said, so that they would be known to each other.

Suppose Carter was now marked.

Boom, boom, boom.

But the voice of the old man that vibrated Carter's belly was calm and kind, and it said, "Friend, there's a story Jesus tells us in Luke about a man from Samaria. You all know about the Good Samaritan—about how a man on the road to Jericho was set upon by thieves who robbed and beat him and left him for dead. Two travelers—the man's own people—saw him on the road and did not come to his aid. Then, there came along a man from another country, a man from Samaria, a stranger, and he took pity on that poor bleeding man. He bandaged his wounds and took him to an inn and paid the innkeeper to look after him. This man of Samaria could not tarry in Jericho but he promised, 'When I return, I'll pay you any additional expenses you might incur in caring for this man.'

"You all remember that story, don't you, friends? What you may not remember is who asked the question that prompted Jesus to tell that little story. The answer is: a *lawyer*. This lawyer, you see, understood that to gain eternal life he was to love the Lord with all his heart and all his soul and all his strength and all his mind, and his neighbor as himself; but he had a question for Jesus, and that question was, 'Who is my neighbor?'"

There were Bibles, Carter knew, in the bedside tables of motel rooms; still, he felt shy, like an imposter, as he checked the little shelf below the bedside lamp—

Naked girl bound to an office swivel chair. Giant brown nipples. Thighs spread—

Carter hurried the magazine into the trash before he returned to the Bible that had lain beneath it.

The motel Bible was a fancy thing with a golden cover. In the front was a list of readings under the title "HELP IN TIME OF NEED." The first item on the list was "The Way of Salvation" with suggested readings of Acts 16:31 ("Believe on the Lord Jesus Christ, and you will be saved, you and your household") and Romans 10:9 ("That if you confess with your mouth the Lord Jesus and believe in your heart that God has raised Him from the dead, you will be saved").

"I believe," Carter said, going down on his knees beside the bed. He strained toward the meaning contained in the words. The words were a kernel he needed to apply heat to, to make it pop. At AA, people said it was okay just to be willing to believe, but surely God knew the difference, and judged accordingly. Maybe being willing to believe got you on the right track, but if God was going to forgive your sins, surely you had to give God the real thing.

Boom. Boom. Boom.

And how were you supposed to know if God forgave you? Did you feel it in your bones? Did a light switch on in your head?

But a light had not burned in him *before* the accident.

He read from the motel Bible. On his knees. To show he was

trying. Trying showed that you at least believed there was a good chance somebody watched, right? He listened to the Christian channel. Prayed. All three activities were preferable to what filled his mind when he stopped.

Boom, boom, boom.

At first light, when he finally tried to rise, he found that he felt weighted down, as if he had burrowed into the mattress, and now had to struggle to the surface. On his knees, he made his way to the window. Peeked out from behind the curtains.

No police. No nobody. One car down by the motel check-in. His van parked under a big old cottonwood across the quiet road.

Dawn, he thought as he moved out from under the motel's overhang. He carried the gold Bible under his jacket—though it was true the stamp inside the cover read THOSE IN NEED ARE FREE TO TAKE THIS BOOK. He gave a shiver. Low on the horizon, a molten spoonful of light tipped toward him.

An extravagant word: *dawn*. Carter was not sure he could afford to use it. Somebody might pull the rug out from under a man like Carter while he thought about himself using a word like *dawn*.

Dawn. Salvation. Eternity.

Several birds shot past overhead. Flying west, Carter thought. Pointing the way to Bradenton. It made sense to him, just then—granted, he was sleepy, hung over—it made sense to him that the birds might know that he had hurt innocent people, *killed* a good man, and that the only thing he could do now was try to make things right.

7

There have been times in Carter Clay's life when, for no discernible reason, Carter has thought of a minor intersection where one of the several roads that enter his hometown of Fort Powden changes from fifty-five miles an hour to twenty-five. He sees the complete background of the spot (trees in leaf, their great trunks rising from grass to sky; a food distributor's warehouse; a small bridge topping a drainage ditch). There will never be revealed some deep or hidden reason for Carter's thinking of this spot, whose only claim is that it is a place where, if a person travels in one direction, he must slow down; and, if he travels in the other direction, he is allowed to speed up.

Still, Carter thought of that intersection as he drove toward Bradenton and the hospital holding the girl and her mother. He noted that unbidden memory. Then—because he was on the way to a hospital?—he tried to remember his own stay, a year ago, at the VA in Tampa, and the events around the stabbing.

While Carter was at the VA, and for a time afterward, he believed that his memory of the night he was stabbed—clearly an important night—would come back to him if he worked at it. However, try as he might, he never could piece the thing together. Too many holes too full of alcohol riddled the view. He had not paid much attention to the stranger who was supposed to have been his assailant; embarrassing to admit to the police that all he really remembered was that the guy had worn one of those silky Indy 500 jackets that Carter had always admired.

The evening of the stabbing, when Carter arrived at Shelter #6, the new man was roasting hot dogs over the garbage barrel, passing them out to anyone who was hungry. A nice thing to do, and Carter felt bad that he had to point out that the roasting sticks came from oleander bushes, and, thus, were full of poison. Some of the men—R.E. and a few others—had already eaten the hot dogs by then. They were angry with the new man, and then the new man was angry with Carter. Carter offered the man a drink. He had just been paid for several days of yard work, and he had three bottles of Cuervo Gold to share.

"Fuck off," the newcomer said.

Carter let the matter slide—when you were as big as Carter, you often let things slide. Carter and another regular, Louie Konigsberg, took two of the bottles of tequila and the carton of salt they kept stashed in the shelter rafters, and they set out to scout lemons and limes in the neighborhood trees. Louie—Slim Louie—was wearing a Confederate soldier's cap, and he was getting into that hat, talking with a southern accent. He and Carter managed to end up lying around in the grass with a couple of women who had wandered off from a family reunion.

After that, Carter's memories of the night were vague. According to the police who came to question him at the hospital, Carter had defended R.E. in some argument with the man in the Indy 500 jacket. Supposedly the stranger pulled a knife on Carter. Carter decked him. Then the man lay in wait for Carter and stabbed him on the service road.

As for Carter: when he came around at the hospital, he believed he was lying on top of a burning Willy Pete, and all that mattered was to squirm away from the thing before it blew.

Certain men—R.E. and Louie Konigsberg and a few others—Carter had a vague memory of them visiting him in the hospital in Sarasota before he was transferred to the VA in Tampa.

But Carter did not even remember how the fight at Shelter #6 started. He did not remember the wind high and blowing moisture from the nearby canal; or how, when he and Louie returned to the shelter that night, the man in the Indy 500 jacket stood on one of the concrete benches, holding forth on the storming of the Citadel at Hue. He did not remember interrupting the man in the Indy jacket in order to say, "The Citadel? Did R.E. tell you he was there, too? He's got great stories about fighting in the wrecks of all those bombed-out buildings. And the fire—there was fire on the river there, right, R.E? The Perfume River, right?"

"What kind of bullshit's that?" The man in the Indy jacket took a seat on top of the picnic table. He was still mad over that hot-dog-stick business. "Half an hour ago, R.E. here was telling me how he was a big shot at Khe Sanh with Colonel Lownd's 26th." The man shot a quick glance in R.E.'s direction. "You couldn't have been at Hue *and* Khe Sanh. They're two different places, man. One of you—or both of you—is full of shit."

R.E. laughed his distinctive laugh—a kind of old man of the West whoop and cackle; then, as if the man in the Indy 500 jacket had rendered him hopelessly amused, R.E. let himself roll right off his own piece of bench and onto his knees. "Must have imagined all those people shooting at me, man!" he said, still laughing. "Oh, man! Better check your history book, man!"

Carter and the man in the Indy 500 jacket glared at one another. "You owe me and my friend an apology," Carter said.

The man in the Indy jacket looked scared, but determined. "I don't apologize for other people's bullshit," he said.

R.E. rose to his feet. Waved a hand in the stranger's direction. "Let it go, Clay," he said.

"Fuck him, R.E.! He's calling you a liar, man!"

The man in the Indy jacket trembled—his hands, his shoulders, even his cheeks. "Anybody that was over there without his head up his ass would know you couldn't be at the Citadel and Khe Sanh at the same time," he said.

Carter's neck tugged at his collar. He recognized that feeling and the tight rocking that accompanied it. Rocking in time with his pulse. His shoulders and chest and head tilted back, then rocked forward, back. "I was over there," Carter said.

The man looked at Carter and away. Looked back. Eye to eye. Murmured, "Like I said, man."

The men at Shelter #6 often carried weapons or had a weapon tucked away somewhere, so it was no surprise that the man in the Indy jacket carried a knife, or that he pulled it out when Carter stepped close; but, that night, Carter was drunk and energized by his defense of his friend and himself. Just as R.E.'s gun would later infuriate him on Post Road, the knife of the man at Howell Park infuriated him, and he caught the wrist of the man's knife hand and snapped it back before he whipped a boot-kick into the man's groin.

Carter remembered almost nothing of that fight, or what followed: the newcomer's bellow of pain, the knife flipping into the dirt, the letting loose of a blow that cracked shut the man's teeth and dropped him in the dirt next to his knife.

The other men who had been drinking and smoking at the shelter stayed back while Carter, R.E., and Louie looked down at the man.

"Don't pull no fucking knife on me," Carter spat. His lips and tongue were swollen with anger. He kicked at the knife where it lay in the dirt and pebbles and bits of grass.

"Woo-whee!" R.E. cried. "Fucking A-team, man!"

Louie Konigsberg, however, said a slurred but somber, "That's enough," then held out the remains of one of the bottles of tequila to Carter. "Here."

Carter took the bottle; but before he drank, he bent down and picked up the knife and flung it off in the direction of the canal.

"Bastard," R.E. said. He gave a kick at the downed man, nothing too brutal, but Louie raised his elbow, hard, into R.E.'s chest, and said a gruff, "Leave him be."

"He's a fucking liar!" R.E. protested.

"Maybe so," Louie said. "Maybe so, R.E., but right now, we want to keep things quiet. We don't want cops."

Louie took the bottle from Carter then, and sat on one of the picnic tables. Carter—trembling, sore with tension—joined Louie, but R.E. stayed where he was and leaned against one of the shelter's support timbers and rubbed at the spot where Louie had elbowed him.

After several minutes, the man in the Indy jacket opened his eyes. He got up on his hands and knees but could not quite raise his head. "Fucking bullshit," he mumbled.

"You better take your ass away from here," called a voice from inside the shelter, and someone else agreed, "Haul buns, man!" There were a few laughs, but they did not come from Carter or Louie or R.E.

Awkwardly, the man in the Indy jacket made his way to his unsteady feet. Then he stuffed his pack with the things he had taken out, slung the pack over his shoulder, and straggled off into the bushes.

Carter raised the last of the bottle of tequila toward R.E. He felt bad about Louie elbowing R.E. so hard. "Cheers," Carter said, as if they had just shared a memorable occasion, but, basically, all he would remember was a man in an Indy jacket. Not the fight in which people said he defended the honor of his friend and fellow veteran R.E.

8

According to Jersey's occupational therapist, M.B. Milhause really should think about taking one of the hospital's classes on home care for the paraplegic. The doctor—young, overweight, poorly shaved—nods in vigorous agreement:

"The time she spends at the rehab center will go by fast. You want to be ready."

The three of them sit in a room of the hospital that does not seem to belong to anyone—a gray-carpeted space with a long table, chairs, a rubber plant that has outgrown its pot and now tilts precariously toward the room's single, narrow window. M.B. and the perky therapist drink coffee from disposable cone-shaped cups suspended in reusable plastic holders. M.B.'s holder feels rough in her hand, as if someone has chewed on its handle.

"She's so lucky to have you!" the therapist says.

M.B. makes a thin smile. She knows that the therapist knows that she is twisting M.B.'s arm. Trying to force a yelp of enthusiasm from M.B.

For what?

On one of M.B.'s favorite television shows, real people experiencing gruesome trials—broken spines, amputations, an assortment of horrors—*those* people pray for, and regularly receive, miracles. Loved ones recuperate, wonderful healing occurs in the family, renewed relations, faith in God—while *her* daughter remains in a coma and *her* granddaughter is crippled and sullen with no end in sight.

So wend M.B.'s thoughts as she makes her way down the corridor to Jersey's room.

And Jersey? Just then Jersey is wondering, could the laugh she has just heard from the corridor—a laugh that sounded so much like the laugh of her father!—could it have been some sort of mental ventriloquism? A message to Jersey that her father could deliver only via some more functional passing body?

Once, Jersey's mother said to Jersey, "Just remember, honey, the way your dad and I love you—even if we die—our love will be with you."

Jersey protested, "But you don't even believe in that stuff!" To which Katherine Milhause replied with a laugh, "Well, I do when it comes to you!"

Sometimes now, it is true, Jersey does feel her mother's and her father's love. At the same time, however, she suspects that this feeling may be a trick she plays upon herself. But suppose it is *not* a trick. Worse: suppose that from some notion of intellectual integrity, she were to actually extinguish a wonderful gift? Such thoughts make the girl grind her teeth, wake in the mornings with a sore jaw and raised welts running along the insides of her cheeks.

"M.B.," she says, "did you hear that laugh?"

M.B.'s no is no surprise. Lately, it seems to Jersey that the universe has selected her as a test case of some sort. Nights, in her own hospital room, she hears sounds hidden from her in the past: the chatter of air molecules in collision, plus certain terrible gnawing and digesting sounds that she fears are the din of full consciousness.

Who can she ask about such things?

In the night, the dark sparkles. The bedsheets are granular. She understands the bitter scent that rises from the stiff wrappings on the hospital mattress to be the odor of betrayal.

"I heard a laugh. It sounded just like my dad."

"Hm," says M.B.

That evening, no sooner are the lights turned off in her hospital room than an image arrives, unbidden: herself bringing down a hatchet on a neck that she knows belongs to the driver who hit her parents and herself. Chop, chop, chop. It is no dream but she cannot stop the image—chop, chop—and when the night nurse comes into the darkened room, Jersey whispers, *May she, please, have more medicine? To help her sleep?*

Not without doctor's orders.

The night nurse—Nurse Aguasvivas—is a young and very pretty Cubana whose Negroid hair forms a saintly nimbus in the light from the hall. Nurse Aguasvivas has come to check Jersey's catheter, and to turn her.

Turn her?

To prevent the pressure sores to which Jersey is subject now that messages for movement and feeling are no longer transmitted through her spine to her legs, every two hours a nurse or aide must move the girl into a new position.

So hard to imagine: that simply *not* moving can lead to damage, amputation, even death. Later, while staying at St. Mary's Rehabilitation, Jersey will learn how to shift and elevate her weight in her wheelchair for one minute out of every fifteen. She will begin her own daily inspections of legs and feet and—with a hand mirror—buttocks and hips for that first hint of red that can go dangerously fast to the bluish-black that means a trip to the hospital and possible surgery. At present, however, she is still new to all of this, and shy, and to absent herself from Nurse Aguasvivas's ministrations, Jersey now concentrates on the tiny plastic flashlight that sways from a string around the nurse's neck. In the dark room, the light shining through its translucent blue rim reminds Jersey of a magical glow-in-the-dark Virgin a classmate once displayed at show-and-tell.

Does Nurse Aguasvivas disapprove of Jersey for asking for more medicine? Jersey hopes not. She wants the nurse to think she is fun, to stay and talk, and so she teases Nurse Aguasvivas about her anesthesiologist boyfriend. "How's Dave?"

When the nurse only snorts in reply, Jersey continues, "Better be careful! He probably never told you, but the first person to ever become addicted to IV drugs was the wife of the guy who invented hypodermic needles!"

Another snort from Nurse Aguasvivas. "Now where'd you hear that?"

Because she detects a note of censure in Nurse Aguasvivas's voice, Jersey says, "I don't know." But she does know. It was in her family's very own kitchen, back in Seca. Jersey's mother laughed as she read the tidbit to Jersey's father—but *not* as if what she read were silly; rather, as if she hoped both to prove something serious and to entertain at the same time.

"So, your grandma come to see you today?" Nurse Aguasvivas asks.

In the dark, hidden, Jersey dares to make a face when she says yes. She knows what the hospital nurses think: grandma, granddaughter, cookies and milk, and isn't M.B. a kick with her snappy clothes and bright red hair—

"That's cute, the way you call her 'M.B.,'" says Nurse Aguasvivas.

Jersey does not explain that M.B. forbids Jersey's calling her "Grandma"; that M.B. made Katherine stop calling her "Mom" as soon as Katherine turned ten years old. Instead, Jersey explains to the nurse that Katherine can—could?—fill her mouth with sugar water and let a hummingbird hover right before her lips as it feeds.

"Girl, you got too much imagination!"

"No! I have a picture! Back home! You know what a broad-tailed hummingbird is? Their wings make a whistling noise, they beat so fast. Their backs are iridescent green. You know how come? You know how iridescence works?"

"How iridescence works?" The young nurse laughs, then takes a deep, appreciative whiff of the bouquet of red roses that sits on Jersey's bedside table. "So who's your sweetheart that sends you all these roses, hm?"

"Oh," Jersey says. "Anonymous."

A freind, the sender signs his cards—which excites Jersey's grandmother. *Look at the way the person misspells* friend! *That's just the way your grandpa did it:* f-r-e-i-n-d. As if she wants to believe the roses come from Jersey's grandfather Lorne.

Well, who is Jersey to sneer at such wishes? Still, she hates the roses; the way, all day long, they form a terrible clot in the corner of her left eye. At night—dark and jagged and menacing—they become a demented watchdog that hangs above her, insisting she acknowledge its unfailing loyalty.

During her first week in the hospital, many people from Seca—family friends and classmates, even strangers—sent boxes of candy, flowers, tiny blue and yellow teddy bears clutching shiny Mylar balloons: GET WELL SOON! The weekly bouquets of roses, however, have never stopped coming.

"Hey," Jersey blurts when Nurse Aguasvivas starts to leave the room, "what if—since I can't sleep—could I write in my journal for a while?"

"Fifteen minutes."

"Half an hour? 'Cause it's a story."

▪ ▪ ▪

"Demon Hands," Jersey writes in that journal her father once bought her on a trip to Chinatown. "Demon Hands" was a story her father told as the family drove to Florida. Joe remembered "The Demon Hands" from an old radio show; a little 1940s spookiness that felt tame in the nineties. In her recording of the story, Jersey hopes to capture something of her family; not just Joe and his exuberant tale, but also a whiff of that magic that came off herself and her mother when they sang "Down Yonder Green Valley" or made their lists (every candy you can name, the ten books to take to a desert isle, plans for perfect days).

The car that Joe and Katherine rented for the trip had air-conditioning, but the family took in the sea breeze of nighttime Biloxi while Joe told of that genial but mediocre pianist whose hands are crushed when his carriage collides with the carriage of a murderer—just then attempting to flee the scene of one of his many dastardly deeds.

"Working feverishly through the night," Jersey writes—didn't her father say that? and give her a parodist's wink?—"the brilliant but slightly mad Dr. Von Hegelstein replaces the pianist's hands with the hands of the deceased criminal!"

Should Jersey insert into her journal story the way her mother whooped in delight at the Pepe le Peu accent Joe gave to the pianist, Bernard? Maybe it is enough that, on the same day, over breakfast in a Texas café, Katherine seized Jersey's journal in order to record in the margin (page 17) a remark that had made her snort coffee through her nose:

> "I guess my philosophy of life could be summed up in two words: Martin and Lewis."
>
> Joe Alitz (August 4, 1993)

"*Crrreak*," said Joe as, under cover of night, Bernard entered the conservatory. Joe hummed a bit of the "Moonlight Sonata," then cried in the voice of Bernard, "'*Mon dieu!* My playing is filled with a fire I could only dream of in ze past!'"

At this, Jersey's mother groaned, but Joe continued on, relating how Bernard's new hands allowed him to play music that won the love of the beautiful Marie. Alas, the hands also began to distort his good nature. He stole a priceless diamond necklace, then penned a note that implicated his talented rival, Jacques. "CLANG!" cried Joe as the prison door swung shut on Jacques.

"'What a zhame!'" said the secretly delighted Bernard. "'Now Jacques's great concert must be canceled!'"

But, no. As head of the conservatory, the beautiful Marie's father insisted that Bernard perform in place of Jacques.

Joe whistled and thundered his feet against the floorboards of the car to suggest the appreciation offered by Bernard's audience, and, alone in his dressing room, Bernard declared, *sotto voce*, "'Ze actions of ze hands are evil, but surely zey are not my responsibility! I have triumphed!'" Just then, however, Marie entered the room, weeping. She and her father had learned the truth about both the hands and the necklace. "'Bernard, you must confess!'"

Jersey does not record that Katherine interrupted Joe to ask, "Why does Marie have to sound so wimpy?" or that Joe did not answer, but continued in that same voice: "'Bernard—your hands! You're—choking me!'

"'Marie! I—I can't stop! Help! Zomeone! Murderer!'"

While Katherine and Jersey giggled, Joe pummeled the steering wheel to indicate the knocking of Marie's father and the musicians at the dressing room door:

"'Put a shoulder to the door, men! Break it down!'"

There followed a brief round of terrible choking noises, then a crash followed by gasps of both horror and relief. Marie was alive! Joe explained, but Bernard—Bernard was dead, strangled by his own hands.

"'F-father?' said Marie"—Katherine began to protest the voice again, but Jersey broke in, "She just about got choked to death, Mom! You can't expect her to sound too lively!"

Joe cleared his throat: "As I said: 'F-father?'

"'Yes, Marie, it is I. But do not look at Bernard. Best for you to remember Bernard as your savior, for it is certain our old friend managed to call upon his best self to subdue the hands that meant to rob you of your life!'"

Jersey does note the question her mother asked after the story—"So what's it mean, guys? Mind over matter or matter over mind?"—and her own response: "Just—you can't be what you aren't. If you try to be, you'll end up paying for it."

"Well, that's good," Katherine said. "I can accept that."

"But no need to make it a morality tale," said Joe.

Katherine laughed. "Of course it's a morality tale! And what do you think would have happened if the criminal had received the hands of the pianist? Would he have become a better man? How come we never get that story? Why aren't people even interested in that story?"

▪ ▪ ▪

Long before, and up to the day of the accident on Post Road, Katherine Milhause had wondered how she—with her lucky life, knock on wood—would respond to misfortune. Say she lost *her* hands? Would she be brave? Suppose something terrible happened to Jersey or to Joe, or she herself were ravaged by disease, or thrown into a concentration camp? Would she be able to remain sane and helpful to others if she were tortured?

Brain damage, however, was never on Katherine's disaster list, which suggests that she intuitively understood that a person could hardly hope to adhere to—or even recall—a course of action or a philosophy selected by a differently composed mind.

Jersey, of course, does recall the mind of the mother of the past. Jersey remembers lying with her mother in the sweet dark of her Seca bedroom; her mother telling a little Zen story that she said she sometimes used to calm her own fears:

"Today is the day of a man's execution. One thing you should know about this man: he has trained himself to pay attention to each moment. Though he knows he will soon be hanged, he watches the dawn with great interest. He watches the sun light up the bricks of his cell. He sees that even though the bricks are a brownish red, when the sun shines on them quite brightly, they change colors, some even become white. The man feels the cool morning air, and he notices that, hm, it feels a little different on his scalp than it does on the back of his neck and his hands. The man smells rain in the air. A good, clean smell, and he can take it right inside himself when he breathes. In the air, he can smell the leaves and the dirt of the region. He hears a set of keys jingling. The door to his cell opens. It is the people who have come to take him to his execution. Still, he stays in each moment. As he walks outside, he observes the way his feet move, and how it feels to put down the heel, and then the ball of his foot, and then his toes. He notices that his knees feel wobbly with fear of his execution. A breeze moves across his scalp, and the sky is a bowl of pale turquoise in a golden frame.

"He passes a woman who presses one of her feet forward. Tan dust coats a smear of dried mud on her shoe. Ocher mud. His heel goes down and then the ball of his foot and then his toes. Heel, ball, toes. He pays attention to the moment, and it's not so bad, going to be hanged, when he is in each moment."

Her mother sounded calm, contented, when she finished telling her story of staying in the now, but Jersey does not forget that there were also times when her mother stood in the middle of the kitchen and clutched her head and said to Jersey's father,

"How about giving me a lobotomy? Just for the evening? A temporary frontal lobotomy?" Usually, she laughed after she said this; usually, Jersey's father frowned.

He also frowned the night he walked by Jersey's darkened bedroom and heard Katherine telling Jersey the execution story.

"I don't know what you see in that story, Katherine," he said from the doorway. "Somebody can make up a story like that—it may comfort you now to think a story like that would help you out if you were about to be hanged, but that doesn't mean it helps you know how to live."

Katherine did not look Joe's way but stared up at Jersey's ceiling, which was covered with the dabs of glow-in-the dark paint that she and Jersey had put there: stars of the Northern Hemisphere in the summer sky. "It does help me, though, Joe," Katherine said.

"But that's not the way *you* live. Living like that—it would be like living on tepid broth."

Jersey kept quiet while her parents talked back in forth, but she agreed with her father. The execution story struck her as depressing. Still, in the hospital, and for a long time after, it is the execution story, and the execution story alone, that proves the bedtime story that helps her to sleep.

9

Prior to 1968, the year he entered the Marines, Finis Pruitt did not realize that, in their attempt to give biblical names to all eleven of their children, his parents had mistaken the last five letters of their home's only book for something akin to Elam, Mordecai, and Naomi, the names of children eight, nine, and ten.

Finis.

Pronounced *fine-us* in that backwater New Mexico town.

A bookish, if not religious, sergeant major first brought the senior Pruitts' error to Finis's attention. That was on Finis's first day in boot camp. The following evening, the sergeant major took pains to explain the joke to the entire mess hall. As several men in the mess line had already dubbed Finis "Mule," owing to the size and shape of his ears, he proceeded to spend almost a week as Fine Ass—until the group rejected that moniker as too complimentary, and he became simply Rear End.

Certain draftees might have found this hard to bear, but eighteen-year-old Finis Pruitt knew that though he was a poor boy from an absurd family in a dinky town just then in the process of being devoured by an open-pit copper mine, he was also a good deal smarter than most of the people he met. In addition, Finis Pruitt had discovered, long before boot camp, that there were definite benefits to viewing life as a series of private jokes. He awarded himself a point his third morning in camp when he got out of his bunk and said, without evoking any response at all from the dull fellow dressing by his side, "This is the day that the hoard hath made, let us read Joyce and be cads in it."

Ten points when he sneaked a puppy corpse out of the garbage bin of a local pet shop and installed it in the locker of the literary sergeant major.

Rear End's career as a Marine ended before he ever left the United States (the upshot of several issues, including his implication in the suicide of a fellow recruit). He was not sorry. He was eighteen. He imagined himself eventually emerging in some amalgam of London, New York, and Paris as a darker, more elegant sort of Kerouac (dark suits, dark ties, playwright as opposed to novelist).

In the eighteen years following his discharge, however, whenever he looked about, Finis found himself in one university town or another, taking classes, selling stereo speakers. Now and then, he would establish himself in a college coffee shop or bar as an eccentric young professor of drama. He managed to stage the occasional play with the help of enthusiastic students; but though there was some pleasure in acting the temperamental director, he never felt he had found his true role until one fine Sunday afternoon in Omaha, Nebraska. Early autumn, 1987.

NAM JAM IV!
FREE MUSIC ALL DAY!
ROSENBLATT STADIUM!

So read the neon orange posters that veterans' groups and their families and friends had tacked up on telephone poles and buildings all around that lovely green town. Finis calculated that where there was free music, there would also be girls, and he was just then abandoning a period of thought that included celibacy as one of its tenets. (Why not, given that sex was so hard to come by and usually made him want to screech?)

The day of Nam Jam IV, he managed to arrive at the baseball stadium early enough to stake out a spot behind the first base dugout. The day was mild, the grass was green. As a private joke, under his jacket he wore a T-shirt upon which a long-lashed, pink-bowed Persian lay preening above Valentine-red lettering that read A LITTLE PUSSY NEVER HURT ANYONE. Local bands replaced one another hourly on the black-curtained, black-aproned stage erected behind second base. During the changing of the bands, veterans and local dignitaries made announcements, gave testimonials, read speeches. The emcee—a tall, shirtless, sunglassed vet—crowed, "Man, we got a crowd here of upwards of three thousand!" An exaggeration, but the crowd roared with delight.

It was the crowd that interested Finis, not the bands on the stage or the hypothetical female he had meant to seduce beneath the bleachers. That crowd—its ebb and flow of the pathetic (or debased) and the heroic—that crowd revived and inspired him. Vets. Neo-hippie children of vets. Cattle-fed moms and dads. Wives and girlfriends. Brothers and sisters. Everybody's brother and sister, father and son, grandma and gramps. It was a family reunion, a neighborhood block party, a carnival, Homecoming and the Fourth of July, all done up with primitive pageantry. This was no costumed Renaissance Fair. People ate their crappy food and drank and danced and puked it up and engaged in the occasional brawl. Aging vets handed out brochures and flyers, sold flags and bandannas, T-shirts, pins and patches and bumper stickers—both for and against the long-gone war. A guy hawked homemade cassettes of songs by Hendrix and the Doors and the Airplane. *The War Years*: so the man had titled his cassettes, which rattled around in a splintered plywood box that dangled from his neck by a piece of twine. Five dollars a cassette. Volume One. Volume Two. Songs every oldies station played all day long, yet the cassettes sold like hotcakes.

In the evening, Finis worked his way around the cars and campers and pickups holding tailgate picnics in the parking lot. Most people had set up barbecues—Smokey Joes, hibachis—but a few free spirits had gone right ahead and built fires on the asphalt. Lawn chairs and folding tables. Tappers and open coolers. Finis fell in with one group, then another. He listened to war stories. The bad fight. The good fight. The death of the buddy. The Dear John. Some of the vets had repeated a story so many times that it had worn flat, become the spare change in the vet's pocket that would not buy him a thing worth having; others, however, jumped and spun while they told their tales. They drew the eyes and ears of their listeners, and on the edge of one such group, during a lull, Finis turned to a vet at his side and tried out a story he had heard back in Lincoln:

"I didn't give a rat's ass he was my c.o.! I told him I'd shoot him! You don't drag a good soldier around like a piece of lumber just 'cause he got his fucking head blown off!"

The man nodded appreciatively. "*Fucking right!*" he said, and Finis felt so alive in the man's eyes that he had to take himself away from the group. His knees trembled. His stomach felt warm as a bowl of pudding. From a bank of grass at the edge of the parking lot, he stared at the spectacle in front of him. The white-blue overhead lights of the parking lot turned the revelers to cold steel, while the fires cast up something molten, hot. The vets were variously humble and self-righteous; drunk and sober; glamorous in old fatigue jackets, grotesque in their mutilations. Some were sacred and some profane, and their very variety made Finis laugh with delight.

Cackle was the word he liked. *Cackle* had a properly diabolical ring.

A nearby pocket of vets began to shout out a drill song ("I'm going to go to Vietnam / Kill myself a yellow bird!") and Finis understood that the dark Kerouacian fantasy of his twenties had grown out of the deeper, more elemental shit of yearning to be Vic Morrow on *Combat*, and wouldn't a classic role for the late 1980s be the two combined in the Hero Scorned? Vietnam vet Private Rear End?

▪ ▪ ▪

He moved to Texas. There, the big fatigue jacket worn by so many veterans proved useful not only for sleeping outdoors but as an instant costume. He learned how to take advantage of all opportunities to display a "rage" that would have left a genuine veteran depleted, but that invigorated and amused Rear End. The brotherhood of one vet for another—what fun to simulate such cornball feelings! What fulfillment in pretending to be an enraged drunk suffering from, say, the effects of Agent Orange, or PTSD.

While he panhandled around Austin, he reread Nietzsche, and Artaud, to whom he had once been exposed in a university class called Theater of Communion. He came to think of himself as the pinnacle of a street actor, a mummer observing perfect dedication to his craft. But there was more: in the role of R.E., Finis Pruitt was released from the burdens of life. He renounced the self and its natural instincts; he did not need to be—serve—Finis Pruitt any longer.

▪ ▪ ▪

For the last five years, then, Finis Pruitt had introduced himself to new acquaintances as Private Rear End, lighting the insult so brightly that it seemed an incognito; and, indeed, many people believed they glimpsed the outlines of a hero through that incognito's glare.

You had to be careful, of course. Once, Finis allowed himself to get drunk in front of Clay, which was unwise but, fortunately, had only amusing repercussions. (*Why*, Clay asked the next day, *had R.E. kept saying that the motto of Superman was "No compassion for anyone?"*)

Generally, however, Finis stayed sober, and sensitive to his audience. The bio of Private Rear End was outfitted with pockets and zippers that could be opened and closed according to who was listening: zip, and here was an ember-lit scene of nighttime street-fighting in Saigon; or zip, good guy Rear End digs a well in a remote village that, zip, appears in another story, for another kind of audience, as the setting for a rare barbecue of gook babies who, Rear End was only too happy to report, tasted "just like rattlesnake."

Remember the footage of the bombing of the U.S. embassy shown on television during the Tet offensive? Remember the guy who managed to toss a lifesaving pistol to Colonel George Jacobson as one of the commandos sneaked up the stairs? None other than the intrepid hero Rear End.

Really, Finis Pruitt's descriptions of his fictitious stint in Vietnam—a compilation drawn from literature and film and the lives of other men—were much more coherent and vivid than Carter Clay's accounts of actual time spent in the place. Clever Finis could offer up place names, geographical features, dates, and savvy—if somewhat over-the-top—political comment. Yes, he had been intimate with a Confucian whore who helped him understand the mind-set of the Vietnamese people. He could make you see how, when it hit, napalm splashed along on the ground like a wave on a beach. He could tell you, with a wry smile, that he'd nominated the *thorn* for national flower of Vietnam, and that the best way to remove the plentiful leeches of the Trung Bo was to burn them off with a cigarette. If you had come into Vietnam at the busy air terminal at Tan Son Nhut, Rear End had arrived on the beach at Da Nang or at Cam Ranh Bay. You were Infantry? He was Navy. Marine? Air Force. If you were there in '68, he was part of Operation Linebacker, mining Haiphong Harbor in '72, or an early carpet-bomber in Operation Rolling Thunder.

Yes, Finis had presented Clay with the soldier who both fought at Hue and was one of Colonel David Lownd's 26th Marines at Khe Sahn. His special value to the colonel had been his rare ability to spot a subtle disruption in foliage or rock patterns that might indicate the camouflage of an enemy installation.

"Shit, man," Rear End said, his grin signaling an acceptable mix of pleasure and self-depreciation, *"the VC considered me so much trouble, they put a price on my head!"*

Rear End knew payloads. That a good C ration heater could be fashioned from a tin of peanut butter and insect repellant, and that if you were fool enough to leave a shell behind, Victor Charles would be happy to fill it with gunpowder and bits of metal, seal it up, and place it in a bamboo tube with a nail ready to detonate it from below. The converted shell was a *dap loi*, and Rear End could tell you exactly how Charlie buried it in the ground, and how, if you were unlucky enough to step on the mother, you were damned lucky if it blew off only your foot.

Carter Clay still shivers over his own, genuine memories. Landscapes scorched black and white as a photographer's negative. Pools of blood left behind after the VC dragged their dead from the shell-pocked mud. The sewage-stink of triple-canopy jungle. Sleeping in water with his face covered by his tarp so a rat wouldn't take a bite out of his cheek. He had seen that—a rat taking a bite out of another soldier's face. He knew cowardice—his own and others'. He had smelled the smoke of burning villages that were home to kids and women and old people who maybe were or were not the ones who planted the booby traps in the sand—booby traps everywhere, so just walking made you crazy with fear that you might end up like that package of screams you'd seen rise on the trail ahead of you, no arms, no legs, no dick. But there had been real bravery, too, men risking their lives to save other men—and the kids and women and old people who maybe were or were not the ones who planted the booby traps in the sand—

When Carter tried to speak of such things, people tended to grow embarrassed. Carter was too sad. Carter lacked a vocabulary, a sense of pacing and narrative—those qualities that made Finis such a success as Private Rear End, Vietnam vet.

▪ ▪ ▪

But what had happened to Rear End that left him looking so battered and down and out on the day that he came to Sabine to visit Carter Clay?

If Finis Pruitt had been willing to explain, which he was not, he would have told you: *Carter Clay* was what had happened to Rear End.

With Clay, Rear End had reached his pinnacle. With Clay, Rear End had become a deck of cards with which Finis built any number of unlikely constructions. How exhilarating to hover, with the intimation that Rear End had served in Military Intelligence! To watch Clay's eyes to see if they betrayed any misgiving about Rear End's adding MI work to an already multifaceted career as Medivac operator, grunt, and bomber!

Well? Could Finis add the card without the whole toppling?

Yes! Yes! That was cowed admiration in Clay's eyes, not doubt!

Good Dog: Finis's private name for Clay. *Good Dog*, *Good Dog*.

And, oh, how Good Dog's lower lip trembled when Rear End revealed the story of his own mom's demise! Rear End had been only five at the time, and had to watch her fade, fade, fade—

"A terrible wasting disease," Rear End replied after sad old Clay asked what killed her; then Rear End had to quickly concoct a sob to disguise the hilarity that threatened to erupt at the thought of the true Mother Pruitt, painted like a whore for square-dance suppers at the Las Cruces Senior Center.

Well, running that constant show for Clay had been Finis's first error. The repository of all of Finis's inventions: Clay. Finis understood this in a flash that night the guy in the Indy 500 jacket showed up in Howell Park. Finis saw, then, that Clay had become a monster who had to be expunged lest he forever threaten the existence of Rear End. Clay was no simple audience of the Now. He had become—the parrot who learned a secret password without knowing it, and thus had the potential to scream the password out at any time, day or night.

Finis's second error?

Not making sure he had actually killed Clay. And, of course, that meant he should have used a gun, not a knife. Which error had to be excused, right? Since it was that knife-toting Indy 500 guy—the perfect scapegoat—who inspired Finis to run back to the Port-a-Shed for his own knife. To hide along the service road, waiting for sodden Clay to make his way back to the shed.

The third error, however—not clearing out after the stabbing—was a true error.

The day after the stabbing, Finis and the other men from Shelter #6 were questioned by the police. That was to be expected. It was Finis, among others, who gave the police their description of the man in the Indy 500 jacket. Finis who told the police about the knife Carter Clay had thrown off toward the canal. Finis who led the Shelter #6 delegation to the Sarasota hospital for a visit to the comatose Clay. Finis who later learned—and relayed to the group—the news that Clay had been transferred up to the VA in Tampa, and would apparently be there a good long while.

Talk of Clay died out in the two weeks following the stabbing—the men were focused on a meth dealer who had taken to hanging at Howell—yet Finis thought of little but Clay's possible return (*What if Clay figures out I'm the one who stabbed him, and he returns for revenge*? versus *This time I'll do it right*).

The former fear was his first thought that night the men at Shelter #6 rose in a group at his approach. For a moment, Finis tried to look as if he meant to veer off casually toward a group down by the canal, but when the men from the shelter began to run his way, Finis began to run, too.

In their fury, the men were a dark cloud of blows and kicks, grunted threats and accusations. ("Lying son of a bitch!" "You ain't no vet!" "Your damn lies nearly got your own buddy killed") Finis did not understand what-all they had learned or how, but it was clear that they no longer believed in the existence of Private Rear End, and that they had determined themselves to be the only war of which he might rightly declare himself a veteran.

Who knows how long that beating lasted? Probably not terribly long, but when the men finally dispersed, every inch of Finis hurt. His nose was broken and so was one hand. Two fingers. Four ribs. Through the mush of his mouth he felt a slippery absence of teeth.

He had been beaten before, but not like that. That beating took away his sense of humor and left him shamed. Under the viaduct where he took refuge, he formulated a new notion of the perfect revenge on Clay: somehow, he would convince people that *Clay* was the false vet. Stir them to such rage that they ripped and tore at Clay until there was nothing left of Clay at all.

But how to effect such a thing?

He bought a Colt .45 at a pawnshop.

Telephoned the VA in Tampa to learn when Clay would be discharged.

"Mr. Clay has been sent home," said the operator who took his call.

"Home?" Finis yelped, then added, ever so sweetly, "And just where would that be?"

The hospital operator was not authorized to give out such information.

Home?

Suppose that right this very minute, Clay was on his way back to Sarasota?

Immediately, Finis hauled his aching self out to the highway and stuck out his thumb. He had no cart or encumbrances in those days. It did not take terribly long for a pickup truck to stop. The man inside looked Finis over. "I'm going south," he said, "if you don't mind riding in the back."

After that—leery of "Rear End," and feeling too old and damaged to invent a fresh role—Finis descended into the dankly anonymous atmosphere of the New Life Mission in Oneco. The people at the New Life Mission got him help at the charity clinic (stitched lip, cast, tape), but there was no help for the fear that followed him now. Sometimes, at night, when he finally did fall asleep, he woke with a shout, certain that one of the men from Howell stood over him and, at any moment, would hit or kick him again. Bits of smelly curd came up in his mouth without warning, perhaps because of his lost teeth; and his lost teeth—they made his speech clownish in his own ears.

▪ ▪ ▪

The audience supreme: so Finis Pruitt had considered Carter Clay. Finis had been intoxicated by his power to trade false experience for the admiration of a man of true experience.

At the New Life Mission, Finis did not seek an audience. At New Life, without Rear End—in a role Finis came to think of as Persona Non Grata—Finis did not talk to anyone. Because he was quiet and took the occasional job of yard work without complaint, the mission let him stay on. One of the mission volunteers—an innocent widower with cobwebbed eyes—mistook Finis's furious silence for shyness. Would Finis allow the volunteer to buy him a small pet, a rabbit, say, or a guinea pig? Finis could keep it at the volunteer's garage. Would he like that?

While the volunteer talked, Finis rubbed at his chin and studied the pattern of dusty shoe prints that marked the red tile floor of the mission. Perhaps, Finis thought, in time this volunteer might invite Finis to move in, might become Finis's own private volunteer. Hadn't Finis wanted a ferret as a kid? A creature capable of attack? He remembered reading with some fascination about the habits of such creatures: their clean, cozy houses; their larders stocked with live animals rendered helpless by a bite through the brain.

"Well, a *ferret* would interest me," Finis told the volunteer.

A European polecat. *Mustela furo*. The weasel thief. Males were called hobs, explained the book Finis consulted in the Oneco library. Females were "jills." Disappointing to learn that the creature—a beautiful gray tube of nastiness—had grown so dependent upon those who used it for sport that it could not survive more than a few days without human care.

"Are you finding what you need?" the librarian asked Finis. A fish-faced hag. Wanting him to move along, move along, now.

"*Bona note,*" Finis replied, then gave the woman a wink that made her step behind the reference desk—though, in fact, he was ready to leave, anyway. His chair—some hideous fifties thing—made a satisfying screech as he pushed it away from the table. A mystery: that people had actually paid money for such ugly items. Could you explain it as a species of bragging? *You think I can't bear blond furniture and linoleum? Well, watch this!*

The librarian watched as he started for the door. He let his fingers trail insolently over the carrel that held the latest *Reader's Guides*.

But was that open atlas of the United States perhaps an invitation? He hesitated, then took a seat, and soon he had calculated the distance from Oneco to Fort Powden, Washington: 3,196 miles.

A funny name, he thought, as he went for the pay phone in the foyer and asked directory assistance for Fort Powden.

Two Clays were listed—a Duncan and a C.L.

"Mr. Clay, sir? This is Craig Towley with the VA. You are the father of Carter Thomas Clay, are you not, sir?"

Duncan Clay made a rustling noise very much like the noise Finis's ferret made as it turned about in its cage.

"Sir, we have several pieces of correspondence for your son. We hoped you might be able to give us a current mailing address?"

With thickened tongue, Duncan Clay managed to explain that he could not help, no, but maybe the sister could.

Yes. Once Finis managed to get hold of Cheryl Lynn Clay at the bowling alley where she worked—Rex's Bowladrome—Cheryl Lynn was only too happy to talk to Craig Towley. Her "little brother," she called Carter. "He's such a good person," she said in a teary voice, "but I got to tell you, your damned war screwed him up!" Oh, Cheryl Lynn worried about Carter. If he contacted the VA, would they let her know? Could the VA at least give her brother a message to call his sister?

Finis's voice of official decorum was phlegmy, high-pitched. He reminded himself of Gayle Gordon as bilious boss to Lucille Ball's scattered Mrs. Carmichael. "Though the VA can't serve as a message center," he said, "I will make a personal note on the case, Miss Clay, and perhaps be in touch from time to time."

For this false bone, the woman was—like her brother—stupidly grateful. Good Dog, Finis thought, but then he heard someone in the background whistling "Proud Mary," and it occurred to him that Clay could be at the bowling alley, listening in at his sister's elbow, *knowing* it was Finis pretending to be from the VA. Suppose the bowling alley had one of those devices that revealed the number of the caller and Clay traced it and he came to Oneco and beat Finis to death?

This notion frightened Finis so much that he gave up all thought of a second call to Cheryl Lynn. He spent his days doing the yard work doled out to mission residents or reading in the volunteer's garage. Without asking the volunteer for permission, he began to leave a Winn-Dixie cart in the garage too. It had been a long while since he had allowed himself to acquire things, and, after a time, he began to take pleasure in selecting not merely what he wanted but what he thought the homeless Persona Non Grata might want, too.

Really, life was not so bad until the middle of July, when a drugstore owner beat Finis for shoplifting the Advil he needed for the aches and pains he still suffered from the beating at Shelter #6. Sometimes, after that second beating, during the evening services at the mission, Finis found himself wanting to shriek—actually, to *caw* like a crow—which he knew would be a terrible mistake, despite the immediate relief it would provide.

The throat-clearing and leg-crossing of the other mission residents made him shiver with revulsion. The promise of an afterlife with such scum made Finis's left eye twitch. *Give me another chance to kill the motherfucker and I'll do it right this time*. Such was as close to prayer as Finis ever came during mission services, and one day in early August, he heard news that made him wonder if his prayers might soon be answered.

It was noon. Finis was consuming a swampy lentil and carrot soup in the mission dining hall. "Private Rear End!" A man who reeked of both circulating and processed booze plopped down at the table, and whooped, "Private Rear End! Who ran over you?"

Hayes. A baby bull veteran Finis had known in Austin during his early days as Rear End. *Yeah*, said Hayes, *he'd finally got tossed out of Texas altogether, and then, lately, he'd had some trouble in Sarasota, so he'd decided to come south*.

Finis did not much like Hayes's gleeful eyeing of his battle scars, and he said, affecting that bit of a British accent with which he could best ladle out an air of noblesse oblige, "Sarasota, you say?" He slid his soup bowl and forearm over the section of the map of Washington that he had been inspecting before Hayes sat down.

Had Hayes ever met a guy named Carter Clay while he was in Sarasota?

Hayes laughed. *Not in Sarasota, but he'd been at Recovery House in Tampa with Clay! Shit, man, he'd lived right across the hall from Clay!*

Finis folded the little paper napkin that came with the mission lunch of peanut butter sandwich, soup, two cookies, and coffee. Hayes was jaundiced. Yellow cheeks, yellow eyes. Going, going, gone. Sit back. Let the fool talk.

And talk he did: "The minute I got out of that zoo, man, I bought myself a drink, you wouldn't have believed those AA bastards would whip Clay around the way they did! A big guy like that. Somebody said it was 'cause he almost died." Hayes grinned. "Put the fear of the devil in him. You know about him getting stabbed?"

"Clay got *stabbed*?" said Private Rear End.

Hayes leaned forward. "He didn't remember the details—I guess he was all fucked up—but he got into it with some guy who pulled a knife on him. Supposedly another vet. Clay decked the guy, but later the guy came back and stuck him, like, I don't know, ten times."

Difficult for Finis not to smile at Hayes's story. He had to take up the folded napkin and use it to scrub at his mouth before he allowed Private Rear End to say a relatively somber—if appropriately astonished—"Crazy!"

"Anyways, last I heard"—Hayes sneered—"Clay's a cook or something in Sabine."

Rear End smoothed the crease in his map of Washington with the bowl of his soup spoon. Cleared his throat. "Is that up in the Northwest? Where he used to come from?"

"Hell, no!" Hayes laughed. "Sabine's half an hour—forty-five minutes—from here, man. Head east and you can't miss it."

Part Two

10

In the original *Invasion of the Body Snatchers* (1956), with the help of the police and the National Guard, the hero foils the aliens' attempt to take over the world. The remake of 1978, however, ends with a bitter surprise: we see the fugitive hero, Matthew—charmingly portrayed by Donald Sutherland—all alone in the city's central plaza. We suppose brave Matthew to be the only human being whose body and soul have not yet been taken over by the space aliens, but then a voice calls out, "Psst! Matthew!" and who is it? *Nancy!* Matthew's good friend! About whom we have assumed the worst! Up starts Nancy to Matthew. Bedraggled, broken by all that she has witnessed, Nancy still manages to smile a brave smile at her old friend. We smile, too. But then the mouth of *Matthew* opens wide, and, oh, no, *Matthew* breaks forth in the aliens' hideous piglike squeal of denunciation. Matthew is now one of them.

The film's final shot: a movement into the void of that open, squealing mouth until the screen is black, black, black.

Joe Alitz preferred the original *Body Snatchers*, not knowing its optimistic ending to be a last-minute paste job. Jersey and Katherine preferred the apocalyptic remake of 1978, and watched it many times.

So it is that as Jersey sits playing chess in the dining section of M.B.'s living room (color scheme: bittersweet orange, powder blue), Jersey recognizes the odd sounds that come from M.B.'s television—weird rumbles, whispers of solar winds—as the beginning of the remake.

"Wait!" she cries, for M.B. is in the process of changing the channel from *Home Shopping Network* to *Rescue 911*, complaining as she goes, "What's the deal with all these TV shows where everybody talks Spanish? *I* can't understand a word they're saying!"

"M.B., go back! You passed a great movie, and it's just starting!"

That odd grouping of heavenly objects that hangs above the rough rock horizon informs the viewers that the horizon belongs to an unknown planet—*not* earth, not anything in our solar system. Note the unfamiliar colors and webs and fogs that enshroud the planet's surface, the triumphal protozoa spinning off into space.

Jersey maneuvers herself closer to the switch that controls the dining area's overhead light. Her wheelchair is Model 504 from Theralife, a "super-lite," with wheel covers decorated by Jersey's own hand (Arizona sunsets, saguaro cacti, a Gila monster nosing in from one edge of a tire rim).

"I want to watch *Rescue 911*," M.B. protests.

"Please? I promise you'll love it?"

Jersey smiles back at frowning M.B. A pretty girl, M.B. supposes, though those dark eyebrows above the blue eyes are a too potent reminder of her father, and, with her long skirts and beads, she looks like a hippie girl from the sixties.

"Well, all right," M.B. says. Her voice is calm, but the cords in her neck are tight, and in a most uncalm way M.B. is thinking, *Now it is the month of March*.

In August, when Pastor Bitner said, "The Lord has his reasons for this accident," and "This is your cross to bear," M.B.—who has always believed that the goal of life is to get *rid* of crosses, not take them on—M.B. did try to make herself humble. After all, who on earth would not have wanted to do everything possible for her own daughter, and her one and only grandchild? And she did bring Jersey home after rehab, didn't she?

This morning, however, while her coffee perked, M.B. tore off the spent page of her kitchen calendar, and what did she discover? The month of *March*—with a grid so sharp and dizzying it seemed a thing upon which a person might fall and cut herself up into thirty-one squares. How could M.B. explain to Pastor Bitner, let alone anyone else, that a page from a calendar could make her grab for her kitchen counter, and hold on tight?

Of course, the calendar did not explain that at three this morning, M.B. woke to the sound of the girl crying in the bathroom—and, oh, what a stinking mess, followed by two hours of cleaning wheelchair, nightclothes, grout, and tile.

"It wouldn't have happened if you'd gotten the safety bars installed!" That was what the girl shouted at M.B. "Stop worrying about putting screws in your damned tiles and get the safety bars installed!"

M.B., however, has counted on Kitty's improvement; on mother and daughter's eventual return to their own home in Arizona. M.B. has believed that safety bars around the toilet would not only be an eyesore in her lovely guest bath, but also a possible jinx on Kitty's recovery.

At any rate, tonight the girl smiles as she asks, "See that mucilaginous stuff on the plants, M.B.? That's how the aliens spread themselves. A flower grows from it, and the flower turns into a pod, and a copy of a human being grows from the pod."

Musa-what?

A collection of needlepoint pillows that declare M.B.'s preferences and loyalties sit about the living room. "A penny saved / Isn't worth much." "My other pillow / Is a sofa." M.B. leans away from her game of solitaire and rests the small of her back against "Life is short, / Eat dessert first."

Musa-something.

The girl's mother and father used words like that. Indeed, the first time that Kitty brought Joe Alitz home, M.B. supposed many of the words the two of them used were a trick, some pig-Latin kind of way of excluding Lorne and herself. When Joe finally went out to buy cigarettes, M.B. fetched the dictionary from Kitty's old bedroom. She meant to force Kitty to admit that the words did not exist. Well, that was not a pleasant memory: Kitty standing in the kitchen, looking sad and sorry. Pitying M.B.!

Exiguity. M.B. remembers the word because, afterward, she wrote it in pencil on the bottom of her lingerie drawer. And did she ever in her life hear it used again? No.

"See how the camera looks smeared, M.B.? Like some of the slime fell on it? Isn't that great? Like, everything's being affected by the aliens, you know?"

Jersey turns in her wheelchair to smile at her grandmother. Who sits—as always—in the orange leather recliner that would have been the special chair of Jersey's grandfather had he lived. How many times has M.B. told Jersey this? Many times. Lorne this, Lorne that. Lorne didn't like rhubarb pie, but, oh, he loved strawberry. Lorne believed there ought to be committees in the public interest set up to vote on whether or not a woman had good enough legs to wear shorts, and if you couldn't get a tan car, Lorne said white was second best.

Does Jersey appear sweet and tractable as she speaks to her grandmother about the movie? ("You see, it's supposed to be happening in San Francisco, M.B. See the hills and all?") After last night's overwrought bathroom scene, she certainly does mean to sound sweet. She knows well enough that M.B. does not want the job of Jersey's caretaker.

"What if she stayed on as a boarder? And I come by for daily visits?"

So Jersey overheard M.B. ask the director of St. Mary's Rehab on the day that M.B. was to take Jersey home. At the time, Jersey was hidden behind the reception area's fish tank, but she could see the face of the director. Blanched. Clearly ashamed for M.B. *"It isn't appropriate for a bright, healthy girl to stay on in an institution, Mrs. Milhause."*

The time that the physical therapist showed the patients and their caretakers the slide show *Decubitus Ulcers (Pressure Sores) Stages I-IV*—that time, M.B. knocked over her folding chair long before the slide that showed the teacup-sized hole in the blackened buttock of a young patient. In fact, M.B. fled the darkened room after a slide of a relatively minor sore—one on the back rib of an invalid who had spent too many days with his torso twisted, just so, while he stared out his front window.

The Grandmother Queen of Frogs. Isn't that what M.B. resembles in her lacy bathrobe and the lacy cap that is a twin to the cover—strange in itself—that she keeps on a roll of toilet paper in the guest bath? In the dark pool of the living room—with her wreath of cigarette smoke wafting upward in the halogen light, her chair a bright lily pad upon which she sits cross-legged—couldn't M.B. be a creature in a fairy tale?

"You ever been to San Francisco, M.B.?"

"I never been anywhere much out of Indiana, but, say, don't those things drive you crazy?" M.B. draws a hand up to her own forehead to indicate the minute braids that Jersey has made in her long blond hair, and that now hang over her face like so many stalks of wheat. M.B. does not understand how the girl can bear to have such things in her face when M.B. herself can scarcely bear to see them—

Jersey chuckles, then gives the braids a shake.

To calm herself—distract herself—M.B. takes out the bottle of Jergen's Lotion she keeps in the drawer of her coffee table and begins to work lotion into her skin—hands, arms, elbows, then back to the hands, push up the cuticles.

At first the lotion's almond scent evokes its usual sweet association for M.B.—Lorne rubbing her back—but then something new and unpleasant arrives: yesterday's visit to Kitty at Fair Oaks Care. Kitty's roommate had a bottle of Jergen's Lotion on her own bedside table. Old Mrs. Radosovich—with her hearing aid and her Confidence panties that are really just diapers.

M.B. hustles the bottle out to the kitchen. Pitches it in the trash.

Fair Oaks. Plantation life. Shade and genteel comforts. Lemonade. Polished wood floors and balconies and handsome visitors. These were the images that the name *Fair Oaks* initially suggested to M.B.; in fact, she carries those images with her still, though Kitty's Fair Oaks is actually brick ranch-style, linoleum, walkers and wheelchairs and hospital beds, a bleached-bone yard (no oaks at all, just two empty planters, and a single palm stump whose tiny tonsure gives a pathetic flutter on days when a breeze stirs).

Couldn't M.B. have found a nicer place? So Joe Alitz's brother asked on his visit, but what help did he give, and suppose Kitty lives another fifty years? No matter what anyone says, money does have to be considered.

March.

Seven months have passed since the accident, and Kitty—also in Confidence panties—spends most of her day staring at the acoustical tile ceiling above her bed, or playing with bits of fuzz she picks off her blankets. Yesterday, when M.B. arrived at Fair Oaks, the aide directed her to the courtyard, and there she found Kitty, collapsed on a lounger, looking so pale and bony and lifeless she might have been the old canvas cot that Lorne always aired on the lawn before fishing trips with his pals.

I should have had another child. So thinks M.B. as she returns from the kitchen to the living room. Surely if she had had the foresight to bear a *second* child, then child number two could at least take charge of Jersey.

If only the girl were more—lovable! A regular girl with regular interests.

It hurts M.B. to think she may not—well, *love* the girl. And who's to say she doesn't? M.B. refuses to think about something that is so uncertain, when she can think about something that is definite, something that she can say with confidence: "I am not equipped"—she likes the word *equipped,* its suggestion of outfitting rather than competence—"not *equipped* to provide care for an invalid."

This morning, on the telephone to Pastor Bitner—the door to the master bedroom closed so the girl could not hear—M.B. tried to explain: "It would have been easier—I never told you, Pastor, but at the hospital I asked God to take me, please, just make them well and take me! I really did!"

And what was Pastor Bitner's response? A laugh! "Looks like God didn't give you the easy way out, doesn't it, Marybelle? But, you know, you oughtn't do a thing you can't do with a song in your heart!"

M.B. understood, of course, that Pastor Bitner did not mean she had his permission to stop visiting that stranger at the nursing home, or taking care of Jersey. On the contrary, Pastor Bitner meant that she must get a song in her heart. A song in her heart as she hefts her cross.

Oh, the cross. Pastor Bitner is more fond of the idea of the cross than any minister M.B. has ever encountered. The cross, the cross. *Folks, if you imagine you don't have a cross to bear, you haven't looked hard enough! If your life is so fine you haven't got a cross, look around for that person whose cross is too heavy for him to carry alone! That's your cross, folks! That's your cross!*

"M.B."—Jersey points at the TV screen—"see that woman in the trench coat? She's the heroine: Elizabeth. Brooke Adams. That's the actress's name. I really like her."

"Mm." M.B. rises to make her way to the ringing telephone, saying as she goes, "What do you bet it's the Breather?"

■ ■ ■

"The Breather" is Carter Clay, calling tonight from a pay telephone that roosts on one leg in front of an Exxon station.

Carter Clay has prayed to God for forgiveness for the disaster on Post Road. Still, he yearns to say—albeit anonymously—"Please, forgive me" to the girl and her grandmother. "Please, please, please." Carter Clay—in his red-hot desire for forgiveness—does not understand that for M.B., perched atop the mountain of the accident's outcomes, the idea of *the driver* is merely a dark seam on some lower slope: laboring mule train? crevasse? shadow from an overhead cloud? Up here, where the snow is blinding, and the winds freeze your breath and sometimes threaten to carry you right over the edge, who cares about the driver?

Well, Jersey does.

The accident, in effect, not only has robbed Jersey of her parents, and the use of her legs, it has made her (at least in thought) murderous. Mentally, Jersey has executed the driver many times in many ways. Bullets, axes, trucks, fire.

Once, Jersey informed M.B. of these thoughts, and M.B. felt obliged to speak of forgiveness; still, she could not help admiring the girl's spirit.

One thing M.B. has to grant: her granddaughter has spunk. The way she whips around in that wheelchair as if she does not even notice how people stare—that's spunky, and M.B. thinks of herself as having spunk, too. She feels quite spunky as she asks the Breather, "Enjoying yourself, buddy?"

Though M.B. refers to Carter Clay as the Breather, Carter Clay makes no sound during his calls. Hand over the mouthpiece, he waits for himself to confess. He thinks that maybe if the girl answered the telephone—he has seen the girl at a distance several times now, in that wheelchair that always gives his gut a wrench, on her way to the library or to Fair Oaks to visit her mother—maybe if *the girl* answered the telephone, he might be able to speak.

"Bye, now!" With a bang, M.B. hangs up the telephone, then says to Jersey, "The heroine—her husband's cute, ain't—*isn't* he?"

Jersey says a noncommittal "Mm," in order to avoid pointing out that the man is the epitome of mindless conformism, a beer-swilling watcher of TV sports who will be one of the first humans taken over by the aliens. To switch the subject, she says, "You hear that little squeal in the background, M.B.? That squeal lets you know the aliens are chasing someone, somewhere. Only, if you haven't seen the movie before, you don't really notice it, see? It works on you almost subliminally."

■ ■ ■

In the Exxon station parking lot, as Carter sets the telephone receiver in its cradle, he realizes that he has been standing with one foot on the front bumper of his van, and—full of shame and fear, like a man who has accidentally stepped onto a fresh grave—he stumbles back. He knocks into the window of the Exxon station, inside of which the attendant and a friend sit in lawn chairs, watching *Invasion of the Body Snatchers* on a TV that they have balanced on a pile of radial tires. Carter looks in at the TV. He recognizes the movie's hero. He likes his face. Its homely self-acceptance reassures Carter in the same way that the faces of Abe Lincoln and Walter Cronkite and Walt Disney reassured him as a boy, and so he stops and he stares at the hero through the gas station window.

In 1966, when Carter heard on the radio that Walt Disney had died, he felt even worse than he had felt when President Kennedy was shot. Only his mother was home at the time, and Carter did not know how to tell her that he was upset at the death of a stranger who dreamed up kid shows and cartoons. He left the house and he walked. It was December, cold and damp, and he ended up at the Bowladrome. He bowled a few games. But even the Bowladrome seemed damp and cold that day, and when none of his friends showed up, he headed for home. He went up the little alley behind the house, and used the backdoor. His father always complained that Carter was too big for the house: Didn't anyone else notice the noise the kid made on the stairs? The amount of food the kid put away? The way he grew out of clothes?

That December afternoon, Carter concentrated hard on being silent as he passed through the house. Everything was so quiet that he assumed his mother had gone out for an afternoon job or she was maybe taking a nap. It was pure luck that he needed to use the bathroom; otherwise he would have missed the pinkish water that slipped, like an SOS, from beneath the bathroom door, and he would not have been able to call the ambulance in time.

▪ ▪ ▪

An effect of his poor hearing: at first, Carter does not understand that the movie on the gas station TV has been interrupted by a noisy truck advertisement. Carter only sees a pickup bound across a rough rock landscape, then rush toward the camera, shove a wave of gravel in the viewer's face.

▪ ▪ ▪

Jersey, watching the ad in M.B.'s living room, recognizes the advertisement's horizon, those red rocks: the Moenkopi Formation, where, on several occasions, she tagged along behind her father and his university students as they examined Triassic trackways.

M.B. looks up at the small moan that escapes the girl. As a reward to herself for not saying more about the girl's braids, she decides that, just once this game, she'll let herself flip the fourth card, not the third, and that little bit of a cheat brings her an ace, and then lots of moves, and makes her happy enough that she asks, "So what do they look like, Jersey? These aliens?"

"Like—people. They take over people."

"That fella, there, has he been taken over? He looks kind of like your dad, don't he?"

As M.B. has made it clear to Jersey that she found Joe disagreeable, Jersey answers coolly, "That's Matthew, the hero. He looks more like my Uncle Sam to me."

"Mm." A painful subject to both M.B. and Jersey: Sam Alitz. A stage actor who made of his post-accident visit to Florida a kind of demonstration of his inadequacy for the task of taking Jersey into his bachelor household. Upon arrival at M.B.'s—Jersey was still in rehab at the time—Sam announced that he could not eat the lovely rolled flank steak that M.B. had prepared for their Sunday meal, and would M.B. mind if he just went out to the kitchen and whipped himself up one of his health food concoctions in her blender?

M.B. stayed at her place at the dinette, but raised herself from her chair to peer into the kitchen from the pass-through. She was astonished—and somewhat pleased—that a person twelve years her junior could look older than herself. She also noted that the main ingredient in Sam's blender drink—a sprinkle of brewer's yeast, a dollop of yogurt and honey—was the Glenlivet he carried in what she would have had to call a purse. "Truth to tell," Sam called over the blender's little roar, "I never cook. That's probably why I've developed such an odd repertoire of tastes!" Well, Sam could smile as he carried his drink to the dinette, but M.B. felt silly and furious over her efforts on his behalf (potatoes and gravy, meat, green beans, molded salad). Really, she wished he would just shut up, but on he went: *M.B. was lucky to be so firmly settled. Why, he hadn't been home more than two days running in months!*

Before Sam's arrival, M.B. had practiced saying to her bathroom mirror, "Sam, we need to figure out a way for us to care for the girl when they send her home." Once Sam arrived, however, she saw that he could not (would not) take care of the girl.

The truth: Sam knew Jersey even less than M.B. did. The longest stretch of time that Jersey had ever spent in her uncle's presence was the night she sat in front of a television set for ninety minutes while he appeared in an American Playhouse performance of *Job's Children*.

Still, on that Sunday afternoon when Sam loped into the recreation room at St. Mary's Rehab, his resemblance to his brother affected Jersey deeply.

At St. Mary's, for consolation, Jersey sometimes imagined that her father was her opponent in her solitary games of chess. She was involved in such a match when she looked up and saw Sam. At that moment, Joe's face blurted out of death's dark like those ghost landscapes—swollen trees, rush of lawn, flowers, shed, swing set—revealed by the flash of late-night lightning. Jersey wept and threw her arms around her uncle's neck, and would not let him go. M.B. wept at the sight, as did a physical therapist who happened to pass by the open door. Sam wept, too. Though the changes he had seen on his visit to Katherine had made him almost ill, his niece was still charming. Her disabilities, however, terrified him, and he itched to leave St. Mary's almost as soon as he arrived.

"I've got a message machine," he told the girl. "You call me whenever you need to, okay?"

She looked up at him with sad and lovely blue eyes. Doves, he thought of, and seashells, and clouds and ice. Three times he had played the role of Tom in *Glass Menagerie*, but it was a shock—well, he had known it would be bad, but it really was a different thing altogether—to disentangle himself from a girl who lived a life of loneliness and paralysis as opposed to an actress who portrayed such a thing.

Was he right to leave her with M.B.? It was true, he drank too much. He *was* rarely at home; and though his third-floor apartment in the West 70s was a nice airy place, it consisted of one room that could be reached only by a set of steep granite stairs.

And M.B. and Jersey do have fun together sometimes: picking out nail polish at Walgreen's; making elaborate sundaes; listening to old musicals, which, to M.B.'s delight, the girl likes as much as M.B. herself does. The first time Jersey sang along with a recording of "On the Street Where You Live," M.B. remembered something she had forgotten: Kitty used to like to sing along with the musicals, too.

At any rate, it is M.B. with whom Jersey lives, and M.B. with whom she watches *Body Snatchers*, and M.B. who asks on her way to the kitchen, "You want anything, kid?"

"No, thanks."

M.B. turns on the kitchen overhead, transforming the pass-through into a square of trembling fluorescence through which M.B. pokes her head to cry, "I can't believe your mother let you watch such a movie!"

Jersey wonders: Does M.B.'s shock refer to the nakedness of the actor now struggling to rise from a mud bath? The quaking of his muddy buttocks, as the kindly bathhouse attendant, Nancy, guides him to the showers? Or is this expressed shock really just some excrescence of M.B.'s guilt over the fact that she—a lifetime teetotaller—has gone to the kitchen in order to get a little tipsy on MD 20–20?

"This was one of my mom's favorite movies," Jersey says—then corrects herself—"*is*. My dad liked the original."

"Your grandfather wouldn't have allowed me to see such a thing!" says M.B. "He thought too highly of me. As a lady, see? He thought there were things a lady shouldn't see."

"I guess we aren't ladies, then," Jersey says with a sniff, while, on the screen, the fat customer asks Nancy to turn off the recording of classical music she plays in the bathhouse. Jersey, who has seen the movie five times, knows just how Nancy will respond, and so she wonders: if she could rent a VCR and show her mother

Body Snatchers, would that repetition of experience help bring her mother back?

Recognition is easier than recall. Jersey has read this in several of the brain function books she has consulted since the accident, and, listen: as if to provide an example, M.B. now hums along with the soundtrack recording of "De La Tromba Pavin"—though had someone asked her to hum a few bars of "De La Tromba Pavin," M.B. would not have known that she knew the piece at all.

Dum, dum, dee. M.B. is always nervous while fetching her wine. To cover any possible clink of glass against glass, she hums a little louder while she extracts the bottle from behind the Cascade and the Lysol Disinfectant. Task accomplished, she calls out, "There's that darned owl again! You hear that, Jersey? It gives me the shiver-shakes."

On the television screen, a not quite fully formed alien has begun to stir on one of the bathhouse massage tables, and the sight makes Jersey squirm. Still, she rouses herself to make a response to her grandmother.

"It wouldn't hurt you, M.B.," she calls, quite certain of herself, for on several occasions, with the help of M.B.'s shish kabob spears, she has managed to gather—and inspect—a number of the plugs regurgitated by the great horned owls that roost in a line of eucalyptus trees above parking lot H. Amber-clawed rodents, tiny-skulled birds, and frogs—these seem to make up the diet of the great horned owls.

How beautiful the owls were when they tilted the gorgeous plates of their faces to look down on Jersey in the parking lot! To be in the presence of such grandeur made Jersey gleeful, and she called to the birds, "Well, aren't you the prettiest things ever!" Just like her mother. That was how she sounded. She heard it herself, and felt pleased and dismayed: how much of herself could be given over to housing her parents before she found herself with no room to grow?

M.B. peeks through the pass-through once more. Making certain that the movie still occupies the girl. Yes. And, in addition, the girl now practices what she calls "popping wheelies"—tipping herself back in the chair to balance on its big wheels. This, according to the girl, is something the physical therapists *want* her to do—

"Suppose the owls got in your hair, though, Jersey?" M.B. takes from the cupboard a large novelty mug that she recently purchased at Walgreen's. (IF YOU DON'T LIKE MY PEACHES, HONEY, DON'T YOU SHAKE MY TREE!) "I guess you never heard Patsy's story about Princess?" M.B. unscrews the wine bottle's noisy lid. "How they tried to grab Princess when Patsy had her out doing her business?"

Jersey smiles as she lowers her chair. She loves all dogs, even the ancient Princess, whose old poodle eyes are full of a chocolatey goo that stains her white cheeks, but she doubts Patsy's story. "M.B.," she calls, "you're missing everything!" The movie's hero—aware that the heroine is in danger—now begins to break into her house to rescue her. At the same time, the aliens are coming, and tonight, in their piglike squeals, Jersey hears something new: the chilling sound of fast tires trying and trying to come to a stop.

"Don't worry about me, kid. I'm gonna do my pillbox and mop up where the darned dishwasher leaked, maybe play a little cards."

On a few occasions, after the girl first moved in, M.B. had put up with the girl's joining in on the cards. Double solitaire. Which was not solitaire at all, in M.B.'s book. And then M.B. caught Jersey starting a new column with any old card, when *everybody* knew you could only use a king! Luckily, after that the girl never tried to play with M.B. again.

On the kitchen counter, M.B. sets out a collection of bottles marked Beta Carotene, B Complex, C, Goldenseal, Echinacea, A, E, Cod Liver Oil, Zinc, Calcium, Magnesium. These are the pills she will drop into the twenty-eight now empty partitions of her plastic vitamin tote (SMTWTFS. BF, LUNCH, DIN, BED) between sips of wine from the mug that she has positioned behind the flour canister, too far back for the girl to reach, should she enter the kitchen unexpectedly.

The bottle of MD 20–20 that M.B. pours from is not the bottle that Patsy Glickman brought over to #335 two years ago, but

M.B. still thinks of it as Patsy's bottle. In fact, on her twice-a-week—lately, sometimes thrice-a-week—visits to the Winn-Dixie, M.B. thinks of *each* bottle of the fortified wine that she sets in her cart as the bottle left behind by Patsy.

As she must. Because M.B. Milhause does not drink alcohol. Has never been a drinker. Neither she nor Lorne. M.B. comes from a long line of nondrinkers.

Dark, sweet—while she gets down on hands and knees to wipe up the spill from the dishwasher, M.B. can feel the wine begin to work its way into her tense scalp, her fingertips, her toes.

Two years ago, when Patsy came by with that first bottle of wine, M.B. stuck to iced tea. She felt gratified that she was not such a fool as Patsy—drinking wine, telling loud jokes, wearing gold flip-flops and a muumuu cut low to show the tops of her crinkled old boobs. As if anybody wanted to see!

Still, after Patsy departed that evening, and left the wine behind, M.B. felt awfully dull, and so she decided to see how much of Patsy's high spirits came from the bottle.

Pure panic: that was what M.B. felt the morning after. She could remember enough—dancing around #335, grinning at herself and her grape-blackened tongue in the bathroom mirror, deciding to stay drunk forever—she could remember enough of *that* to be stunned by the discovery that such bliss came at the price of such misery. Her vow: not another drop as long as she lived.

Three days later, however, while squeezing loaves of bread at the Winn-Dixie, M.B. made a startling discovery: the bread section sat across from the liquor section.

Up until that time, M.B. had lived her entire life passing by liquor stores and liquor sections in much the same way that she had passed by the churches of strangers (face forward, never taking a look in). Now, however, it seemed that the plain old Winn-Dixie had thrown wide open the gates to a secret and sublime pleasure dome, a magic palace whose treasures (sparkling bottles of red wines and white and great walls of beers) delivered more than any doctrine M.B. had ever met. Alcohol was not the paradise of Jesus, no, but it could erect an earthly paradise for a time, and that was surely some kind of miracle.

M.B. grabbed a loaf of bread and put it in her cart and started down the aisle toward crackers and chips; but not quite so fast that she missed the chance to form the question: *What would she tell Patsy if Patsy stopped by for the rest of her wine?*

The answer that presented itself: *M.B. would simply have to purchase another bottle.*

That day, as soon as she reached home—swiftly, feeling efficient and managerial—M.B. opened the new wine, and dumped into the drain the amount of wine (two orange juice glasses full) that Patsy Glickman had consumed during her visit. After M.B. poured the two glasses of wine down the sink, she planned how, the very next time she saw Patsy, she would say—so casually—"You want me to get you that wine you left at my place? It'll just go to waste otherwise."

That very evening, however, M.B. helped herself to a generous portion of the new bottle, and so had to hurry out the next day to buy another in order to bring the level of the first back to where it ought to be. After the second purchase, M.B. poured wine from the new bottle into the older bottle, but then it seemed—since she would never, ever again have alcohol in the house—that she might as well drink a glass or two from the new bottle rather than pour it *all* down the drain.

With slight variations, this scenario repeated itself some dozen times over the next two months: M.B. promised herself not to touch the wine; then evening came, as evening does, and M.B. found herself walking toward a pale and shrunken figure in order to draw the living room drapes against the night. When the drapes moved along the traverse rod, they made a sound like a crowd of insects or birds or bats. She was alone in the world, and unsafe. Her knees and her bunions ached. Surely one glass of wine would not hurt. The news reports said wine was actually *good* for the heart.

Then came the accident, and M.B. began buying bottles often enough that she canceled home delivery of the *Gulf News* so that she might purchase a copy on her way into the Winn-Dixie and, while she shopped, use it to hide the bottle in her cart.

These days, M.B. no longer bothers to funnel the new wine

into the old bottles. Once she even spoke of the MD 20–20 to the checkout girl. "It's Jewish wine," M.B. told the girl—babbling, she knew she was babbling—"for my Jewish friend." She felt a stab of guilt, then, and added a lame, "Not that she's a big drinker, not at all, only I like to be able to offer her something Jewish when she comes by."

At the kitchen table, M.B. glances at the morning paper's TV schedule to see how late Jersey's movie will run. Because of the early tranquilizing effects of the wine, M.B. has begun to feel—as she often does at this point in the evening—quite sorry for her poor granddaughter; thus, when her shirtsleeve sticks to a smear of jam on the table, why, M.B. just fetches a sponge and does not even make a point of removing the shirt, soaking the sleeve, hanging it up so the girl would have to see it.

Either because of some unevenness in the floor, or the length of the table legs, the kitchen table does not sit quite right, and it taps against the linoleum while M.B. wipes up the jam. She hopes Lorne would have approved of the table. The table is the only piece in the unit that she picked out on her own. Except for Kitty's old twin set in the guest room, Lorne and M.B. picked out everything, brand-new. Powder blue for the carpet and tiles, bittersweet for his leather recliner, a paisley featuring both colors for the living room curtains, the sofa, and the dinette's upholstered seats. When the two of them left Indiana, they donated most of their belongings to Goodwill: tweed sectional; easy chair of beet-colored vinyl; maple hutch whose too-short drawers forever dumped their contents onto people's toes; six black TV trays decorated with gold and red cornucopias; blond oak bedroom set with an always grimy-looking grain.

It is painful but good to remember Lorne testing the leather recliner in the showroom, sitting back and closing his eyes, and M.B. does her best *not* to consider the fact that the chair in which Lorne sat was a floor model, and almost certainly not the chair that now sits in the living room; if M.B. thinks otherwise, she begins to wish she could retrieve the sectional and maple hutch and bad bedroom set. She starts to wish that they had never left Indiana. In Indiana, perhaps Lorne would still be alive, and if

Lorne were still alive, Kitty's accident would not have occurred, because one did follow the other—

"M.B.," Jersey calls over a noisy, hyperkinetic ad for a cola drink, "aren't you going to watch this at *all*?"

M.B. sucks hard on her wine-stained lips, straightening and smoothing the syllables she means to use in her reply. "I'm fine, dear. I've got my cards."

Jersey sighs. She does not understand why her grandmother's drinking is a secret, but she knows that she is not supposed to know about it, acknowledge it.

While the advertisements play on, Jersey moves closer to the large piece of furniture that houses the television set. "Lorne's shrine" is how Jersey thinks of the thing. A tiny man with a baseball bat on his shoulder decorates the trophy her grandfather received for high school baseball. Next to the trophy: an 8 by 12 sepia photo of Lorne in army dress, skin an eerie bisque, cheeks' blush and blue eyes courtesy of Meyers Studio of Gary, Indiana. And here is Lorne, fishing. Lorne cuts up a watermelon on the front steps of the house that he and Jersey's mother and M.B. shared in Indiana. Lorne and M.B. wear New Year's hats and dine out with friends. A windblown Lorne and M.B. hold hands in front of the sign that marks the entry to Palm Gate Village.

To one side of the "shrine," half-hidden by a plaque announcing that Lorne Milhause made a hole in one, there sits a color photo of Jersey, Joe, and Katherine. This is a "family portrait," taken at Montgomery Ward's, at M.B.'s insistence, one day before the accident.

Katherine, seated in the studio's decidedly flabby rattan throne, is flanked by Joe and by Jersey. The photo's background is all golden aspens, apparently meant to trick the viewer into believing that the family vacations in autumnal Colorado. On photo day, M.B. did not approve of any of the clothes that the family had brought from Arizona, so she dispensed costumes from her own closets: for Katherine, a suit of bumpy lime bouclé; for Joe, a plaid sports coat that had belonged to Lorne; for Jersey, a cocktail dress of bronze satin. The effect is ridiculous: the long limbs of Joe and Katherine poke out from sleeves and hems; the darted front of M.B.'s cocktail dress has collapsed against Jersey's twelve-year-old chest. At the studio, when the trio could not stop laughing at themselves, M.B. snapped at the photographer, "Do you think they're funny? *I* don't think they're funny."

In the photograph, it is true, they do not look funny. They look—pathetic, impoverished, their skin the greasy ocher of people who must live on the streets and panhandle with creased bits of cardboard that read HUNGRY WILL WORK FOR FOOD.

Jersey's mother used to give money to such people, afterward whispering to Jersey, "We have to remember, that could be us." *We have to remember*. When they saw the poor. The morbidly obese. People with appalling scars or missing limbs. Blind people. The man who held his mouth open wide and screamed *cuntcuntcunt* as he made his way down the street. People in wheelchairs.

That could be us.

Tears often swarmed in Katherine's eyes at such times. Though Jersey understood the tears, she resented her sense of being trained for disaster, and so did her best to short-circuit the moments by grabbing Katherine's chin and turning it toward herself as she teased, "Are you *crying*, Mom?" Which made Katherine laugh, and apologize. "Sorry. Sorry for being morose, honey."

But that was the Katherine of the past. That was the Katherine who believed it was wrong to feel superior to other people, and also acknowledged that she felt superior quite often. That was the Katherine who said (page 25 of Jersey's journal), "I travel a small circle some days. Puffing myself up, recognizing it, deflating myself again."

Since the accident, the engine that drives Katherine's smiles and grimaces now produces such different effects that often even her face seems altered; indeed, a great patch of red now marks her left cheek—a typical blemish for the head-injury patient, the doctors say. Too: Katherine's gaze is slightly cockeyed, and the bright tracheostomy scar at the base of her throat gives her the look of someone rescued from hanging or torture.

"Arrh!" For quite a while, "Arrh!" made up the whole of Katherine's vocabulary. She graduated to "Shit!" at about the same time that she stopped having spasms—slashing motions of the right hand that, before restraint, dug bloody gouges across her chest. "Shit!" Shouted at the Fair Oaks aides and residents and visitors and walls and a light in the eyes or a dish of lime gelatin dessert—

Everyone gave a nervous smile when Katherine first said, "Shit." As if they believed she would never have known such a word before the accident. As if her injuries had made it possible for the word to enter her vocabulary in much the same way that they had allowed in the infections that left her packed in ice for almost two weeks.

Jersey knew better. She had a mother who said "Shit" at missed turns, mislaid briefcases, spilled milk. Sometimes, in fact, Jersey found Katherine's language a bit of an embarrassment: Irked by a fad in expensive T-shirts that declared that the T-shirts' owners felt NO FEAR, Katherine borrowed the manufacturer's ragged calligraphy to write on a T-shirt of her own, SCARED SHITLESS. Worse, she insisted upon wearing her T-shirt to the university on the day she gave her undergraduate group its spring final.

Usually, it is true, after Katherine said "Shit" in Jersey's presence, she apologized. Still, Jersey would have liked to defend her mother's use of the word, to insist that it was a sign of returning health rather than an aberration. But suppose that, knowing this, the hospital personnel liked her mother less. There were plenty of people who didn't like her mother when she was whole, before the accident; and now she really needed all the friends that she could get.

"Shit," says Jersey as she sets the family photo back on her grandmother's entertainment center. "*Shit.*" Quite loud.

M.B.—just then washing down her vitamin C with a gulp of wine—looks up, both guilty and shocked. "Jersey?" She makes her voice a little sharp. "Did you say something to me?"

"No."

True but not true enough, and the lie in the answer leaves the girl painfully empty. No one knows her anymore, and because no one knows her, she no longer seems to know herself. Who is she now? She has gone out into the world and discovered that she is A Girl in a Wheelchair, and that the grip of this image chokes the breath from every other possibility. Jersey understands that the fact of her body in the Theralife 504 makes people think of things they would rather not think of at all—*that could be us*—and so Jersey has put away her body. It has become a thing to be attended to, like the cage of a dumb pet (hamster, turtle). Before the accident—though she would not have admitted it—she liked to go without socks so she could see her pretty ankle bones, which looked almost chipped from stone. Now, those slim ankles are gone forever, replaced by something mottled and soft that she does not want to see at all. The beginnings of breasts—she had been fond of them, too, but now she finds them loathsome, obscene. In February, when she began to menstruate, she did not telephone her best friend back in Arizona, Erin Acuff, although the two had shared an intense interest in all such matters, had stolen the literature accompanying the tampons in their mothers' cupboards, and been mutually confounded by the pale cross section of the woman who demonstrated, one thigh raised, knee bent, the insertion—*where*?—of that plug of cardboard and cotton.

Together, Jersey and Erin Acuff had enacted scenes from *Little House on the Prairie* and the other Laura Ingalls Wilder books; one Christmas, they exchanged the deliciously humble gifts that Ma and Pa Ingalls had given to Mary and Laura (a tin cup, a penny, a piece of peppermint candy). Later they became obsessed with learning the whole of *A Little Night Music*, *Into the Woods*, and *Sweeney Todd*. They took Saturday classes at the Seca Children's Museum and, all through fifth and sixth grades, carpooled to swim club and home again each weekday morning at five-thirty. Just that June they had finally received permission to walk to day camp at the university on their own.

These days, when Erin Acuff and Jersey speak on the telephone—an event that occurs less and less often—Jersey can scarcely hear Erin because of the noise raised by the facts of her own life: squeals and bangs, the sounds of the rodent trapped within her racing round and round on its wheel. To shut out that racket, Jersey must almost shout. And speak very fast. While Erin and Jersey talk, twin drips of sweat trace Jersey's rib cage, draw moist seams along her edges. Recently, after a particularly awkward conversation, Jersey steeled herself and immediately punched Erin's number into the telephone once more.

"Erin," she said, "it's me again. I just—you know, if there's anything you want to ask about, like my wheelchair or anything, feel free."

Erin Acuff did not know what to say to her old friend. Perhaps she could have borne to read a book that explained the details of Jersey's altered body and life, but she was terrified of entering too intimately into Jersey's new world. Also, it seemed to Erin, now, that she had been feeling distant from Jersey even before the accident, hadn't she? She had a feeling—irrational, but deep—that in becoming a cripple Jersey had gone and done something that kids their age were not supposed to do.

These were things, of course, that she could not say, and in an attempt to draw Jersey back into the world they had shared before the accident, Erin teased, in the voice of Angela Lansbury as *Sweeny Todd*'s Mrs. Lovett, "I'm sure it's a perfectly lovely chair, dearie! But promise you won't run over me foot when we meet again!"

▪ ▪ ▪

In *Invasion of the Body Snatchers*, the aliens chase the hero and his friends through a tunnel. Always a menacing place, a tunnel, there being only the beginning and the end as points of escape. The aliens who pour from the tunnel look like anyone—Jersey, M.B., you, me. One of them bears a remarkable resemblance to Finis Pruitt, who is, indeed, a kind of body snatcher, though of his own devising, his own invention.

By 1975 the site of Finis's birth had been completely devoured by open-pit copper mining and no longer appeared on the maps. Finis enjoyed the fact. To commemorate the occurrence—and as a goof on Gertrude Stein—he composed the following two-line poem:

There:
Air.

It would have pleased Finis immensely to have been able to tell someone that he had invented his own past, but who would have made a sufficiently appreciative audience? Stein herself? God?

Who knows? And wouldn't it have depended on Finis's mood?

After all, on the day of the accident, when Finis came to behind the tangerine-colored garage, his mood was such that he cried. The pale patches of dusk beyond the privet hedge baffled him completely: were they so many handkerchiefs spread out to dry? And where was he?

On the pile of firewood belonging to the garage owner. On a pallet fashioned of what seemed to be the softer items from his cart.

His entire head hurt—though Finis often pretended to drink, he rarely did—but it was the sparking and combusting pain in the right side of his face that made him remember the day, the accident, and his failure—once again—to kill Carter Clay.

"Jesus fuck!" he cried. At that moment, there was not a crumb of improvisation left within him. With caution, he climbed down from the woodpile and made his way toward the dull glimmer of the shopping cart. Something crinkled as he moved. Beneath his jacket. A twenty-dollar bill and a note, both attached by tiny holes to the buttons on the front of his shirt. In the dim light, he struggled to read:

Sorry about your jaw, buddy. Had to take off.

What the hell? Finis flipped the note over. The reverse side gave mimeographed instructions on how to get to an upcoming picnic for AA members and their families.

"Nietzsche? You here?"

Carefully—though without much hope—Finis went through the items that Clay had piled back into the cart. Found the ferret's makeshift cage, broken and empty. "Nietzsche?" After a bit more searching toward the core of the cart's contents, Finis's hand closed around a familiar, solid weight that made him shake his head in wonder:

The Colt. That crazy Clay had left him the Colt. Discreetly wrapped in a T-shirt and a pair of boxer underwear.

11

On their trip from Arizona to Florida, the Milhause-Alitz family stopped in Texas to view Shankar Chatterjee's fossils of *Protoavis*. In *Protoavis*'s pneumatized skull, modified temporal region, and relatively large braincase, Katherine saw a primitive bird. A specimen that predated *Archaeopteryx* by at least seventy-five million years. A bird coeval with Triassic dinosaurs.

Joe, on the other hand, saw a specimen whose reconstruction he believed to be a botch. While Katherine oohed and aahed, Joe squinted out a window at a scissortail just then perching on a handy strand of telephone wire. Joe remained on excellent terms with the theory that had established his and his colleagues' reputations twenty years before: that little flycatcher, just then so carefully preening against the Texas sky, was—like all birds—*descended* from a dinosaur, perhaps *T. rex* itself.

Did Joe's training of Katherine provide for the possibility of his own overthrow? Yes. This, of course, is the proper path of scientific knowledge.

In his reluctance to admit change, then, Joe was very much like the pastor of M.B.'s church.

Silver-haired Pastor Bitner of Vineyard Christian is a nice man, a true friend and servant to his parishioners. However, Pastor Bitner's desire to protect the biblical world—its oil lamp lighting so lovely, so golden; its ability to examine minutiae limited to what can be observed by the naked eye—Pastor Bitner's desire to keep that world from advancing into the chillier and more brightly lighted domains of scientific theory and discovery moves him to perversity. With indomitable—and uninformed—authority, Pastor Bitner's sermons render the theory of evolution mere fodder for the generation of Sunday sermon belly laughs. For the amusement of his parishioners, Pastor Bitner is only too happy to grin and rub his hands together while he extrapolates from the oh-so-funny thoughts of molecular physicists.

"Get this, folks: *God* didn't make you! Hydrogen gas made you! That's right." Pastor Bitner wags a playful finger at the congregation that spreads out before him in a fan of pews made of that same blond oak Finis Pruitt hated so in the Oneco library. The members of Vineyard Christian are a mixed group, but they give an overall impression of homogeneity due to a predominance of clothing the color of party mints and made of fabrics composed in large part from materials that decayed in permeable sediments laid down during the Tertiary era—an era in which Pastor Bitner's parishioners do not believe.

Pastor Bitner's parishioners believe in nothing more than a few days older than Adam. How pleasant they find the notion that they are descended from no one but that old boy and his gal, upon whom God bestowed dominion over all the beasts of the earth.

"Now don't laugh, folks," Pastor Bitner says—laughing—"this is what the evolution scientists would have you believe!"

Giggles erupt here and there. The children of the congregation do not understand what is funny, but they want to laugh, too. Dads are laughing. Some moms are laughing, while others—this group includes M.B. Milhause—only allow themselves faint smiles, believing a good Christian woman doesn't show her teeth during Sunday service.

"But seriously, folks," Pastor Bitner continues, "you and I know that the Bible tells us, very clearly, how God created man, and, folks, the Bible does not lie. You cannot believe you were created in the image of God *and* created by a bunch of hydrogen gas. You cannot believe that there were creatures on earth who lived and died before the creation of man! *Death* was God's penalty for Adam's sin! But Jesus came to take away the sins of the world, folks, and when he took the sins away, at that precise moment, and only at that moment, did he restore us to grace and eternal life!"

On their own, the members of Pastor Bitner's flock rarely worry about the validity of the theory of evolution. M.B. herself was surprised the first time Pastor Bitner raised the subject. M.B. assumed evolution to be some queer obsession that only her daughter and a few other odd ducks gave the time of day—a little like listening to opera, or studying a foreign language.

However, M.B. finds Pastor Bitner's arguments against evolution—unlike Kitty's arguments for it—just plain fun. They make churchgoing feel like those school field trips where getting educated involved eating glazed doughnuts at the bakery or sliding down the firemen's brass pole.

"The evolution fellows want us to believe that since a human being's genetic material is ninety-seven percent the same as the genetic material of a chimpanzee, you and I only missed being a chimp by three percent!" Pastor Bitner laughs. "Folks, to clarify the holes in this kind of thinking, consider: a cloud is one hundred percent water while a watermelon's ninety-seven percent water. Would that convince you that a watermelon missed being a cloud by only three percent?"

This time the entire congregation—minus one soul—laughs along with the preacher. And who *is* that large man of shaven head and indeterminate age who sits in the next to last pew and looks so grave?

Carter Clay. Who has not only begun working as an aide at Fair Oaks Care, and continued to remain sober, but—upon determining that Vineyard Christian was Marybelle Milhause's church of choice—taken to attending services there each Sunday, and then again on Wednesday, potluck night.

Carter Clay's body still vibrates, now and again, with the blows that his van delivered to the Alitz/Milhause family; hence Carter Clay takes Pastor Bitner's sermons seriously. On his first visit, Carter came close to tears when Pastor Bitner spoke of the parable of the laborers in the field. Carter *saw* those laborers and their master bathed in a pure and liquid light, a mercurial shimmer that outlined their edges at the close of the working day, and he understood that Pastor Bitner was saying: even at the last minute of the hour, the man who came to believe could receive God's treasure in full.

Thus far, however, Carter has failed to gather the requisite courage to speak to Marybelle Milhause at either Vineyard Christian or Fair Oaks Care. Thus far, the girl, Jersey, has not come to church with her grandmother. But Carter feels certain he will find a way to meet both girl and grandmother soon.

At Fair Oaks, Carter has twice managed to be the one to help Katherine Milhause to the dining room, and on a number of occasions, while Katherine dully waited in the hall, Carter changed her bedding or mopped her floor—praying all the while: *Forgive us our trespasses as we forgive—*

Carter does not *like* to see Katherine Milhause, of course, but he recognizes that she is, as Pastor Bitner would say, his cross, and that he must welcome all opportunities to help her. Really, until a week ago, Carter tended to see Katherine as more messy and moody than ruined. He was badly shaken, then, last Wednesday, when a couple came to call on her. Carter first caught a glimpse of the pair while repositioning an old fellow across the way, and then later he saw the couple again, in the hall, looking around as if for help. A man and a woman. Both of them younger than Carter, but appearing worn, almost ill. The man explained that they had come all the way from Arizona to visit Dr. Milhause. They wanted to show her some slides—the man held a slide projector in his arms, and he raised it, as if for proof. Would it be possible, he wondered, for them to borrow a sheet for a screen?

Carter was saying sure, no problem, when without warning the woman pressed her face into the man's shoulder and began to cry—deep, hard sobs. Her companion shook his head. Voice low, he said to Carter, "We were close friends of Dr. Milhause."

Carter nodded, but as he hurried off to fetch a sheet, he felt a chill at the way the man spoke as if the Katherine Milhause he and the weeping woman knew were dead; it was only from loyalty to *that* Katherine Milhause that they meant to treat the resident in #112 as if she were still among the living.

▪ ▪ ▪

Had Carter happened to go to the church the Sunday *before* the accident, he would have seen, only inches from where he now sits, the intact Katherine Milhause smiling and nudging her mother as she whispered, "This is so crazy! Your minister guy looks just like the nut who preaches outside my office!"

"Pastor Bitner is not nuts!" said M.B., and Katherine sighed, and said, "Of course not," and felt sorry she had thought to offer up poor St. Tom to her mother at all.

Pastor Bitner paused in his sermon. Was he smiling at Katherine? Just in case, she smiled back, though she was a little alarmed by the pastor's teeth. So white-white! Were they really real?

"Disease, injustice, economic slavery"—Pastor Bitner made a wild flourish, drew both hands to his chest—"these are the fruit of man's decision to reject God in order to be"—he raised his fingers to scratch quotation marks in the air—"'*independent*.' Folks, are you saved? Will you go to heaven when you die? The Bible tells us: Ye must be born again. All this talk today about self-esteem!" Pastor Bitner screwed up his mouth and cringed. "They're asking, 'Do you feel good about yourself?' Folks, feeling good about yourself will take you straight to hell if you're not saved!"

Katherine smiled and turned to her mother to whisper, "So did you tell him I was coming today?"

"Sh!"

Katherine continued to smile. Despite—or because of—a tendency toward gloom, Katherine insisted upon exhibiting both humor and optimism whenever possible. Proof: in attending services at Vineyard Christian with M.B., Katherine believed absolutely—and mistakenly—that her polite interest in M.B.'s church would lead her and M.B. to respect of one another's views.

("So, M.B.," she had said as they came into view of Vineyard Christian—a young but weary-looking building the color of baked salmon—"so what exactly does your church believe?"

M.B. bent down to crumble the frowsy tip of a juniper branch that poked out into the sidewalk. "Someone should chop that thing down," she said, because actually she had little idea what Vineyard Christian believed, and felt the need to practice a tone of hauteur before replying, "It's *Christian*, Kitty. We believe the Bible. That's the main thing.")

M.B. did not want her daughter to know what she hardly acknowledged herself: that she had initially resumed going to church in order to counter Patsy Glickman's talk of "temple"; and that she had selected Vineyard Christian as her church for the same reason that she had selected Walgreen's and Winn-Dixie for her drug and grocery stores—all three were within walking distance.

Having to explain the latter to Kitty would have meant revealing to both Kitty and herself that she had not been able to bring herself to unlock the doors of the white LTD in lot H since Lorne's death. Why? Because the LTD was Lorne's car? And in the past, M.B. had always asked Lorne for permission to drive the car? Could that be it? M.B. did not think so and preferred not to think of the matter at all. She had learned, thank you kindly, to think about her eternal salvation rather than to worry over how independent a woman she was; and Pastor Bitner seemed to know just what she needed to hear on that score.

"Folks"—Pastor Bitner lowered his head in a way that M.B. could appreciate for both its dramatic flair and its modesty—"there's something a whole lot better for us to do than sit in front of our mirrors and tell ourselves we're fine and dandy. I don't know about you, folks, but I think I'm better off down on my knees, spending part of my day in the presence of God. That way"—Pastor Bitner grinned—"when I get to those pearly gates, I won't be in danger that the Savior's going to take a look at me and ask, 'Now, who might *you* be?'"

At this bit of fun, the congregation laughed in delight. Katherine laughed, too, and M.B. felt some relief that her daughter's visit had not fallen the week before, when Pastor Bitner had gone on at length about his miraculous prayer-based recovery from a five-inch-long festering wound he had received while a high school hurdle jumper; and his opinion that a person should avoid drinking from plastic cups. However, when Katherine whispered a shamefaced "Sorry," M.B. realized that Katherine had *not* been laughing along with Pastor Bitner—she had been laughing at a teenage boy three rows up, who wore a T-shirt across the back of which he had painted in an ugly scrawl, FEAR GOD.

M.B. stared at Katherine. A grown woman, yet her cheeks vibrated with suppressed laughter. *Fear God*. M.B. did not see anything at all funny about that.

12

"What's your name?"

"When's your birthday?"

"Where are you?"

Standard questions, but only the first two receive correct answers; the third makes Katherine Milhause's eyes grow large in alarm and what Subhas Mukhergee suspects is shame. Subhas pats Katherine Milhause's arm. A sad case. He has read her very interesting book of 1991, *Rethinking the Evolution of Birds*, alongside an essay she has more recently produced for her occupational therapist:

<u>BIRDZ</u>

I lik birdz. Therz blak birdz in the gardun. I giv tost. to them.

End.

A sad case.

In a wheelchair, in a corner of this shadowy room, the patient's paraplegic daughter sits with fingers pressed hard to her own lips, as if she must *physically* prevent herself from answering the questions posed to her mother. The daughter is the one, Subhas understands, who made the big sign posted above the easy chair in which the patient sits:

PLEASE, SPEAK TO ME, and REMEMBER I CAN HEAR YOUR WORDS.

Surely the girl and her grandmother do not need to witness this depressing examination again and again. Even the aide—a big fellow who must have observed plenty of similar scenes—the aide gives a heavyhearted sigh as he fiddles with the blinds.

In an attempt to bring a smile to the face of the patient's daughter—a bright, pretty child; no doubt ill-served by her cranky grandmother—Subhas points to the big book in the girl's lap. "Pretty heavy going, that!" he says.

As if she has been called from somewhere, the girl looks up at Subhas for a blank moment before she smiles and nods and says, "It is!"

Subhas smiles, then turns back to the patient to ask, "How about the month, Katherine? Do you know what month it is?"

She gives him a withering look.

Which her mother protests. "Stop that, Kitty!"

"Kitty" sticks out her tongue.

The mother—an odd little creature—steps close to the patient's bed; she slips her watch off her wrist and presses it into the patient's hand. "Now watch that little skinny thing, Kitty. That there's the second hand and when it moves, that means seconds are passing, see? There's sixty seconds in a minute. That's what this other hand's for. The seconds add up to minutes, and minutes add up to hours, and then days and months. Doctor wants to know what month it is. The *month*. If last month was March, then this month is—"

The old lady holds her mouth open, ready to help the patient to say *April*, but the patient looks away.

■ ■ ■

And wonders about the girl, who rolls about in the ugly chair and never, ever stands up. Is something tucked beneath the girl? Hidden?

"Stand up! Stand up!" she shouts, but the girl will not do it. The girl says, "I can't, Mom. No way."

■ ■ ■

"Kitty," says the patient's mother, "look at the watch!"

Subhas is aware that the patient's mother has some crazy notion that the patient and her paraplegic daughter will soon be back at home in Arizona, with the patient teaching at the university again, and the granddaughter riding bikes and going to dances—

"Kitty?" The patient's mother wraps her hand around the patient's hand. She closes her eyes and says in the mournful croon of a fortune-teller, "Every morning, Kitty, the sun rises up in the east."

"But not *really*," says the patient's daughter, then apparently decides to be less finicky, and so adds, "In Arizona, Mom, at home, east is outside your bedroom window."

"Your dad—Lorne—remember how he sang that song about 'East is east,'" the patient's mother asks. "You loved that when you were a little girl, Kitty. 'Buttons and Bows.'"

The patient blinks at all of them, then, before the aide can leave the room, she calls to him, "Were you the'?"

The man flushes and looks to Subhas as if for help.

"In the *askident*?" the patient says. "Were you the' too?"

The patient's mother turns to the aide and pats his big shoulder and whispers, "She asks everybody that, hon."

"It's okay," says the aide, but the patient shouts, "HEY!" and points out the window toward a large anonymous building in the distance. "Meet the-re!" she says to the aide. "Bring me can-ny bar!"

"Kitty," Subhas says, "what is it that's so interesting over there?"

From her spot in the corner, the patient's daughter murmurs, "She likes to be called *Katherine*."

Subhas nods. "Katherine. What would you like to do over there?"

The patient looks at her daughter as if she is a terrible annoyance, then, ignoring Subhas, she signals for the aide to draw near, and she hisses, "We run 'way."

The aide gives Subhas a nervous smile, then says to the patient, "You need to stay here. Till you're all better. Ain't that right, doctor? If there's anything I can do to help get you better, I'd be glad—if the doctor's got a suggestion."

Subhas nods, then tells the patient, "I'll be back next month. You see that these fellows get you walking every day!"

▪ ▪ ▪

The way that Katherine Milhause does not respond to the doctor—just turns her head and looks at the wall—makes Carter Clay think of his own mother. When she died, his mother was about the age of Katherine Milhause; had she lived, it occurs to him, she would now be about the age of Katherine Milhause's mother. This realization leaves Carter feeling stretched between fact and possibility, for him always a painful location—the most likely spot from which to reach for a drink, a drug.

As the three visitors move out into the hall, Carter follows them, trying to hear their conversation. He lingers at the water fountain. One short drink. Straighten. Swallow. Bend for another.

"So, is Kitty any better?" Marybelle Milhause asks the doctor.

The doctor looks embarrassed. He rests his hand on the shoulder of the girl—a nice girl, Carter feels sure—and he gives the girl's shoulder a squeeze. Carter can feel that squeeze, its friendly assurance, and wishes he were the one dispensing it, inspiring confidence in the girl.

"Kitty—Katherine needs to get involved in life," the doctor says. "And to get around more. I have to tell you again, Mrs. Milhause, I don't believe this is the right place for her."

The girl makes some response, but Carter misses what she says because, just then, she turns his way.

Does she stare at Carter or merely at the felt banner above his head?—*Today is the first day of the rest of your life*. Carter would prefer that he felt more keenly his remorse at the fact that he is the driver than his fear that, as in a movie, the girl or her mother will look at him—if not now, maybe later—and say, "You!" To his regret, the two feelings continue to hang in balance, and as he hurries down the corridor, he tries hard to generate a more acute remorse: Because of him, the wheelchair, the scars on the mother's neck, and let's face it, both of their lives loused up forever. Because of him. Because of him.

As a kid on a swing or a teeter-totter uses the ground to boost himself into the air, so Carter uses his rock-hard fear of disclosure to boost himself into the loftier realms of remorse, but he understands that he, on his own, cannot keep himself suspended indefinitely.

13

After his discharge from the service in 1970, when Carter returned to the upper left-hand corner of the country, he knew exactly how to find the sea-foam green rooming house into which his father had moved after the suicide of Carter's mother. Everyone in Fort Powden knew the place because of the large, cartoonish sign nailed to the front porch: BRENT'S ROOMS FOR MEN, announced a dialogue balloon above a monkey who held a banana in what many took to be a suggestive position.

Imagine Carter imagining a nervous but poignant reunion scene in which he puts out of his mind his father's blows, the terrible things Duncan had said about Carter's mother and Carter and Cheryl Lynn (*slut faggot bastard asshole shithead twat bitch jerkoff fucker*) so that he and Duncan Clay can embrace, man to man, soldier to soldier. After a few embarrassed tears—tears? no tears?—Duncan and Carter go out for a drink. They talk about the suicide of Carter's mother. Duncan explains that her death has opened his eyes, he misses her something awful—

No. Drinks with Duncan would be a bad idea. Duncan, drunk, tended to grow sullen, not sentimental. So, no drinks. They would sit in the rooming house and talk—Carter, perhaps, perched on some lumpy bed while Duncan sat in a chair. A straight-backed chair? An easy chair? Soft light coming into the room?

Carter smoked a joint before he left his motel room for his visit with Duncan. In high school, he and a girl named Sharon Scott had come to this motel—the Adelphi—a few times. He suspected that he might even be staying in one of the rooms he and Sharon Scott had used. Was that strange? Was it anything? In a town with only three motels, wasn't it likely you might end up in the same motel room someday?

Autumn. Everything deep green and bushy behind the bits of fall color. Without his weapons, walking the damp gravel road that ran beside the Adelphi and toward the bluffs overlooking downtown, Carter felt naked, as if an ambush awaited him behind each tree. He could smell the paper bag plant. If the day had been clearer, he knew—at least in theory—he would have seen the Cascades. If he kept going toward the water, he would eventually pass through the concrete and iron remains of the old fort, where he and his childhood friends had played war, and he and his high school friends had gone to drink.

Actually, there was a faster route to Brent's Rooms than the one Carter took, but he wanted to see the town, the old Victorian houses, the stores. Neff Morgan and a few other people had taken him past the high school and down London Street and up on the bluffs the night before, but he needed to walk on London Street in the daylight.

Innocents. That was what Carter thought of Neff (exempted for asthma) and Cheryl Lynn and everyone else who had not been in the war. He was glad of their innocence, really, because when he was with them it was not necessary to know what he knew. That was one of the worst parts of the war, what all of you knew together and could not pretend *not* to know.

The small white hexagonal tiles that still led the way into Fuller Drugs soothed Carter. The yellow and white cardboard display of Jean Naté After Bath Splash still sat in Fuller's window, though it seemed dustier now. Becky Pattschull had worn Jean Naté. The house of Becky Pattschull still pushed its great gray breast out over the bluff, and though it broke his heart a little, it was good to see that great dove of a house. While he had been away, it sometimes seemed to Carter as if Becky and anything else clean and normal might be things he had dreamed up altogether.

He had written to Becky Pattschull from over there but she never answered. A number of people from the high school did write to him. And his sister wrote, and his mother, too, before she died.

At Brent's Rooms, a man with a cotton swab dangling from each ear helped Carter find his father, who was not only drunk but vomiting into a Folger's coffee can.

"You jackass!" Duncan Clay declared when Carter tried to help. After he began to feel a little better, Duncan threw a gooseneck lamp at Carter—a feeble toss, but, nevertheless, eight stitches were required to close the gash left on Carter's jaw.

The next day, Carter and Cheryl Lynn went together to visit their mother's grave. The weather was rainy and cold. The grave marker was a square of metal that looked like the lid from a canned ham.

Was that the best they could do? Carter wondered, but he said nothing, as Cheryl Lynn was already on the verge of tears.

Cheryl Lynn was a nice enough girl, but it was not easy being her younger brother. Cheryl Lynn was loud and crude and had a reputation for being a fool in love. Let Cheryl Lynn fall in love—and she was always falling in love—and she would be a happy idiot, writing the boy's name on anything at hand, playing songs she connected with the boy over and over and over, and, in general, planning her entire life around the newest jerk's likes and dislikes. Every breakup was a major catastrophe, with Cheryl Lynn blubbering in her room and at dances and the Bowladrome, her cheeks streaked with black makeup. Carter could have borne that, but he sometimes did feel angry at Cheryl Lynn for not knowing more about the world. She should have known, for example—and let Carter know—that a girl like Becky Pattschull would laugh her tinkling laugh when Carter said his sister was going to cosmetology college. ("Cosmetology *college*, Carter? Do they major in things like permanent wave techniques or what?") That you did not order pie à la mode with ice cream. That a Fort Powden girl considered a pearl ring a ridiculous gift unless she was ready to be "engaged to be engaged."

In her drafty old Fairlane, on the way home from the cemetery, teary Cheryl Lynn wanted Carter to talk about the war. Clearly she wanted to think that Carter was a hero, or some kind of wild man; that Vietnam was a World War II movie, or that it was an orgy.

"Did you carry a bullet with your name on it, like I told you?"

Carter nodded, although he certainly had not been that dumb.

"Maybe that's why you're alive, you know?" A little sob escaped Cheryl Lynn, but then she laughed, and said, "Sorry," and talked about how skinny Carter was, on and on. She wanted to talk about the protesters, too—*little college shits, what do they know?*—but to Carter, Cheryl Lynn looked as if she could have been one of them. She wore bell-bottom trousers, and her hair was long and straight. While he was away, Cheryl had gone to Seattle, to the cosmetology college, but now she was back in Fort Powden, working at the bowling alley.

"So what happened in Seattle?" he asked.

"Oh, they was all stuck on themselves, and you know how good Rex and Maggie always been to me. When I come home—after Dad called about Mom—"

Cheryl Lynn shook her head, then reached up to the Fairlane's battered visor and pulled out a joint tucked there. Carter was relieved. He thought maybe Cheryl Lynn meant to change the topic. He should have known better. Even though he and Cheryl Lynn had never smoked dope together, he should have known that Cheryl Lynn, stoned, would not turn all light and lively.

"That fucking bastard." Cheryl Lynn rubbed the back of her hand across her nose, and growled, "He drove her to it." Carter could feel her sneak a quick look his way. "You don't know, Carter," she said, then began to cry in earnest, her voice tiny, a tiny thing. "Their bedroom. That's where she did it." Cheryl Lynn's shoulders worked up and down convulsively, and Carter said, "Hey, you want to pull over, maybe you should pull over," but she shook her head and kept driving, as if they were headed somewhere important.

"Maggie helped me—clean." Though she kept her eyes on the road, Cheryl Lynn leaned a shoulder toward Carter to hiss a furious, tear-filled, "And all the while we was working, Dad's out in the hall, ragging on about how that bitch Betty fucked up his precious gun, that bitch got his gun all bloody! I was crying my head off, and Maggie says don't listen, and that I could just think of her and Rex as my parents, you know?"

Carter did not nod to show understanding, but he began to wipe at his steamy window as if he needed to see something out there in the rain—maybe a certain gas station, or the swing set at Fort Powden State Park.

Cheryl Lynn taking on other people for her parents? What the fuck was she talking about? He wanted out of her car, now. He felt as if he were hacking his way through jungle, and he wondered—not idly—how much skin would a person lose in a roll along the road's gravel shoulder?

Before he could jump, however, Cheryl Lynn pulled up in front of the Adelphi Motel. "*Anyways*"—she gave him a wobbly smile—"I'm having a welcome home party for you! A tea."

A tea?

When Cheryl Lynn insisted he wear his uniform, he began to get the general idea.

Cheryl Lynn had rented the social hall of the Moose Lodge. The refreshments were dishes of colored mints and mixed nuts and a ginger-ale punch with an ice ring of strawberries and pineapple chunks floating on top. She and her best friend, Donna Hale, were decked out in matronly party dresses and hairdos stiff and lacquered as cinnamon rolls.

Carter cheered, along with the majority of the guests, when his friend Neff Morgan turned down the lights and began—one bottle per hand—pouring vodka into Cheryl Lynn's fruit punch.

"Neff!" Cheryl Lynn protested from across the room. "This ain't that kind of party!"

Neff had topped off each punch bowl by the time she reached him. "The rest's for you, man," he told Carter, and handed over the bottles, each still a good third full.

"Thanks, buddy." Carter took a swig. He tried to act as if he were having a good time, but everything irritated him. The dark social hall felt like a garage. Several of the girls who had written to him while he was gone tried to get him to dance. *"I don't dance no more. Not me, girls,"* he said. Still, he did not understand—because he did not see the new way his eyes darted around the room, even when he talked about things he had always talked about—he did not understand why he kept finding himself standing alone.

Eventually, he took what remained of his vodka out into the alley behind the lodge. It felt like a wonderful escape, a brilliant move. In the dark, there, he leaned against a concrete wall and closed his eyes and smoked one of the several joints people had pressed upon him. A light rain fell, and the rain in the streetlights was a beautiful thing to see, and the chill in the air distilled the smell of the pulp and his damp uniform to a kind of syrup coating the back of his throat.

On foot, he started toward the Adelphi Motel. Then he changed his mind and backtracked, making his way across town toward the little white rental where he and Cheryl Lynn had grown up. Where his mother had tried and tried to kill herself, and finally succeeded.

Carter had no idea who lived in the little white house now. The dark windows suggested that no one was home. A lawn chair, folded-up, sat propped against the front steps.

He walked around the corner, then up the dark back alley, overgrown with raspberry brambles, bits of fence pitching this way and that. The house surprised him when he saw it from across the open backyard. Because it was the same? Because it did not seem to know that his mother had died there?

A window on either side of the back door, a window in the door. A black wire swung down from a power pole and entered the house just above the left-hand corner of the door. He did not remember whether or not the door used to be black, and this bothered him. He had *lived* there, for Christsake. His mother *died* there. He wanted the house to mean something. He wanted to be able to seize that something, and to store it in his heart for all time.

But, man, as he stood there in the alley, staring at the house, his heart was already full of something, and it was the wrong something. The weight of it rolled upward and tipped him forward, hands on his knees. It contorted his face, and he found himself straining to make the contortion bigger, uglier, more distinct so that he could expel it, oh, please—

The moan that rose from his mouth took him by surprise. It made a red and turquoise and purple pressure behind his eyes and grew to a roar that filled the little yard. He was hot. He was wet, his uniform—

"Who's out there?" someone called from the back door of the house. "Who is it?"

Carter backed into the alley, turning his ankle in a rut. There had been a rabbit warren in the alley when he was a boy. One morning, right where he now limped, he had seen a baby rabbit. When he drew close to the creature, it hopped away, but not before Carter saw that the top of its skull was missing. A beautiful little gray rabbit, big enough to have fur, and there was its brain, exposed, and a fly was feeding there. Carter wanted to catch the rabbit, to help it, but the rabbit was scared of him, and hopped away into the alley's mess of brambles and bushes. On hands and knees, Carter tried to get to the rabbit but it did not matter that the strip of brambles and bushes and rolls of old fencing and piles of rusted tin cans never was wider than six feet, the rabbit could always move back and forth in the strip faster than Carter could move to catch up with it. The poor thing, it was terrified of Carter. He began to feel as if he might make the creature's heart explode, and finally he had backed out of the bushes—on his way, cutting his knee badly on a piece of broken jar.

Now, it was night. The alley was dark. He walked toward the floodlight that shone over a backyard garage. He had never seen the woman who lived in the house to which the garage belonged. He had heard she had flippers for hands. He stopped by the garage, and he yanked his shirtfront into the light. An oddly disappointing moment. He had known that his entire uniform was soaked, but had formed a notion that it was blood that he sweated, and that blood would have done him some good.

14

You cannot imagine what it's like—

So begins the little speech that M.B. Milhause practices while sitting at her kitchen table, applying Plum Cider polish to her fingernails, and trying to ignore the bone-jarring sounds that periodically reverberate in the stairwell closest to #335.

When my husband died—

I am sixty-four years old and suffer from a variety of ailments myself—

A shuddering crash—that might be the best description of the stairwell's noises. Sounds sufficiently alarming that they cause certain Palm Gate Village residents to open their doors and call out in frightened voices, "Anybody hurt?"

Jersey's echoey reply—"Just practicing moving my wheelchair on the stairs"—of course brings offers of help, and makes M.B. indignant. As if M.B. would not help the girl move her chair if she wanted help!

To her would-be helpers, Jersey calls, "No, thanks! This is something I have to do on my own."

Which is *not* true. M.B. would like to print up an announcement indicating that it is not necessary for the girl to practice manually moving her chair up and down the stairs—a procedure that involves her having to slide out of her chair and onto her bottom, then haul her body up or down a step, then haul the chair up or down onto the step beside her. All this when there is an elevator ten yards down the balcony, for heaven's sake! M.B. feels certain there have already been complaints to the association about her having a person under nineteen living with her, and why the girl should torture everyone with all that worry and racket is beyond reason.

"It's important to know how to do it, in case I ever get stuck someplace. Say there's a fire and the elevators don't run." So Jersey insisted, and she just laughed when M.B. told her there was bound to be trouble with the association.

Well. Another stroke of Plum Cider, then M.B. half-rises from her chair to take a peak out the window. She cannot see the top of the girl's head yet, which means it will be a good ten minutes until she returns.

She sits. Dips the brush back into the polish. Wipes the excess back into the little bottle before she makes her next stroke. One wide stroke for the middle of the nail, then over the top—so, so carefully—and then a stroke on each side. She has done this hundreds, thousands of times, yet the rule presents itself to her anew each time, and she finds this annoying. If she did not think of the rule, would she botch the job? No. But still the rule comes, will not let her alone.

Other rules: Cut the stems of roses at an angle the minute you receive them. Use bleach to get rid of tea stains in your cups. Encourage large mums by the removal of early buds. A pea-sized dab of petroleum jelly worked into freshly cleaned skin will do as much for the complexion as the most expensive of lotions—

It seems to M.B. that she could have looked back on her life and judged it a good life if only these last years had turned out differently. Everything that she and Lorne worked for is in place—retirement in the perfect retirement home with everything just so—but the set is being used for the wrong story, a story of disaster, the set rearranged into ugly angles to make paths for a wheelchair.

What no one at all seems to understand: M.B. must protect what little she has left. These demands upon her from Jersey and Katherine will make her run out of life even sooner.

I do the best I can but, of course, I'm not equipped—

She caps the bottle of nail polish. Stands. Smiles.

Perhaps it is her nature, and cannot be helped, that, all day long, M.B. lies to her God. She would be startled if you pointed this out to her. Ask M.B. if her God knows all and she will say, *of course*; still, she persists in going about #335 in a rage over this or that—while smiling for her God-audience. For God, she pretends that she has done all she can for Katherine. Though she has moments when she asks forgiveness for her drinking, most of the time M.B. believes that if her makeup is right, and her clothes are ironed, and she wears a spot of Chanel No. 5 behind each knee, God, too, will construe the wine she takes from the cupboard as, say, a graham cracker, a piece of fruit. Just as now, watching M.B. take a glance out the window, walk to the guest room, and, using her elbows to protect her damp nails, remove the girl's little red book from under her pillow—God will view M.B.'s reading as a sign of responsible parenting.

M.B. That is what M.B. looks for in the journal, but does not see.

On the stairs, the girl's chair booms, then shudders. Boom, shudder, then silence as the girl rests in preparation for the next riser.

Grants. M.B. recognizes that name. The Grants live downstairs. But, no, after she reads half a page, M.B. realizes that Jersey is writing about a family of scientists and their study of the evolution of finch bills—finch bills!—in someplace called Galapagos.

> She still doesn't want to hug me or anything.
> Usually she'll let me kiss her when I visit but . . .

That would be about Kitty. *M.B.*? No *M.B.* but M.B.'s eyes do alight upon a *Grandma.*

> Today, from the TV, Grandma ordered something called a "jewelry armoire." I love it! Eight individual felt-lined drawers for $159! As usual, she tried to hide me

when her friend Patsy came by. She's afraid I'll say something disgraceful and the police will haul us both off to jail. After Patsy's visit, we visited Mom. Then Grandma watched Pat Robertson on TV. She thinks he's the one we ought to have as our next president. What a jerk! She thinks it's some great compliment to say he looks like Lorne.

Who did the girl call a jerk? M.B.? Lorne? Pat Robertson?

"*Com-ing,*" M.B. calls. That will be the girl at the door. Carefully, carefully, using her elbows, M.B. sets the pillow back in place on top of the little book.

Beyond the storm door, binoculars held up to her eyes as if M.B. is some giant bird she longs to see, Jersey waits. Her face is red, and she breathes hard from her exertions.

"Very funny," M.B. says through the screen.

"M.B."—Jersey grins and points to the way M.B. struggles to turn the door's little knob with her palm in order to protect the wet polish—"M.B., you're denying yourself the use of your opposable thumb!"

"Oh, hush." M.B. holds the door for the girl. "Joan Rivers you ain't, kid."

"You might want to know"—the girl lowers her voice as she rolls her chair over the threshold and into the hall—"a bunch of people are out there. On the balcony. I think something's up."

After a quick peek out the door, M.B. grins at Jersey. "Probably a party, and, of course, I'm not invited! Hah!" she says. "Hah! But I got me an idea." She gestures for Jersey to follow her to the guest bathroom, where she steps into the tub and with a great show of care—shoulders drawn up, finger gesturing for silence—slowly slides open the frosted window that lets out onto the balcony.

From the hall, Jersey whispers, "What do you think it is?"

M.B. turns, shakes her head. "Not a party, kid. Looks like it's that Mr. Welty. Like his calendar's out of date."

From the tub, M.B. narrates: First, the debate over whether to call the man's children in Illinois, or the manager. Next, the arrival of the manager with a key. Then, the hushed entrance of an ambulance into the parking lot.

From her spot in the hall, Jersey can hear the loose rattle of the folded gurney's parts as the attendants make their quick trip up the stairs; and, a few minutes later, the whisper of the gurney's freighted wheels as the attendants guide the body along the balcony and into the elevator for the trip down.

"Is he dead?"

"I think he is, kid."

When M.B. finally leaves the tub, she discovers that Jersey has moved herself off to the guest room. "So"—M.B. peeks in at the guest room doorway—"I guess that'll be me one of these days if I'm not careful."

Jersey looks up from her journal. That'll be all of us one of these days whether we're careful or not, she thinks; however, she knows it would be impolite to say such a thing to someone whose "day" is probably much closer than her own, and so she just smiles at her grandmother, and returns to her writing.

▪ ▪ ▪

Before receiving the Chinese journal, during the course of her life, Jersey has purchased or received: one journal of leatherette the color of olive wood, one of handsome paisley, several plain numbers picked up at drugstores or OfficeMax, one of quilted lavender calico (a gift from M.B.), one of corduroy, one—a gift from her friend Erin—of green rep cloth atumble with golden retrievers chasing after gay red and yellow balls.

Before the accident, each time a new journal came into Jersey's life, she put it on the table beside her bed. Every night, before sleep, she cracked the stiff binding and wrote for fifteen minutes. Such discipline made her feel strong. Journal-writing threw loneliness into relief, yes, but in the act of writing, loneliness could be transformed into *aloneness*, which felt not merely less onerous but sometimes even desirable.

After a few weeks of disciplined journal-keeping, however, a night invariably came when she carried the latest journal out of her bedroom with the notion that she might make her writing time pass more quickly in front of the television set. Or, looking for company, she carried the journal down to the jumble of a room her mother and father called their study. That evening would soon enough be followed by an evening when the journal could not be found, and by the time the thing turned up again (behind a bookcase, under a pile of magazines, deep in the crack of a sofa and covered with crumbs and dust), another had taken its place, the promise of day following day was marred, and so she let the rest of such journals remain a blank.

The Chinese journal has led a different life from its predecessors. The Chinese journal's pages are swollen like old dollar bills, soft and worn and dingy with much handling. This journal no longer shuts tight. Not just opinions and information and stories, but the physical facts of lead and ink and finger-grime have leavened the journal's pages.

The Chinese journal is a refuge. It is also a vehicle that takes Jersey closer to her parents. Even the simple act of accumulating detail brings them near; so much so, in fact, that when thoughts do not come to the girl, she sometimes copies into the journal bits of text from library books: hints for the family of the brain-injury patient; tidbits regarding mitochondrial DNA; the horrible but oddly consoling news that children incapable of feeling pain have been known to push their own eyeballs right out of the sockets. Really. That pain in Jersey's tethered spinal cord, there is a reason for it. *Really*.

Jersey appreciates the way in which facts help a person make sense of the world. Facts have implications, yes, but they can also break free of their implications and sit on a table before you, neat as any cup with a sliver of reflection dancing on its rim. Facts may vary with the times, and that in itself is a fine thing, isn't it? With facts, a person can expect advancement. Once upon a time, Aristotle—Father of the Scientific Method—did some careful observing and deduced that dirty rags generated mice. Other splendid thinkers were convinced that nasal secretions came from the pituitary gland. "Pituitary," Jersey has noted on the sixty-third page of her Chinese journal, "originally meant 'slime.'"

Jersey enters the details of the death next door, then goes on to record the fact that, because he checked the appropriate square of his driver's license, today parts of her father now wander through the world in other people. *What* parts, Jersey does not know. Would she want to know? No. Instead, she tries to wrap herself up in the general notion that he is out there. Tries to make that a comfort. Someday, on the street, perhaps a nice young woman will glance Jersey's way through Joe's cornea. Or maybe, right now, the cells of Joe's liver assimilate the nutrients from a beloved boy's lunch, store his sugar and glycogen and keep him in the world.

Surely, Jersey thinks—though she does not write this in her journal—surely there is a sense in which this means that her father is not totally dead.

15

Such is her frame of mind on a Wednesday night outside of Vineyard Christian when she glances up and catches sight of the tree trimmers across the way, and she thinks: a vision.

In part, this is because, initially, she does not see the tree trimmers themselves—only the blue and red balls that are, in fact, the men's baseball caps. Visible, then not. Like something tossed up and down in ocean waves. For one happy moment, those dots of color form a sign of a previously unknown wholeness adrift in the world, and, heart leaping with the possibility of the impossible, she puts out her hand to M.B., and breathlessly points—

"Tree trimmers," M.B. explains. She and Jersey are on their way to the Wednesday night service and potluck. "Things are always growing here. You can't stop them."

Of course. Now Jersey, too, can make out one of the men, his T-shirt, his jeans. She understands that he rides a ladder, and that the ladder is attached to a truck obscured by a high hedge of white oleander.

The hour is five-thirty. Five-thirty in the afternoon in early May, with the Florida sky blazing such a nacreous white that the fronds of the big palm trees flash in an afterimage on the eyes. That sky—it is a duplicate of the sky in the charged mural with which Joe Alitz once covered an entire wall of Jersey's Arizona bedroom. Joe painted that mural just after Katherine published *Rethinking the Evolution of Birds*, a refutation of much of the work that had made Joe famous. A tension-causing bit of decoration. Begun and completed while Katherine lectured in Rome, the mural contained two examples of what Joe considered to be the oldest known bird, *Archaeopteryx*. Befeathered in hypothetical blues and greens, the mural's *Archaeopteryx* perched on cycads, while *Pterondons* careened above the horizon; and, for a moment, Jersey hears the swish and crash of the trimmers' falling branches as the sound of a grand sauropod lumbering through the mural's swamp. She replaces the small boy who bends to retrieve his toy car—there, in the right-hand corner of her field of vision—she replaces him with the mud-brown paint her father hoped would suggest sediments fine enough to immure the bones of *Archaeopteryx*.

"We'll just wait outside until the others get seated," M.B. says. She stops on the sidewalk near the parking lot and lifts her chin in greeting or defiance—Jersey cannot tell which—as a small family passes by and into the church.

Because it is Wednesday, many of the women who enter the church wear oven mitts (plain, calico, in the shape of fish and lobsters and cacti) to protect their hands from the hot dishes they carry. Many of the parishioners smile at Jersey and M.B. as they pass by the pair and into the church. Do they acknowledge her only because she is A Girl in a Wheelchair? Jersey alternately does her best to smile back, to pretend she and her chair are not really there. She is there, of course. Each time the others open the church door, Jersey feels a puff of air-conditioned air.

WACKY CAKE

Mix in a 9 by 13 pan (ungreased) 3 cups flour, 2 cups sugar, 1 cup cocoa, 2 t. baking soda, 1 t. salt. Stir in 1 t. vanilla, 2 cups cold water, 2 T. vinegar, 6 T. salad oil. Bake 30–40 minutes at 350°F.

This is the recipe affixed to the lid of the cake pan that rides in Jersey's lap. The girl notes that M.B. decided against revealing her secret frosting (fifteen Pearson's mints laid across the cake's top just before it comes out of the oven) and opted, instead, for writing across the bottom of the recipe card, "Chocolate icing always a nice addition."

"Mrs. Milhause?" Down the steps of the church taps a sweet-faced old fellow in a suit the color and texture of wasps' nests. He smiles at Jersey and, as if they were already inside the church, whispers, "They're getting started inside. Can I help this young lady?"

M.B. nods, then says to Jersey, "See him?" She points toward the church parking lot. There, a very large bald-headed man doffs a cowboy hat in their direction.

M.B. waves at the man, then whispers, "He look familiar?"

Jersey stares at the man's wrists and neck, how they strain against the snaps on his western shirt when he stoops to retrieve the Stetson hat he has dropped in the gravel. Like the man's jeans, the shirt appears an insufficient package. The effect is cartoonish: the bull got up in the clothes of the cowboy.

"He works over to Fair Oaks," M.B. whispers. "An aide."

Jersey nods, yes, he was in the room the last time Dr. Mukhergee came to test her mother. She just did not recognize him in this getup, this location.

▪ ▪ ▪

In an effort to ignore all looks from the parishioners, once she and her chair are parked behind the last row of pews (and M.B.), Jersey squeezes her eyes to slits. She transforms the shifting members of the red-robed choir into embers pulsing in a grate. This is a trick with which she formerly amused herself when her parents took her to the symphony (the rich wood of the stringed instruments, the black of the musicians' dress clothes, the musicians' gestures—all metamorphosed into a monarch butterfly, fresh from the cocoon and drying its wings with small throbs of movement).

Still, Jersey cannot help registering the fact that Pastor Bitner looks so much like poor St. Tom from outside her mother's office building in Seca. St. Tom, of course, was always somber. St. Tom had a low and lovely voice—really, a better voice for sermonizing than that of Pastor Bitner.

"Folks," Pastor Bitner is saying, "let's not have any confusion about this. Genesis 25:23 says, plain as day, that the Lord told Rebekah, even before Esau and Jacob came into the world, that the *elder*—that is, *Esau*—would be ruled by the younger! So when we see Jacob and Rebekah arrange for Jacob to receive the blessing of Isaac, what we are seeing is their *fulfillment* of God's plan! Jacob and Rebekah *lie*! Yes, they do! We can't call it anything less than an out-and-out lie when Jacob pretends to be someone he is not, can we? When he drapes the kidskins on his hands and neck so his father will mistake him for the hairy Esau, he *lies*. Rebekah, aiding him, *lies*. But in no way does the Bible suggest that Jacob or Rebekah should be *censured* for their lies! Jacob and Rebekah do that which makes the prophecy of *God* come true, hence their actions find approval with the Lord."

Pastor Bitner goes on to list other examples of sanctified lies (Rahab the harlot's concealment of Joshua's spies from the king of Jericho; Joseph's hiding the golden cup in Benjamin's pack) and how those stories just might be taken as endorsement for the use of deception in fighting the godless abortion promulgators of today.

Three times, Jersey leans forward in her chair to whisper to M.B., "You can't believe *that*!"

M.B. does not respond, but, after the third time, Pastor Bitner meets Jersey's eyes and holds them for a moment—which is something, it occurs to her, that poor St. Tom could never do.

Once, Jersey went to the university with her mother to pick up a batch of papers at Earth Sciences, and she witnessed her mother's attempts to stop the students from heckling St. Tom. He was outside Earth Sciences, preaching in the middle of a ring of students, and as Jersey and Katherine came down the building stairs, Katherine pulled Jersey to a stop.

"How'd you get to be fucking Tom the Baptist, anyway, man?" one of the student hecklers shouted, and another:

"Hey, Tom! Your wife satisfies, man!"

"Kegger at Tom's after the baptism, everybody!"

A handsome boy wearing a baseball cap backward entered the ring on his knees, teasing, "Baptize me, Tom, man! Come on, man, let's do it!" At this, the crowd roared with laughter. Jersey could feel her mother's anger toward the hecklers rise, and she thought, as she had many times in the past, that, yes, it was nice that her mother liked to defend underdogs, but it was also scary. "Let's go, Mom," she pleaded, but then the boy on his knees wrapped his arms around St. Tom's legs, almost toppling the man, and Jersey's mother flew down the steps, her black bag banging against her thigh as she broke through the circle, and grabbed the big boy by the sleeve.

"Knock it off!" she cried.

A horrible moment: that big boy rising to his full height, his cheeks going bright red with embarrassment, and then fury, before he drawled, "Hey, why don't you go fuck yourself, bitch?"

Several people cheered the boy's suggestion. Jersey's mother glared at them, and then—trembling, but still a little scary-looking herself—she turned back to the boy and said an uneven, "Yeah, and why don't you act like a human being, you big ding-dong?"

Ding-dong made the boy and his admirers whoop with derision. St. Tom—oblivious—continued his crisp and crazy litany: "If John Locke were here, *he* would come forward. Where are the Jesuits? I'm not asking that ten Jesuits come forward. I'm only asking that one Roman Catholic priest step out!"

Slowly, Jersey approached the circle. Her mother had set down her bag and now stood with her hands outstretched to the boy. "How would you feel," she asked in a low voice, "if your dad were sick, and some kids came and made fun of him?"

Hisses and boos and obscenities were the answer from the crowd. Jersey's mother lowered her head, and shook it; but then she took a deep breath and she raised her face and she smiled a terrible smile. "Oh, I get it," she said. "I get it now. Before, I didn't realize you were all a bunch of assholes."

Unlike *shit, asshole* was a word that Jersey had never heard her mother say, and the fact that she said it, just then—it frightened Jersey so that she began to weep.

Most of the students stood silent while her mother made her way out through the circle and wrapped her arm around Jersey's shoulder, but soon they were tittering again, and by the time the pair had begun to make their way to the parking lot, a good number of the students were hooting. Katherine's own eyes jiggled with tears, but as she and Jersey walked, she said in a fierce voice, "Just don't you be ashamed of me, Jersey Alitz. Don't you dare be ashamed."

▪ ▪ ▪

"I HATE THIS CHURCH!"

Jersey, digging her pencil into the pages of her journal, apparently makes enough noise that she attracts the attention of M.B., who now sits, neck craned, glaring over the back of the pew at the girl.

Jersey pretends to be unaware of her grandmother's gaze—but then she hears Pastor Bitner ask, "Do we have any newcomers with us today?" and she hisses—while M.B. rises to her feet—"M.B! No!"

"Why, Marybelle Milhause, we know you!" Pastor Bitner says with a laugh, and a number of other people join in. Then, still smiling, Pastor Bitner explains that he is only teasing Marybelle; Marybelle has brought along her granddaughter today. "Jersey. A lovely young lady, and she's away back there!" Pastor Bitner tilts his head to the side to smile around M.B. to Jersey. "Hi, neighbor!" says Pastor Bitner, and the others turn and smile, and say "Hi, neighbor!" too.

What a relief when the congregation turns away to greet an entire family of newcomers; mom, dad, daughter near Jersey's own age, all on their feet, healthy and whole. The young dad hoists a tiny, adorable girl in rucked-up skirt and ruffled underpants. Ah, says the congregation, in automatic delight; while Jersey recalls a little mnemonic device taught her by her dad: *My very educated mother just served us nine pizza pies*. Mercury, Venus, Earth, Mars, Jupiter, Saturn, Uranus, Neptune, Pluto.

▪ ▪ ▪

At the potluck, because his hands are full—paper plate, cup of coffee—Pastor Bitner extends his greetings to M.B. by carefully lifting his elbow and tapping it against her arm. "This is a special day, isn't it, Marybelle?"

M.B. smiles, then launches into a tale of Jersey's lack of religious education, a terrible, terrible thing. Pastor Bitner offers the girl a sympathetic smile. He doubts it is easy, living with Marybelle.

"I'm reading the Bible," Jersey tells Pastor Bitner. "My mom always wanted us to read it together, so I'd at least know the references and all, but we never got around to it. My parents and I did read some Greek things before. I guess I sort of expected the Old Testament to be a little bit more like that—like Plato or something."

M.B. has taken up a position behind Pastor Bitner from which she waves at the girl and gives her looks of horrified warning—please, don't start in! Pastor Bitner just smiles. "When you have the word of God," he says, "you don't have to bother with Plato, Jersey, but, here, let me introduce you to some of our members," and he calls, "Come over here, Lloyd. I have a young lady for you to meet!"

Lloyd is an elderly gentleman who raises his tangled eyebrows in a show of delight, and, then, with a boy's spry step, heads their way.

"And there's Mick, too," Pastor Bitner says. "Mick, come say hello to Marybelle's daughter and bring that platter of cookies, too—"

"Granddaughter," Jersey murmurs.

Pastor Bitner gives the girl a hard wink. "Your grandma looks so young, somebody might take her for your mom, though!"

"Oh, my." M.B. grins. "What do you say to that, Jersey?"

Jersey says nothing, only smiles at poor pale Mick, who apparently has suffered some accident himself. Fire? Half of his face is tight and strange as a portion of shrink-wrapped veal—

"Cookie?" Mick says. Jersey says thanks and selects a ball dusted in powdered sugar. Meanwhile, a stocky blond identified as Mrs. Trevor has arrived to offer details of the youth choir and the Christian Teens' upcoming trip to the roller rink—oh! Mrs. Trevor's lips twitch in mortification: is it terrible for a person to mention roller rinks to a paraplegic?

Jersey is touched by the woman's obvious tenderheartedness but also wants to deflect her pity, and so she pretends curiosity in another matter: to whom does Pastor Bitner now wave?

The big bald-headed cowboy that M.B. identified as the aide from Fair Oaks. Coffee cup and full paper plate in hand, the cowboy seems reluctant to join the group. His face has turned an astonishing red, like something cooking.

"Another new member of our congregation," says Pastor Bitner. "But, Jersey, you may have met Carter—Mr. Clay—over at Fair Oaks."

While Jersey shakes the man's great humid hand, M.B. smiles, and says, "Well, hello, again!"

"I enjoyed your sermon today, Pastor," Mr. Clay says. There is a tremor in the man's voice, and Jersey appreciates the way Pastor Bitner works to put him at ease, asks him this and that—how's Fair Oaks, and has he tried any of that cherry salad stuff? Oh, do! Great stuff, Carter, just great!

Jersey remembers that there was something about Mr. Clay that gave her a chill the time she saw him at Fair Oaks. Perhaps he looks like someone she has seen before? Certainly the rose-colored scar that marks his forehead—that diamond-shaped pucker—reminds her uncomfortably of the tracheostomy scar at the base of her mother's throat.

"Them powder sugar ones are good, ain't they?" Mr. Clay says, then bends with his napkin to mop up a spot on the floor where he has sloshed a bit of coffee.

The man's grand and shining head is almost on a level with Jersey's own, and when he glances her way and mutters, "I'm clumsy," she smiles at him. A shy man, she thinks, and feels sorry for him—until he leans closer to whisper, as if they are old friends, confidantes, "So, you have to use that chair all the time? I mean, do they think maybe you'll walk someday?"

The idea that a stranger would ask something so personal of another human being! Flustered, hurt, she immediately backs up her chair. She murmurs, "Excuse me, Mr. Clay. I'm going to get some dinner."

An array of food covers several big folding tables. Parishioners cluster around the tables, carrying paper plates that sag with the weight of potato salad, casseroles, brownies. The first dish that Jersey encounters is something made of corn chips and kidney beans, and this she scoops onto her own plate.

Roatley Handel, she thinks, as she sneaks a look back at Mr. Clay—now leaning against the wall once more.

Roatley Handel is a man whom Jersey never met but whose photo hung in her mother's office. A cement contractor, Roatley Handel one day went out riding an all-terrain vehicle on his property near St. David's, Arizona, and what did he find sticking out of the rocks but several fossils of *Eohippus*? This Mr. Handel sat down and posted Earth Sciences a photograph of himself and the fossils—along with a note requesting twenty-thousand dollars for his find. Katherine Milhause telephoned Mr. Handel to let him know that the university would dearly love to receive his fossils but could not possibly come up with such a sum. "Is that right?" Mr. Handel said, and then a great noise arose at his end of the line. The noise, Mr. Handel shouted, was the sound of his rock pulverizer, and did Dr. Milhause want to reconsider just how much money she had to spend? Katherine had said no more than two panicky sentences—both containing the absolute truth about the Earth Sciences budget—when she heard the fossils hit the bowl of the rock pulverizer, and rattle and whine as the machine broke them to bits.

Afterward, Katherine hung the photo of Mr. Handel and his *Eohippus* fossils next to the photograph of Darwin that already hung on her office wall. Darwin all in black, very grave, his mouth a dark line drawn hard in the white of mustache and beard. A viewer could hardly help imagining that the man who replaced the stairway to heaven with a chute to the bacterial stew now pondered the mortality to which he had, in effect, condemned himself.

According to Katherine, hanging up a photo of Darwin with a photo of Roatley Handel was a little like hanging up a picture of Jesus with a picture of one of the thieves; and soon after, a friend who overheard her offer this analysis brought in a thumbtack and one of the garish 3-D postcards of Jesus and his bloody heart that were sold at the nearby mission.

"Now you really do have Jesus," the friend wrote on the postcard's back, and Katherine, after giving the matter some thought, found a fourth image—a postcard of René Magritte's *La Tentative de l'Impossible,* in which a painter is shown in the process of painting into existence the arm of the otherwise complete woman who stands before him.

16

> Had so many of us not been so very charmed by the notion that the shy sparrows eating millet at our feeders were the descendants of *Tyrannosaurus rex*—the large and brutal become the small and shy, the earthbound taking flight—surely our understanding of avian origins would not have been befogged for so very long. But we were. And it has been.

So began the prologue to Katherine Milhause's *Rethinking the Evolution of Birds*. The year was 1991. *Rethinking the Evolution of Birds* was well received in certain quarters, vilified in others. Katherine escaped both the good responses and the bad (and the stony gaze of Joe) by taking off for a dig in the Ischigualasto valley of west central Argentina (rare Middle Triassic remains, including *Pisanosaurus*).

In the Ischigualasto valley, Katherine worked in the field each day from dawn until sunset. In the evening, by the light of kerosene lanterns, she busied herself cleaning specimens, cataloging, writing letters to Jersey and Joe that were, in part, a spirited continuation of her argument: *Archaeopteryx* belonged to an extinct subclass of birds and was no ancestor at all to *Aves*. "Joe, the orientation of the pubis in the London specimen appears *backward* only because of errors in the postmortem rotation!"

Once, while Katherine was in Argentina, Jersey accompanied Joe on a nighttime errand to his office. The evening was damp, the air filled with the pungent odor of creosote bush. Her mother would have talked about the smell. Her mother loved the smell of the creosote, orange blossoms, verbena. Jersey grew lonely for her mother on that walk across campus. Had her mother been there, she would have been holding Jersey's hand. The old Earth Sciences building, with its globe fixtures and darkly varnished wood, increased Jersey's nostalgia, and as a way of "visiting" with Katherine—while Joe went to the main office to check his mail—Jersey went to the collections room to inspect the cast that had been made of England's *Archaeopteryx* fossil.

Of course, what was preserved in the wood and glass case no more resembled the live *Archaeopteryx* than any skeleton resembled its living self—Jersey understood that. Big eye orbits, struts raised—the cast had a demonic look, to Jersey's mind. When Joe joined her in the collections room, she pointed to "the London" and said, "It always reminds me of Las Momias." On a trip to Mexico, the family had visited that odd museum in colonial Guanajuato, where it was possible to view case after case of disinterred corpses, mummified by the peculiar soil of the city's old burial grounds. It was at Las Momias that Jersey first saw how, when all of its engineering was laid bare, the human skull conveyed only the purest expressions: terror, agony, some species of maniacal joy.

Joe unlocked the case of "the London" with a little key from the heavy ring hooked to his belt. "Their nature led to their perfect preservation," he said, then pointed with his pen to what he explained was the bird's lack of a well-developed keel. "That made them weak flyers, and sometimes, out over water, they drowned. Their bad luck, our good fortune. When they drowned, their lungs filled with water, and the weight made the corpses sink before they could decompose."

Jersey nodded. "But what was Mom talking about in her letter?"

"Oh, that? That was—treason," Joe muttered, but then he laughed and gave Jersey a hug, so she was not sure whether he was truly angry with her mother or not.

Of course, when Katherine rejected his theories, it did hurt Joe. Before, in all things, Katherine had been Joe's fan. When she took her own stand as a scientist, suddenly the scientific became personal. Worse, he feared that not just Katherine but many people believed he held onto his ideas out of stubbornness or vanity.

But he was a scientist! A scientist must be ready to make way for the new.

The verification of truth. This, both Joe and Katherine always told Jersey, was science's greatest and most noble aim.

▪ ▪ ▪

Today, for Katherine, science is not an issue. For Katherine, the world is a fraction of its former ingredients. It is a sheet covered in trees, grass, the blind blue eye of the Fair Oaks swimming pool, and the sky. The sheet does not pucker like a curtain in a breeze. Its edges do not lift. But behind it, the rest of the fraction tumbles and fuses and concocts a significance that lies out of reach. Is it fire? Whatever, it is something that begets a roar, and to reduce the sound, Katherine yearns for a smaller fraction; sometimes, the tiny square world of the Fair Oaks television set will do, sometimes not, and then she has to turn herself outside in. Like a glove.

Today, Katherine does not remember the bulk of *Rethinking the Evolution of Birds*, teaching, growing up in Indiana, raising Jersey, marrying Joe. To clarify: the extent of her injuries was such that she now remembers her own life the way you or I might remember a language we studied long ago and have not used for years.

Is Katherine, then, still Katherine?

If a person no longer remembers most of her own past, or even what she agreed to ten minutes before, is it possible to think of her still as "herself"? Maybe a sense of allegiance compels someone like Jersey or M.B. to answer yes, but what—if she could formulate a reply—what would Katherine's own answer be? (And what of, say, a case like that of the Russian, Shereshevski, who possessed such freakishly prodigious powers of memory that, as a child, he sometimes failed to leave his bed to go to school?

And why? Because the strength of his memory of other days of rising, eating, and attending class led him to believe he had already experienced the new day as well. Who is Shereshevski to those who see him sleeping while he sees himself living his day? Who is he to himself?)

This morning, according to the Fair Oaks aide who telephones M.B., Katherine has signed a contract stipulating that she will wash her hair. *On her own!* says the aide. Very loud. Very enthusiastic.

M.B. holds the receiver away from her ear and makes a sour face at the voice issuing from it. M.B. can scarcely abide contact with Fair Oaks—all those old women, bundles of rags with joints swollen big as the clubbed steer bones that M.B. and Dicky used to find while out playing in the hills. M.B. would like to make Jersey promise to just *shoot* M.B. if anyone ever threatened to put M.B. into such a place; but, then, how can M.B. say a word against Fair Oaks, given that it is where Jersey's own mother lives?

The telephoning aide—M.B. loathes her. A good fifty pounds overweight, and yet she waddles down the halls of Fair Oaks as if she finds her heft some sort of dreamy treasure she thought up all on her lonesome.

"First time she'll have washed it herself since the accident, right?" the aide asks.

M.B. glances across the room to Jersey, busy with a game of chess. M.B. supposes she does not have to answer every question the aide asks. She can allow certain questions to hang in the air where perhaps their general stupidity will be revealed to their owner. On the table of the dinette sits an article in *To Your Health,* which explains that the bulk of free radicals in our systems are toxic oxygen molecules, which might be thought of as making our bodies "rust." This is what M.B. was reading when the telephone rang, and as the aide rambles on, M.B. senses quite clearly that, yes, she does need to add selenium, ginkgo biloba, and flavonoids to her day. *Rust.* She can feel it, some sort of robbery going on in her system. To distract herself, she plucks at the dinette's bouquet of silk iris. Fifty dollars on Home Shopping Network, a good price, but M.B. is distressed by the bouquet's plastic stems. She must remember to purchase a spool of green silk ribbon. She will wrap that ribbon around the stems, top to bottom, so the plastic does not show.

"Miz Milhause? You still there?"

"Yes. I won't be coming in today." M.B. blinks, and turns her shoulders just enough that she can see Jersey at her game of chess. "I'm not feeling up to snuff. My back. Too much lifting, I suppose."

Did Jersey hear that? Though M.B. supposes that she *did* mean for Jersey to hear, she knows the impulse was wrong, and feels guilty while the aide commiserates.

"You poor thing! But, oh, I got back trouble, too, honey, let me tell you—"

"Is that Kitty I hear crying?"

"Mm. Lost her fuzz. You know how she likes playing with that blanky fuzz, and now she's lost her blanky fuzz somewheres."

M.B. feels the girl's eyes upon her—fervent as a setter's, waiting—and so she says, peremptorily, "Can't you help her?"

The aide chuckles. "Honey, I ain't got time to be searching for bits of fuzz!"

To Jersey, M.B. mouths *stop staring*, then snaps into the telephone, "I guess if you've got time to jaw to me, you've got time to help a woman that pays two thousand dollars a month for care!"

This last draws a moment of silence, followed by: "Just giving you the report on your daughter, ma'am. See you around."

After she sets the telephone back in the cradle—ignoring the stares of the girl—M.B. takes up her magazine article once more. Underlines "Taking four hundred micrograms of selenium at noon will allow ample time for digestion before the evening meal."

"So"—the girl—"what was Mom crying about, M.B.?"

"Oh—who knows? She couldn't find her fuzz. And the big news is"—M.B. lifts her index finger, makes a little twirling motion in the air—"she's going to wash her hair today."

"And you're not going?"

In the margin of her magazine, M.B. draws her usual doodle (profile of a girl with upturned nose, long lashes, pouty lips). "I guess I seen enough people wash their hair in my life," she says. "*Have* seen. I guess I washed *her* hair a couple thousand times when she was little."

Jersey flushes at the thought of her own bath times, all the angry silence and shame and exasperation between herself and M.B. as M.B. helps her—naked—out of the wheelchair, onto the special stool that straddles the tub, and then into the shower chair, and then the whole business in reverse.

"Well, I'll go," Jersey says.

M.B. gives the girl her boldest smile to make it quite clear that she will not be made to feel guilty. Then, "Excellent," she says. "*Excelente*, *magnifico*, *terrifico*," and moves across the room to sit in Lorne's leather recliner. She takes her deck of cards from her pocket, shuffles. "It's just too bad your grandfather isn't here."

Jersey is weary of M.B.'s constant references to the wonders of this grandfather who never cared enough to come to Arizona to visit her mother or herself, and she does not mind sounding a bit snappish when she asks, "Well, what would *he* do, M.B.?"

"What?"

"What would Lorne do that we're not doing?"

M.B. gives a low laugh and blows a blast of cigarette smoke in the girl's direction. "If I knew that, kid, wouldn't I be doing it?"

17

The wheelchair ramp that leads to Fair Oaks' front door is bowed plywood covered with black corrugated rubber. *Brunk*, *brunk*, it rudely announces the arrival of Jersey's wheelchair, and she does her best to appear unaware that the sound makes the yellow-haired receptionist, Cherie, poke her smiling face out the window of her drywall cubicle even before the automatic door opens.

"Howdy-do, Jersey!" Cherie holds needle and thread and a piece of cross-stitch canvas that depicts a computer monitor whose "screen" will soon read:

But when I bought this thing
They said it did Windows!

Cherie explains that she recently saw Jersey's mother in the TV room, and Jersey says thanks, and wheels into the nursing home's now familiar territory.

"Nuh!"

A resident—also in a wheelchair—makes his way toward the girl. David: nineteen years old, afflicted with cerebral palsy; retaining enough of his good looks that in his face Jersey spies the face of a famous American heartthrob—but lifted from a newspaper photo with Silly Putty, then stretched by a cruel hand.

"Cah!" David says. Jersey knows what he wants: for her to come close so that he can thump out a message on the smeared word board lying across the arms of his wheelchair. Today, however, Jersey is too weary to stop, to crane her neck in an effort to read the words that David spells out with such difficulty, and so she only smiles and says, "Got to get to my mom, David. See you later."

Slits of Florida sunshine make a brilliant frame around the TV room's drawn shades, and in the half-light provided by the shades, Jersey makes out a retarded man by the name of Mr. Fleiss; her mother's roommate, Helen Radosovich; and her mother.

Though Katherine has regained most of the thirty-five pounds she lost after the accident, she continues to look so unlike herself that Jersey still suffers a shock at the beginning of each visit. Before the accident, Katherine was not so fashion-conscious as certain of the mothers of Jersey's friends. She sometimes complained that her thighs were fat or whatever, but she looked nice in her long skirts and T-shirts, hair pulled back in a soft bun, big silver hoops in her ears. Today, Jersey cannot stop herself from noticing that Katherine (stretch-waist skirt, dull gaze, pasty skin) looks like the Mutter that came with the expensive German dollhouse that Jersey received from her Alitz grandparents one Christmas.

And Jersey herself? In her equally ugly easy-off-and-on clothes (Velcro fasteners and wide necks and dark prints that hide "accidents"), Jersey does not doubt that she is Mutter's daughter, Anna.

"Katherine?" Smiling at Jersey, tiny Mrs. Radosovich leans forward to lay a hand on Katherine's knee. Mrs. Radosovich wears an attractive jade-green suit and matching jewelry and holds a purse in her lap. As far as Jersey can tell, there is not a thing wrong with Mrs. Radosovich beyond a certain frailty and—as M.B. says—"wetting" problems.

"Katherine!" Mrs. Radosovich says. "Here's your Jersey, dear."

Katherine's laugh—who knows what provokes it?—is the laugh found in comic strip bubbles over the heads of big bullies. *Har, har, har!* It makes Mrs. Radosovich put her little hands over her ears, and wince. "That hurts," she says, then smiles faintly at Jersey. "Literally, it does something to my eardrums."

Jersey nods in commiseration—she hopes Mrs. Radosovich won't ask for another roommate—then turns to her mother.

"Mom?"

Since the accident, Katherine's right eye tends to wander, and her efforts to focus her gaze make her appear suspicious of her visitor, but Jersey leans across the arm of the wheelchair and lays a kiss on Katherine's cheek. "I've come to see you, Mom."

Katherine looks back at the television. Her loss of memory is not nearly so entertainingly transformative as the amnesia of TV and movies. Damage is what one sees in Katherine. Big D.

Mrs. Radosovich gives a tug to Jersey's sleeve. "She was supposed to get that hair washed today, weren't you, Katherine?"

Katherine makes a nasty face, then raises one of her slippered feet and gives a kick in Mrs. Radosovich's direction. "I gow ouw towe!" she says irritably.

"Mom"—Jersey pats Katherine's arm—"you head to your room for your shower, and I'll go get you a Coke. For when you're done."

Immediately, Katherine stands, and offers Jersey her ruined smile, and booms, "GO GEH COH!"

▪ ▪ ▪

Carter Clay is in Terence White's room, cutting Terence's pork patty into tiny bits, talking to Terence's mother, when Jersey rolls past. That nervous drumming in his chest when he sees the girl—it feels a little like the way he remembers feeling when he saw Becky Pattschull in the halls at high school. A little like the way he always feels before first blows are exchanged in a fight.

"You see? Nineteen sixty-seven?" Terence White's mother points to the date printed along one edge of the photograph in her hand. A view of Terence, home from boot camp. "His hair was lighter then, of course."

Carter can tell that Terence's mother worries that Carter might not believe that Terence ever had a life other than this one, in which slack-faced Terence lies in a bed, crippled with MS or MD or some such thing.

Of course, Carter believes it. He has to believe it. "Good-looking guy!" Carter says, then turns his attention back to Terence's plate. Apple crisp, mashed potatoes, pork patty, carrot coins. When the Fair Oaks staff make up their menu, they always call cooked carrots *carrot coins*, just the way Carter's school did when he was a boy, and though he knows it is silly, Carter still feels cheated each time he sees cooked carrots, and not some sort of treasure.

▪ ▪ ▪

Yes, Katherine has returned to her room by the time Jersey gets back with the sodas. Seated on her bed, back to the door, she rolls a bit of blanket fuzz between her fingers. From the doorway, however, it is clear to Jersey that Katherine has not showered, and, quietly, Jersey moves the Cokes from her lap and into the carryall that hangs from her chair, before she wheels herself into the room (sprigged yellow wallpaper and matching curtains, print of *Pinky* on the wall).

"You need help with your shower, Mom?"

Katherine turns her way. "Where Coh?"

"You'll get Coke after you wash your hair." Jersey wheels to the window. Tries to appear nonchalant, interested in the view. At the end of the driveway, a little man sits perched on top of the dumpster, and Jersey calls to Katherine, "Mom, come look at this guy."

That could be us. That was what her mother would have said in the past, and she probably would have darted out and given the man a dollar or two.

"Come here, Mom. He's got on a Yankees cap. Remember the Yankees?"

"No."

"They were Dad's favorite team."

"NO."

Jersey hopes she does not show that she is a little afraid of her mother. Recently, she read in a book called *States of Mind* about a woman whose left hand continually rose up to her neck in an effort to strangle herself. The woman insisted she had to sit upon this murderous hand to quell its impulses, and after her death, sure enough, an autopsy revealed that the woman had a damaged corpus callosum. The two sides of her brain were disconnected; and, disconnected, they considered themselves at war.

"Coh, *now*," Katherine says.

Jersey nods—a distraction—before she says, "If you don't want to wash your hair before you have your Coke, how about doing some flash cards instead? Flash cards, then Coke?"

Katherine stands. "NO WAY! NO WAY! NO WAY!" she barks; then she grabs the metal bar at the end of her bed and begins to rock it, back and forth, bam, bam, bam.

"Mom!" Jersey grabs for Katherine's hands. "Stop it!"

"What's going on here?" In the doorway, hands on her hips, stands the ferocious nurse that Jersey knows as Mary: wild black hair, pinpoints of red on her white cheeks and the great white sheaves of arm that push out from her uniform.

"It's okay," Jersey calls above the din. "I'm going to read to her. I'll read from your book again, Mom. How will that be?" The girl reaches into her carryall for *Rethinking the Evolution of Birds*. "I brought your book, see?"

"COH!" Katherine shouts.

"That's enough, you," warns the nurse.

"Here. Wait." Jersey begins to read where she left off during her last attempt—something about crocodiles and convergence—

"NO!" Katherine plugs her fingers in her ears and makes a terrific noise, a grinding whine, like the sound of a child pretending to be an airplane.

The nurse peers over Jersey's shoulder. "WHY READ HER THAT?" she shouts above Katherine's sound effects. "SHE DOESN'T UNDERSTAND THAT!"

"SHE WROTE IT!" Jersey shouts back.

Katherine's bedside clock, thrown through the air, hits neither Jersey nor the nurse, but—harmlessly—the wall just to the pair's right. Still, in an instant, the nurse has Katherine by the front of her ugly blouse, the fabric choked up around her tracheostomy scar.

"SO YOU WANT TO BE SEDATED!" the nurse shouts.

Jersey pulls at the nurse's skirt. "Please! She just wants her Coke! I have her Coke! It's my fault—I was trying to get her to wash her hair—"

The nurse, clutching the flailing Katherine, glances down at the girl. And receives a slap from Katherine. "You'll be sorry for that!" the nurse trumpets, and releases Katherine's collar, and starts for the door.

"You're not supposed to sedate her!" Jersey cries. "Call Dr. Mukhergee! All she wants is her Coke!"

The nurse does not respond but pushes her way out through the little group drawn to the door by the commotion: David in his wheelchair, an angel-haired lady with a walker, the large aide that Jersey met at her grandmother's church, Carter Clay—

"My mom—she's not supposed to be sedated!" Jersey cries to Carter Clay; then turns as, behind her, the closet door slams and Katherine shuts herself up inside, and screams, "I KILL MYSELF!"

"Out of my way," says the returning nurse, needle and syringe in hand.

"Mary." Carter Clay lays a hand on the nurse's shoulder. "How about you let me and the girl try and quiet her first? Give us a few minutes?"

The nurse stares at the hand on her shoulder until Carter Clay removes it; then she informs him that he is *not* a doctor and patients at Fair Oaks are *not* allowed to act out. But go ahead. Try. By all means. Be her guest!

"Thanks, Mary," Carter Clay says, and pulls the door shut behind himself and Katherine and Jersey.

"Katherine? It's Carter Clay, here."

Behind the closet door, hangers ping. There is a rodentlike scratching.

Carter Clay smiles at Jersey. "You got to come out, Katherine," he says. "Nobody's going to bother you, but you got to settle down."

"We won't let anybody hurt you, Mom," Jersey adds.

"Tell Jers go 'way!" Katherine calls. "Go and leave Coh!"

Carter Clay gives the girl a sad smile. "She don't mean that," he whispers.

"I wan' go home!"

"I know you do, Mom. That's why you can't have temper tantrums. The sooner you stop, the sooner you can come home! You and me—back to Arizona. Won't that be nice? Swimming every day?"

When Katherine does not respond, Carter Clay pulls something from his back pocket: a pulp magazine, which he displays to Jersey. *Josannah!* read the red-hot letters on the cover. "Hey, Jersey," Carter Clay says in a loud and enthusiastic voice, "what do you bet your mom would like to see this new issue of *Josannah!*?"

Jersey remembers reading *Josannah!* at the home of a grade school classmate whose family believed in Jesus, the devil, the NRA, and killing doctors who performed abortions. She longs to tell Carter Clay that Katherine would not have the slightest interest in his comic book. She also recognizes that his stagy announcement is a ploy that she ought not to damage, and so she keeps her mouth shut, and, sure enough, the door handle turns and a slice of Katherine's face appears in the crack between the wooden frame and the door.

"Hey!" Carter Clay holds up the comic book. "You want to come out and I'll read you this?"

The noise Katherine Milhause makes is not a noise of assent. It is neutral as the creak of a branch, which sound it resembles. Still, her expression is her own and particular, and Jersey recognizes it—though not from a time before the accident, no; this is an expression of the new Katherine.

▪ ▪ ▪

The story Carter reads to Katherine Milhause tells of a brother and sister who fall into bad ways after being raised without religious instruction. It is impossible for Carter to say if Katherine listens. She lies back on her bed and closes her eyes, sips at her soft drink, strokes and rolls one of her fuzz balls, and eventually—Carter has started a second story by then—drops off to sleep.

The girl—Jersey—thanks Carter after she has followed him out into the hall. She gestures apologetically toward his street clothes. "I guess you were on your way home?"

"I'm glad I was here," he says. Which is true, but now he wishes he could flee. He feels nervous in the girl's company since they do not have Katherine to focus upon. "I'm—glad your family's coming to the church."

The girl responds in a voice so low that Carter must ask her to repeat herself.

"I was saying—well, maybe you know." She stares out the patched screen of the hallway's track window. "My family was in an accident, here. Really, we live in Arizona. And we're not Christians, really. My grandma—she makes me go to church."

"Well, that's good, though, Jersey. 'Cause you can learn about the forgiveness of sins and—oh, eternal life and all."

The girl shakes her head.

"What?"

"If your God exists, there's probably plenty of things I'll go to hell for. I mean, if somebody told me that I could kill the person who killed my dad—if I could kill him, or her, even by just *thinking*, I'd do it."

Carter crouches down beside the girl, who looks away and begins to pick at the folded-over edges of the screen's patch. "I guess I understand that," he says, and then, his heavy heart carrying him further than he intends, he adds, "but maybe someday you'll forgive him. Maybe you'll get better, both you and your mom. I pray for both of you, and—Pastor Bitner says it's okay to pray for *anything* at all—as long as it's not evil, I mean—since God's only going to give us what's in his plan."

"So—if God's only giving us what's in his plan, what difference does your praying make?"

Carter rises shakily to his feet, dusts off the knees of his pants. "I'm kind of new at this, Jersey, but—well, you can get to know God better through prayer. And you can pray to live according to what He wants for you."

She pushes the window forward on its tracks, then pulls it back. "But if your God wants me to live a certain way," she says, "why doesn't he just *have* me act that way?"

A noisy milk truck passes by, bringing supplies to the home, momentarily casting the pair in shadow and roar, and it is when the truck moves on—as if it were a curtain pulled aside—that Carter sees R.E. panhandling in the next parking lot, not fifty feet away.

Should he go out to R.E.?

But suppose that R.E. hates Carter for slugging him and then ditching him after the accident? And what if R.E. feels that he should let the girl know the truth about who crashed into her and her family?

"Is that what you're saying?" the girl asks. Her voice is higher. She is upset. "That God wanted some creep to drive into my family?" She blinks back furious tears, and he tries to think of what to say to comfort her, and also of what he might say to R.E.

"It's because of that free will business, Jersey. He wants us to have free will."

"Free will, but everything's planned?"

"You know, though"—Carter sneaks another look out the window. Discovers that R.E. has disappeared from view—"I guess—" He means to start for the door to the parking lot, but when he turns, he finds that the girl now has lifted her weight off the wheelchair's seat, and that she holds herself in the air, suspended by her arms.

Her breath squeezed with effort, she tells him, "Go on with what you were saying."

He shakes his head. He holds his breath until she finally lowers herself into the seat; and even then he is quiet while she uses her hands to reposition her legs, her feet. "I'm sorry," he says. "I was staring, wasn't I?"

She does not answer, but he can tell she wants to get away from him even before she says good-bye, and, quick, he pulls the copy of *Josannah!* from his back pocket. "Here," he says, "take this. It says things better than me."

"Thanks," she says, but Carter can tell she is not truly grateful, and for a moment he feels a little angry. It seems unfair that she does not feel bound to him as he feels bound to her.

"But wait," she says, then reaches into the bag hanging off the side of her chair, and pulls out a book and hands it to him. "I appreciate you being nice to my mom, and—she wrote this before she got hurt. If you'd like to see."

▪ ▪ ▪

It is a relief to Jersey to get away from Fair Oaks. Even the busy street in front of the nursing home feels relaxing after her scene with her mother and that intense—and odd—conversation with Carter Clay.

While she waits for the crosswalk light to change, she glances at the cover illustration of the *Josannah!* in her lap: an international jumble of fireman, nurse, grandma, grandpa, telephone repairman, lady in a kimono, homemaker, factory worker, turbanned gentleman, chef—all of whom march together into a heaven that looks very much like the drawings of national parklands that appeared in those booklets Jersey and her classmates always received during Fire Prevention Week.

Never debate the issues with an idiot. So her father always said. As if you always had a choice. As if being smart were always an advantage.

In the past, at school, Jersey was sometimes ridiculed for being smart, but now she needs to be much smarter than ever before. When she and her mother get back to Arizona, she means to hire tutors from the university to come work with her. To make her so smart that by the time she gets to college, no one will imagine that she is weak or pathetic just because she uses a wheelchair.

Spinning across campus. That's how she sees herself. Always moving fast. A silvery blur of competence.

18

M.B.'s rule: no wine before 8 P.M. Tonight, however, she has broken the rule because, she reasoned, she woke up an hour and a half early this morning, and that meant that 6:30 felt like 8, and besides, it was a bad day.

Red nine goes on black ten. Black three on red four, and there's an ace of clubs!

At M.B.'s "Ah-hah!" Jersey looks up, teary-eyed, from her reading in one of M.B.'s ladies' magazines—some irritatingly heartwarming article about a woman who adopted thirteen handicapped and biracial children. Jersey knows—having spied the inky lining of her grandmother's lips—that M.B. started drinking early tonight, and so Jersey feels particularly abandoned, nervous. She has no intention whatsoever of telling M.B. about this afternoon's scene at Fair Oaks, and she hopes no one from Fair Oaks will mention it either.

Please.

Are such hopes a little like a prayer? Once, Jersey saw a photo of a Tibetan prayer wheel, a prayer-inscribed brass drum that revolved in the churning force of a white and navy river. The photo was on a wall calendar that hung in the kitchen of her friend Erin Acuff. According to the calendar's caption, the prayer wheel's believers counted on the force of the river to send up their prayers in the same way that it milled their grain—not merely to save time but to multiply what was humanly possible. Such shifting of spiritual work to river-power struck Jersey as somehow wrong, or lazy, but when she said so, Erin's mother laughed and said, "What a little Puritan you are, Jersey!"

A Puritan. At the time, Jersey was pleased to have grabbed Via Acuff's slightly flaky attention, but could not decide whether to take the remark as insult or compliment (though Via, Jersey understood, meant it as a goad, a suggestion that Jersey needed a new attitude).

A Puritan.

These days, it seems possible to Jersey that she has inscribed her very own *brain* with pleas on behalf of her mother, herself; perhaps, even while she sleeps, her faithful blood courses over her pleas like the river that does the work of turning the wheel.

"Hey!" Hearing the girl sigh deep and long, M.B. looks up from her cards. "For crying out loud, kid! Cheer up!"

Sober up. This is what Jersey would like to say to M.B. Instead, however, she says what is more important: "We've got to get Mom out of there."

M.B. makes a sour face. "What's this?"

"We've got to get Mom out of Fair Oaks."

M.B. picks up her mug. She eyes the girl over its rim as she takes a discreet sip. "Look at it this way, kid: we get her *out* of there, I'll end up *in* there, and then where will you be?"

Jersey meets her grandmother's gaze. There is a pain in her chest, as if M.B. has just driven a flag into her heart and declared her conquered land. To take a breath, to retaliate, is essential, but, nonetheless, it hurts the girl to say, "Well, I suppose you could try to send me back to St. Mary's."

M.B. sets down the mug and inspects the top card of the next trio from her deck as if it absorbs her completely, but Jersey hurries on, "I heard you that day they made you bring me home, M.B. When you asked Mrs. Carlyle if they couldn't keep me on like a boarder. I *heard* you."

"I don't know what you're talking about," M.B. says, then turns and begins poking around behind herself in the cracks of the leather recliner. "Where is that darned lighter?"

"I wouldn't be surprised if you tried putting me in Fair Oaks, too! Why should you deal with me if Fair Oaks can do it?"

M.B. blinks at the girl. "I don't—why, when you were in the hospital, I prayed to God to take me instead of you and your mother!"

"Really?" The girl looks back at the book in her lap as if the conversation with M.B. has gone on long enough; she is finished, but then she adds—the lid she has placed on her emotions rendering her voice almost sensuous—"Maybe you should be more careful what you pray for, then, M.B. Maybe it's your fault we're alive."

▪ ▪ ▪

Only when she can hear M.B.'s knock rattle the storm door of Patsy Glickman's unit—only then does Jersey begin to cry. "Bitch. Lousy, crummy bitch." She wheels herself over to the footstool and whisks M.B.'s unfinished game of cards onto the floor. A petty gesture, she knows, and it only makes her feel worse. She sits back in her chair. Stares at the cards on the floor. Lifts M.B.'s coffee mug from the little side table. She has tasted wine but only tiny sips from her parents' glasses of special-occasion champagne. For M.B.'s dark potion, she holds her nose and downs the stuff in one great gulp.

Arrh! She shivers. Arrh! But that does not stop her from heading toward the kitchen, and the cupboard under the sink, which she long ago realized held M.B.'s stash.

The glimmer of glass at the back looks promising, but it is not easy for her to reach such a distance. First she must fetch a spatula from the utensil drawer and draw forward the boxes of dishwasher detergent and Spic and Span. By the time she switches over to the long-handled broom for the actual retrieval of the bottle at the back, she is in a sweat, but the broom does finish the job. With a sturdy clink, the bottle falls forward. Then it is within reach of the spatula, and the wine from the mug has begun to take effect, and she just has to *laugh* in delight.

"A toast!" she says, and ferries the bottle to the mug in the living room.

How interesting her face feels. How interesting. And her lips, too. In five gulps, she downs the contents of the second mug.

"Oh, me, oh, my, Erin, I'm drunk out of my mind!" This is what she means to cry out when Erin Acuff answers the telephone in Seca, where it is still early—Jersey knows exactly how Seca looks, the rosy ring of mountain sunset, the Acuffs eating dinner on their patio, tiny bats zooming down to the swimming pool for drinks and bugs. Surely Jersey's wild call will drive out any idea Erin might have of Jersey as crippled girl and replace it with something entirely new, and interesting—

But the Acuffs are not at home. The Acuffs have installed an answering machine, and over the opening of U–2's "With or Without You," Erin's big brother says, "Leave a message, dude."

Jersey hangs up and, immediately, with a huff of breath meant to stop any slopping over into untoward emotions, she punches in her own number in Seca. Counts the rings. In a way, she is there, isn't she? Holding onto the telephone, she is, at the very least, connected to the ringing telephones in the Seca kitchen and in her parents' study and in the front hall. And who is to say, then, that she cannot send herself through the telephone and right into her own bedroom—there's the *Archaeopteryx* mural, and her own of the twin beds into which she can surely climb, yes?

Eventually, this notion depletes itself—*there* is not *here,* after all—and she hangs up. She feels lonely. When will M.B. come back? She pours and drinks another splash of wine, then moves into the middle of M.B.'s living room. Pops a powerful but inept wheelie. Comes down hard and laughing. "Chugga, chugga, choo, choo!"

Can they hear her next door?

Up on the chair's big wheels! And this time she *holds* the position, the way they taught her at St. Mary's, balancing, balancing, she is a tightrope artist, an aerial queen, she has never, ever held a wheelie this long, yes, the wine has bestowed amazing grace.

"A-ma-zing grace," she sings, sweating a little. But then she tips her head back too far, and gravity asserts itself, sends girl and chair slamming backward into the floor, breath knocked high as the ceiling.

She cannot cry, only moan around the loaf of pain in her chest, and then laugh at the idea of M.B. coming through the door just now. To the empty unit, she calls, "I'm drunk!" She spreads her arms on the floor. She has never been down here before, and the baby blue carpet feels nice against her palms, like the gentle prickle of the fur on a teddy bear.

"DRUNK!"

Dragging herself out of a wheelchair that has tipped over is not a maneuver Jersey learned at St. Mary's, but in time, she does manage to free herself, right the chair, and haul herself up into the thing once more.

. . .

The hisses and pops on Patsy Glickman's thirty-year-old recording of Tony Bennett singing "I Wanna Be Around" are sounds of wear and tear that Patsy associates with the crooner's own aging, and so she loves and laments the intrusions in much the same way that she loved and lamented the late Milt Glickman's sags and wrinkles; they showed he was still alive, yes, but also predicted his demise.

Patsy would not think of replacing her Tony Bennett record with a new copy. Even the songs she did not care for so much in the early years have become friends she would now miss. She did replace her hi-fi when it could no longer be repaired, but in her own move to Florida, she remained faithful to most of her New Jersey furnishings (the *mamasan* and *papasan* chairs she and Milt bought on their trip to Hawaii, the French provincial dining room set, the rattan of the master suite).

M.B. thinks Patsy's furnishings show a lack of good taste. Worst of all are the orange table lamps that almost scrape the living room ceiling, and feature bases designed to look like candleholders upon which great quantities of wax have dripped. While Patsy talks on about a book she recently read (farmwife has an affair with a sexy photographer), M.B. imagines herself telling a sympathetic friend, "Her lamps look like something out of *Mickey and the Beanstalk*! Every time I'm there, I imagine Mickey peeking out from behind them, watching for the Giant!"

Actually, now that Lorne is dead, Jersey is the only person to whom M.B. could say such a thing, and M.B. does not want to think about Jersey, though it is hard *not* to think about the girl, given the thump of rock and roll from #335—

"Let me tell you," Patsy says, "that book made my heart go pitty-pat!"

While Patsy grins and fans the air in front of herself, M.B. rolls her eyes. Patsy laughs as if M.B. does not mean her exasperation, but M.B. *does* mean it. M.B. considers Patsy and her romantic notions hopelessly silly. As if Patsy were not forty pounds overweight with a perm that appears to have been modeled after the coat of her ancient poodle.

("Let's go be volunteers for the blood drive!" Patsy will say. "What do you bet there's some widowers there?" Or: "There's going to be a talk on bonsai trees. *A talk on Indian jewelry, mangrove conservation, what to do in the event of a hurricane*." "How about *Barefoot in the Park*, M.B.? That's a cute one! And we'd probably find some lonely hearts out in the lobby during intermission!")

"You wouldn't believe the fight Jersey and me had tonight!" This is what M.B. longs to say to Patsy. But as she cannot tell Patsy what the girl overheard at St. Mary's, the tale of the evening's quarrel is impossible. Patsy would never understand M.B.'s hoping that St. Mary's would let the girl stay as a boarder. Patsy adores her own grandchildren. Of course, Patsy's grandchildren have normal kid interests *and* do not live with her and require a wheelchair and need help taking a bath—

The poodle hops down from her spot in Patsy's lap to sniff at M.B.'s feet. "No, you," M.B. says, and then, "I was reading today about these free radical things—"

"Free radicals?"

"It's like—oxygen, you know? We've got to have oxygen, but some of it's poison too. It makes our cells rust."

"Princess, no!" Patsy scolds, as the poodle drags her wet ribbon of tongue across M.B.'s instep. "Just take off your shoes, M.B., and tuck your feet up so she can't get at them."

M.B. does as she is told, but the dog stays, little mop of coat aquiver as she inserts her nose into the now empty shoes.

"Princess." Patsy slips off her own shoes—gold sandals, studded with fat, fake jewels—and extends her feet. The dog immediately stops sniffing M.B.'s flats, and trots over to Patsy. Ick, thinks M.B., as the dog licks Patsy's toes, but she also feels somewhat abandoned.

"I know it's pathetic, but she doesn't have many pleasures, poor baby."

M.B. nods, and soon after, she makes her excuses and heads back to #335.

In #335, Jersey is driving her chair back and forth across the framed photos of her grandfather that normally sit on top of M.B.'s entertainment center. Even before M.B. has the door open all the way, she hears the sound of the glass breaking against the carpet—a kind of crisp *crack*.

"What are you doing?" she demands, though now she can see.

The girl looks up. She is crying, but she also grins and says, in mush-voiced imitation of Tweety Bird, "I cannot tell a wie! I dwove acwoss da pwitty pitchers wid my funny wittle car."

M.B. yanks the wheelchair back from the smashed frames and photos. "What have you done?" she asks. "My pictures! You—monster!"

Ineffectually, the girl tries to slap M.B.'s hands away. "Just you remember," she shrieks, "you'll never get me in Fair Oaks! Never!"

"The neighbors!" M.B. says, but Jersey goes on, her face twisted and dark.

"I'd kill myself first! I'd kill myself now, if it weren't for Mom! And that fucker that hit us! I'm going to find that fucker and kill him, too!"

"Quiet!" M.B. drops down on her knees in the wreckage and, from that vantage point, spies the bottle on the coffee table. "You're drunk!"

Jersey neither agrees nor disagrees, merely lets her head loll forward. She has never before been called a monster, never said the word *fuck.* The words are claws. They rip something in her chest. They tear at her temples.

"That wine"—M.B. tries to sound utterly reasonable as she gathers up the photos and broken frames and pieces of glass from the carpet—"that's Patsy's. Oh!" she breaks into a wail. "Look!" She holds up a photo in which Lorne's face has been torn in half by the weight of the chair's wheels.

Jersey sees, then, that what she has done is terrible. Her grandmother: an aging woman who has lost her husband, and she, Jersey, has increased her hurt. Of course, this is what Jersey meant to do, and so she can only sob from blue-grape lips, "I'll fix them, M.B. I'll fix them."

"Fix them?" Now it is M.B.'s turn to shriek. "You can't fix them! The only thing I have left—you'll never get near them again in your life!"

▪ ▪ ▪

The two do not speak to one another until the next evening, when Pastor Bitner comes by, drawn to the condo by a tearful telephone call from M.B.

A most unsatisfactory call, as far as M.B. was concerned, but Pastor Bitner winks at M.B. as she comes to answer the door, and he says in a jolly voice, "Just in the neighborhood!"

Though Pastor Bitner always tries to be cheerful, tonight he is rather tired, having just come from a painful session with another parishioner, the new man, Carter Clay. ("*But how do you know when you're really forgiven and loved by God*?" Clay pleaded. "*Does God talk to you, or give you some kind of sign in your heart, or what?*")

When M.B. shows Pastor Bitner inside, Jersey is seated at M.B.'s dinette, taking apart an owl plug she recently found in the parking lot. She flushes as she looks up to say hello. She feels certain that M.B. would not have told Pastor Bitner about last night's drinking episode—M.B. would not want him to know she kept wine—but she might have told him about the photos.

"And what have we here?" asks Pastor Bitner.

"It's what an owl spits out after it's digested all that it can digest of its prey." Because most people do not like to see the pulverized fur and feathers, she points only to the little rows of ribs the size of eyelashes, tiny yellow teeth and claws, the weight-sparing bones and skulls of the small birds upon which the larger dined. "It shows you what the owl's been eating."

"At my table!" M.B. means to sound both amused and put out, but suspects she succeeds only at the latter.

"Good to have a hobby," says Pastor Bitner. Pastor Bitner has considered his speech beforehand, but feels on slightly shaky ground with this particular girl. "Jersey?"

She looks up.

"You know your grandmother loves you, don't you?"

The girl clasps her hands in her lap, and looks down.

"Isn't that right, Marybelle?" Pastor Bitner says.

"That's right."

Pastor Bitner explains what he and her grandmother discussed on the telephone: the need for Jersey to face the fact that her mother lives in Fair Oaks; the need for Jersey to start school here, in the fall, and for her grandmother to put the Seca house up for sale.

Jersey looks at M.B. M.B. does not appear happy with what Pastor Bitner says, and so, without arguing, Jersey wheels herself down the hall and into the guest room—which is not her room, will never be her room—and there she picks up several of the books and articles on brain injury that she has collected, and she wheels herself out into the hall and back to the dinette, where she looks right into Pastor Bitner's blue eyes while she explains that Fair Oaks is doing nothing to rehabilitate her mother. That plenty of rehabilitation is possible. That the brain-injury patient will do best when surrounded by the familiar. That recognition is easier than recall, and, also, that helping her mother would provide Jersey with an excellent cross to bear.

Straight-faced—meaning it—Jersey says, "If she were here with us, Pastor, I'd see that she got to church at least twice a week. And out for walks. She needs to go for walks. My grandmother shouldn't sell the Arizona house yet"—here Jersey looks M.B. in the eye—"because, you know, my mom and I should go home, eventually, if we can. M.B. could come, too, if she wanted." Her lips tremble, but she goes on. "There's a clinic in Phoenix that could maybe even help me—and I don't see how we'll ever know what my mom can do while she's at Fair Oaks. They dope her up, Pastor. They're not supposed to do that—"

At this, M.B. interrupts to say, "That's for her seizures!"

"I don't mean the stuff for her seizures—"

"Well, maybe they need to—give her things!" M.B. protests. "She can be wild, Pastor, believe me. And I only put her in Fair Oaks because—you don't know! Those physical therapists at the rehab hurt her. I was there once. She was *screaming*!"

"She screamed because it hurt!" Jersey says. "But they were *helping* her get better!"

Well! Pastor Bitner has an idea! *How about you girls give weekend visits from Katherine a try?* Pastor Bitner knew a couple whose son did just that till he got well enough to go home for good.

Jersey nods. Her voice fogs with emotion. "I'd go get her and take her back, M.B. That way she'd get a good walk both ways and you wouldn't have to do anything."

M.B. does not respond, but busies herself with folding up one edge of that sheet of aluminum foil upon which the girl was making her owl pellet mess.

"Did you two ever think"—Pastor Bitner picks up an amber rodent's tooth from the foil, turns it this way and that—"maybe you're here to bear each other up?" He smiles expectantly though neither female looks his way. "Be strong and cheerful when the other one's weary and downhearted?"

This notion so clearly refreshes Pastor Bitner that M.B. knows she is licked, and, sure enough, not ten minutes pass before Pastor Bitner is on the telephone to Fair Oaks, establishing that Katherine will spend the next weekend at Palm Gate Village with M.B. and Jersey.

"This ought to be good," M.B. mutters to Jersey while Pastor Bitner talks to Fair Oaks. She means to sound funny—like a comrade. She gives Jersey a wink. Jersey, however, keeps her eyes on Pastor Bitner. Holds her head cocked to one side, as if she is an attentive pooch who cares only for the words of her master.

19

In the fairy tale "Rumpelstiltskin," the trouble all begins when, to make himself look important, a miller brags to the king that his daughter can spin straw into gold. The king asks for a demonstration, noting that he will kill the girl if she fails to do this thing her father says she can do. By great good luck, the girl is saved when a little fellow appears to her and, for a price, performs the magical spinning each of the three nights the king sets the girl to the task. The first night, the manikin spins straw into gold in exchange for the girl's necklace; the second, he spins for her ring. In some versions of the tale, after that second night, we learn from the narrator that the king is a greedy fellow, and that it occurs to him: *with such a girl for my wife, I would always be rich*. The third night, then, the king promises to marry the girl if she spins a tremendous roomful of straw into gold.

However, by the third night, the girl has nothing left to offer the little man in exchange for his spinning.

"I will spin for you this night if you promise to give me your firstborn," says the manikin, and the desperate girl agrees.

Time passes, as time will. The girl, now queen, bears a child, and the little man comes to fetch the baby. Frantic, the queen offers him all of the land's riches if he will only let her keep the babe, and from pity the manikin makes the queen this allowance:

if she is able in three days' time to discover his name, he will let her keep the child.

On the third day, after the queen has guessed all the names of which she can think, and after her minions have gathered novel names from far and wide—each the wrong name—one final scout returns from overhearing, at the end of the forest, a ridiculous little fellow singing a song that announces that he bears the name Rumpelstiltskin.

Thus the queen is able to tell Rumpelstiltskin his name; he loses his claim to the baby and becomes so furious that he tears himself in two.

▪ ▪ ▪

Is it the continuing rescue of the girl-queen from disaster that makes this story such a favorite?

But consider who put her in the initial position from which she needs to be saved: her father! And consider who rescues her: Rumpelstiltskin!

A question: shouldn't the miller have been the one threatened with death? Or is the story a warning to parents? *Don't be like the miller—or, for that matter, his rash baby-promising daughter—and put your children in positions of danger.*

No. "Rumpelstiltskin" turns out to be, by and large, a tale of luck and magic, and of pity that comes from the most unlikely source. The miller's daughter and her child are saved not by a demonstration of bravery or morality or intelligence but by (1) Rumpelstiltskin's magical ability to spin straw into gold, (2) the unanticipated pity that moves Rumpelstiltskin to change the terms of the bargain, (3) the incredible good fortune of the scout's passing by as Rumpelstiltskin sings out his improbable name, and (4) the fact that, apparently, the king never again asks the girl to spin straw into gold.

▪ ▪ ▪

As a boy, the fairy tale that Carter Clay—and Joe Alitz, too—liked best was "Rapunzel." Both wanted to be the brave prince who climbs up the rope of the beautiful princess's hair into the tower of her imprisonment and kills the imprisoning witch. Neither Joe nor Carter was familiar, however, with those grisly versions of the tale in which the witch throws the prince from the tower into terrible brambles that scratch out his eyes and leave him to wander, blind, through the forests for seven years.

Katherine and M.B., no doubt to their detriment, longed to be Cinderella, while Jersey—who encountered the Greek myths some years before the Grimms'—considered Cinderella a wimp and identified with the brave and adventurous Perseus.

It would be a convenient lie to say that "Rumpelstiltskin" was a favorite of Finis Pruitt's. Finis, however, never liked to think of himself as a person with favorites. Or alliances of any kind. He had, rather, "enthusiasms," "positions in relation to." In high school, for instance, in tandem with reading Kerouac and Ginsberg and Henry Miller, he completed all—and mentally staged many—of the plays of O'Neill, Ibsen, Shaw, and Arthur Miller. *Just to get a feel for them,* was how Finis thought of it. For a time after he was booted from the service—before he discovered that someone else had created much the same sort of publication—he threw himself into creating a parody of his high school yearbook. During another period, for several months, he moved back into the New Mexico home of his cleaning-woman mom with the idea of organizing—and pitching to some tony New York gallery—an art exhibit made up of the discards that his mother received from her employers (wives of the three major hotshots at the copper mine). There would be porcelain Virgins missing, say, nose or hand; half-filled containers of bath powder; rusted lawn chairs; a defunct cuckoo clock; a stuffed doggy made of genuine raccoon fur and sporting a plaid tam; the odd piece of glassware or eating utensil; a cabinet that once housed a television set; electric hair curlers; wood and metal wall ornaments made by somebody's son in "shop"; a laminated picture of Jesus, bubbled from a houseguest's careless transfer of a space heater to a dresser; several space heaters; a box of bath oil capsules that had melted into a kind of gorgeous jam; daisy bedsheets and bedsheets that looked like bandannas; striped towels that came, free, in boxes of

Duz detergent; assorted pieces of ugly or defective jewelry; bathrobes; a set of salt and pepper shakers in the shape of an eggplant and a tomato; a large framed photograph of Venetian rooftops; extra envelopes from boxes of note cards; wire hangers; battered lamps; incomplete craft projects—

No!

He would make his parents' *house* the exhibit—complete with his parents! And the paneled wall in the little front room that held, along with photos of his many brothers and sisters, a senior photo of Finis himself (who had practiced the pursed-lip expression he believed made him look like Kerouac, but had no control over the lemonade-colored hair of his ancestors, the skin pale as that bleached flour from which most of the Pruitt meals were made).

A wonderful exhibit, he felt certain, but the next thing he knew his mother was chasing him from the house with a red-hot curling iron—or was it an electric charcoal briquette starter? Some dangerous discard, at any rate—and soon after, the mines ate the land upon which that house stood, and the Pruitt parents moved to Las Cruces, and Finis sallied out into the world once more, alone.

20

On the back of the book jacket of *Rethinking the Evolution of Birds* is a photograph of Katherine Milhause. In his lavender room, beneath the light from a pole lamp that the hair salon's owner has loaned him, Carter considers this photograph. The fact that the Katherine Milhause on the book jacket appears entirely different from the woman at Fair Oaks makes Carter feel much worse than the fact that the former Katherine Milhause was a person capable of writing a book of science. The book, after all, makes no sense to Carter. He even wonders: are there really people to whom any of this *does* make sense? Or do a bunch of them just pretend it makes sense because that's supposed to mean they're smart?

Which is not to say that Carter imagines he has simply robbed Katherine Milhause of her looks. It has never occurred to Carter to study the brain or its processes or why people say that the woman will never be able to resume her career; still, he understands the idea of *damage*. He understands the idea of some specific destruction of which he is guilty.

However, even after he turns off the light, it is the photograph of Katherine Milhause that keeps him awake. She was smiling at her husband when that photograph was taken. The little sideways name alongside the photo read *Joe Alitz.* She looked—amused. He has never seen her look amused.

He thinks about the conversation he had with Pastor Bitner after he learned that Katherine would be going to Palm Gate Village for the weekends. "I've come to think of her as my cross, like you talk about. If she leaves—I mean, for good, what should I do, Pastor?"

Pastor Bitner did not understand what Carter meant. Carter could tell this by the way Pastor Bitner smiled and nodded as if he had a little itch he held off scratching.

"There's others at Fair Oaks that will be your cross, Carter. You're helping people all day long. It's a fine job for a Christian—and, of course, you can always pray for Katherine—and her little girl, too—to continue to be healed. 'Whatever you ask the Father in My name He will give to you.' Remember that, Carter."

Carter nodded. He could not explain to Pastor Bitner that he owed Katherine and Jersey more than he owed the other residents. Jersey and Katherine—he owed them a life. And the love that he had robbed them of—surely he owed them that, too: the love of a father, and a husband, too.

He tosses back the sheets on his bed. He wants to *love* Katherine and Jersey, but when he thinks about love—what love feels like—he thinks of Bonnie Drabnik and her chubby, laughing kids. Becky Pattschull tossing her blond hair over her shoulder. And, of course, his mom and Cheryl Lynn and, years ago, his dad. Neff Morgan. R.E. Some of the men he served with in the war.

He brings his knees up to his chest. *Dear God*, he prays, *help me to do what's right, Lord. To be your obedient servant. To love Jersey and her mom. This is the day that the Lord hath made, let us rejoice and be glad in it*.

His thoughts drift in and out the rest of the night—prayer, dream, prayer, worry—until six o'clock, when his alarm rings and he clatters down the stairs to the salon's little bathroom and cleans himself up for his first AA meeting since before the accident.

▪ ▪ ▪

Outside the putty-colored building that is apparently the AA clubhouse, two men smoke cigarettes. "How you doing?" Carter says as he walks up to the entrance. The men scarcely look his way.

They are arguing over which of them is responsible for removing the concrete block that props open the clubhouse door.

"I didn't put it there!" says the one; and the other, "Well, that don't mean you can't *move* it, man!"

From the foyer, Carter can see into what is clearly the meeting room: clusters of people, folding chairs, a length of counter with a stainless steel coffeemaker and bags of Styrofoam cups.

He pours himself coffee. "Have some cake, too," says a woman at his elbow—cute, but with a disturbing number of rings in her ears.

"Is there a kitty?" Carter asks.

"No, I brought it. Help yourself!" The woman grins at a young man measuring scoops of ground coffee into a filter. "Ron, there, brings donuts but they disappear fast so I have to bring cake if I want to eat."

Carter is too nervous to enter into the coffeepot banter, but he smiles and says thanks. From one of the folding chairs, he reads the familiar Steps sheet at the front of the room, focusing on Step Nine:

Made direct amends to such people wherever possible, except when to do so would injure them or others.

"How you doing, there?" A burly older man with a strawberry nose and silvery Elvis Presley hairdo sits down next to Carter and holds out his hand. "Tom. Welcome."

Carter shakes the man's hand. "Carter."

Tom smiles. "That Jeanie makes a mean cake, don't she?"

"Real good."

Tom laughs. "My mom—us kids would have her make a cake kind of like that for our birthdays. Chocolate sprinkles on top. We called it 'Birthday Cake.'" He laughs again and gives his head a fond shake. "That always irritated her—my mom. 'Don't call it that!' she'd say. She worried people'd think she'd given us the impression she owned the trademark recipe or something."

Carter nods, though he hardly attends the man's words. *I'm supposed to make amends*, Carter thinks, *but if I make amends and then Jersey and Katherine hate me, I won't be able to help them at all.*

And wouldn't that be an injury to them?

And the accident was God's will. And God forgives me. So if I just do right by Jersey and Katherine—

He does not have a chance to play out this old argument any further because a hand comes down on his shoulder and he must turn in the folding chair to see to whom it belongs.

Louie Konigsberg. Carter has not seen the skinny, loose-limbed Louie since that night two years before when they each drank a fifth of tequila and Carter ended up stabbed and dying along Howell Park's service road.

"Slim Louie!" Carter cries, and, laughing, jumps up from his chair. For one hot moment, Louie's somber expression makes Carter fear that R.E. has seen Louie and told him what happened on Post Road—but, no, it turns out that the somber expression stems from Louie's feeling that *he* needs to make amends to Carter.

"Sorry I didn't visit after they moved you up to the hospital in Tampa." Louie glances at the man named Tom, then breaks off. "I meant to, but I was too much in my disease, I guess."

Carter raises his hands. "No problem, Louie."

Louie sighs. Though he is younger than Carter, his skin is gray and pitted, as if all those years of using left him corroded. "Will you excuse us?" Louie says to Tom, then signals for Carter to step down the length of a few chairs so they can talk alone.

"Catch you later," Carter says to Tom, who lifts his Styrofoam cup in a kind of toast.

"You look good, man," Louie whispers. "So I guess you heard we took care of that fucking imposter Rear End, huh?"

That fucking imposter Rear End?

The words knock against Carter like a stick dragged across a picket fence—rat rat rat rat. He bends over and rests his hands on the back of a folding chair before he asks, "What're you talking about, Louie?"

"Oh, man." Louie rubs at the pained grin on his face. "Man—you don't know about Rear End?"

Carter wets his lips. Brings the folding chair onto its back legs, holds it there.

"Carter," Louie brings his face close, "the fucker wasn't even *in* 'Nam. He got the boot before he finished camp! Can you believe it? Un-fucking-believable or what?"

▪ ▪ ▪

There is a buzzing in Carter's bad ear. A silvery something that is not quite a noise, but what else can he call it? He sees the old Elvis-guy, Tom, look his way—worried at what he sees on Carter's face?—and so turns back to Louie. "You're telling me that R.E.—"

"—is a fucking imposter, man! All lies. All of it. Kasik—you remember Kasik?"

Carter gives a dull nod.

"Me and Kasik, we'd always wondered about Rear End, but we never said nothing to you 'cause you two were so tight. Anyways, after you got stabbed, the police ran a couple of sweeps at Howell and had everybody show ID. That's how we learned Rear End's real name: Finis Pruitt. Then, a couple weeks later, Kasik shows up at the shelter with Rear End's service record." Louie shakes his head. "The fucker never even finished boot camp, man. So the next time that little prick showed up, we took care of him good. Wostachec was all for killing him, man—I mean, 'cause Wostachec and Kasik figured it was Rear End who knifed you."

Carter jerks at the words. "What?"

"Well." Louie squints at the floor. Scratches hard at the back of his head. "Nobody proved it, man." He gives an anxious glance toward the front of the room, but no one has taken the spot at the lectern yet. "You didn't know any of this, huh?"

Carter shivers. He wants to get out of the room, fast, but he has to ask Louie, "Why would R.E. want to knife me, man?"

"Wostachec's theory was you knew too many of Rear End's stories." Louie laughs and gives Carter a brotherly slap on the arm. "Rear End. Maybe he made that name up, too. But, hey, man, the best part's you're alive, right? And sober, too, huh? Both of us sober. It's a fucking miracle—oh, Jeanie's about to get us started here. Better get to my seat."

Carter looks up as the woman who offered him cake steps to the lectern. She smiles and her eyes move back and forth across the room, sweeping up the group's attention before she calls, "All right, everybody. How about let's have a moment of silence for the alcoholic who still suffers, followed by the Serenity Prayer?"

In the foyer—to explain to himself his departure from the meeting hall—Carter knocks on the door to the rest room. No answer. Blindly, he tries the handle. When it does not turn, he leans against the foyer wall; paneling so thin it buckles beneath his weight, and he quickly stands straight once more.

Someone might smile over the ironies in all of this: how, after the accident, Carted wanted R.E. to kill him, but Carter could not even ask the favor of R.E., as Carter had knocked R.E. out. Perhaps the accident, in effect, saved Carter's life. But Carter has neither an eye nor an appetite for irony. He feels ill. And grief-stricken. And disloyal for even considering that his friend could be the one who knifed him and left him for dead. R.E. never made it through boot camp? Did that make everything he ever said to Carter a lie?

No. It was impossible that R.E. could have known all that he knew without having been there.

Several people enter the AA clubhouse while Carter stands outside the rest room. Some of them nod and greet Carter as they hurry into the meeting. "Going to join us?" asks a man of about his own age, and Carter nods: "Just waiting for the john."

According to the foyer bulletin board, one of the AA groups is having a fifties party. Had. The flyer is out of date. Another flyer announces a benefit dance for scholarships for the children of police officers.

Carter glances back toward the meeting room. Louie Konigsberg waves and points to the empty chair beside him. Carter nods, mouths *just a minute.*

"Hello, there, young fella!" An elderly man—smiling, wearing a sporty hat—steps into the foyer. "Hello," Carter says, and—

as the man sets his hand on the knob of the rest room door—"That's occupied, sir."

The man—hearing aid in each ear—does not register Carter's words, and he gives the door a tug. When it opens, he smiles back at Carter. "Were you waiting?" he asks, as he reaches inside to flick on the light.

"You go ahead," Carter says, and he slips out of the clubhouse and into the parking lot as soon as the man pulls the door shut behind him.

▪ ▪ ▪

When West Central Land began developing the site for Palm Gate Village Retirement Living, the partners—young men out of Pittsburgh—were delighted by the utter flatness that makes Florida's west so well suited for the golf games and wheelchairs of retirees. The site needed only the slightest modifications after bulldozers bladed the native scrub and grasses that attracted local fauna but did nothing at all for humans in search of an expanse of lawn, bright blossoms, handsome shade trees.

It did not occur to the developers that the golf course site contained no trees because it could support no trees; that the sturdy saplings they plugged into the ground in 1987 would, seven years later, remain so puny that the four retirees who play the course this May morning have a well-established ritual of rotating turns beneath the trees' tiny umbrellas of shade.

The day is sunny, as are most May mornings at Palm Gate Village. The red-faced golfer now taking his turn in the shade of hole 8's little scholar tree has misplaced his sunglasses. Axel Barkely. Lately, more and more often, Axel misplaces things (sunglasses, keys, checkbook)—or so it seems to Axel. According to an article read by his wife, we *believe* we misplace things more often as we grow older simply because we are constantly on guard for signs of senility, dementia, Alzheimer's.

To avoid the sun's glare, Axel turns from the game entirely and watches the odd pair who now come down the asphalt path.

People at Palm Gate Village talk about this pair: the little girl in the wheelchair; the awkward, limping woman (Axel once saw her break into loony laughter while watching a groundsman work with hedge trimmers). Mother and daughter, some say, and both are blond and fair and long-boned, but it is hard, catching sight of the two, not to imagine them wayfarers bound to one another by affliction rather than affection or family ties.

▪ ▪ ▪

When the man in the baby blue golf clothes—baby blue shirt, pants, cap—turns her way, Jersey is sure he will be the one to speak to her, but it is another from his group who calls out: "May we help you?"

Tick, tick, tick. The wheels of her chair strike against the little rocks on the asphalt path, and the path passes close enough to the green that she can imagine the men hear the tick too. Tick, tick. An advance warning system. Like the alarm clock that ticked inside the crocodile in *Peter Pan*.

People at Palm Gate Village often ask Jersey, "May I help you?" and some mean just that, and some mean, "Do you have any right to be here? May we help you leave?"

As there is no reason to suspect that she needs help, Jersey supposes the golfer is in the latter group, but she cannot be certain. There is something confusing about his face: the way the murky yellow tint of his eyeglasses gives one segment of his otherwise very rosy face a depressed and sickly look.

"It's okay," she calls to him. In the hospital, she learned that "It's okay" was a good phrase for allaying people's fears. "It's okay. We're going to feed the ducks." She lifts from her lap the two cellophane bags of popcorn that she purchased at Walgreen's the day before.

"Well, that's fine, sweetie," the man says with a cheer as prickly as her own, "but during daylight savings time, nongolfers are prohibited from the course between 7 A.M. and 6 P.M."

Jersey pretends not to hear this last remark, and she presses on, while Katherine—a few feet ahead—stops and turns and arranges her own face in what seems an imitation of the man's expression of amused dismay.

"Jersey"—Katherine bends to whisper when Jersey draws up alongside her—"do I rememer him?"

"Maybe," Jersey whispers back. She is relieved that M.B. is not there to hear Katherine's question. This morning, when Katherine could not recall how one went about making water flow from the kitchen faucet, M.B. rolled her eyes. Angry, Jersey threw a sponge at M.B. But the truth of the matter is that Katherine sometimes frustrates Jersey, too.

Just the night before, Jersey tried to get M.B. and Katherine to take part in a game from one of her books for families of brain-injury patients. This game involved one person's holding an orange under the chin, and passing that orange along to another person, neither making use of their hands ("Improves cooperation, coordination, and intimacy skills," said the book). While Jersey read the instructions aloud, Katherine hummed "She'll Be Coming 'Round the Mountain," and M.B. went right on laying out her game of solitaire, only looking up once in order to mutter, "*Ri-dic-u-lous!*" Jersey finally drew M.B. down to the master bedroom to discuss M.B.'s lack of cooperation, and by the time the pair returned to the living room, Katherine—her chin dripping juice—had finished off the last bite of the orange.

Another failure to arouse Katherine: the weekend before—over M.B.'s objections—Jersey borrowed a VCR from the public library so that she could show Katherine *Invasion of the Body Snatchers*.

Movie under way, Jersey turned to Katherine to ask, "Do you remember any of this?" Katherine shrugged from her spot on the couch. Her own interest was focused upon the hard candies set out in the bowl on the coffee table before her: cinnamon balls, butterscotch disks. The candies' transparent wrappers—red and gold—lay scattered about her on the couch, and rustled each time she reached for a new sweet.

Really, Katherine seemed quite content just to roll candies about between her tongue and the roof of her mouth. Jersey, on the other hand, was depressed: *why did she not have a movie of her father?* Try as she might to imagine her father at any particular moment in his life, and what did she come up with? A reconstruction. Because in life, things happened only once.

Each moment passed. On the other hand—and this struck her as grossly unfair—as the watcher of *Invasion of the Body Snatchers*, she had witnessed, at least six times, the way the Chinese laundry owner's mouth turned down at the corners as he tried to explain that the woman who *appeared* to be his wife was *not* his wife.

"She wrong," the laundry owner said of the woman lurking at the back of the laundry. "*That* not my wife."

Also, Jersey knew precisely how the movie's heroine complimented the hero's cooking: "This is delicious. You're a great cook." Something so particular, so charming in the way the charming heroine swallowed her delighted and delightful laugh, and emphasized *you're,* and slurred *delicious.* In fact, Jersey not only could *recognize* such moments, she could *recall* them. She could *anticipate* the moments that lay ahead because she could *recall* them: gestures, sets, smiles, lighting, dialogue; and she turned to her mother and demanded—her voice a small shriek—"Do you even *try* to think of Dad?"

An abrupt and accusing question that not only frightened Katherine but reminded her that she was not what she once had been; and when Katherine shrieked back, "I *do*!" Jersey felt more dreadful than ever.

Why did she not have a movie of Katherine?

All that she remembered of the beloved, pre-accident mom was slowly being effaced by this other Katherine. Trying to love this woman who sat amid candy wrappers and twiddled her bit of fuzz—Jersey knew this woman deserved her love, too, but sometimes, when summoning love for her, Jersey felt that she performed a discipline rather than acted from her heart. A strange and lonely sensation. She might have been one of Pastor Bitner's parishioners, taking up the cross for any suffering soul.

▪ ▪ ▪

A pair of wood ducks, several buffleheads, a common goldeneye, and a number of lesser scaup—these are the ducks on the golf course's largest water hazard today, and while Jersey opens the bags of Walgreen's popcorn, she makes the sort of polite conversation with the ducks that her mother would have made in the past, asks about their health, and tries to remember some of the duck facts that she read in the bird book back at the condo.

"So these are tippers rather than divers, right, Mom?"

Katherine stands by the bindweed-covered fence that runs between the edge of the golf course and the street. Katherine seems more interested in the passing cars than the ducks; still, she nods at Jersey's question. Perhaps some bit of old knowledge has entered her atmosphere once more, and now burns its bright path across her inner sky?

"I like bir-ds," Katherine says.

Jersey nods. For a moment, her heart catches. One hand on the fence post, looking intent as she watches passing cars, Katherine appears, just then, very much the way she used to when, say, watching for Joe and Jersey to meet her outside a baseball game, a store, the symphony. A little intimidating, that watchful look, even if you knew that it was done on your behalf and would vanish straightaway once she clapped eyes on you, had you safely within her protective gaze.

"Jers-*ey*?" Katherine says. The pair has spent part of the morning working on Katherine's enunciation—particularly the troublesome ends of words.

"M-hm?"

"You know Car-er?"

Jersey hesitates. "Carter Clay? From Fair Oaks?"

Katherine points toward the road. "He wa-s there."

Absently, Jersey nods. "Spread out your popcorn, though, Mom. You've got it all in a heap."

Katherine begins to flatten the noisy cellophane bag against her chest. "I like Car-*ter*. He walk-s me. He says I get better."

Jersey glances at the golfers, now heading up the path. Soon they will pass by her and her mother, and she will be obliged to drum up another pleasantry. "Well, I think so, too, Mom," she says.

"There! Car-er!" Katherine points across the street, where,

sure enough, Carter Clay is now climbing from his rusty van, waving, heading their way.

"Hey!" he calls. "How you doing, ladies? I thought—driving by—I thought that was you two!" He smiles at the ground as he makes his way through the knee-high grass on the other side of the fence. "Feeding the ducks, huh?"

"Done!" Katherine says, and holds up her empty bag for proof.

"Looks like fun!"

When he reaches them, Carter Clay asks Katherine if she is enjoying her weekend, and so on. Though he is kind, Jersey feels awkward in his presence; particularly as it seems to her that her mother is trying to *flirt* with the man—

Is that what the tilt of the head is all about? The giggle behind the hand? Flirting?

If so, it is lost on Carter Clay.

For the past five hours—ever since leaving the AA meeting—Carter Clay has been driving around Bradenton. He thought of calling Pastor Bitner, but what could he tell Pastor Bitner? "Pastor, it may be that the man who was with me when I killed Joe Alitz, and left his wife and daughter smashed up on the road, is also the man who knifed me two years ago when I was a homeless alcoholic/addict/bum"? What could Pastor Bitner do with that beyond telling Carter to turn himself in?

So Carter drove. And, eventually, he wound up in the neighborhood surrounding Palm Gate Village. He hoped he might see Jersey and Katherine out for a walk, or maybe running an errand at the shopping center, and here they are, out on the golf course. Pure luck.

■ ■ ■

While Katherine babbles away with Mr. Clay, Jersey, bored, plucks at the sedge that rims the water hazard. *Sedges have wedges*. She remembers only that much of the ditty, and nothing of the nature guide who delivered it, but she can evoke the spot in the Everglades where she stood as the guide spoke: the dock from which, moments later, Jersey would see a log resolve into an alligator. After *that* event—in commemoration—she drew a three-panel cartoon in her journal.

In the first panel, something—dark, scaled, mostly submerged in a lagoon—lies close by a group of feeding flamingos. In the second, the flamingos fly off, several looking back, wide-eyed, at the signs of agitation that now mar the water around the apparently emerging "something." In the third and last panel, the "something" is revealed to be a suitcase on a conveyer belt, with several other suitcases following it up and out of the lagoon to the line of commuters who have gathered on the opposite shore.

Jersey liked the way she transformed the *experience* of "log turning into alligator" into a depiction of a faulty *expectation* of "log turning into alligator." The harmless turns out to be the dangerous; the dangerous turns out to be the harmless. The drawing was not so great, but the flamingos were very expressive. Today, however—even after her experience of the Everglades and the drawing of the cartoon—she stares directly at an alligator of the same type and size as the one she saw a year before, and she mistakes it for a concentration of old leaves and twigs at the bottom of the water hazard.

"Lis-en," Katherine says, clearly addressing herself to Mr. Clay, and not to Jersey. He holds up his hands, okay. Katherine smiles her damaged smile—higher on one side than the other—then makes what Jersey recognizes as a common refrain in the call of a mockingbird.

In response to Katherine's call, a mockingbird flies out from one of the golf course's dinky trees, and it lands—with the breed's characteristic balance-seeking wobble—on a post a way down the fence.

"Hey!" Mr. Clay laughs. "That was good!" He smiles at Katherine, then at Jersey, who feels taken aback, once more, by his interest in her mother and herself.

"Do you know any more calls, Katherine?" Mr. Clay asks.

"Actually"—Jersey tilts her head in the direction of the condominiums—"we have to go inside now. For lunch, Mom?"

"Jers, Car-er wans to *talk*!"

With her hands on her hips, Katherine appears an adult imitating a child who hopes to sound like an adult. The effect unsettles Jersey, but she says, as firmly as possible—hoping to sound adult herself—"You'll see Mr. Clay at Fair Oaks on Monday."

He grins. "I hope I'll see you at church tomorrow."

This does not satisfy Katherine, however, who complains so loudly all the way back to #335 that M.B. asks, the moment they come in the door, "What's going on?"

Katherine plunks herself down on the couch. Begins to wreak havoc on the wool of one of M.B.'s needlepoint pillows. "Car-er came and Jers *ma-de* me lea'!"

"Carter?" M.B. comes out from the kitchen. "Here, here, give me that!" She removes the pillow from her daughter's reach, and opens the coffee table drawer where, just for this purpose, she keeps a skein of mohair yarn and a pair of scissors. "Here." M.B. snips a length of the multicolored yarn into Katherine's lap. "Now." She takes a breath. Looks at Jersey. "Carter Clay came to see your mom?"

"He saw us feeding the ducks and stopped to say hi, M.B."

Katherine shakes her head. "He my *boyfrien'*," she says in a superior, correcting tone that makes M.B. and Jersey exchange a startled glance. "I see him 'morrow at chu'ch."

M.B. starts to roll her eyes for Jersey's benefit, then stops herself. "Let's just say he's your friend, kid," M.B. says. "Now how about Jersey reading you a Bible story while I finish making lunch?"

Katherine picks up the Bible that sits on the coffee table and holds it out to Jersey. "Pas-or Bi-ner says Go-d's go-t plans for me. He says the aski-*den*'s par' the plan."

Jersey takes the Bible without argument, but who would be surprised to find that the passage she chooses to read aloud is one she finds not only beautiful, but to her purpose (the Letter of James)? And that she raises her voice so that her grandmother is sure to hear?

> If anyone thinks he is religious, and does not bridle his tongue but deceives his heart, this man's religion is vain.

> Religion that is pure and undefiled before God and the Father is this: to visit orphans and widows in their affliction, and to keep oneself unstained from the world.

"Isn't that nice?" M.B. says, as she looks out at the pair from the pass-through; and when the telephone rings, she tells Jersey, "You keep on, hon, I'll get it."

For a moment, because of the silence on the line, M.B. thinks, *the Breather*, but then the caller gives his name: "Carter Clay." He hesitates, then adds, "From church? And Fair Oaks?"

"Of course!" M.B. feels a growing lightness in her chest, a sense that something crushing has just been removed from there, and she calls, "Kitty, Carter Clay wants to talk to you!"

Katherine looks up from frizzling her bit of yarn. "I don' wanna talk now." She waves a hand in the direction of Jersey. "You be quiet, too," she tells the girl. "I wan pie now."

M.B. covers the receiver. "Don't be ridiculous! Come to the phone!"

Katherine folds her arms across her chest and does not budge.

"What do I tell him?" M.B. hisses to Jersey, who cuts her eyes at M.B. and hisses back, "What're you doing, M.B.? Tell him she doesn't want to talk right now."

M.B. glares at the girl—even while she manages a merry laugh for the benefit of Carter Clay. "I guess she can't come to the phone just now, Carter, but we'll all be here tonight, if you feel like dropping by!"

■ ■ ■

If Carter had a button—say, in the palm of his hand—that he could push and, *boom*, his head would explode, he might have pushed that button after M.B. Milhause answered the telephone.

Before he even placed the call, he must have picked up the receiver twenty times, then returned it to the cradle.

It was not that he lacked nerve, but, rather, that he felt a terrible, sodden hopelessness. Seeing the pair on the golf course: Katherine, who would have been lost without Jersey; Jersey in her wheelchair—and there was no getting around the fact that it was he and nobody else who had brought things to this pass. He was responsible.

Dear God, he prays, *help me be willing to help them.*

And dear God, he adds, *let them let me help*.

21

"I can't believe you did that," Jersey says.

"I was just being polite," says M.B. Which is not entirely true. M.B. does hope that Carter Clay will come by the condo—*could* he possibly be interested in Kitty?—and so she experiences only a minor twinge of guilt alongside a good deal of satisfaction when the doorbell rings that evening.

The scene: Katherine on the couch, making dangerously defective pot holders; M.B. in the recliner, playing solitaire; Jersey parked in front of the VCR, watching a videocassette.

"Oof-uh!" To conceal her anticipation, M.B. makes an assortment of dramatic noises as she works her way out of her recliner and onto her feet to answer the doorbell. "My poor bunions!"

Jersey does not turn from the videocassette to show her grandmother the skeptical look on her face, but it is there, it is there. "*One hundred trillion neural connections,*" says the scientist of Jersey's video. Hemmed in by tremendous models of the left and right hemispheres of the brain, the host makes his way down a grand corpus callosum.

Carter Clay seems nice, M.B. thinks. Someone you could talk to. *And* a Christian. And nice to look at. Beneath M.B.'s yellow buglight, with his shaved head, Carter Clay is pure gold; he could be a figure on one of Lorne's trophies.

Out of the corner of her eye, Jersey watches to see if either her videotape or the arrival of Carter Clay makes any impression upon Katherine. Apparently not. Katherine appears engrossed in her pot holder, breathing hard.

In the hallway, M.B. yelps, "Don't be silly! The girl's watching something, but me and Kitty are relaxing."

There follows the sound of the man's polite scraping of his cowboy boots on the doormat (as if, Jersey notes sardonically, he comes in from a dusty trail ride, and Old Paint's tethered to the front porch).

"It's Carter Clay, Kitty!" M.B. calls.

Though her mother does not look up at this announcement, Jersey notices that the corners of her mouth do rise as she works a loop of red over a loop of blue, under a loop of green, over, under.

There are presents. For M.B. and Katherine: scarves. "Isn't that nice, Kitty?" M.B. asks. "What do you say?"

Katherine bobs her head. "Thank you, Car-ter."

And "Thank you," says Jersey as she examines her own gift—a new journal, in which Carter Clay has written on the first page:

Dear Jersey,

I saw you write in one of these before. Maybe you'll need a new one someday!

Your freind—Carter Clay

"Hey, Katherine, let me show you something," Carter Clay says, and holds out the brown paper bag in which he brought his gifts. Obediently, Katherine puts down her loom and takes the bag. "See how it says *Fort Powden*, there?" Carter Clay asks. "That's my hometown. Most paper bags you get in the stores, they come from Fort Powden. My dad worked at the pulp, there, till he had too many back problems and all."

When Katherine only gives a nod, M.B. supplies a friendly "*Hm!*" then starts to the kitchen to fetch Carter Clay a cup of coffee.

"M.B."—Jersey wheels after her grandmother, and in the kitchen whispers—"why's he coming here?"

Though M.B. is pleased by the appearance of Carter Clay, it is not easy for her to sound entirely convincing when she whispers back, "Guess he's sweet on your mom!"

Really, the idea makes Jersey woozy. Mr. Clay is not worthy of her mother, of course not. Still, the idea that he would be romantically interested in this version of Katherine—Jersey senses that it is absurd, and somehow creepy, too, and she whispers a pleading, "I can't believe that, M.B., and he's—not *smart*."

M.B. makes a face. "As if being smart ever did your mom a lick of good!"

Jersey stares up at her grandmother—now briskly opening and closing cupboard doors. "Well," she says, finally, "that was mean."

"Oh, *mean*! You just come out and behave yourself!"

The information contained in a simple virus would fill a book of one hundred pages, exclaims the video host, but M.B. crosses in front of the set and places Carter Clay's cup of coffee on the dinette, and does not give the host a glance.

"I been thinking, Carter," M.B. says, "maybe we could hire you to give us some help around here sometimes. Now that Kitty's coming home, weekends?"

Carter has just been noticing how nice M.B.'s apartment is—like a model room in a department store: pretty sofa and chairs, matching tables with matching lamps—and, instantly, he looks up in distress and repentance. "Oh, I couldn't take money! But I hope you ask me to help. Any time. Really."

"Well, fine!" says M.B. "So! What do you think about this Holy Land tour Pastor Bitner's planning?"

Carter is still unused to conversations relating to church life, and he feels especially shy in front of the faithless Jersey; but he studies his big hands and ventures to say, "I guess they'll see Mount Quarantanin. Pastor Bitner says that's supposed to be the site of the Temptation. That'd be something, wouldn't it? Though, according to Lloyd—you know old Lloyd from church, right?—Lloyd believes you only have to travel to Missouri to be where they had the Garden of Eden. I can't remember the name of the town, but Lloyd says it's in Missouri."

"Branson?" M.B. says. "No, that's the entertainment place, isn't it? Bobby Vinton—'Roses Are Red'?—he's got a place there. A bunch of big stars do."

Carter flushes at this swerve in the conversation, then gazes at Jersey's video as if he is suddenly vitally interested in what the host has to say. Once upon a time, Carter loved the songs of Bobby Vinton—"Blue Velvet," sure—but should he know of a place called Branson? Sometimes, at church or at work, when people mention this and that as if they are *givens,* he feels a gap as plain as the one left behind by a lost tooth.

And hey: does Jersey *really* understand this video?

In pure agitation, Carter rises from the dinette with his cup of coffee and—careful not to block the girl's view—crosses the room to inspect the lone photograph on top of the entertainment center.

Woman, man, girl. Immediately, Carter realizes it is a family photo of Jersey, Joe, and Katherine, and he turns away with a guilty start that M.B. registers—and is only too happy to mistake for a sweetheart's unhappiness at seeing his girl with another guy.

"Oh!" she says with a little laugh. "That's—a bad picture! I don't know why we even have it out!" She rushes across the room and sets the thing face down on the entertainment center. "Anyways, have you ever been to Missouri, Carter? You ask me, it can't hold a candle to Florida. Did anyone ever grow an orange in Missouri? Give me a break!"

"M.B.," Jersey says, "you make a better door than a window."

"So turn the darned thing off! We got a guest, for crying out loud!"

"No," Jersey pleads, "please?"

M.B. looks to Carter for sympathy. "The part of science that's to do with electric lights and telephones and all, that I don't mind, but *this*"—M.B. waves a dismissing hand at Jersey's videotape—"this isn't anything anybody needs to know."

Carter nods. "Sometimes I wonder if we're even supposed to know all the things we know today."

"Right." M.B. sighs. Really, what she would really like is to return to her game of cards, and in order to resist the urge, she stays away from her recliner, takes a seat at the dinette. "But try to tell Jersey that!"

Jersey turns away from the show. "You rang?"

M.B. nods. Lights a cigarette. Hopes Carter Clay does not object to cigarettes. Good grief. Should she put it out? To deflect attention from herself, she continues, "I just wish you could hear all Pastor Bitner knows about science, Jersey—how fossils are a trick from the devil and all."

The girl bugs her eyes. "A trick from the *devil*?"

"That's right." M.B. lifts her chin to give strength to her position. "The devil tries to make people—like your scientists"—she glances at Katherine, still absorbed by her pot holder—"he wanted them all to believe the wrong dope, so he made fossils, see? So's some people would get tricked into believing there wasn't the Creation. They'd think it happened real *slow*, over millions of years and all, instead of the seven days"—she claps her fingertips to her mouth—"*six*, I mean!"

Jersey turns her chair in the direction of her grandmother. "So that's what you think my mom was doing? The devil's work?"

"Now, I didn't say that, Jersey."

"Of course, you did!"

"You never let me finish. What I was going to say—the scientists who claim fossils show there's no Creation, *they're* the ones I'm talking about! Your mom—she just got taken in by Joe and them when she was a girl. And, you know, toward the end there, I got a feeling she thought some of your dad's ideas were wrong. It's just a matter of time before somebody figures out she's wrong, too." M.B. turns to Carter Clay to smile. "She wrote a book—about birds and dinosaurs?"

Carter Clay nods. "Jersey loaned me it." He smiles in the direction of Katherine, but Katherine does not seem to notice. "It's a long one!"

Jersey gives a bitter laugh. "You don't understand, M.B. Scientists—they may change their ideas, but they always try to work from evidence."

"Well!" M.B. brings her hands together in a merry clap. "Don't that tell you something? There's the devil's trick, right there! Evidence—but it keeps changing!"

Jersey points the remote control at the television screen to lower the volume of the videotape. "Anyway, if you believe the devil can trick people, why wouldn't you think God could eliminate the trick?"

M.B. looks to Carter Clay, to see if he might tackle the question, but Carter is now busy fishing for something in his back pocket, and M.B. grows impatient and answers herself, "He could! But He wants us to have faith!"

"In *what*?"

"Hold on," Carter Clay says—now unfolding an index card he has taken from his wallet.

"Faith in Him, silly!" says M.B.

"That's right!" Carter Clay holds up the card, then reads from it: "'By a man came death.' Corinthians 15:21. You know how there's all that talk about how fossils are real old, Jersey? Like, before there was even people?" Carter Clay smiles. "The thing is, you can't have fossils of dead creatures from *before* the Fall, because 'By a man came death.' There wasn't death before the Fall."

Carter Clay mistakes the girl's embarrassment for him as embarrassment for herself, and he feels a little sorry for her. Her eyes are such a bright-bright blue, he thinks she may begin to cry. Instead, she speaks: "We do have fossils before man, Mr. Clay." She takes a little breath of air and looks away from him. "The Bible doesn't prove fossils are wrong. The fossils prove you can't use the Bible as a science book."

Carter studies the writing on his index card, then moistens his lips before reading on, "'The Bible is the word of God. Good men said so and good men don't lie.'"

To Jersey, the idea that this man quotes such trash-thinking is not just confounding but scary, too, and she offers in return, "Good people, like my mom and dad, they say the fossil record contradicts what's in the Bible."

He gnaws on his lip. "But"—he speaks slowly—"then they ain't good people. I mean, unless they're just deceived. But if they're deceivers, then they ain't good."

M.B. nods. "That's right."

"No," says Jersey. "Look at the moon and the sun. We'd think they were the same size if someone hadn't figured out ways to measure them. Well, people have also figured out how to measure the age of really old things."

Carter Clay takes a deep breath as he tucks his index card back into his wallet; then he asks, "Jersey, you don't want to be atheist, do you?"

In response, she rolls her eyes.

If Carter had rolled *his* eyes like that—hell, his father would have tossed him right into a wall.

"Anyways, Jersey"—M.B. tries to sound kindly, calm—"you'll never be saved if you're atheist, Jersey."

"Well, boo hoo hoo!" Jersey cries, and, realizing that she sounds like her father when he was being silly—relishing that resemblance—she repeats, "Boo hoo hoo!"

Which makes Katherine laugh, and imitate Jersey—or possibly Joe: "Boo hoo hoo!"

"Kitty!" M.B. cries. "Shush!"

"*You* shush," says Jersey; and then, cheeks flaming at such daring, she adds a mumbled, "She has a right to laugh."

Really, the speed with which M.B. springs from the recliner startles even M.B.

"Hey," Carter Clay says, "hey, now—" but M.B. has already got hold of one arm of the girl's chair and begun to shake it as she shouts, "If you weren't in that thing, Jersey Alitz, I'd slap your face! You ought to be ashamed!"

Jersey closes her eyes. Her voice is small when she says, "God's the one that ought to be ashamed. Any reasonable human being would have prevented what happened to my parents and me if he could have. *You* would have, M.B.! Think about that! If God exists, you're nicer than God!"

Though she has never in her life been slapped across the face, Jersey does not cry out at M.B.'s slap. Instead, quite evenly—despite the way her own mother now wails *no, no, no*—Jersey continues, "Don't you think that if your God wanted me to believe in him—that he could make me, M.B.?"

No one answers this question, perhaps because frightened Katherine now noisily works her way into the narrow space between couch and wall. Ducked down, out of sight, Katherine calls a trembling, "I luh you, M.B.! I luh you!"

"I love you, too, Kitty," M.B. says in a determined if shaky voice. She steps between an end table and the wall. "Come on out, kid." M.B. crouches down, then whispers, "What'll Carter think? Come on out now."

The couch shifts as Katherine tries to find a way under it. "Don't hurt me!" she cries.

"Nobody's even near you, Kitty!" M.B. says, then flashes a look of fury Jersey's way.

"I luh everybody!" Katherine squawks, and Carter Clay looks at his hands and wishes himself far away. What the girl said about the accident and God—he wishes he had not heard that. In one of the pep talks he conducted as he drove to Palm Gate Village, Carter told himself: *If things are bad, just pretend you're in a cell, praying. Just pretend you ain't there at all.*

Fat chance of that.

Again, Katherine squawks, "I luh-v everybody!" and Carter, his own voice quaking, says, "That's good, Katherine. That's what Jesus wants us all to feel. And we all love you, too."

"*Please!*" Jersey lifts her hands high in the air, wags them over her head. "I mean, I'm sorry, Mr. Clay, but—she only said that because she's scared."

"No." M.B. backs out from behind the end table, in the process setting one of the ivory lamp shades tapping, tapping, and she glances at it—yes?—before continuing on: "What you don't understand, Jersey, is Kitty's got faith in Jesus now. She don't ever have to be afraid again."

"*Jesus?*" Jersey stares at the trembling couch, its irregular shakes and jumps. "You want to know what she thought of Jesus before the accident, M.B.? She thought if Jesus was the son of God, and he really did save people, it was because God knew he needed to *apologize* for the mess he made. She considered herself a—pagan! That's what she said! She was a pagan, because she worshiped order in the nature of things, not some big old God on high!"

"Whoa," Carter Clay murmurs, "whoa." He waves a silencing hand at the girl, then goes to the end of the couch and calls, "Hey, Katherine, why don't you come out now?"

A moment later, Katherine's face comes into view—smiling, if teary-eyed—and Katherine takes Carter Clay's proffered hand and steps out from behind the couch.

"That's better now, isn't it?" he says.

Jersey stares at him, hard, when he keeps hold of Katherine's hand and twists the wedding band back and forth on Katherine's third finger. "Safecracker," Jersey mumbles.

"What?"

Her audacity astonishes her, but is she to be polite when she feels their lives are spinning out of control?

She holds up her own hand and imitates the twisting motion that Mr. Clay makes with her mother's ring. "You look like a safecracker," she says, "trying a lock."

He looks down at Katherine's hand in his. "I didn't neither," he says. "You just thought I did, I guess."

As if he has said something extremely foolish—outrageous, even—Jersey widens her eyes and laughs. In fact, Mr. Clay is at least partly right, and she knows this is so. It is unlikely that her comparison of him to a safecracker would have occurred to anyone but herself, and it may have occurred to her only because she is trying so hard to find a way to understand what on earth he is doing in their lives, and how he got there in the first place.

"Well, I suppose I better head home," he says.

M.B. glances at the girl, now turning her chair back to the television: so rude! Still, M.B. manages to summon a pleasant smile for Carter Clay and to say, "We certainly do thank you for coming by! Taking time from your busy life—"

"LRHHHH!" The voice on the reactivated videotape jumps at them. Everyone startles. "Sorry," Jersey says as she lowers the volume to a normal level.

"You'll have to come back soon," M.B. continues.

"I hope to do that."

Katherine looks up at Carter Clay. "You go-ing?"

"I'll see you tomorrow. At church. And you too, Jersey."

Jersey lifts her hand in a wave without turning away from her show.

"If you like," says M.B., "you could stop by after church, and tell us what you thought of the sermon. I think Katherine'd like that, wouldn't you, Katherine? Have some pie and coffee?"

Katherine smiles at Carter Clay, who says, "Sounds like a plan to me!"

"That Jersey," M.B. whispers as she sees Carter Clay out the door. "I apologize."

He shakes his head. He feels a little dizzy. "No need," he says. "She's got—a hard thing. It must be—hard."

"I do what I can, but I'm a little late in life to take care of the both of them."

"Well"—he hesitates, then plunges on—"that's what I'm here for, though. I want to do all I can to help. Katherine—" It is a false start and he finds he cannot take it anywhere. "So, goodnight, then," he says.

"One good thing, though," blurts M.B., "I mean, for her and Jersey's future, she's got money. From insurance and all. And they got a house and all—"

He shakes his head. "That's good," he says, but he does not want to hear more, and he takes a step backward, and turns and hurries to the stairwell.

For a time, M.B. remains on the balcony, afraid to go inside, afraid of what Jersey might see on her face. *She's got money. From insurance and all*. How much did I shame myself then? she wonders.

When Carter Clay appears in the parking lot below, whistling "Blue Velvet," M.B. makes him into a stranger, no one who has anything to do with her life. She holds onto the wrought iron railing of the balcony and it carries her back to the railing on either side of the front stoop of the house in Gary. Lorne repainted those rails every year. A shiny black like fresh tar. It took forever to dry. She remembers watching him paint the rails. He wore a pair of old wingtip oxfords when he painted. His painting shoes. So ancient they were hard as flint. She could look out the window of the front room and see him painting. He was not the sort you told, "*Hey, you missed a spot there.*" He would make you pay for that sort of thing, and, anyway, you could be sure he'd find every spot before he finished. Even now, when he is dead, M.B. remains slightly astonished that Lorne—Lorne Milhause—married her. Not that she mistook him for the most wonderful man in the world and not that there were never other men who wanted to marry her and not that she wasn't a hard worker and careful with money and clean and all. Still, that someone married her and stayed married to her forty-two years—it is so extraordinary, it often feels like something that must have happened to somebody else.

22

Though it is not impossible to train wild birds to eat from your hand, the process requires patience. First, provide a regular and plentiful supply of seed on a feeding station attached beneath a window. Be patient. After establishing a regular feeding schedule, add a glove and hat to the station, and place seed on *only* the palm of the glove and the crown of the hat. Be patient. Eventually, the birds will take seeds from the glove and the hat. After they have done so for several weeks, open the window, and while still standing inside, place your hand in the seed-filled glove on the station. Be patient. Be still. Eventually, the birds will feed from both the hat and your gloved hand. After several weeks of this, go outdoors. Stand beside the empty feeder with the seed-filled hat on your head. Lay your gloved hand, full of seed, on the feeder. Be patient. Be still. Do not try to look the birds in the eye. Do not allow the birds to see you swallow; they may take you for a predator, and flee. Practice. Be patient. Eventually, the birds will fly to you when you walk out of your house wearing your hat and glove. Practice more, and, if you are very lucky and very patient, the birds may one day fly to your bare head or shoulders or hands.

Jersey knows these procedures, as they were the ones followed by her mother in order to establish a relationship with the birds of the family's Arizona neighborhood. Thus when Katherine first started coming to Palm Gate Village for weekends, Jersey tried to convince M.B. that a feeding station at the kitchen window would be good for Katherine. M.B., however, protested: the other residents would have kittens over such a mess on their balcony, and she was already in dutch over their staying at her place!

Though she has no feeder, early each evening Jersey goes out on the balcony, closes her eyes to slits, and sits with seed-filled hands resting on the arms of her wheelchair.

Not expecting much—no Florida bird has ever come even close to taking a seed—she sits there now. It is quiet. The men who were spreading tar and gravel on the roof of carport H have taken their radios and departed. Now the only sounds are birdsong and the noise of cars moving through the parking lots that wind among Palm Gate Village's many buildings. Jersey thinks of her father, and how, at a time like this, he would say, with a sigh,

> It is a beauteous evening, calm and free,
> The holy time is quiet as a Nun
> Breathless with adoration—

What did it come from? Who was the author?

The Hannigans and the Munros, who go out for the Early Bird Special each Saturday, advance down the balcony in her direction, and, to avoid striking them as too odd, Jersey opens her eyes wider and smiles. Hello, she says, and the adults say hello, too—as moved by the solemn girl in her wheelchair as she is moved by them in their clouds of perfume and aftershave, the men in blazers and plaid pants, the women in silky dresses whose belted skirts fall in soft folds. (M.B. often makes fun of the Hannigans and Munros. When M.B. rises up on tiptoe to imitate the mincing way the women walk in their high heels; when she giggles behind her hands at their trumped-up girlishness, Jersey laughs along, but also supposes—correctly—that the women lead the sort of sweet retirement life that M.B. meant for herself and Lorne.)

The next noise in the parking lot: the arrival of Carter Clay's old van.

It unnerves Jersey that she can feel Carter Clay come up the concrete stairs. The vibrations of his tread travel up her wheels, into the chair frame, and, then, into her own skeleton.

"Hey!" he says when he reaches the balcony. Hey, he's just come from working on a doohickey that will let Jersey come for a ride in his van! A brace kind of thing. "I read how to do it in a library book," he adds, then gives her a happy and conspiratorial wink, as if to say the library is just one more thing they have in common these days.

Jersey does her best to smile. She does not notice the way Carter Clay holds onto the balcony railing as he speaks—squeezing so hard that the knuckles in his hands bleach white. She cannot know that Carter Clay is still upset from a conversation that occurred when Pastor Bitner asked him to come by his office today. Pastor Bitner wanted to warn Carter that Katherine Milhause might "mistake" Carter's special friendship toward her family for romantic interest in her.

An unpleasant series of moments for Carter: when he said that he hoped eventually to ask Katherine to marry him, then witnessed the astonished and suspicious look that clouded Pastor Bitner's face before he asked, "Why are you doing this, Carter?"

Carter had assumed Pastor Bitner would approve, and so he felt hurt and looked away when he answered, "A husband's supposed to take care of his wife for better or worse, right?"

Pastor Bitner put his hand beneath the big leaf of the plant that grew in a pot beside his office desk. Pastor Bitner lifted the leaf with the back of that hand, lowered it. "But—you're not her husband, Carter."

"Right! She needs a husband, though! If her husband were alive, he'd take care of her. Not that I'd mean to—you know, it wouldn't be with sexual relations. I'd just be there to take care of her and Jersey."

It had occurred to Carter in the past that some people might suppose that he was a pervert or money-grubber if he married Katherine; but he had never worried that Pastor Bitner might be one of them.

"Jersey"—Carter plucks a few of the girl's sunflower seeds from her open hands and sets them, one by one, on the balcony's wrought iron railing. "You know I care about you and your mom?"

Sometimes, when Jersey throws the sunflower seeds in her hands over the railing, she imagines that, one day, she will look over the railing and find the giant faces of sunflowers poking up from the evergreens below. But not now. Now, she wipes her hands on her skirt and says, as politely as possible, "You really don't know us, though, Mr. Clay."

He shakes his head. "That don't matter."

"Of course it matters!"

In Mr. Clay's company, Jersey finds the air suddenly dense and spongy. Though she would like to wheel away from him and this conversation entirely, she lowers her voice and she says, "Look, Mr. Clay, before the accident, in the morning, my mom listened to Bach and did the *Times* crossword. She—was a vegan! She was a volunteer bird-bander. Her idea of fun was trying to figure out how a fossil, broken in a million pieces, could be fit back together again."

Carter nods. Though unnerved by what the girl says—he has never heard of bird-banders or whatever that V-thing was—he knows he has a card to play, and he plays it now without hesitation. "But, Jersey, if your mom's not herself now, maybe I know who she is now better than you do."

Jersey peers out over the balcony. It is possible, looking to the east, to see into the streets of the nearby neighborhood of modest single-family homes, rooftops blanching silver as the streetlights tremble to life.

It is a beauteous evening, calm and free—

When she looks up at Mr. Clay again, the sadness on his big face startles her—sometimes, that sadness of his almost makes him seem a kinsman—but she feels a pressing need to turn the conversation in another direction, and she says, "What would you bet I can guess any number you think of between one and one million within twenty-five guesses?"

"Twenty-five guesses?" He smiles at M.B., who has now

appeared behind the condo's storm door, smiling. "Twenty-five seems like a lot of guesses, Jersey!"

Jersey ignores the sound of the storm door opening. "A lot?" she says. "Do you know how much a million is? To count to a million requires eleven days and four hours—"

"None of us is interested in that, Jersey," says M.B., her voice a little strained by the fact that she is now pulling Katherine—awkward in spaghetti-strap dress and high heels—onto the balcony. "Don't she look pretty, Carter?"

He nods. "Real nice. You ready for dinner, Katherine?"

Katherine does not nod or shake her head. She likes this Carter's face, his rosy lips and blue eyes. Still, she wonders if maybe she should go back inside to the television set for company, reengage her fingers with their bit of fuzzy wool. She does not like outside, the way outside's clouds boss the trees and houses. See? Still, there is one good thing: Jersey is not invited to go to the restaurant with Katherine and Carter. Jersey is staying with M.B. Katherine likes that. Jersey always pushes Katherine: do flash cards, take walks, listen to music, look at books and birds. Once, Katherine got so tired of Jersey's prodding that she hit Jersey in the face with a big book. Blood came out Jersey's nose and she cried, but Katherine said, "Don't you tell!" and Jersey never did.

■ ■ ■

"How's your weekend going?" So Carter asks as he opens the door of the van for Katherine. Katherine does not answer—merely looks back at the balcony, where M.B. stands, waving good-bye.

"M.B. like you," says Katherine, "but not Jers'!"

Though he is not sure whether Katherine means that M.B. does not like Jersey, or that Jersey does not like *him*, Carter asks—in the interests of keeping the conversation going—"Why not?"

"Sec-*ret*," Katherine says.

While she laughs her noisy, gulping laugh, Carter makes his trip around the van to the driver's door. *Secret*. The word affects him bodily. He wipes at his upper lip. He thinks again of his conversation with Pastor Bitner. *I guess I must look like a suspicious character*, he said to Pastor Bitner, and Pastor Bitner did not say, *no, no, of course not, Carter*.

"Hey, Car-*ter*." As he climbs inside the van, Katherine—now serious—reaches over to tap his arm. Opens her eyes wide. "Want to know the sec-*ret*?"

"Well"—he sets his elbows on the steering wheel, and looks out the windshield—"you sure you should tell?"

"It's jus-*t*"—Katherine lowers her eyelids and sighs—"Jers' thinks you are no' *smar-t*."

Carter busies himself with backing out of the parking lot. The way he figures, God must help people learn to love their wives in places like India where marriages are arranged. So if he marries Katherine, he can pretend they have an arranged marriage. A marriage arranged by the accident. Or, you could say, *by God*, who never really let anything happen by accident, right?

Right. This is a solid, happy thought to swallow: a marriage arranged by God.

The restaurant to which Carter and Katherine go for dinner is called Mr. Ribs. Hunter green and burgundy decor. Booths with high backs that ensure privacy. A place suggested by M.B.

Blinded by the restaurant's mood lighting and his extreme self-consciousness, Carter stumbles after the hostess and Katherine. *I did this to her*. He wants to confess to the pretty young hostess: *I did this to her!* But he also understands that a good part of his urge toward confession springs from some rotten longing to deny Katherine as his choice of dinner date.

"You want the ribs?" he asks after the hostess departs.

Katherine peeks out from behind the corner of the grand and glossy menu. She swallows the bite of muffin in her mouth, then says, "M.B. tol' me fry chick-en. 'Cause"—she makes a little face, then twiddles her fingers in front of her—"I not so goo-*d* wit fork."

Carter nods. A buttery crumb of muffin speckles Katherine's cheek, and the sight of it there—though it is just a crumb, and, damn it, any woman eating a muffin might have a crumb on her cheek—the sight of it makes Carter queasy.

Does he only imagine the stares of the couple in the booth opposite? *Custodian*. That is the message Carter finds himself trying to project. *Caretaker. Kindly social worker*.

When he catches himself at this, however, he feels ashamed, and he reaches across the table and lays his hand on Katherine's.

Does Katherine remember whether or not she has ever been to Washington? No, and Carter fills a large part of the meal with talk of Fort Powden: the deer that graze in the meadows near the bunkers where he used to play war as a kid, the marion berries, the perfect skipping stones that come in along the Sound.

Katherine looks out the window while he talks. She is quite solidly inside her own thoughts, just then. Her open eyes merely hold her place in the ongoing world—they are a thumb stuck in a book in which she has temporarily lost interest. Sometimes, she forgets Carter altogether, despite the pleasant heft of his big hand on hers.

Halfway through dinner, she looks up to say, "On the cliffs, we ki-*ds* play Cas-ro. Cas-tro. He chase-d us. Once, a girl fell. On a cliffs. Deb-bie Mil-ler. Her mom put . . ." Katherine makes wide eyes, then raises her hands to imitate stitching motions. "In 'er head." She pauses, as if deciding whether to say more, then scoots out of the booth and murmurs an urgent, "I nee' go to bafroom! You hel' me!"

"Oh. Just"—Carter stands—"let me tell the waiter not to take our stuff."

"No! I can' wait, Car-er!"

"Okay. Okay." He takes her hand and begins walking her toward the front of the restaurant. "No need to get excited."

"I can' go 'lone!" She pushes her head into his shoulder. "I nee' help."

"Come on, now, Katherine." He guides her behind the wall separating the rest rooms from the lobby. He tries to sound patient but firm. Courtesy and Compassion: the Fair Oaks slogan. "You go by yourself all the time at Fair Oaks, Katherine."

"But no-t *here*!"

"Manager-in-Training" reads the tag of the tiny frizzy-haired woman who peeks around the edge of the wall.

Katherine holds onto Carter's arm as she leans into the swinging door of the women's rest room and hisses, "I can' wait, Car-er!"

"Ma'am," Carter says to the frizzy-haired woman, "I'm this lady's aide at Fair Oaks. She needs some help in the bathroom, and I wondered if I—"

The woman gives a quick nod. "Go ahead. Please."

"Oh!" Katherine wails. "Oh, no!"

"We'll take care of it, Katherine," Carter says. "Go on."

Things are not so hard when he treats Katherine the way he would treat her at Fair Oaks. At Fair Oaks, he regularly helps with bedpans and changes diapers. Over the Fourth of July holidays, when Fair Oaks was short-staffed for three days, he had to remove and insert tampons for a lady quadriplegic. That poor lady—she tried to pretend she was not there; that her body was like a car left behind for service.

Katherine leans back against the sink while Carter tries to dry her underpants with the little blower unit attached to the wall. "You hay me now," she says.

He is responsible for that, too, isn't he? He shakes his head. He says, "No, I'm glad I was here to help."

23

Vast deposits of limestone make Florida an ideal spot for the development of caves, and a *sinkhole*—as that morning's *Gulf News* explained—is simply an underground cave that makes its presence known when its roof collapses.

Over breakfast, when Jersey read the piece on the sinkhole now developing not far from Palm Gate Village, she liked the notion of those unknown caves, and of the need for a different name for a cave that opened at the top rather than from the side. However, when she noticed that the newspaper artist who had diagrammed the collapse of the sinkhole was the same artist who had illustrated the injury to her mother's brain, Jersey put down the newspaper. And now she does not join in the discussion of the hole as Carter Clay drives her and her mother and M.B. past the thing.

A strange, oppressive day.

The pale sky with its layers of gray and tan reminds M.B. of the grease her mother used to collect in jars at the back of her stove.

"Now, Carter," M.B. says, "does weather have anything to do with these sinkholes?"

Carter Clay wishes he knew, but he don't, sorry.

One entire section of strip mall has tipped into a crater that is not visible from Carter's van. A pair of mannequin legs sticks out from what was formerly the window of the Tog Shop. The tilted and heaved-up crusts of sidewalks and parking lot reveal sandy undersides, rough and crumbly as streusel topping, and there, against the broken brick front of the Chowder House, a man cautiously sets great fang-shaped shards from the Little Switzerland sign that M.B. knew in its past life, lit up from within, shaped like a wedge of Swiss cheese.

Pleasure, M.B. thinks. *I am taking pleasure in that mess*, and she feels a stab of guilt, which she tries to dispel by leaning forward to say to Katherine, seated in the front of the van, "I bet you'll want the chocolate shake, Kitty! You always liked chocolate."

And Jersey—Jersey wonders what her father would think if he saw them now, going out to eat at McDonalds in Carter Clay's van. "As goes McDonalds," her father liked to say, "so goes the world."

Would he think less of them if he saw their lives today? But that would be too harsh, surely. Surely he would understand that they do the best they can. Her mother, after all, seems to prefer the company of Carter Clay to that of anyone else.

"Jersey"—while Carter sets up the ramp for the wheelchair in the McDonalds parking lot, M.B. leans over to whisper—"what was that German word you taught me once? Remember? You used it about that Mrs. Reynolds at church?"

She gives her grandmother's face a slightly suspicious once-over. The little wrinkled face, the quilting around the eyes. "*Schadenfreude*?" she says.

"That's a terrible thing, isn't it?" M.B. whispers.

To avoid being accidentally touched by Carter Clay, Jersey draws her arms in as close as possible while he removes her chair from the restraining device he has installed in the van's floor. "I don't know much German," she murmurs to M.B., "but I know *Schadenfreude* is better than *Lustmorde*. And worse than *Haferflocken*."

Carter smiles. "What's *Haferflocken*?" he asks.

To include Carter in this exchange with M.B. distresses Jersey, but he means well, and so she says, "Oh, just—oatmeal."

▪ ▪ ▪

In the McDonalds play area, a toddler sits neck-deep in a box filled with thousands of lightweight, brightly colored balls. He laughs and laughs as his father perches on the box edge and—looking like any adult testing a child's bathwater—swishes his hands through the loose balls.

While Carter has gone to the counter to place their orders, the others have taken a seat near the play area. Jersey, eyes on the toddler, whispers, "Isn't he cute?" and M.B., still feeling remorseful, agrees with some vehemence, "Adorable! Kitty"—she means to call Kitty's attention to the toddler, too, but Kitty gawks, wide-eyed, at something across the room—

A filthy little troll of a man who wears on his head the sort of bowler children wear to St. Patrick's Day parties (black plastic, an elastic under the chin).

"Panhandler," Jersey whispers. "And I think he's drunk."

M.B. whispers back, "He's trying to sell something. A—grapefruit spoon?" Yes. Shrink-wrapped on a piece of cardboard.

The troll moves from table to table, shoulders shifting and dipping like a boxer's. Customers bend low over their hamburgers or stare out the big windows to the parking lot, trying to ignore the man and his sales pitch, which becomes audible as he winds closer to the trio in their booth by the window.

A veteran. Disabled. Out of work. Homeless.

"You hear that, Jersey?" M.B. whispers. "A veteran. Like your grandpa, but I put my money in the offering at church."

"Mom." Jersey nudges Katherine. "Don't stare."

▪ ▪ ▪

It has already been a year since Carter Clay knocked Finis cold on Post Road. Two years since Finis received the beating at Howell Park. In addition, there have been other—altercations, scuffles, thrashings since Finis has been on his own out in the world. It is no joke, then—no part of a carefully crafted disguise—that he pumps himself a tiny paper cup full of ketchup and proceeds to flatten the cup, the contents spurting into his mouth.

"He must be starving," M.B. says, and she slides out of her booth and makes her way to the counter and Carter Clay. "There's a fellow here," she whispers, "just behind us. A veteran. You think you could give him some change and—I'd pay you back."

"Where?" Carter Clay turns to scan the room.

"Don't stare," M.B. says, "but by the condiments."

At that same instant, the little man turns their way. He is wiping his mouth with the back of his hand when his face registers the sight of Carter Clay. As if by instinct, the little man ducks and takes a step toward the side door. Then—just as abruptly—he claps his hands together and he says, "Clay! What happened to your hair, man? I almost didn't recognize you!"

"Sir," the girl behind the counter says. "Your food, sir?"

A dazed-looking Carter Clay turns to M.B. "Nice talking to you," he says, and something in his tone makes M.B. turn and walk back to the booth—though she does look toward the counter again, where Carter Clay now shakes his head at the tray full of burgers and drinks in the hands of the countergirl.

"I don't know what's going on!" M.B. whispers to Jersey; the countergirl, lips puckered in annoyance, has begun to remove the food from the tray and put it into carry-out sacks.

They both turn to watch as the little man leans in close to Carter Clay. Does Carter Clay answer? M.B. cannot tell, but once the countergirl hands him sacks of food, what does he do? He starts for the door! Without a glance toward their table!

The little man continues to dog Clay's steps, pull on his sleeve. Clay pretends to ignore him until he reaches the door—where Clay drops the sacks of food, and spins around. The little man begins to retreat, but not fast enough, and now Clay has him by the shoulders and he leans into the little man's face and shouts, "*Back off!*" Then—boom—Clay exits through the restaurant door and out into the parking lot.

For a moment, the restaurant crowd sits perfectly quiet; the little man's head remains cocked backward, as if Clay holds him, still—but, slowly, the man straightens and turns and scowls at the patrons.

Is it true that his gaze stops at M.B. and seems to suggest recognition? Frightened, M.B. slides out of the booth. "Let's go, girls, come on," she says.

Katherine shakes her head. "I wan' ea-*t* here!"

"Wait, M.B." Jersey has her eye on the parking lot. "Mr. Clay's coming back—"

But not inside. Up to the junipers outside the window. Waving his arms. *Come on*, he mouths. *Let's go*.

Even before the little man sets his grimy hand on her shoulder, M.B. begins to turn—something about the look on Carter Clay's face has warned her. Nevertheless, she lets out a shriek of surprise—and sits back down.

"Hello to you, too!" the little man says, then adds in a hoot of delight, "Jesus, I know who you all are!"

He is still smiling when the door crashes open, but at the sight of Carter Clay, the little man covers his face with his arms. He darts backward, hits a bolted swivel chair that sends him crashing into the booth across the aisle.

"*Don't get up!*" Carter Clay stands over the little man, pointing one of his big fingers in the man's face in such a menacing way that, for a moment, M.B. actually mistakes the finger for a gun. "*Don't move. Don't open that lying trap of yours. Don't. Don't. Don't.*"

Could a finger be a gun? Carter Clay keeps the thing trained on the troll as he glances at M.B. and says (his hoarse breaths as frightening as any threat), "Let's go, M.B."

"Sir?" It is one of the teenage boys who works behind the counter. He stands a few tables in back of the booth in which the little man lies curled, eyes flooded with bridled rage. "Sir?"

Carter Clay turns the menacing finger toward the boy, who immediately retreats to the counter. "We're just leaving," Carter Clay says, then glances at the man in the booth. In the now quiet restaurant, it is possible to hear the crisp snapping noises made by the plastic bowler as it presses into the booth behind the little man's head. "Not one word," Carter Clay warns, and then, after a quick glance at M.B., "I said let's go."

M.B. steps out of the booth. "Come on, Mom," Jersey whispers.

"Wha-t wrong, Car?" Katherine asks.

"It's okay," he says. "Just go."

Two large adult males, one wearing a rainbow yarn Rasti hat, have come to stand next to the boy in the McDonalds uniform. "I saw him walk over and grab at the older lady," the man in the hat says to the boy, then he turns to Carter Clay to ask, "Everything okay, man?"

Carter Clay nods. "We're just leaving," he says, and he takes Katherine by the arm and points her toward the door. "Go. I'll be right out."

The McDonalds worker asks, his voice a squeak, "Do you want me to call the police?"

"No, man," says the Rasti, but Carter says, "Go ahead." He is trembling. He looks dead in the eye at Finis Pruitt—Finis, who has somehow managed to rustle up a bit of smugness from somewhere and now uses it to stroke one finger against the other: *naughty, naughty*.

"Go ahead," Carter repeats. "I'll kill him before they get here."

"Easy, buddy." The Rasti man's companion sets his burger on a table. "The guy's just a drunk."

At this, Finis Pruitt laughs and flails a leg at Carter, who instantly finds himself pressing a thumb on Pruitt's windpipe.

"Don't be crazy, man! Let up!" say the voices at Carter's back, but Carter presses his thumb deeper—Pruitt's eyes become a rheumy slough before Carter removes his thumb and takes one step back, and then another, keeping his eyes on Pruitt until he is outside and can quickly cross the parking lot.

There are only two keys on Carter's key ring, but in his agitation he fumbles with them before he can fit the right one into the ignition and start the van.

"Mr. Clay!" Jersey cries as he backs out of the parking space. Her chair rolls forward and strikes the back of Katherine's seat. "I'm not locked in!"

He brakes. The chair rolls backward, slams into the service door. "Stop!" she wails.

"We got to get out of here, man!" He wriggles over the stick shift and between the two front seats, jerks the chair into its runners, locks the wheels.

"What's going on?" M.B. wants to know, and Katherine asks, "Where my hambur'? I hun-ry!"

They are stopped at a second light before Carter speaks again. "That guy—he's got some mental problems. I knew him—before I was saved." He shakes his head, then checks his rearview mirror. "Let's head to your place," he says as they start through the intersection; then, after a moment's thought, he adds, "Maybe not. Maybe my place. No, your place is better."

"Where my ham-bur-er?"

"Sh," says M.B. in a tiny, tiny voice. The terrible weight that lifted when Carter Clay first began to visit Katherine has settled on her chest and shoulders once more—and if anything, perhaps because of the respite, it feels heavier. "Not now, Kitty. Carter wants quiet now."

None of them speaks again until they are in the little front hall of #335. There, Carter Clay bows his head and says, "I'd like to pray."

"Lord," he begins—M.B. tries to give Jersey's shoulder a pinch when Jersey fails to bow her head, but the girl manages to roll out of reach—"please, forgive us our sins, and let Your graciousness shine on us all this day. Us humble servants. Help us see the way as we seek to do Your will and pray for Your continuing love and forgiveness. In the name of Your Son, Jesus Christ. Amen."

"Carter," M.B. says, "are you okay?"

He nods. "I better go, though."

"Don't go!" Katherine throws her arms around his chest and tries to pull him into the living room.

"Kitty!" M.B. says. "Stop that! If you stop—if you calm down, I'll call Fair Oaks and see if you can't stay an extra night. Then maybe Carter'll come back and see us later, right, Carter?"

"Well, I'd *like* to," he says.

Which is enough for Katherine, who releases him, and smiles, and says to M.B., "I'm calm, see? Calm as a cu-cumer. See?"

▪ ▪ ▪

After Carter Clay left the McDonalds, Finis Pruitt extricated himself from the booth where Clay had held him captive. He made a show of dusting off his pants with his preposterous hat, and the swinging of his arm and the actual dust he managed to raise had the not unintended effect of clearing a little space for himself.

On the sidewalk outside the restaurant, he stretched in the sunshine. Smiled. He felt—weak, but in a pleasant way. As if he had just stepped from a sweat lodge or survived some astonishing train wreck. Really, the theater of the last ten minutes—could it have been even that long?—that degree of theater had been too much even for Finis. He could have sworn the rush of adrenaline he experienced in there had zapped this past year's rotgut residues right out of his brain. His thoughts were clearer now than they had been at any time since before the beating in Howell. The world sparked with purpose. Ever since Howell, he had been dull, hadn't he?

No more. On the molded plastic seating of McDonalds, he had undergone another metamorphosis. Before, he had been Persona Non Grata, the Guy Who Lost His Role. Now he found he had wings, a larger, grander part: the Dark Avenger.

Thank you, Carter Clay. Thank you, thank you.

Who would have thunk you had it in you to be so fucking scary?

Bright-eyed Finis threw open the restaurant door for the alarmed lady who headed inside. She tucked her child in close to her hip. "Good day to you, miss!" Finis crowed as the pair hurried past.

Finis was not the man to comprehend what drove Clay to associate with that threesome, but he could bet that neither grandma, daughter, nor grandchild knew the truth about the accident, and, clearly, Clay wanted to keep it that way.

To be so deliciously vulnerable—well, *that* feature of Clay's situation did not surprise Finis.

Something with an M? Finis felt certain that he would know the older lady's last name if he heard it. All of their names would have appeared in at least one of the newspaper articles about the accident. He might have the clipping still. Or he could look it up at the library. Get his gun. How difficult could it be to find an address if you had a name?

He opened the sack that held Clay's milk shakes in their lidded, now sweaty containers. Took out one plus a straw. Stuck the straw through the lid. Chocolate.

Of course, he reflected, as he sauntered off down the sidewalk. Clay's audience (crippled kid, old lady, head case) was not the most challenging audience in the world. But Mr. Nice Guy had to be a challenging role for a fellow to play for a family he had pretty well destroyed. Not to Finis's taste, true, but still an accomplishment of sorts; a treasure Finis certainly did not intend to allow Clay to keep.

▪ ▪ ▪

In his lavender room above the hair salon, curled up on the too-short bed, Carter Clay listens for the faintest stirrings of sound in the alley below. He supposes it is only a matter of time before R.E. shows up at his door. Or M.B.'s door ("Mrs. Milhause? I think there's something you ought to know").

Carter pictures the scene at the restaurant. As it happened. As it might have happened otherwise. Just now, a version breaks through in which he has not only killed R.E., but slipped past a police blockade after ditching the van for a stolen car.

Katherine and Jersey are with him in that car.

Or: they are *not*. Alone in the stolen car, he drives fast. Pedal to the metal. Hands tight on the wheel. Alone in the car, there is no need for conversation, explanation. The dark night fills his chest like a hit of good dope—

The sound that makes Carter jump back into his life in the lavender room is the opening of the hair salon's alley door. Click of a light switch in the hall below.

"Just me, Carter!" Jeri, the salon owner. "Forgot my purse!"

"Okay," Carter calls back. He sounds calm enough, though he had readied himself to do murder, throw himself out a window, or maybe just—combust.

24

That night, when Carter Clay does not return to #335, Katherine Milhause panics. She spends the night prowling the condo, flinging Jersey and M.B. from sleep with various explosions: cupboard door slams, incoherent tantrums, frightening bursts of high-volume TV, crash of dishes dropped in sink, machine-gun discharge of popcorn into metal salad bowl.

Again and again—after M.B. has identified the source of the latest noise, after her heartbeat has begun to settle a bit—M.B. calls, "Come on, Kitty! Get in bed!"

Still the noise continues. M.B. stares at her bedroom's drawn curtains—Vanilla Creme, pinch-pleated, selected with so much care. The curtains seem to bloat with the coming dawn, and M.B. shivers and thinks: life is trying to steal life from me.

Then falls asleep once more, and is in Wyoming, in her childhood bedroom, the briny patches of wallpaper rough under her hand as she tries to make her way to a window. There is no air in the house! She breaks open the window and sticks her head outside in order to breathe—

Panting, she wakes up and knows she made a mistake. That is clear. She dropped a stitch. Her life has unraveled. But what was the mistake?

It was not having Kitty or marrying Lorne. Not leaving school after grade nine. That could not be helped. Not that stupid Ferris wheel ride on which it seems she has pinned so much. Not Kitty's accident. Those were *happenings*, and what M.B. feels is *absence*, as if her life could be summed up by that hideous and mushrooming light now pushing out from between the pale curtains' darker folds.

More noise from the other room. Kitty running M.B.'s hair dryer?

What Kitty does not yet know, and M.B. does: Last night, when Carter Clay did not return, M.B. slipped into her bedroom and sat down on her bed and called Fair Oaks to ask for Carter Clay's telephone number. And learned that not only did Carter Clay not have a telephone, he had quit his job that afternoon.

A great palm pushing down upon her chest—that was the effect of such news upon M.B. Long after the Fair Oaks receptionist had hung up, M.B. stayed flat on her back on her king-size mattress. *Dear Lord*, she prayed, *make Carter come! Please, Lord! Help us!*

That man at the McDonalds—what did he have to do with Carter?

Her little bedside clock—a thing of gilt and pretty turquoise glow-in-the-dark hands, a gift from Lorne—reads six-twenty. She could call Pastor Bitner. Pastor Bitner could comfort her. He could restore her faith. If only she could first admit to him that she has lost it. Maybe never had it.

At the rattling of the front door, M.B. pushes herself up on her elbows. There: the yawn and click of the aluminum combination. Quick, she grabs her bathrobe and starts toward the hall.

"Mom?" Jersey calls from the guest room.

M.B. does not answer, but calls, "Kitty?"

The creaks from the guest room signal that the girl is moving herself into her wheelchair. "What's going on, M.B.?"

"I'm checking."

There is no way to separate from one another those feelings of weariness, despair, and mortification that come over M.B. at the sight of Katherine crouched on the balcony, staring down at the parking lot through the wrought iron rails.

"Come inside, honey," M.B. says. She does not turn as the wheelchair's footrest taps up against the storm door behind her. "Come inside and I'll make you French toast."

No. Katherine shakes her head. At some point in the night, she must have put a couple of M.B.'s hot rollers into her hair, for several sausages of curl lie across her crown. She has been crying. Her eyes are swollen, red; the skin beneath them is creased from lack of sleep.

"Pancakes? Waffles? An omelette?"

Katherine extends her throat to bleat, "I wan' Car-er!"

▪ ▪ ▪

It is almost seven-thirty by the time M.B. has eaten her own breakfast and cleaned up the various spills and messes that Katherine created during the night. Seven-thirty is late enough, she decides, that she can reasonably slip into her bedroom and call Fair Oaks and ask them to have someone fetch Katherine.

"Oh?" says the receptionist, a young woman who drives M.B. wild with her habit of speaking in questions. "But we don't do that, Mrs. Milhause. I guess we figure you'll bring her back yourself?"

The morning sky over parking lot H appears plundered, as if it could not support a single breath. After nodding to a neighbor who politely pretends to think nothing of Katherine's occupation of the balcony, M.B. crouches down to say, "Kitty, you need to get dressed so Jersey can walk you back to Fair Oaks before lunch. There'll be trouble if you ain't there by lunch."

Katherine grabs the top of the balcony railing and yanks herself to her feet. "I *wanna* go!" she says indignantly. "I see Car-*ter* there!"

Because M.B. does not have the heart to tell the poor thing otherwise—let them tell her at Fair Oaks, she thinks—she simply holds the door open for Katherine to pass into the unit, but, lo and behold, before Katherine is even inside, here comes Carter Clay, pulling into the lot below in his rusty, dented van.

A rotten apple. Jersey once said the rusty van made her think of a rotten apple, and today M.B. can see what she meant.

▪ ▪ ▪

Desperate embraces are something Carter has grown accustomed to receiving at Fair Oaks, but though he pats Katherine

Milhause's heaving back as patiently as he would pat the back of any Fair Oaks resident, his heart constricts with the bitter knowledge that he is no longer merely the anonymous source of so much of this woman's misery; no, now he has made his own self important enough that his *absence* can actually increase her pain.

Over the top of Katherine's head, Carter looks up to the balcony. There is M.B., watching Katherine lift Carter's hand and kiss it and hold it to her cheek.

"Katherine." Carter restrains her busy hands in his own. "You know how we talked about you getting out of Fair Oaks? Well, I come to see what you'd think about me taking you and Jersey back to Arizona."

Katherine's first response is a whoop that could easily be mistaken for a sign of pain, but when she turns to M.B., she is all smiles. "Car-er's here to take me Ar-zona!" she calls.

Carter's face blazes under the full force of M.B. and Katherine's attention. He is exhausted from his sleepless night, but does his best to sound alert and reasonable when he reaches the balcony and speaks to M.B.

Katherine and Jersey want to go back to Arizona, and he's been thinking, he could take them there. Just to see how it would go, you know? And take Jersey up to that clinic in Phoenix?

For a moment, the look in M.B.'s eyes alarms Carter—*Rear End called, she knows everything*—but then M.B. is pressing her hands to her cheeks and laughing, holding open the door to #335, come in, come in.

"Where's Jersey?" Carter asks.

"Oh, she's feeding the ducks." M.B. waves toward the big windows that overlook the golf course. "But let me think," she murmurs. "Let me think."

Carter steps over to the windows. The golf course and grounds of Palm Gate Village are so clean and organized that he feels as if the outdoors might actually be indoors.

There is the girl, sitting in her chair by the little water hole.

"When did you mean to go?" M.B. asks.

"Well, right away. Right—now, I thought. If that don't seem too nuts."

M.B. looks at his face as if it is a clock and she needs the time, then, just that quickly, she turns away. "But I don't know that Jersey'll go with you," she says. "She should. It's what she's been wanting—to go there." M.B. drums her fingers against her lips. "Would it be too awful—because she's so stubborn—"

Anyone could see that it is with some effort that M.B. laughs. "—I mean, what if we just throw everything in the van before she gets back? You three go out for a ride, and after you're a ways down the road—well, a few hours, I guess—you tell her you're taking her to Arizona. So it's—a *surprise*, see?"

"But tricking her"—Carter breaks off as M.B. rushes down the hall to the guest bedroom.

"You tell her you're taking her to that clinic in Phoenix," M.B. calls over her shoulder. "That'll get you on her good side. But, hey, grab that box of garbage bags under the kitchen sink, and we'll pack in them so Jersey don't see suitcases. And, Kitty, you watch the window and tell us when she starts back, hon!"

"I don't know," Carter says, but he hurries to the cupboard under the kitchen sink and reaches for the box of bags—in the process knocking over another box, which then causes an unnerving clink: glass hitting glass in the recesses of the cupboard.

Carefully, he pats his hand toward the cupboard's rear wall and finds he has not broken, only tipped over, the bottles. Mad Dog 20–20. One full, one half-empty.

"Didn't you find them?"

Carter jumps as, coming up from behind, M.B. grabs the box of bags from his hand.

"I just—" he begins, but she is already hurrying off, and he closes the cupboard doors, and leans against the sink for a moment to catch his breath.

"Hi, Car-*ter*." Eyes still swollen, Katherine waves from her post at the windows when Carter passes through the living room.

"How you doing?" he says, and smiles and waves back.

In the guest room, M.B. stuffs into a garbage bag: books, colored pencils, a ball of fuzzy yarn, bright clothes still on their hangers, shoes, the JERSEY ALITZ knapsack that strikes a blow to Carter's belly. M.B. looks up—a little breathless—and points to a bag by the door. "Take that down, too. That's Kitty's purse. It's got her house keys and all. Do you need money?"

"I'm okay."

"'Cause she's got money, you know."

"We'll be fine."

On his fourth or fifth trip to the van—they have almost finished the job—Carter veers off into the kitchen. "Thirsty," he calls to Katherine when she turns from the windows to smile at him through the pass-through. "Keep your eye out for Jersey!"

The fake cheer in his voice disgusts Carter, but that disgust does not prevent his turning on the tap and noisily opening a number of kitchen cupboards, including the one beneath the sink, as he mutters, "Glass, glass, where's a glass? Okay, here's one!" He lets the tap fill one of M.B.'s tumblers while he nestles the unopened bottle of MD 20–20 into the least full of the bags in his charge.

"She come!" Katherine sticks her head in the pass-through just as Carter closes the cupboard. "She com-ing, Car!"

Carter's big heart never ticks the nervous tick of a small heart, but it does beat harder. Boom, it goes. Boom, boom, like a ship banging into a pier. A big tree hitting the ground after a long fall.

Boom, boom, boom.

"Let's go, let's go!" M.B. runs into the hall with a last bag for each of them. "Let's go!"

▪ ▪ ▪

When Jersey comes around the corner of building H, out of the shadow of building I, and into the summer's white light once more, she finds that her mother and Carter Clay and M.B.—still in her bathrobe—stand in the parking lot beside Carter Clay's van.

"Well, hello there!" croaks M.B., and even Katherine smiles, and Carter Clay says, "Hey, Jersey! I was just showing these guys how, last night, I improved that doohickey I made—for your chair? Want to give it a test drive?"

Only politeness, and the eager look in her mother's eyes, makes Jersey agree. M.B., however, cries, "Well, great!" and then, in a burst of emotion that gives the girl a start, bends down to press a kiss onto the top of Jersey's head.

"Hey!" From the balcony, Patsy Glickman whoops, "Hey, what's going on down there? I heard you all tromping up and down the stairs—"

"No!" M.B. whirls around. She flaps her arms. She cries, "I'll be right up, Patsy! Don't—wake the neighbors!" She turns back to the others. "You all get going," she says, and smiles—a little maniacally in Jersey's opinion—before she darts forward to kiss Katherine's cheek and even give a hug to Carter Clay.

"Have fun now," M.B. calls from the stairwell. And then, from a few steps higher, "Drive carefully!" and then, from the landing, "Take care of my girls, Carter!"

The van is damp and smells of pine cleaner. In the seam at the top of the seat in front of Jersey—her mother's seat—is a skinny, still-moist line of foam cleanser. Cloudy streaks reveal where someone—presumably Carter Clay—worked over the dusty dashboard with a rag. Also, Jersey notices—while he fidgets with her wheelchair restraint—Carter Clay not only has stubble on his chin but a pale blond fuzz on his scalp. Apparently he is bald by choice.

"There you go!" He gives her shoulder a little pat before he jumps out to close the cargo door.

Jersey says, "Thanks, Mr. Clay," but is relieved that once they are moving, he inserts a cassette of Bible stories and turns it up so loud that conversation is impossible.

They drive for half an hour, forty-five minutes, an hour. Farther north than Jersey has been since the accident. Because she has no window of her own from which to look out, she fixes her gaze on the windshield. Which proves difficult; she must hold her head tilted to the left, and even then one corner of the back of her mother's seat still blocks her view.

"So, hey." Carter Clay clears his throat. "Jersey, tell me some more about this clinic in Phoenix you want to go to—for your legs."

Always mortified when Carter Clay raises the issue of her inability to walk, Jersey automatically glances at Katherine for help—and finds that Katherine holds in her lap the big black purse that Jersey has not seen her carry since the accident. Katherine is inspecting the contents of her wallet: pictures—Jersey, Joe—and credit cards, driver's license, membership card for the Arizona-Sonora Desert Museum—

"It's supposed to be best for what you got?" Carter Clay says.

"Yeah."

"What do you think, Katherine?" Carter Clay asks.

When Katherine waves a preoccupied hand in the air, Jersey feels annoyed, and says, "*I'd* like to go to Arizona, period."

Carter Clay laughs, and looks in the rearview mirror to catch her eye. "Well, that's good, 'cause that's where we're taking you!"

"What?" Jersey looks out at the flatlands in which they move; which come to her in frames, click and click. Though the interstate highway's green mileage signs have gone silvery in the elements, she can make out Tampa. Coming up. Tampa.

"Mom!" she cries. "Where are we going?"

Smiling, fanning her credit cards like a hand of gin rummy, Katherine says, "Ar-zona! I don'*t* have to go *Fair* Oak *an-y-more*!"

"We're—you have to stop!" Jersey cries. "*Stop! Mom!*" Jersey reaches forward, fingertips grazing Katherine's shoulder. "Tell him!"

Katherine laughs. "M.B. help us pack!" She turns in her seat to point to the heap of plastic bags in the rear of the van. "See?"

Jersey leans as far forward as the restraints allow, and makes an ineffectual grab at the shoulder of Carter Clay's shirt. "Are you going to stop?"

He pats the air in her general direction. "It's okay. Don't upset yourself."

Yes. Because panic is useless. Jersey tries to think. Remember: *Christmas tree*. "Mom? Christmas tree?"

Katherine smiles over her shoulder, and offers in response a question of her own: "Jin-le bells?"

"Exit," Carter Clay announces. "We can use the facilities and talk about what's on our minds."

Katherine holds out a handful of credit cards. "Car-er! Look!"

He shakes his head. "I ain't got any use for them things, Katherine."

Jersey is too smart not to sense some connection between today's trip to Arizona and yesterday's encounter with the man at McDonalds, but the idea of a connection—it is too disturbing for her to confront it directly. Instead, once they have parked beneath the station's service canopy, and Carter Clay has guided her chair down the ramp and onto the cement pad, she murmurs to him, "You tricked me!"

"But you want to go to Arizona!"

The crackle of injury in his voice is only part of what makes Jersey afraid to crane her neck and look up at Carter Clay directly as he begins to push her chair toward the rest rooms. Still, she forces herself to speak. "Stop pushing me! And I want to call M.B.!"

Carter Clay removes his hands from the back of the chair but he steps around in front of it to speak to her, his voice low. "What your mom said is true, though, Jersey. M.B. did help us pack. She said we should make the trip a surprise."

While Jersey tries to absorb and understand the significance of what Carter Clay says—without crying over the betrayal—Katherine nods and smiles, and calls out, "Surprise! Surprise!"

"And you thought this was a good idea?" Jersey asks Carter Clay.

He rubs his palm over the fuzz on top of his head. "I wasn't so sure about the surprise part, myself. But I knew your mom wanted to go to Arizona and that you did, too."

"Did M.B. hire you?"

"No! I want to help, Jersey. I'm your friend."

"Take us to an airport, then," she says. "If M.B. wants to go this route, just put us on a plane and we'll fly to Arizona."

"You'll need help in Seca. I'm going to help you."

"Mom," Jersey cries, and reaches out a blind hand to grab at Katherine's shoulder.

"Go on, Katherine," Carter Clay says. "Take her hand, there. She's feeling bad."

Katherine obeys Carter Clay's command, but she sighs as she does so. She rolls her eyes a little, too—a gesture she picked up from her mother long ago, but one in which she has not indulged for almost a year.

Part Three

25

The leisurely trip made by Jersey and her parents recoils on itself with the snap of a New Year's Eve noisemaker. This time, there will be no visit to the Florida Museum of Natural History where, with the museum's permission, Jersey could open and close charming wooden drawers filled with shell samples and bird specimens (American kestrel, purple gallinule, kingrail, each one with its eyeholes stuffed with a bright blind dot of cotton wadding). There will be no detour to the Devil's Millhopper; or to Gadsden County, where the family ate a picnic lunch at the Lake Seminole Overlook and, at the base of a small bluff, Jersey discovered—all on her own—several nice chunks of fossiliferous clay (steinkerns, endocasts, permineralized bits of shell) that had recently come unhinged from the bluff's overhang.

The only concession Carter Clay makes to Jersey is the fifteen-minute stop that she has read a paraplegic must make for every hundred miles of travel. "To prevent pressure sores," she explains. "You have to get in a different position. Off your—ischial tuberosities? You know?"

He nods. He does *not* know, but he remembers seeing an old fellow at the hospital with holes in his heels that somebody said were pressure sores. Carter does not want Jersey ending up with something like that, and so they stop every hundred miles, and he lays her down on the garbage bags of clothes, on one side for seven minutes, the other, eight.

It is midnight when they exit for Mobile. He pulls the van into a place called the Big 9 Motel. The office is constructed of a transparent material so flimsy that Carter feels as if he stands inside a plastic corsage box. In and out, the walls heave in the stern breeze that blows off Mobile Bay.

From the front seat of the van, Katherine announces, "I see Car-ter. You see, Jers?"

"Mom?" Jersey tries to sound—just interested in a friendly sort of way. "What do you think of Carter?"

Katherine nods without turning the girl's way. "He taking me to Ar-zona. No more *Fair* Oak-s."

"Is he—your boyfriend?"

Katherine looks back over her shoulder at the girl, then sticks out her tongue, and says, "None your beeswax!"

"You can't love him, Mom! You can't!"

Fingers in her ears, Katherine sings, "Car-er thinks I fine! *You* don-*t* think I fine!"

"Oh, Mom!" Jersey presses her fingers against her closed eyes, bringing up a second star-spangled night. "He'll get himself his own room, won't he?"

Katherine does not answer, but points across the street to the familiar building and signs of a fast food outlet. "Taco Bell. Bea' bur-ri-to. Sixy-nine cens."

In the van once more, Carter Clay says, "So I can be there to help, I got one room, but you two get the bed. That way, we save money, okay?"

Jersey waits for his eyes to turn up in the rearview mirror, but this time they do not, and so she plunges ahead, albeit nervously. "My mom and I can pay for our own room, Mr. Clay. Or we can sleep in the van, and you can have the room."

Carter Clay does not respond to these alternatives until he has driven the van across the lot and parked in front of a unit marked 18. "Katherine"—he is trying to sound amused, Jersey guesses—"you want to sleep in the van?"

"No!"

Carter Clay nods. "If having me in the room's a problem, Jersey, *I'll* sleep in the van."

His voice buzzes with weary irritation. Jersey hears this, but she steels herself against whatever fear and sympathy it arouses, and murmurs, "Okay. Thanks."

▪ ▪ ▪

I feel like pizza. You guys like pizza? Pepperoni pizza?

Carter slams on the brakes just in time to avoid smashing into the teenage couple who lurch out of the late night gloom to cross the motel's driveway. Their headlight-bleached faces snarl his way, and both offer Carter a familiar middle-finger salute.

I could bring a pizza back here. A pizza with everything?

Carter suspects that, somehow, his offer sounded all wrong, like a lie, a cover-up, an escape plan.

Well? Is this a surprise? The relief that swells in Carter's chest as the motel shrinks in his rearview mirror has everything to do with the way in which going out for pizza clears a path to the bottle of MD 20–20 nestled in the rear of the van. The thought of the wine blotting out his worries over Finis Pruitt and Jersey and Katherine—it fills his groin with an anticipation not unlike what he recalls of true love.

He wishes wine were love. That love could let in air and light as well as a drink can.

"Goddamn that R.E.!" he cries. "And Jersey, too!"

Then prays that God will forgive him for swearing. And that God will help him not to be afraid of R.E. Finis Pruitt. *Help me, God, to not drink and to be brave and calm! Please*.

Carter finds Carol's Pizza Pie a familiar sort of place. The ceiling's fluorescent lights unapologetically reveal an indoor-outdoor carpet gone slick with grime, and Carter is well aware that the counter at which he takes a seat would be called a bar if it were set a tad higher from the floor—which helps him to shake his head when the server (a plain girl, heavy thighs testing the limits of her new blue jeans) asks if he wants a beer while he waits for his pizza.

At the other end of the counter sit two women. Both wear some sort of stiff white martial arts uniform and their hair braided and coiled over their ears. Mother and daughter? Big sister and little? The pizza maker himself is visible in the pass-through to the kitchen. A scrawny, unappetizing fellow. The lump of Band-Aid on his forehead scarcely covers the great blue carbuncle beneath.

The road to Hell is paved with good intentions.

Someone has burned this message into a long plank of varnished wood that hangs above the pass-through, and the women in the martial art uniforms laugh over the message, and debate its meaning.

"Here you go."

Carter looks up as the countergirl sets a beer in front of him.

"Hey," the younger martial arts woman calls down the counter, "he *told* you he didn't want a beer, Louise!"

"That's okay." Carter sets his hand around the wasp-waist middle of the beer glass. "It's okay," he says to the server.

"You sure?" She cocks her head to one side, and puts out her hand to suggest that she will take the drink back if he wants.

He lifts the glass and takes a sip. "Sure." He smiles at her but not at the martial arts woman, who shrugs and turns back to her companion.

While he drinks the beer—not really his beer, because he did not order it, and what is *one* lousy beer at a time like this when he would need a case to put himself under—while he drinks the beer, Carter fixes his gaze on the window where the pizza maker spins and tosses a ball of dough into a thin disk.

Now how does a fellow learn to do that?

That's really something, isn't it?

You got to admit, probably not everybody could do that.

Carter practices these lines of appreciation, and smiles, and keeps his eyes on that activity that has nothing whatever to do with the fact that he is drinking the glass of beer, it is almost gone, he wants the next one already.

That's really something, isn't it?

If the martial arts women look his way again, he can nod toward the pizza guy, and say, *That's really something, isn't it?* But the women do not look his way, and, finally, when the countergirl comes by again, he lifts his chin for her and says, "That pizza guy's really something, isn't he?"

She shrugs. "He's my dad. You want another one of those? It'll still be about ten minutes."

Carter knows, even before they do it, that the women at the end of the counter will turn his way and smile and wait to hear his answer, and so he says—though it breaks his heart—"No, thanks. But I guess I'll step out for a smoke while I wait."

What he feels after that one beer: odd, unfamiliar, *better*. He is a dog who has just given a shake to his wet, cold coat.

Though the parking lot of Carol's Pizza Pie is dark—the only light a parallelogram of white coming from the kitchen window—it is easy enough to locate M.B.'s bottle of wine (last row of bags, familiar shape and heft). He does not remove the bottle from the bag, however; he only touches it through the plastic as he prays, *God, please help me not to drink. Please, help me to help Jersey and Katherine, and not be an asshole.*

It is not nice to leave the pizza behind, unpaid for, but he cannot go inside that place again without getting drunk, and so he returns to the Big 9 Motel, and he parks in back, then hurries to the pay telephone at the front of the motel.

"Go dump the bottle, hon," says the lady volunteer who takes his call. "I'll wait."

Carter actually does go so far as to walk back to the van. He stands there for a time looking at the van's rear door. He whistles the first half of "Born on the Bayou," then returns to the dangling telephone receiver.

"Okay. I'm back."

"Good for you, darlin'!" The woman tells him the location of the Welcome the Dawn group, and that she has arranged for one of the local members to meet him for coffee at a nearby restaurant in half an hour. A nice lady. Carter agrees to everything, but, for now, the best he can do is leave the bottle in the back of the van, let himself through the chain-link fence surrounding the motel's tiny pool, lie down in the webbed recliner there, and stare at the stars and pray until he finally falls asleep.

▪ ▪ ▪

The next day, the dark muck of Louisiana exudes a scent that reminds Jersey of the digestive smells of Fair Oaks and the fact that her mother is *not* in Fair Oaks, and this makes Jersey feel a twinge of gratitude to Carter Clay, and she tries to strike up a conversation with him. "So, Mr. Clay, did you ever visit Arizona before?"

Carter Clay is just then concerned about an unfamiliar noise—a sound in the engine? the transmission? the undercarriage? Because of his bum ear, he can never say from which direction a sound comes.

Arizona? He doesn't think so. He's pretty sure he's been to Arkansas, though. Has she ever been to Arkansas?

No.

Is that the end of the conversation? The best either of them can do? Jersey stares out at the tall trees that sit far back from the road, beyond the sloughs. Because of the moss and vines that grow on them, they look dead, rotting, but she knows they are alive.

When she and her parents passed through this region traveling east, Joe lectured Jersey on the marshes' deposits of oil and natural gas. "Pumping history" was the phrase that Joe applied to the slow, menacing dance of the region's oil derricks, and—just to see if it stirs a memory in Katherine—Jersey now says a falsely casual, "So—pumping history, Mom."

Katherine says nothing, but Carter Clay reads aloud the tall black letters painted on the side of a diner up ahead—" 'God is love' "—then adds, "That looks like as good a place to eat as any."

Perhaps it is Jersey's wheelchair that causes people at restaurants and gas stations to smile so much. Perhaps it is Carter Clay, who does not allow his basic shyness to keep him from striking up a conversation: "Look like the high school'll have a good group for football this year?" he asks the diner's owner.

The owner is a friendly fellow himself, with sideburns that are simultaneously so skinny, so furry, they appear fake. In Jersey's past, those sideburns, the restaurant's paintings of country singer

Willie Nelson (in Indian chief headdress, cowboy hat, bandanna), the gumball machine that contains not gum but a bouquet of blue plastic flowers—all of these would have been items to evoke a private smile between Jersey and her parents. ("But let's be nice," Katherine would say if anyone threatened to laugh. "Be nice.")

"Mom"—Jersey closes her eyes as Carter Clay settles her in the van once more—"remember last year how we stopped in Baton Rouge and visited your friend Dave?"

"Dave?"

"He took me to that dinosaur exhibit?"

Katherine does not remember, but she jabs her head between the seats and nods agreeably. Carter Clay nods, too—which is maddening, in Jersey's book—and then, as he finishes locking Jersey's chair in place, he adds, "Pastor Bitner told us how dinosaurs are really just what you hear called Leviathan in the Bible. Just alligators or crocodiles."

"Mom, maybe you'd like to call Dave."

"No," say Katherine and Carter Clay in one alarmed breath. Then they reach out between the seats and squeeze each other's hand. Smile.

"We want to get to Arizona, right?" says Carter Clay, and Katherine nods, "Righ'."

That day and the next, Jersey spends in limply reading from the Turquoise Motel's gold-covered Bible, every now and then stirring herself to ask the pair in the front seat, what do you think of this or that?

"If you're a leper, you have to make a *sin* offering. You're supposed to buy the idea that it's your fault you've got this terrible disease. Anything goes wrong with you, it's your fault, because God is just and if you'd done everything right, you wouldn't be sick—"

"Whoa!" says Carter. "What you're reading, it's a book *God* wrote, Jersey."

"Just let me have one of my own books," she says with a sigh. "Then I'll be quiet, okay?"

"Jersey." After a quick glance at Katherine—now absorbed in a copy of *Josannah!*—Carter says, his voice low, "Without God, Jersey, what'll you do when your dark days come?"

She meets his eyes in the mirror. Each word bitten off, she says, "You think I haven't seen dark days? You think, since my parents—"

"Sorry," he murmurs. "Okay? I'm sorry."

She nods. "Okay." She does not want to fight. Things are bad enough. "Hey, Mr. Clay. That—should the motor sound like that?"

Carter listens, shakes his head. "I don't know. It's old. It sounds that way every now and then."

After staring out the windshield for a few minutes, Jersey says, "I guess you've seen dark days, too."

He nods, yes. "In the war, you see your buddies get killed and all. And my mom—she killed herself while I was over there."

"Oh! That's—I'm sorry. Your *mom*."

■ ■ ■

Will there ever be a better moment for Carter Clay to say, *I'm the one who hit you*? Probably not, but just then the van begins to lurch and lunge and buck, and Katherine starts to cry, and the engine dies, and there is nothing for Carter to do but pull off on the shoulder.

"What hap-pen?" Katherine asks.

Carter glances in the side mirror at the cars and trucks that buffet the van in their passing. Maybe God did not want him to confess just then? Is that the message? Or is he *supposed* to confess now, when the car cannot move and he cannot be distracted by driving?

"Mom, you should have one of those AAA cards," Jersey says. "Let me see your wallet."

"I look!" Katherine says.

And Carter: "We'll just sit tight and see if it don't start up again."

During last year's trip to Florida, Katherine explained to Jersey that the pronghorn antelope that feed on the hills along the interstate have keen vision; and big windpipes and big lungs so they can take in great quantities of oxygen. That their blood is rich with hemoglobin and their body mass contains proportionately more muscle cells than that of the average mammal; and that these muscle cells are particularly rich in the mitochondria that help them to use all that oxygen more efficiently. "In effect," Katherine said, "pronghorns are running machines, built to escape predators in a land with minimal cover."

Now, however, Katherine knows only what she sees, and so she looks at the dark-eyed creatures that browse on the hills and says, "Pretty."

"Mom? Remember this?" Jersey takes her journal from the side pocket of her chair and, leaning forward so Katherine can see, holds the journal open to a cartoon she drew on the trip to Florida: Nighttime. A groggy man in hunter's garb climbs from his car while a bemused woman in a bathrobe—presumably the man's wife—stands in the front door of her house and peers out at the sign strapped to her husband's crumpled bumper: DEER CROSSING.

"I drew it last August. When we were driving to M.B.'s, remember? We kept seeing Deer Crossing signs?"

The August before, Katherine laughed and laughed over the cartoon. Now, the way she merely stares out the window of the broken-down van makes Jersey want to cry.

Carter Clay, however, leans sideways to stare at the cartoon in Katherine's lap. Carter wonders: Should he say something about the girl's little drawing? Or does she want him to pretend he is not there at all? Sometimes he gets tired of trying to figure out how to respond. "I guess the guy knocked over the sign, right?" he says. "I did that once. Not a deer sign, but one like that, a big yellow sign. I think it was for a crosswalk or something."

"It's supposed to be—funny," Jersey says. "Like, instead of bringing home a real deer, the hunter's come home with a sign showing a *picture* of a deer. The sign's message is, like, 'Watch out 'cause there's so many deer!' but, see, the hunter didn't get any deer when he was hunting. What he got was the *sign*—and now he's got the sign strapped on the front of the car. Like it's a real deer. See?"

"Yeah, sure." Carter turns to smile over his shoulder at the girl. Okay. Relax. Say a prayer. So they're broken down on the interstate. They've put quite a few miles between themselves and Florida, haven't they? The girl's been talking to him. Katherine seems all right.

Still, being stuck on the side of the interstate—it makes Carter feel like a criminal, and when an eastbound highway patrol car slows, and turns around in the grassy median—bump, bump—he has to grip the steering wheel to keep himself from leaping out of the van on the run.

Jersey, on the other hand, views the patrol and all police officers as public servants. Jersey says, "Thank goodness! He can call AAA for us right from his car."

She is correct. The officer—a nice young man—assures them that they will not have to wait more than fifteen minutes for a tow; then he climbs back into his car, bumps across the median again, and resumes his eastern path.

Carter looks at Katherine's AAA card. "It expires day after tomorrow. Just as well, too. I don't like cards. A person can follow you with them. A person can find out where you been and what you bought, all kinds of private stuff."

Katherine turns toward him, her eyes open wide, staring. "I know! A man ha' a gun!" she cries. "Remem-er? A man with a gun!"

Carter stiffens but Jersey begins to smile and nod. "You mean the man who got mad at Dad at the rock shop, Mom? You're right, it was around here. The owner guy took out a gun, and he told Dad, 'I shot people for better offers than that!' That's what you're talking about, right?"

Katherine stares at Carter. "You were there," she says, then frowns and looks confused before she turns to stare out the window again.

But Jersey laughs with delight. She has often thought that if she could see, strung together and sped up, the days since her mother came out of the coma, *then* surely she would notice improvements that are hard to spot because they are gradual—and doesn't this new memory of her mother's testify to her improvement?

"Mom, remember how that guy had his rock shop set up in a kind of machine shed thing? And he had that weird little toy running around on the floor? It looked like a squirrel chasing its own tail?"

When Katherine does not respond, Carter Clay murmurs, "You don't want to pressure her. Maybe she don't remember all that."

"I don't know." Jersey leans forward to rub a corner of Katherine's shoulder. "I don't know, but she remembers I was there, and the guy with the gun. That's pretty good. That's a start."

26

"I guess we don't need to call in an expert for me to know you've got heap big guano between your ears!"

So Patsy Glickman told M.B. on the morning of Jersey and Katherine and Carter's departure for Arizona. Patsy had the advantage; M.B. was still in her bathrobe while Patsy was dressed for the day (turquoise knit under the influence of a vaguely Native American bosom fringe that bounced and swayed as Patsy stomped into her kitchen to fetch coffee).

M.B. immediately regretted that she had settled herself in Patsy's *mamasan* chair, a pillowy affair out of which she always had to fight her way. "Is this why I'm here?" she called after Patsy. "To listen to insults?"

"What do you even know about this guy, Marybelle?"

When Patsy had first learned M.B.'s true name, she had used it, now and then, in a teasing way, pretending to be a kind of mother figure. Lately, however, Patsy had begun to employ Marybelle exclusively, and this grated on M.B.'s nerves.

"Here." Patsy handed M.B. a cup of coffee. M.B. offered Patsy the terse smile she had refined many years ago on customers hoping to return used cosmetics. "Patsy." M.B. held up her fingers to enumerate: "Carter goes to my same church. I know that his mom's dead. His dad and sister live around Port"— M.B. waved in what she thought of as a northwesterly direction but actually indicated the Caribbean—"something. I can't think just now, but it's up there in Washington. His dad worked in the paper mill there and they like Carter at Fair Oaks and he served in Vietnam."

Patsy bugged her eyes at M.B., then kicked off her shoes and plopped down in the *papasan* chair.

Animal, M.B. thought as she stared at the yellowed calluses on Patsy's feet. She blamed Jersey for the thought. It was Jersey who was always lumping humans in with the rest. Just the way Kitty used to. *Bird nostrils*. Just the week before, Jersey and M.B. had gone to a mall not far from Palm Gate Village, and when they stopped in a pet store, Jersey insisted that the nostrils of certain birds were red because they had *colds*. Bird nostrils. And once you saw them, you could never unsee them. Birds had ears, too. Jersey had shown M.B. Pitiful little holes, right under the feathers.

"M.B.," said Patsy, "what if Kitty gets better eventually and here you've married her off to a janitor?"

"There's nothing wrong with being a janitor." M.B. pulled her Salems from her robe pocket and lit up. "Anyway, Carter isn't a janitor. He's an aide. And he's done other things too. In case you've forgotten, my husband was a factory worker! Unless that's not good enough for you."

Patsy reached into the drawer of the end table where, until recently, she had kept her own Kool Lites. She took out a stick of gum and unwrapped it and folded it into her mouth and began to chew very hard, very seriously. M.B. waited. She almost had a sense that Patsy's next words depended on something Patsy was extracting from the gum, but when Patsy finally spoke, all she said was, "Don't be dumb, M.B."

At which M.B. gathered up her bathrobe as if it featured a train and, feeling both queenly and grossly underdressed, headed for the door.

Back in #335, she immediately set to work. There were certain things to do to restore the condo to its pre-accident condition. She removed all bedding and towels and curtains from the guest bathroom and bedroom and began running bleach-heavy loads in the washing machine. Emptied the cupboards, drawers, and closets of both rooms for thorough cleaning. Sprayed down the walls with Lysol, which left streaks on the paint in the bedroom but M.B hardly cared. She doused the bathroom floor with bleach and set to work on the grout with toothbrush and Q-tips—missing the fact, until it was too late, that a bit of bleach had seeped into the blue hall carpet, making a little pile of white clouds along the tile's horizon. No matter. No matter. Though she had done her best to see that every possible item belonging to Katherine and Jersey went into the bags loaded into the van, as she cleaned M.B. kept an eye out for strays: two ponytail holders, a sock that read Southern Arizona Swim Club around its cuff, and a few colored pencils—all of which she dropped immediately into the trash.

The records of Jackie Gleason and his orchestra had been Lorne and M.B.'s favorites—"For Lovers Only"—and she listened to them as she worked. "Dancing in the Dark," "I Only Have Eyes for You," "I'm in the Mood for Love."

Lorne, she knew, would have approved of the way she put the clean laundry right into the linen closet. For now, however, she had to store the freshly washed bedspreads and curtains and shower curtain on her bed. Until she felt the guest room and bath were solely hers once more. *Uncontaminated* was the word that occurred to her, but only in the most private folds of her brain. In that private part of her brain, she wished she could zap the entire unit in a microwave oven; she had read in the newspaper that this was an excellent way to kill germs and bugs in precious documents and books.

It was three in the morning by the time she decided she was done. She went to put on her nightgown; then remembered she had yet to remove the safety rails in the guest bathroom.

Not an easy job. The bolts were in there good, and the holes left behind by her impatient removal were worse than the holes made for the installation, but at least it was done.

She moved the table in the hall back where it had been before there was the maneuvering of a wheelchair to consider.

When, finally, M.B. did set her head down on the pillow, she smiled. But after all that cleaning, shouldn't she remove the old air-conditioning filter and install a new one? Yes. She got out of bed. Then had to rise a second time because it seemed #335 might become recontaminated immediately if she did not carry the old filter down to the dumpster.

Was that enough?

No. Let's face it, it was not, and so she rose—now with less enthusiasm—and emptied the kitchen drawer that held her dish towels, and she set the towels in the washing machine. The next drawer held her spice tins and she removed and wiped down each tin with a solution of Spic and Span and water.

At 8 A.M.—she checked the time when she heard a neighbor go out to change his Today's Date calendar—M.B. thought that she really might need to drink a glass of wine in order to fall asleep. She was opening the dishwasher for a glass when the telephone rang.

A man. Asking for Katherine.

"Oh." M.B. pulled the telephone cord behind her as she opened the cupboard under the sink, stuck out a toe to search for the bottle of MD 20–20. "She—Katherine's gone back to Seca. Moved—home."

"Ah! Would you happen to have her number there?"

M.B. knew it was acceptable to ask for a caller's name; still, she was grateful that the man did not seem to take offense at the question, and while she unscrewed the lid on the wine bottle, she said in her most bright and friendly voice, "Let me just grab my address book, Mr.—was it Arnott?"

"Toby Arnott—*Toby*!"

M.B. hurriedly poured herself a glass of wine while flipping through the address book pages, and when she returned, she said, "Was it the address you wanted, or the phone—"

The caller laughed lightly, then said, "I suppose both would be helpful, wouldn't they?"

27

In the mornings, now, the front hall of the Alitz/Milhause residence (glass brick, white walls, red concrete floor) appears brighter than during its past life. This is because a pale layer of desert dust covers the floor. Dust, in fact, now coats the entire home and all of its objects. Beneath the hall table upon which the family members formerly dropped keys and mail, the husks of a number of dead Indian crickets are almost immured in dust, their features delicately veiled.

M.B. has been fooled. Ruby Hinkey, the woman located by the family lawyer, and paid to keep the house "up," has not been inside for seven months. Does it make sense to clean an uninhabited house? Ruby Hinkey asked herself this question, and the answer she came up with was *no way*. However, Miss Hinkey does recognize her unearned monthly checks as gravy, and uses them entirely on slots at the Desert Diamond Casino.

The home is a brick ranch built in the late forties on what was once the edge of Seca. It is the only house that Jersey has ever lived in, apart from stays in summer rentals and her time at M.B.'s condo; still, that first morning that she awakens in her Seca bedroom—the ringing of the telephone serves as an alarm—she does not know where she is, and so feels defenseless against the now unfamiliar positioning of walls, and the location of the windows' squares of bright morning light. To complicate matters, she has been put in the wrong bed. Her proper bed is the twin closest to the windows, not to the mural of *Archaeopteryx*. It is, however, the glossy mural that finally informs her: home.

Home. The mere idea of it makes the girl almost swoon with pleasure. She can smell it: home. When the telephone stops ringing, it comes to her that someone has turned on the swamp cooler: the pleasant, woody odor of wet excelsior fills the air. As soon as possible, she will go out to the back patio where, even before she was born, the roots of trees were shoving up the bricks. The Crocodiles, she called those ridges upon which she had so often stubbed her toes. She will rub the leaves of the Diller orange between her fingers, release their scent—

So Carter and her mother put her in bed? From the looks of the other twin, her mother slept in this room as well.

Did Carter Clay sleep in the bed of her parents, then?

"Mom?" she calls. The wheelchair is propped against the wall, all the way across the room. "Mom? You need to bring me my chair!"

Six Easy Pieces reads the title of the library book on her bed stand. Katherine had checked that book out for Jersey. They were going to try to read it together. AUGUST 17 reads the crooked due date stamped on the cover. Almost a full year overdue.

"M-om?" She does not like the fakery of calling her mother for help when, in fact, she is calling Carter Clay. She can, however, justify it as a means of maintaining distance from Clay; she is not so sure, however, that she can bear the self-deception that occurs each time loyalty and optimism lead her to call Katherine "Mom."

"My chair's across the room, Mom!"

Could they be outside? Odd to find herself hoping that Carter Clay is about.

"Mom! I need to go to the bathroom!"

She eyes the floor. Oxblood concrete. True southwestern style. "MOM!" In a fury, trying not to cry, she tugs the top sheet and spread from the mattress in order to make a kind of landing pad of them and her pillow. But how do you do this?

Her first plan—hold onto the headboard, let her legs slide over the edge of the bed—is a fiasco that leaves her sweating and quaking as she looks over the side of the mattress to the floor. The main problem, she understands, is controlling the speed at which the dead part of herself reaches the floor.

So: head and arms first?

Not bad. But her legs—they follow with a dull slam that she knows was a terrible mistake.

"Ass!" she calls herself. "Jerk! Stupid."

You were supposed to wet the bed before you did something that dumb.

"Mom!" She does not stop to examine herself for possible damage, but, crying, begins to drag herself across the floor toward her chair.

She is almost there when she hears the front door open, the familiar whistling ("Born to Be Wild") of Carter Clay.

■ ■ ■

It is Carter who arrives at the bedroom first. "What happened here?" He hurries to unfold the chair and helps the girl into it. "Are you okay, Jersey?"

"I didn't have my chair!" Used to navigating the rehab center, the retirement condo, stores that cater to a wheelchair-using population, she struggles now to move through the bedroom's narrow doorway and into the hall. "Damn it!"

Behind her, Carter tries hard to guide the chair through the door. "What do you want me to do, Jersey?"

"Get me to the bathroom!"

Carter lifts the girl in his arms, and hurries her down the hall. Just now, please, he wishes Katherine would be quiet, but she follows, saying, "We wen' to get wed-ding license, an, bu' they say you can marry now, if you wan', and we di-*d*!"

"You can't have!" Jersey shrieks, and then, "Oh, hurry!"

"Pant like a dog!" Carter says.

"Oh, damn!"

He flinches as the heat of her urine flashes into his shirt front, then, quick, he recovers and says, "Hey, it's okay."

"Just—put me in the tub!" she yelps.

Holding all three of them plus their reflections on the mirrored wall, the bathroom feels crowded, and Carter makes several false starts before he gets the girl properly situated, her back against the slope.

She grimaces up at the two of them. "God," she says, and begins to weep hard.

He feels like a monster. He pleads, "What do you want us to do next, Jersey?"

For a moment, it seems she is going to laugh, but then she stiffens and says, "Get me clean clothes. My mom can help."

It is wrong to listen outside the bathroom door, but he cannot stop himself, and worse than any bitterness he might have guessed at is the *sorrow* he hears in Jersey's voice when she asks, "How could you possibly have married him, Mom?"

"Car-er loves me."

"Mom, you don't even know him! You don't have to go through with this, believe me. It was a mistake—"

"Car-ter brough' us home! You and me. I don't haffa be at Fair Oak, Jers'! Tha's no mis-take!"

▪ ▪ ▪

Think of marrying Katherine as, like, being a monk. So Carter told himself as he and Katherine drove to the license bureau.

Seca's dry yards, absence of grass, the ring of mountains blanched by heat and dust—they made him nervous. *This is the day the Lord hath made, let us rejoice and be glad in it.* He shook at the wedding—the old-timer performing the service noticed and kidded Carter—but Carter is still shaking, even after he has changed his shirt and cleaned up in the smaller bath off the bedroom that held the bed that was clearly that of the parents.

The bed of the man he killed.

Is there any way to tell the girl that though he and her mom are now married, they will not be having sex? *Just in case you worry about that. It's not that kind of marriage, see? It's more a friendship kind of marriage.*

Smelling of some sort of perfumed soap from the parents' bathroom, he makes his way to the kitchen to wait for mother and daughter. He hoped the kitchen might be book-bare—every nook and cranny of the house is filled with books—but it turns out that the kitchen, too, features bookshelves that run above and alongside the cupboards, and even those bookshelves hold extra books fitted into horizontal spaces, like mortar.

Through a window he can see the back patio: ancient swimming pool, wilted hedge of oleanders, rim of uninviting mountains. That the house is *not* the mini-resort that some part of him secretly expected is a relief. There should not, after all, be hidden worldly rewards in the deal.

The jiggles and whispers of the girl's wheelchair tell him that she heads his way, and so he makes his voice happy and calls out, "Guess I better pick up some stuff at the store. Any requests, Jersey?"

She stops in the doorway, then backs up to try to align the chair with the frame.

"Let me help."

"*No.*" Her eyes flash before she looks down and adds a more reserved, "Thank you."

"Just—I'm sorry, again, about this morning."

When she shakes her head, he continues, as calmly as possible, "I know you don't understand me and your mom getting married, but, believe me, being with you and your mom—"

"And here she is now," Jersey says.

Jangling a ring of keys, Katherine comes to stand behind Jersey in the blocked doorway. "Es-cuse me!" she cries. She peers over her daughter as if over a cliff, then roughly pushes the wheelchair through the door.

In her hands, Katherine holds, besides the key ring, her black purse and a dusty briefcase. Over the dress she wore to the license bureau, she has donned an old barn coat that Jersey recognizes as Joe's. Katherine's shoes are a pair of gold spike heels that formed a part of her getup for the costume party that she attended in the role of rhythm and blues singer Tina Turner.

"I rea-y to go to work," she says.

"Won't you be hot in that jacket, though?" Carter asks.

Katherine ignores him, and Jersey—Jersey wheels herself over to the bulletin board that hangs on the door to a closet. She consults a card there, then dials out on the kitchen telephone.

Carter does not hear the message Jersey hears on her Uncle Sam's answering machine—

> You have reached the home of Sam Alitz. We are currently referring to ourselves in the "royal we" due to our starring role in *Dick the Three*—

but he does hear the message that she leaves and its tone of emergency:

> Uncle Sam, this is Jersey. Your niece. I'm in Seca with my mom and—she just got married. Please call.

▪ ▪ ▪

Though you might not know it to look at Jersey as she and Carter and Katherine drive in the van to the Earth Sciences building, there is some joy in her heart. Just to be in Arizona again! To smell the baked dirt and know that the thunderheads along the Santa Ritas mean the chance of a rain. She can almost summon up the smell of rain in the Sonoran Desert, a smell as fine as the smell of the sea: wet creosote bush and something magical that the rain releases from the dirt.

Surely her mother can get an annulment. A friend of her mother's got an annulment once. The friend was a Catholic, but there must be something like that for non-Catholics. There has to be a protection for people like her mother.

People like her mother. She feels guilty for thinking of her mother in these terms, but also knows that her mother—the mother who raised her—would be proud of her for watching out for this other.

▪ ▪ ▪

The Earth Sciences building has led many lives. Its old floors are a gray, glossy granite whose pattern resembles that on the back of the small lizards that dart in and out of the cat's-claw vines clinging to the building's base. The hallway that leads to the professors' offices is dim even at noon, its only source of illumination the whey-colored light that passes through the fish-scale glass of the office doors; and this sense of constant overcast, plus an abundance of dark wood trim, gives the place that air of befuddled innocence so often produced by old age.

Without explaining herself, Katherine takes a seat on a worn swivel chair that someone has left in the hall outside the glass door to her old office, and, there, she begins to work at her bit of fuzz.

As there is no one to whom she can put the question but Carter Clay, it is Carter Clay whom Jersey asks, "So, what now?"

He chews on a nail. "We'll see," he says.

"Hu-uh!" Every now and then, Katherine makes some odd little noise, and casts an angry, sideways glance toward the door of E 186. Looks at Jersey—one eyebrow lifted combatively. At Carter. Then back toward the door. This time, however, an anonymous gray shape behind the milky glass suddenly looms upward, like a breaching whale, and all three in the hall simultaneously draw sharp breaths: hhh!

"Mom," Jersey says, when she has regained her composure, "why don't you show Mr. Clay and me the fossil collection?"

Eyes still on that ghostly shape behind the door, Katherine stands, nods, then asks, "Where we go?"

Jersey leads the way down the hall. Takes the key ring from Katherine's briefcase. "The last two digits on the key are seventy," she says, holding the ring out to Katherine. "That's the year you graduated from high school."

Katherine nods, then turns away with a sniff, as if she has smelled something rank but is too polite to say so.

Cabinet after cabinet of varnished blond drawers, and on top of the cabinets, rusty-looking mastodon bones and teeth, scale models of *Ankylosaurus* and *Ichthyosaurus*, and, then, life-size models of the *Archaeopteryx* and *Protoavis* central to Joe and Katherine's debate.

When Katherine wanders over to look at these last, Jersey and Carter Clay follow. "Those are the fossils she studied most," Jersey whispers. "In her book—"

"Excuse me!" booms a voice from the end of the row of cabinets, and Jersey and Katherine and Carter Clay turn.

This fat fellow bedecked in Navajo turquoise is Max Wheeler, Katherine's former boss, a man with skin so sun-damaged that he resembles a ship's hull covered in barnacles and brine. His white hair has an iodine cast.

"Katherine." Wheeler's voice clogs with tears, but the fact that his former colleague now dandles the model of *Protoavis* as if it were a teddy bear makes alarm join the grief that propels him forward to plant a kiss on Katherine's cheek. "How are you, my dear?"

Katherine leans away from the kiss.

"So you're admiring our model!" Adroitly, Wheeler removes the thing from her hands and holds it up as if he too wants to look. "Yes, yes."

The glance he gives Jersey offers commiseration, but she sees he cannot remember her name, and she offers a quiet, "I'm Jersey."

"Of course you are! And how're you doing, Jersey?"

As if she does not hear—she cannot seem to formulate any sort of answer—Jersey busies herself with adjusting her legs.

"Well! We've missed you terribly, Katherine! And Joe—"

"This is Mr. Clay, Dr. Wheeler," Jersey says.

Carter Clay smiles and sticks out his hand to Wheeler. "Me and Katherine met over in Florida. We was members of the same church. Vineyard Christian. I don't know if you have that here. She wanted to come by today. Just for a bit." He takes a deep breath, then announces, "We got married this morning."

"Ah." Max Wheeler moistens his lips. Without quite meaning to—well, he cannot help it—he glances at Katherine's briefcase, and the enormous pockets of the barn coat she wears. "So, what—have you got some work there, Katherine? Were you thinking about going to your office? Because, actually, I think someone's in there. This summer. Since we hadn't heard you were coming—"

Carter Clay interrupts Wheeler's hemming and hawing with a contemptuous nicker. "We didn't cop any of your fossils, if that's what you think. We just stopped by to look around before we go out for ice cream, right, girls?"

Jersey and Katherine nod as one.

Wheeler protests, "Well, for goodness sakes!" and then Carter Clay adds a gentler though still gruff, "If you want, you can come, too."

"Oh." Carefully, the now florid Wheeler returns the model of *Protoavis* to the top of the case. "Well, thank you—Carter? is that right?—but I'm going to stay here a bit. I'll—lock up after you all. There *are* valuable things here. We have to be careful."

Once the threesome is in the hall again and out of Wheeler's earshot, Carter Clay laughs. "Him and his old bones! Valuable things! That man wouldn't know a valuable thing if it stood up and bit him!"

When Katherine laughs at this, both hands covering her teeth, Jersey feels a terrible ache that she, too, cannot join in their fun.

Distressing was the mild word her father used for moments that left him reeling in pained confusion: *distressing*. The loss of a grant meant to support three years' work. The death of his mother. A friend's suicide. *Distressing*.

In the year that Katherine has been away from the university, the grounds crews have torn out the patch of lawn that formerly led to Earth Sciences' back entrance and, in its stead, inserted water-conserving desert plants: tiny-leaved paloverdes, which manufacture the bulk of their chlorophyll in their green trunks; ocotillos, which leaf out only after a rain; acacias; mesquites.

"Mom," says Jersey, and points hopefully to the silver-haired man preaching in a circle of hecklers at the edge of the new desert plantings. "St. Tom."

Katherine looks, but she now appears gloomy and gives no indication of remembering the campus preacher at all.

"Who's St. Tom?" Carter Clay asks.

"He's—like, mentally ill," Jersey whispers.

The sun sits high in the blond sky, and its hot palm irons the tops of the heads of Carter, Katherine, and Jersey as they stand on the back steps of Earth Sciences and listen to St. Tom.

"There was only one in the land who could baptize Jesus, and that was John the Baptist. There is only one to baptize you now. You must be born again. You must be baptized in water to be clean."

St. Tom shakes his head, then takes a sip from a giant plastic cup that reads 64 OZ. BIG GULP. He wears a robe that appears faintly liturgical but is, in fact, the commencement gown for Arizona University's school of architecture. "Where are the United Methodists?" he asks the crowd gathered around him. "There are ten million United Methodists! Why do you find not even one Methodist who will come out to bear testimony of Jesus? Because the Methodists are cowards!"

Carter Clay starts down the stairs, but Katherine does not follow. Jersey stays beside her, watching for a sign that Katherine may remember something of St. Tom.

"Hey, Tom!" A boy in fashionably baggy shorts and backward baseball cap darts into the circle. He zooms close, bringing his face within inches of the face of St. Tom. Zoom. Moves back. Zoom. Moves in.

"Creep," says Jersey—loud enough that a laughing boy at the base of the steps turns to give her a fiery look—quickly extinguished by the fact of her wheelchair.

"Look at you." Slowly, ruefully, St. Tom wags his head from side to side. "Your body—your body is a whorehouse. You could not stop sinning for twenty-four hours if your lives depended upon it!"

From his bicycle, a passing boy calls, "Super good, Tom!" while, to the delight of the ring of hecklers, the boy in the baseball cap darts forward and sets his cap upon the preacher's head.

"Who is Jesus?" With a stroke of his hand, St. Tom brushes the boy's cap onto the ground. "Who is Jesus? He is Allah! He is the God of Abraham. He is the God of Reuben. He is the God of Moses. He is the God of Queen Esther. He is the God who allows man to fall. He is your God. He is your God"—his voice goes low, then catches in just such a way that, for a moment, Jersey feels some divinity in the man assert itself, clutch her heart—"and unless you become a fool for him, you cannot know your God."

Jersey turns to Katherine. "You remember him, Mom?"

In response, Katherine points back to the circle that surrounds the man. "Look," she says. "There's Car-er."

What makes Carter Clay so intimidating as he joins the circle is not his size but his appearance of having nothing to lose—and of not belonging to that world at all. He looks utterly exhausted, his shoulders hunched, yet even Jersey feels frightened when he walks up behind the taunting college boy. Taps the boy's shoulder as if about to ask him for the next dance.

. . .

"Di' I know them?" Katherine asks as they make their way to the ice cream parlor.

Jersey shakes her head. She still feels shaky from the scene with St. Tom, though mercifully, nothing happened really. The college boy bowed and backed his way out of the ring, laughing while he said, "Hey, he's all yours, mister! You two look like you're made for each other, anyway!"

A bright splash of silver light makes her turn, and who is it but herself, wheeling past the glass doors of the university planetarium? Herself in her wheelchair, accompanied by Carter Clay and Katherine.

Jersey and her parents used to visit the planetarium. Climb the stairs on the side of the building so that they might look at the sky through the big telescopes there. Afterward they would walk to the same ice cream parlor that she and Katherine and Carter Clay enter now.

"What'll it be, Jersey?" Carter Clay asks.

"Nothing for me, thanks." She looks over at her poor mom, stunned by variety. "You've always liked Pralines and Cream, Mom."

In a voice surprisingly sharp, Carter says, "Let her pick for herself!"

"Just trying to be helpful," Jersey murmurs, then looks away, embarrassed before the counterboy. Does he remember her? Probably not. If you remember other people much more often than you seem to be remembered, does this mean you have a better memory than most or that you are simply unmemorable? Now, if she resumes coming to the ice cream parlor, will she be memorable? A girl with long blond hair in a wheelchair?

Peppermint is the flavor that Katherine selects with a point of the finger. "Pink."

"She won't like it," Jersey says, but her voice comes out small. She does not suppose anyone has heard what she said, or cared that she said it, and all that she can think to do is roll back to the store's entry to stare out.

A pay telephone sits on a post just in front of the ice cream shop. She could wheel herself out there. Telephone Erin Acuff. *Erin, it's Jersey! I'm home!* Erin—and other people, too—they would have to let her come to see them.

At her back, quite near, Carter Clay murmurs, "She seems to like the peppermint okay."

She turns, and he jerks a thumb toward the rear of the parlor, indicating Katherine, who is now seated at a little table.

"Mr. Clay." Jersey shakes her head, dull with misery. "I know you're trying to help us, but—what if we met you, and *you'd* been totally changed because of something that happened to you—"

He breaks in, grabbing for her hand. "That's the way it was for me, Jersey! Just before you got to know me, I become a Christian. I was real different before that."

"But what I mean is, you don't know anything about our past, and—well, wouldn't you like us to have some respect for your past?"

"Oh, no!" Solemnly, he goes down on one knee. "The past is gone!" He bows his head. "That's the good news. I have a new life. You can have that, too, Jersey."

Jersey sits absolutely still in her wheelchair. "Yes, well, I do have a new life, but I have an old life, too. That's what you don't understand. I love my old life. Now"—she nods toward the pay telephone—"excuse me, I'm going to call somebody."

"Wait." Carter Clay stands. He seems embarrassed when he realizes that he has used the arms of Jersey's chair for a support while bringing himself to his feet, and the girl wants to reassure him, no harm done, but then he asks, "So, who you going to call,

Jersey?" and the idea that he feels free to ask such a question sets off all kinds of alarms in her head. Worse, her good manners tell her to answer him, and it is only with great effort—the energy required to stop herself seems to leave behind an odor of smoke—it is only with great effort that she is able to say, "Well, that's personal, Mr. Clay."

28

Periodically, a man and a little girl on a tricycle pass by the Alitz/Milhause house. The man is smoking cigarettes and reading a magazine as he accompanies the girl up the street and down. Jersey, in the dining room, looking out, does not recognize the man and his daughter. She guesses from its size and the ratio of print to photos that his magazine is something like *Time* or *Newsweek*. On some of his passes, the man stops to answer a question from Mr. Sheets, who lives across the street from the Alitz/Milhause house, and just now drags his garden hose from one watering basin to another.

Carter Clay is in the kitchen. Jersey can hear him putting the dinner things back in the cupboards.

In the living room, Katherine watches a TV infomercial for an electric sandwich maker. The woman in the ad turns a lazy Susan that bears cartons of various fillings (tuna, sweetened pie cherries, deviled ham) and demonstrates the different snack items she can produce by spreading the filling between two slices of bread and toasting the results in her machine. Katherine nods and smiles and moves her hands in the air as if she too brushes the surfaces of the sandwich machine with melted margarine.

Just a short while ago, however, Katherine was crying.

When they arrived home from the trip to the university—while Carter Clay set up the ramp so that Jersey could leave the van—who should come across the street to say hello but Mr. Sheets?

"Katherine!" Mr. Sheets called. "How are you?"

Well, Katherine wanted nothing to do with Mr. Sheets, and made a point of telling him to go away, even knelt down to pick up a handful of decorative rock with which to ward him off.

Jersey, who knew Jimmy Sheets only as a person with whom her mother shared praise of beautiful sunsets, beautiful days, called out, "She's not up to visitors yet, Mr. Sheets. Sorry."

■ ■ ■

Carter, on the other hand, wanted to talk to the neighbor. To tell him about the wedding. So the neighbors would know that it made sense for Carter to be at the house. Also, it seemed to Carter that if he told the neighbor about the wedding, then he could explain how he meant to take Jersey to the clinic in Phoenix. He wanted to hear himself talk about that to the neighbor, to make it more real. But Jersey and Katherine were escaping up the sidewalk and into the house without him, and Carter worried that he might appear unneeded, and so he called to the neighbor, "We'll talk later, man!" then hurried to catch up to the others.

After dinner—steaks, grilled by Carter on the brick barbecue in the backyard—Carter stayed outside, alone, to poke at the coals for a while. He allowed himself a peek into the part of his brain that screened a jumble of nightmarish possible and past attractions: Katherine lying on Post Road. R.E./Finis Pruitt at the Alitz/Milhause front door, the street behind him blocked with patrol cars. Louie Konigsberg giving Carter the lowdown at the AA meeting. Jersey knowing all, and wishing Carter dead. M.B. giving their whereabouts to Finis Pruitt. Now, while he cleans up the kitchen, Carter works on building up the steam to call M.B. He figures he ought to let her know about him and Katherine, but, more important, he wants to learn if she has heard from Finis Pruitt. If she has not, he means to tell her, "Don't tell folks where Katherine and Jersey have gone"—though he has yet to figure out how he can tell her such a thing without setting off alarms.

Because we're newlyweds and want to enjoy our time together?

"Hey, Jersey." With the kitchen telephone in hand, Carter leans into the dining room. There, the girl sits looking out the front window at the quiet, supper-hour street. "I'm calling your grandma. To tell her about me and Katherine. I'll let you talk, too, okay?"

Jersey makes a face. "Thanks, but I haven't got anything to say to her."

Carter cups his hand over the mouthpiece of the telephone—now ringing through to Florida—and he calls in the direction of the living room, "How about you, Katherine? Want to say hi to your mom?"

When Katherine does not answer, Jersey says, "I think she's watching TV again. And hey, you know it's nine-thirty in Florida, right? Three hours' time difference?"

"I'll hang up if she's—M.B., it's Carter. Carter Clay."

▪ ▪ ▪

Yes, M.B. has been drinking when Carter Clay calls.

And, yes, she was temporarily confused the day that she discovered that her backup bottle of wine was missing; however, she did not give the matter too much thought, as it seemed possible that too much thought might lead to the discovery that she drank even more than she imagined.

Wait: Carter is saying that he and Katherine have gotten married!

Married. Which, of course, was her secret wish. But the news is a blow, all the same. The weight that lifted from her chest when Carter took Katherine and Jersey away in the van—here it comes again.

Still, she says her congratulations. She rambles on about her happiness with Lorne, and her prayers at the hospital for Jersey and Katherine, and, finally, somehow, finds herself talking about the leak in her dishwasher.

While Carter pays a kind of weary attention to all of this, waiting for a chance to say his bit about giving out information to callers, Jersey wheels into the kitchen to whisper a bossy, "What'd she say when you told her?"

"Congratulations," he whispers back.

The girl pivots and leaves the room.

While M.B. babbles on, Carter fingers the objects on the window seat in front of him: not just books, but fossils, a jar of minuscule pine cones, an odd collection of blue glass bottles, a tiny, much-mended plaster of paris handprint bearing the name JOEY ALITZ—

At a click on the telephone line, Carter snaps to attention. "Jersey? Is that you?"

"Yeah." Her voice saturated with tears.

"Hi, kid!" M.B. begins, but Jersey cuts her off.

"Mr. Clay, you know how I thought I didn't have anything to say to her? Well, I thought of something: Traitor. Traitor, traitor, traitor."

After the girl hangs up, Carter apologizes to M.B. Then he mumbles that maybe till they're settled and see how Jersey adjusts to things, maybe M.B. shouldn't tell folks where Jersey and Katherine have gone to, you know?

M.B.—who would like to keep the knowledge of where Jersey and Katherine are a secret from even herself—M.B. considers this a wonderful idea, but, "Oh, Carter! I guess I did tell *one* caller already."

▪ ▪ ▪

The telephone that Jersey used to break in on M.B. and Carter's call was one that sat in her parents' study, and after she has hung up, she finds herself surrounded by her parents' absence, presence. It hurts her to see those things that her father will never come back to: chewed pencils, notes written (a miracle, it seems) in his own hand, cartoons tucked in the border of his blotter. A surprise—a paperback anthology of poetry—lies in the middle drawer of her mother's desk, and Jersey flips through it, and finds, here and there, a discreet pencil mark alongside a line or two. From Wordsworth's "Lines Composed a Few Miles above Tintern

Abbey on Revisiting the Banks of the Wye During a Tour, July 13, 1798":

> . . . Knowing that Nature never did betray
> The heart that loved her . . .

Jersey understands that the black and yellow USED sticker on the book's cover means the margin checks might not be Katherine's, but just then—with the familiar huff of the swamp cooler in the background—the girl feels comforted. At the very least, she is in company with the poets and whoever that reader was who read with a pencil in hand.

■ ■ ■

As he suspected he would, Carter finds Jersey in the cluttered room where he earlier noted the location of another telephone.

"Hey." He drops himself down in a chair so dilapidated that strands of stuffing poke out of its seams. Does he look friendly, casual? He hopes so. Because he has something he wants Jersey to help him clear up.

"Your grandma said a friend of your mom called. She gave him the number here, so whoever it was—maybe he'll call, huh?"

When Jersey looks up, her eyes are red, and Carter feels a surge of woe and worry. "I thought," he says in the gentlest voice he can summon, "you might know who it was. Something, like, Toby Arnott?"

"Toby Arnott?" Jersey thinks for a moment, then gives a weak laugh. "But—it's a joke. You've heard that joke, right?"

Carter pushes a bit of the chair's ancient horsehair back into a rip in the arm. "I don't think so."

"Toby Arnott—Toby?" The girl holds her hands up in the air, as if she waits to catch a ball. "As in *Hamlet*?"

For a moment, Carter is relieved that the ringing of the telephone keeps him from having to pretend to understand the joke, or to ask the girl to explain it; but by the second ring he realizes the much more awkward aspect of his situation: to answer the telephone might be to give away his location to R.E. If R.E.—Finis Pruitt—is also Toby Arnott.

"I bet that's M.B. again," Jersey says. "I'm not answering."

"Well, fine." Carter cannot believe his luck! "Fine, 'cause we can always call her back—"

Abruptly, the phone stops ringing.

"Probably just somebody who realized they'd dialed a wrong number," he says.

"Probably," says Jersey, though she sounds slightly disappointed.

"Car-er!" Katherine calls down the hall. "Car-er!" From the doorway to the study, she smiles the smile of a kid successfully completing a grown-up's job, before she adds, "Fo' you, Car-er."

He hesitates, then—mother and daughter watching—takes up the telephone from the jumbled desk.

"Hello?" he says, but there is only a click, and then the dial tone sounds.

Part Four

29

Once upon a time, during a hike from the floor of the Sonoran Desert into these very same lavender and tan mountains that Carter, Katherine, and Jersey now drive past in such a gassy rush—once upon such a time, right here, Joe Alitz tried to explain fractals to Jersey. A Father's Day hike in the desert. Not long before the fateful trip to Florida. A piece of gneiss lay on the ground, and Joe picked it up and pointed to the mountains of gneiss that rose beyond the desert floor's prickly complications of creosote bush, ocotillo and cholla, opuntia, mesquite, paloverde. Joe held out the rock and exclaimed, "The pattern in the peaks is the same as the pattern in the rock, see? That's called self-similarity, and it's everywhere in nature."

An odd moment for Jersey: when she looked at the rock and the mountains and did *not* see what her father saw. The heavy chunk of gneiss that Joe placed in her hand was striated—dark bands running through a lightly flecked matrix (pale rose, tan, gray)—while the mountains, at least at that moment, appeared a mottled mauve. Still, Jersey believed Joe. That is, she supposed that she *should* see the pattern. She loved Joe. She wanted to please him, and she truly had seen, on other occasions, the phenomenon that he described, and so she nodded. Uh-huh.

Jersey does not think of any of this now, of course; not while Carter Clay whisks her and her mother northward. ("We're going on a camping trip!" Carter Clay announced after last night's phone call, and then he began to add, to the black plastic bags still in the van, every piece of equipment that he could find in the house: tent, Coleman lantern, cookstove, inflatable boat, sleeping bags, even a few bright orange life jackets.)

I will go crazy, Jersey thinks as they drive past fields of irrigated cotton that spark bright green against the desert's glare. *Or die. It must be possible—why not?—to die of misery. It should be possible.*

The pressure of tears behind her eyes causes a wobble in the mesquite trees that border this stretch of interstate. She missed the mesquites while she was in Florida, but they are parched this summer, their feathery leaves—bipinnate, compound—hang limp and gray from dust and lack of rain. The tan clusters of dried seedpods appear so many hands—lopped off, hung out to dry. Pass close enough, and you will hear the bony fingers rattle one against the other.

"Don't be drinking all the time," Carter Clay says with a glance in the rearview mirror. "We don't want to be stopping every few minutes, you know."

Jersey does not bother to point out that she is not drinking at all. She merely stares at Carter Clay's head, shaved to a shine once more.

"Hey"—he ducks to scramble for something under the seat, then comes up, and holds over his shoulder the big road atlas he purchased on their way out of Seca. "Here, Jersey. You be navigator."

She leans forward to take the floppy thing, but whispers, "You can't make me your conspirator, Mr. Clay."

He emits a puff of laughter. "Conspirator!"

■ ■ ■

"I'm not laughing, Mr. Clay." The girl's voice is so cool that Carter must work hard to keep the smile on his face. *Slap you silly*. That was one of his father's phrases, *I'm going to slap you silly*. To remove the phrase from his own head, Carter prays, *Lord, help me know the right thing to do*.

His first mistake—well, he has made so many mistakes he cannot order them, but, sometimes, he does wonder if he should have just confessed to the accident and gone to prison. Finis Pruitt would have had no power then. *Tell! Go ahead!* That's what he could have said to Finis Pruitt. Really, these days Carter has no fear of prison whatsoever. He has thought it through. A bed, food, a place to pray.

If only someone could make him a deal—"Carter, you go to prison, and Jersey and Katherine will never have to know you were the driver"—hell, he would go. Prison would be the easy choice. Prison would mean the end of having to help bear their cross.

But leaving them would not be right. Leaving them would be selfish. So here he is, whistling a little Steve Miller—"Living in the USA"—giving a pat to Katherine's knee. When Katherine smiles, he dips his chin low over the steering wheel and tries to think of himself as a man on vacation with the family; a man appraising fresh scenery. "What do you bet Indians used to live here?" he says. "This looks a lot like places in movies—ha!" Alongside the highway stands a grand saguaro cactus whose upraised arms give it the look of a victim of highway robbery, and Carter points a finger at the thing and calls, "Stick 'em up, pardner!"

Neither of his passengers laughs, which makes Carter feel a little stung, but not long after, Katherine begins to sing a song about a peanut butter and jelly sandwich, and he supposes this may be the result of *his* putting everyone in a vacation mood.

Peanut, peanut butter, jelly! Katherine sings. Jersey joins in—albeit halfheartedly—and, once he understands how the song works, Carter sings along, too. Isn't that good? Isn't that the sort of thing Pastor Bitner would say that a father ought to do? Maybe he could start another song when this one ends? "Bingo"? The one where, as you spelled out the name of the farmer's black dog, with each verse you continued to substitute more and more claps for the letters in the name. But maybe that wasn't a safe song for a driver to lead—

WIDE LOAD reads the yellow banner lashed to the front of a truck now passing in the opposite direction. Its cargo: one half of a gray-shingled prefab house. Though the interior is a blur behind heaving sheets of protective plastic, for Carter it conjures up a poster from the hall of his grade school: a cross section view of an enviably happy home whose inhabitants were shown enjoying the benefits of electricity (kids watching TV in the den, Mom removing a turkey from the oven, Dad using power tools in the basement).

Jersey closes her eyes against the half-a-house and her sense that the shuddering sheets of plastic conceal a brood of big-headed hatchlings, dinosaur babies, aliens.

There is no one of whom she can ask: Is this what it feels like to go crazy? The landscape along the interstate does not appear different than she remembers it. She knows that the straight rows of pecan trees on her right always appear to open like a fan as you pass them by. Still, today they are freshly dizzying, and she thinks, *I will be devoured. Drowned. Undergo some dread metamorphosis, change from human to—*

What comes to mind is something mangy, moss-damp with its own dread secretions. Irrational, she knows, but her life *is* making sly changes, like the shell that looks like itself while, in fact, it becomes permineralized, a fossil—over time, every bit of its original material replaced.

She reaches forward and sets her hand on her mother's shoulder, just to make her turn and smile.

"Hi, Jers," Katherine says. Which makes Carter Clay turn and smile at Katherine, and pat her knee once more. Jersey cannot help liking him for that: for being kind to her mother.

"Hey! We just passed a historical marker," Carter Clay says. "Casa Alma. Read your mother and me about Casa Alma, Jersey."

The girl inspects the paperback guide that Carter Clay passes back to her. JOE ALITZ written on the inside cover. PLEASE RETURN IF FOUND. A knife into her heart.

"'Four-story mud structure built by the Hohokam in the mid-1300s,'" Jersey reads. "'Abandoned about 1350. Later used as a church by Spanish missionaries. Potsherds and tools found in the area suggest that the spot was a gathering place of native peoples as early as the 1100s.'"

"Le's stop!" Katherine interrupts. "I bore-*d*!"

Carter Clay pats her arm. "We got to cover some ground yet."

"'The name "Hohokam,"'" Jersey reads, "'was not used by the tribe itself, but came later from the Pima Indians. Hohokam, in the Pima language, means "all used up."'" The girl leans forward, against her safety straps, and taps Katherine's shoulder. "See that gas station, Mom? Maybe the Hohokam lived on that spot once, too. Maybe later it was a trading post. Remember telling me how, lots of times, cities get built on top of other cities? Remember Jericho?"

Katherine gives the station a bored glance out her window, but Carter Clay laughs, and he looks for Jersey in the rearview mirror. "Jericho's in the Bible, Jersey! 'Joshua took the battle of Jericho and the walls come a-tumbling down.' Like I told you, it's all there! All the science and history you ever need. Here—" He ducks—the van swerves, someone honks—and this time when he rises he passes a Bible with a gold cover over the seat. "Here."

Jersey sighs but takes the book. "Religions get built a lot like cities, too, right, Mom?"

Katherine glances at Carter Clay. "May-be?"

"Not maybe!" Jersey says. "*You* told me about it, Mom. You said how, when people were writing the end of the Old Testament, a lot of them were interested in some Persian god who was a lot like Jesus, and that was how they got people ready for the New Testament. Like, the Persian god was supposed to have been born of a virgin, and shepherds witnessed his birth." She pauses, then snaps her fingers. "And remember? His followers celebrated December twenty-fifth, and he was put in a rock tomb when he died, and he came back to life three days later."

"Hold on!" Carter Clay has just succeeded in the trembling retrieval of his wallet from his back pants pocket. "Here"—eyes flicking back and forth from the road to an index card, he reads, "'A man that is a heretic, after the first and second admonition, avoid.' That's Titus 3:10."

"So avoid me!" Jersey says. "Drop me off at the clinic in Phoenix and I'll take care of myself. That's where we're supposed to be going on this trip, remember?"

"Jersey, just 'cause we're going camping now don't mean I'll never take you to the clinic. And maybe you won't even need the clinic! If you get faith, maybe God'll cure you."

"Ha," says Katherine. "Ha, ha!" Not because she finds Jersey or Carter Clay funny, no, but because she imagines—incorrectly—that if she were to look inside the wallet in her purse she would find the cards that buy things. She imagines that she could buy motel rooms and magazines and good food at restaurants—because she is not aware that, back in Seca, Carter Clay removed all of the credit cards from her wallet into a kitchen drawer.

▪ ▪ ▪

The girl's being cured by prayer—that was not impossible, surely. Didn't Pastor Bitner say to pray for it? And once, when Carter was in Katherine's room at Fair Oaks, and Jersey came in, Katherine shouted at Jersey, "Stand up!" and Carter could have sworn that *everyone*—the doctor who was there, and everyone—they looked at the girl like she could do it if she just would.

A little silvery ringing often starts up in Carter's bad ear when he is feeling tense, or has not had enough sleep. Like now. Now, off and on, the muscles in his thighs twitch. That's something else that happens when he is exhausted. Familiar things, but Carter has never seen a giant dust devil come spinning across the flats off to the west of I–10, and now, when he does, he takes that golden, fast-moving funnel for a sign from God, a pillar of fire. He stops the van—so quickly that the camp stove in back topples over with a *clank*. In indignation and fright, cars and trucks to the rear honk while Carter pulls onto the shoulder and rests his head on the steering wheel.

"Did you see?" he cries, and points a blind finger to the west. "It's a sign!" he says.

"Jus' a dus' de-vil," Katherine says, and Jersey, "Right."

Carter lifts his head from the steering wheel and peeks at the swirling, brilliant thing. "I never seen anything like it," he says, and then, before he pulls back on the road, "Just 'cause you seen them before don't mean this one ain't special. Maybe it's meant to be a sign for you, Jersey. Maybe God's making you an offer, and you need to pay attention."

▪ ▪ ▪

MAN TAKES ON BRAIN-DAMAGED WIFE WITH DISABLED DAUGHTER

Is *that* Carter Clay's story? The sort of thing that occasionally appears in the newspapers when editors believe their readers need a shot of inspiration?

In an attempt at normal conversation, Jersey asks, "So, where is it we're going to camp, Mr. Clay?"

"Somewhere real pretty. Up north. Let it be a surprise."

When he pulls over for gas in Phoenix, she wonders if she is nuts for wondering if she should leave a message on the inside of the handicapped stall of the Chevron station: HELP!

From the stall, Jersey calls to Katherine, "Mom, remember how Carter was supposed to take me to the clinic here?"

Katherine does not respond. She is tipped over the little sink, mouth open as she concentrates on straightening the part in her hair.

"Carter's not doing what he said he'd do, Mom."

No response.

"Remember how you said you'd never go camping again, Mom? You hated camping?"

After Jersey and her chair have boxed their way out of the stall, Katherine lowers her head so that the girl can check the part in her hair. "Wha' else din't I like?" she asks.

The familiar whistling begins outside the rest room door before Jersey finishes her list: expensive cars, Speedo suits on men, Madonna, El Caminos, flavored coffee—

She pauses, listens to the whistling, then adds, "'Stairway to Heaven'"—

A lie. Katherine did like "Stairway to Heaven."

Carter Clay moves fast when he resettles the pair in the van. "But I need to reposition myself," Jersey says. "I need my fifteen minutes now, Carter."

He gives his head a quick shake. "Not now. Wait a while." Then he returns to the food mart to fetch some sandwiches.

"S'too hot," Katherine says.

"Yeah," says Jersey. The car dealership sign that they passed on their way into Phoenix showed a temperature of one hundred and seven. Jersey watches Carter Clay move about inside the station's food mart. A stop at the coffeepot. A few words with a man filling the doughnut case. When he disappears from view, it occurs to Jersey that she would not be entirely surprised if Carter Clay ran off and left them sitting in this van; was never seen again. But, then, she supposes this is no novel idea. She has always felt the potential for abandonment in everyone except her mom. That is, her mom of the past.

"Mom, can't we listen to something besides the Christian channel while Carter's inside?"

Katherine shrugs, then rolls the radio dial to a storm of static through which it is just barely possible to make out a rock and roll beat that causes her to say, "Hey!" and sit back smiling in her seat.

"You recognize that?"

Katherine screws up her forehead painfully, then turns to look out the window and mutter, "I hope Car-er get me can-ny."

"Oh, candy!" Jersey yowls, and when Katherine turns her way, eyes narrowed, lips pursed, Jersey adds, "Get a life, Mom!"

Of course this is shameful; thoroughly ashamed, Jersey stares in misery out the window at the area to the rear of the station: A flaking Adirondack chair. A hose tangled around the chair's legs. The dusty white and blue handle of a pacifier that sticks out from a dried-up mud puddle. A plug, Jersey thinks. Give it a tug and some secret drain will suck everything down, down, down—

She looks up as a teenage boy walks by the van, tossing a set of keys in his hands.

Oh.

She scratches her head, imagining for a moment that she needs to camouflage her thought: *Carter Clay's keys are in the van.*

Carter Clay's keys are in the van and he is in the food mart. There. His head and big shoulders now float along above a shelf of cookies and crackers and chips.

"Mom," says Jersey, "remember, earlier, you were asking about things you didn't like? One thing you always *did* like was driving. You're a good driver. If you'd just slide over, you could drive us back to Seca, or even over to a motel here, and we could get out of this hot old van."

Katherine shakes her head. "They tole me I cou-n't drive!"

"But that was a long time ago. There's no reason you can't drive now."

Katherine turns in her seat to stare at the girl. "We'll as-*k* Car-er."

Jersey pretends to be busy with her colored pencils and does not look up when she says, "It's so hot, though. And you don't need Carter to drive. And—he may be having lunch in there, or something."

"You mea' *leave* Car-er?"

"Well. He might not want to come right now, you know?"

Katherine pushes open her door and scrambles out. "Car-er save' me, Jersey!" she declares, and her eyes fill with fear and she turns and she runs toward the food mart, calling, "Car-er! Help! Help!"

▪ ▪ ▪

This is the route Carter has planned: Seca to Phoenix on I–10; I–17 to Flagstaff; Flagstaff into St. George, Utah on US 89; then interstate all the way—zoom—through Salt Lake, Twin Falls, Boise, Baker City. Take the ferry from Seattle to Bremerton, then drive on north to Fort Powden.

After the scene in Phoenix, Carter is determined to put as many miles between himself and Seca as possible before stopping. He is relieved, then, that the girl asks for the fifteen-minute repositioning stops only twice before Salt Lake. Of course, it is also true that the girl scarcely speaks; that it is Katherine who, as they rush past Salt Lake, complains about the long drive.

"Hey," Carter asks, in an effort to distract Katherine, "you got a favorite movie, Katherine?"

She shrugs.

Well, his is *The Great Escape*. She ever see that?

Another shrug.

He debates whether or not he should ask Jersey if she has seen *The Great Escape*. In the dark, it is difficult to see her face in the rearview, but he feels her presence. She is a strangling vine. A bat, liable to fly out at any moment, flap wings in his eyes, blind him, poison him with her bite.

"We ought to rent it!" he declares. "Back when it come out, me and my buddies must have seen it six or seven times. It's about these Allied soldiers, and how they get put in a Nazi prisoner-of-war camp made just for them 'cause they're all such masters of breaking out. They're from England and the U.S. and such. This one really cool one, Hills"—he turns his head slightly in an effort to make the girl feel included—"you know the actor Steve McQueen, Jersey?"

"No." Jersey's voice sounds raw, as if, instead of keeping silent, she has spent the day pushing rough words from her throat.

"Your mom would know Steve McQueen!" Carter pats Katherine's arm. "*Baby, the Rain Must Fall*. *Cincinnati Kid*—he did that one, too, right, Katherine? In *Great Escape*, though, Steve McQueen is this Hills, an American pilot. He's always got a ball and glove in his hands, and he's always getting in trouble. All these prisoners is good at something; like, one's good at forging and one's good at stealing tools or digging tunnels, see? They got this trick—to get rid of dirt from the escape tunnels they're digging, they all wear little bags inside their pants, and then, whenever they go outside, they dump the dirt while they walk. They're all great guys, too. I mean, you like all of them. A few crack under the pressure, though. One little Scotsman, or maybe he's Irish—he'd been a jockey, and there's a time when they're all set to get out. They've worked and worked on their tunnel, and then one of the Nazis comes in this barracks place where the tunnel starts, and he, like, spills coffee on the floor, and—bam—it goes right through the floor, so he knows, man, and Ives"—Carter's voice cracks a little as speaks through his memory of little Ives' attempt to scale the prison fence—"well, I can't tell you, in case you see it, but, hey, it's a great movie." He pauses. "How about you, Jersey? What's your favorite movie?"

Jersey played this game with her parents many times. Best brownie you ever ate? For Jersey and her dad: the ones from Jersey's swim meet in Yuma; for Katherine, those made by a neighbor named Marion Casey. Best opera? All three of them agreed on *The Magic Flute.* Most beautiful animal of the Sonoran Desert? Puma for Jersey. Trogon for her mom. Gila monster for her dad.

She cannot ignore the fact that her father's favorite movie (*A Man Escaped* by Robert Bresson) is not so far off in title or theme from this movie Carter Clay describes. But her father's movie is a quiet thing, in which the viewer focuses upon a Resistance fighter captured by the Nazis, alone in his cell, and how, ever so patiently, he converts his spoon into the tool with which he slowly, slowly disassembles the cell's wooden door; how he unravels the wires that support his mattress and wraps them around his bedding in order to make himself a rope—

Altogether different, she tells herself. And she does not want to play "favorites" with Carter Clay anyway, and so she returns to a consideration of the Book of Job, which she finished reading just before dark fell. "One thing, Mr. Clay—and Mom? You guys know how at the end of Job, God's supposed to restore Job's possessions?"

Only Carter Clay responds: "Yeah?"

Jersey releases a tired breath. "Okay. God gives Job *more* sons and daughters, but He doesn't bring the dead ones back to life, and that's the most important thing to get back, the ones who died."

Carter Clay is silent for a time. She imagines he is not going to respond at all, but then he releases a long yawn, and he says, "The thing is, Jersey, they'll all be together in heaven. It's in heaven where things'll be made perfect."

"Why?" she asks, then feels a little embarrassed. Her *why* makes her sound like a four-year-old.

"Because—it's heaven, Jersey."

"But why isn't life on earth perfect?"

"Life on earth is a *test*."

"Why?"

"Why should we be tested to find out if we're worthy of paradise?"

"Just—never mind, okay? I'm going to try to sleep."

She looks out at the slice of night sky available from the back of the van. It is dark as a blueprint. Its beauty, she understands, is never banal. It is and it is and it is. Better for God not to have given anything to Job at the end of the story. Better for God to have given his tough old speech to Job and left Job totally bereft than to give him back something and pretend it was everything.

▪ ▪ ▪

"My wife and—daughter," Carter tells the convenience store clerk, "they conked out on me!"

Perry, Utah. Beneath the store's unnaturally bright lights, Carter smiles and pours himself a cup of coffee at the beverage station. The clerk smiles, too. His name is Sandy Lohafer, though his shirt pocket reads BRIAN. Sandy tries to appear blasé while studying the scoop of store and customer contained in the security mirror; fair-skinned Sandy, however, is betrayed by his blotchy cheeks. A small man, and slight, just now Sandy wishes—as he has many times before—that there were laws that prohibited men of a certain size from entering convenience stores at certain hours.

"Almost fell asleep myself!" Carter sets a Butterfinger candy bar on the counter along with his cup of coffee. "It was like I heard a click. Click, goes my brain, and then I feel a tire go off the road—" Carter laughs. He wants to chat with the clerk, and not just to help himself wake up, no, he wants to erase the look of alarm he caused on the clerk's face merely by entering the store. He wants the clerk to understand that he, Carter, is okay.

"I'm a Christian," he says, and smiles, "born again, so I guess I shouldn't worry about cracking up on the highway, but I got to admit, I do—"

Sandy Lohafer nods. He feels dizzy. Unnatural. *Is this it? Is this going to be it*? Two months ago, another clerk was shot and killed right behind the counter at which Sandy now stands. Sandy, coming on duty, was the one to find her. First he found her sandal—one of those thick yuppie flip-flops. She must have lost it when she tried to hide behind the counter.

"I just got married." Carter looks out toward the van. "My daughter—I don't like calling her stepdaughter because it sounds like you're saying you don't like her as much as a regular daughter—anyways, sometimes I get the idea she thinks I'm a weirdo. Because I was in the war. That's part of it, I guess. Her real dad—he's dead—I guess he was against the war. Vietnam, you know, and he wasn't a Christian neither."

"Oh, well. Kids." Sandy means to sound like any commiserating father; it is the wobble in his voice, however, that encourages Carter to continue.

"She's in a wheelchair. I want to help her get out of it. I don't know what you think about the power of prayer"—he pauses to offer the clerk a chance to deliver an opinion on the matter, but then he sees how the man's upper lip and forehead glisten, and—reluctantly—to give the poor clerk some relief, Carter takes his coffee and candy and returns to the van.

What is Carter himself able to believe on this particular night?

We're all sinners but we can choose to be good. God forgives us for past sins, and we'll be with God after death.

So he tells himself, but, in the same breath, his life pitches up against the hard possibility of Finis Pruitt telling all to Jersey and Katherine, and then his faith fails him, and he cannot see why God *would* forgive him.

What kind of God would forgive Carter the terrible damage he's done just the same as He forgives a kid like Jersey for, say, not much liking Carter?

"But, hey, don't go down that road, man." He speaks the words aloud while Jersey and Katherine sleep on. "Ain't nothing for you down that road, man."

He turns on the radio. Grabs at the spunky lyrics of a song on some cowboy station. Rain begins to fall, softly at first, then harder. Behind the noise of the rain, the van is almost certainly making its threatening noise once more, and he wishes Jersey were awake so he could ask, "Do you hear that, too?"

It does not matter that the rest area where he finally pulls off is lit as bright as a stadium. He falls asleep instantly, and he sleeps hard until he wakes to that thumping on the back of his seat. Jersey, saying, "Carter, wake up! Wake up my mom so she can help me to the bathroom!"

30

Since their quarrel over Katherine and Jersey's trip to Arizona with Carter, M.B. and Patsy Glickman have done an excellent job of avoiding one another. Should eye contact threaten in the parking lot, M.B. can easily stoop to extricate a phantom pebble from her shoe. Patsy can always fuss with Princess, or gasp "Oh, dear!" as if she has just remembered an errand in the opposite direction.

So: so much for Patsy. There is no necessity whatsoever for M.B. to tell Patsy about the marriage.

Mistakenly, however, M.B. has assumed that simply staying away from Vineyard Christian would keep her safe from questions in that quarter. Thus, she is taken by surprise by Pastor Bitner's telephone call, which comes in the cool of the morning as she lays out her first hand of solitaire.

"I wondered where you'd all got to, Marybelle! Then I was over at Fair Oaks and they told me Katherine was gone and Carter had quit, and since I haven't seen any of you in church—"

"Oh, well, Carter and Katherine"—does she sound gay, pleased?—"they took off for Arizona, Pastor! They got married!"

The blood in her ears pounds so loudly that she finds it difficult to hear what Pastor Bitner asks next; something about Jersey, she thinks.

"Well, she's with them, Pastor, of course, but you got to excuse me now. My buzzer—"

As soon as she hangs up, she hurries into the master bathroom. Of late, several times a day, she has a bad taste in her mouth, a rotten taste and a smell that she pictures rising out of her gut like sewer gas.

"Good heavens!" she says to her reflection in the bathroom mirror. She offers the face in the mirror a friendly grimace. Pours herself an inch of Listerine. Gargles furiously. Swallows. That will kill the rot in her gut, right?

She takes a seat in Lorne's recliner. With the remote control, she turns on Home Shopping Network. The item under consideration is an exercise device called the Belly-Buster, and the smiling model gives the impression that using it to shape and flatten her waist and abdomen is entirely fun, fun, fun, but, damn it, M.B. is too old to believe the thing can be all that big of a kick to use if it gets results. If it gets results, she knows it must require effort.

Traitor. Jersey called her that. And Kitty called her that once in the past. Maybe Kitty put the word in Jersey's head.

The hostess of HSN takes a testimonial telephone call from a woman who used the Belly-Buster with impressive results. So the audience can see the change the Belly-Buster made in the caller's figure, while the caller talks, the hostess sets out two mounted photos—before and after.

I'm trembling, M.B. thinks; she holds out her hands, and watches them tremble. *My God!* Still, she would probably have been fine in a minute or two had the telephone not begun to ring again. Suppose it's Pastor Bitner, calling back to say, well, didn't M.B. think that perhaps Jersey ought to stay with her?

She will not answer, that's all. But, oh, just in case the neighbors hear the ringing and wonder why she does not pick up the phone, M.B. turns on the television, then darts into the master bath and turns on the faucet and also the noisy blow-dryer she uses on her hair. Pours a small glass of Listerine. Gargles. Swallows. Sings the song that is always closest to her heart, always handy. "I'm in the Mood for Love."

Twenty-two rings.

That evening, after she has had a bit of wine, M.B. practices telephoning the house in Seca. To build confidence, she smiles as she takes up the receiver. "You caught me off guard with your news." That is what she will say. "Of course, I'm happy as can be." And then she will ask, "Can I speak to Jersey?"

May I?

She dials. Hangs up before the ringing begins. Dials. Hangs up. Dials again. She is as nervous as she was when Kitty came home from college for the first time. Combat boots, that was what Kitty wore on her feet, and her skin was brown as wood—except for her nose, which had peeled down to tender pink. *I don't eat meat anymore*, Kitty had written before her arrival, and M.B. could see, even before Kitty finished saying good-bye to the people who dropped her at the curb, that the girl who had come back would never again respect a thing M.B. or Lorne had to say.

For a very long time, M.B. allows the telephone to ring at the Seca house. Maybe Kitty and Carter and Jersey are at a restaurant? Out to dinner? That happy image, however, is immediately spoiled for M.B. by any detail she supplies (Katherine sitting like a lump, Jersey and wheelchair poked out in the aisle), and, anyway, in Arizona, in the summer, it is three hours earlier than it is in Florida. It is too early for them to be out to eat.

One more ring, and then one more.

After she sets the telephone back in the cradle, she pours herself a glass of wine, and wonders if she should call Sam Alitz. See what Sam Alitz thinks about Kitty getting married.

To fortify herself for that call, M.B. downs the last of her mug. The Home Shopping Network is now offering sweetheart lockets, gold with a diamond chip in the center.

Would Jersey like a sweetheart locket?

M.B. tries to imagine this as she pours another drink.

Just to have the drink ready, waiting.

It is Sam Alitz's voice-mail that says, "Hello, this is Sam," but M.B. takes the recording for the real article and begins to speak—

"Oh!" she says when Sam's message speaks over her own. Then she waits until the beep.

"Sam, this is M.B. Milhause. Down in Bradenton. It's just"—for a moment, she cannot speak—"Kitty got married in Arizona, and I wondered if you'd heard anything? Jersey's with her, and, well—I think I made a mistake, letting her go."

▪ ▪ ▪

The next afternoon, it is Patsy Glickman who telephones the Palm Gate Village president to let the man know that the Today's Date calendar on M.B.'s door has not been changed for two days, that the telephone is off the hook, and that Patsy would certainly *know* if her dear friend had left town.

The latter assertion is not true, given that the women have not spoken all week. In addition, it was Patsy herself—to make what she is sure is a bad situation more compelling to others—it was Patsy herself who set M.B.'s door calendar back an extra day.

Wasn't she justified when M.B.'s telephone has given a busy signal for the last twenty-four hours?

The president of the association arrives with a passkey. He is trim and tanned and wears a coral polo shirt that matches his Bermuda shorts. A good-looking fellow, Patsy thinks, but a cold fish. Note how he leans back on the wrought iron railing of the balcony: raises and lowers himself, getting in a little exercise during the emergency call. *Can we get this over with*? So Patsy interprets his clenched and tanned jaw—missing entirely the fact that the poor fellow is scared stiff that he will soon be called upon to view a corpse.

"Just let me check things out," Patsy says. Almost immediately she returns. *She'll take care of things. Marybelle's just a little under the weather. He can leave*.

"Patsy," M.B. calls from inside the unit. "Where'd you go?"

"Coming," Patsy says as she shuts off the television and its raucous sales pitch for fingertip-length beaver coats, and stops to set M.B.'s telephone receiver back in its cradle.

M.B. lies where Patsy found her: on the carpet of the master bath. Crying. The purple stain from her spilled glass of wine matches almost exactly the color of the great bump on her forehead and the swelling of the ankle exposed by her twisted bathrobe.

Patsy kneels on the carpet and takes M.B.'s hand. "I can probably get a doctor to come here," she says. "Or I can drive you myself. What do you think?"

M.B. slowly scoots herself into a sitting position, her back against a bathroom cupboard. "Oh, Patsy. I don't even know where Katherine and Jersey are and—what if you hadn't found me? I'm so ashamed. Jersey hates me, and you think I'm awful, too. Don't you?"

"Awful?" Patsy laughs a little as she holds out her arms to help M.B. to her feet. "My dear, you're such a mystery, how could I tell if you're awful or not?"

▪ ▪ ▪

A good question.

Up until this time, M.B. has tried to trick everyone—including her God and herself—into believing in the face she presents to the world. The effect produced by such a person, of course, is never *precisely* what he or she intends. No presentation can ever be perfectly controlled. Consider Finis Pruitt: Perhaps Finis was more successful as Rear End than Marybelle was as M.B. both because his role was more flamboyant and because he was a better actor. However, in Finis's case, his very success led him to overreach his thinly stretched resources, and, thus, he lost hold of his creation.

Another case: the pre-accident Katherine often wished her true self could be known as well as a character in a book to whom the author, and, thus, the world, had complete access; yet she could never entirely bring inner to outer without distortion.

As there is no perfectly opaque disguise, so there is no perfectly transparent display.

And the Katherine who wanted so much to present her true self to the world—whom did she choose for a mate? Joe Alitz. A person who elected to be mysterious; to say to the world, "You will never receive the entire me." Interestingly enough, in this regard, a man like her father—though it would never have occurred to Katherine to compare beer-drinking, TV-watching Lorne to scientist Joe.

Of course, the Katherine who married Carter Clay is not the same Katherine who married Joe Alitz some twenty years and a life ago. That young Katherine was crazy for distant, brilliant Joe. At twenty, love was crazy. By the time of the accident, Katherine's definition of love had changed to commitment. In a sense, then, the life project Carter Clay received at the Turquoise Motel dovetailed with Katherine's more adult definition. The post-accident Katherine, however, does not know that she is Carter's cross. She would be unhappy in that most unromantic of roles.

As for Carter's view of himself: It is somewhat different from the views of themselves held by M.B., Finis, Joe, and the pre-accident Katherine. Carter, after all, holds out for the wondrous if painful possibility that God knows who Carter is even when Carter forgets. God will always know. And forgive Carter. And love him, too.

God did not even have to *strive* to love Carter after what Carter did on Post Road. Which put God at an advantage, of course. Carter is just a man. As a man, he has come to suspect that striving may be the best a man can do.

31

Out in the Sound, the ferry's lights make misty halos in the predawn fog. They suggest a many-eyed creature on the prowl—something magical that advances, rumbling, toward the shore, to deliver or to destroy.

The van sits in the ragtag line of vehicles that wait to board the ferry. Carter has stepped out of the van, alone. He is exhausted, but also pleased at having come so far, so fast; at being so close to home and the familiar damp and the evergreen smell. With swigs from the gallon of distilled water he keeps in the van for the battery, he tries to swish and spit away the metallic taste of the trip. All those miles—they have worn him down. His thoughts come like simple, terse instructions.

Keep the money for the ferry in your right pocket.

Know where your keys are so you don't hold up the line.

It seems necessary to visualize himself driving the van onto the ramp. Thump. As if, otherwise, he might make some crazy turn and drive the van over the edge and into the water where they would drown.

. . .

In the mid-seventies, when Katherine Milhause was a graduate student, her paper "Estimating Dinosaur Speeds" was accepted for presentation at a convention of the American Paleontological

Society in New York City, and so she was finally able to make a visit to the famous American Museum of Natural History. To her surprise, her favorite exhibit was the great hall of totem poles and masks and carvings of tribes from the Pacific Northwest—among them the Bella Coola, Tlingit, and Salish. On the return flight to Arizona, leaning over the back of her airline seat, Katherine tried to explain to her professor, Joe Alitz, and another student how moved she was, not just by the artistry of the work, but by the idea that, say, eating with a spoon carved with a certain clan sign could make you feel linked to your ancestors and nature and the supernatural. Although Joe did not know it at the time, he was falling in love with Katherine, and—hoping to impress her with a bit of arcane knowledge outside his own field—he said, "Not the most gentle folks, though, Katherine. Did you know, when they really wanted to show off at a party, the hosts would kill a couple of servants for their guests to use as rollers—to keep their canoes on the shore, you see?"

Katherine does not remember that conversation as she sits in Carter Clay's van, waiting for the ferry, but something stirs in her when she considers the contents of the pickup truck parked ahead of the van. The truck bed holds several decorative totem poles and a sign that will apparently be erected somewhere later in the day: FOR SALE!

"To-em poles," she says aloud. "I saw 'em."

Under normal circumstances, Jersey would ask what her mother meant, but after forty-some hours in her wheelchair—in pain, frazzled—Jersey is not feeling particularly solicitous of anyone. Since Salt Lake she has not spoken to Carter Clay except to say "I'm hungry" and "I need to use the rest room" and "I need to see a doctor. From my fall—and the sitting. I'm getting a sore."

"I'm going to have a stretch and look around." Carter Clay's last words before he climbed out of the van. Maybe it was the heavy moisture in the air, or his weariness—or some weariness inside of Jersey's own head—but Carter Clay's voice seemed to twang like a saw that had been flexed and then let go.

I'm going to have a stretch and look around.

Jersey replays the words as she sits in the van, and Carter Clay goes on chatting with some other driver who awaits the ferry.

I'm going to have a stretch and look around.

So what? This, Jersey decides, would be the perfect unspoken response to any remark Carter Clay might make at any time in the future, near or distant.

So what? Who cares? Fuck you. Fuck you, Clay.

32

As they drive up the peninsula toward Fort Powden, Carter does his best not to see what the dawn reveals, here and there, between the little towns north of Bremerton: the narrow bands of trees left as a kind of screen to conceal the disasters of clear-cutting. Dirt churned rough and raw with bits of stump and sprays of root. Nature made junkyard.

He tightens his hands on the steering wheel. In the damp, the layers of grime and skin and oils that have built up on the wheel over the years begin to loosen, come off in crumbs against his palms. He whistles a little of a song that Jersey persuaded Katherine to sing earlier—something Jersey sang harmony to: "Down Yonder Green Valley." A new song for him. Carter whistling a new song in his new life.

How like Carter that he imagines the life of his sister will not have changed since he last saw her! Thus, when he leaves Jersey and Katherine in the van and hurries up the sidewalk to the duplex where Cheryl Lynn Clay lived when he left town, Carter ignores the fact that the duplex, which was brand-new in 1989, now needs paint; that the tidy landscaped yard of six years past has been largely replaced by ragweed and bramble.

It was all a terrible mistake, a terrible accident. This is what he will tell his sister. But *not* to try to excuse himself. *A terrible accident. But my fault*.

How can an accident be someone's fault?

So it wasn't an accident?

But he did not *plan* it. He did not *want* it to happen.

Then—an accident.

I know it was my fault, but it was an accident, and I don't know how to tell them, and if I don't tell them, this other person may, and then they'll hate me even worse.

JIM MINER is the name on the mailbox: a relief. The father of Cheryl Lynn's little boy, James.

Maybe Cheryl Lynn can tell Jersey and Katherine about the accident. Maybe it will be better if it comes from her.

Despite his worries, a silly grin threatens to break out on Carter's face as he waits at the duplex's front door; though, of course, it could be Jim Miner who answers, and Carter never did get along with Jim—

Not Jim Miner or Cheryl Lynn. Still, the woman—scowling, bathrobed—who comes to the door seems vaguely familiar. "You looking for my husband?" she says.

Carter hesitates, then asks, "Jim Miner?"

Carter and the woman proceed to wait for Jim Miner in a hall narrowed to a footpath by, among other things, many five-gallon buckets of paint, a bonnet hairdryer, lots of ladders, a number of disposable diaper boxes filled with what appear to be canning jars, and an artificial Christmas tree—partially disassembled and still bearing a red glass ornament that yields a reflection of Carter quite similar to the one he spied in the convenience mart's security mirror. Carter does his best to step out of the reflection, or at least to position himself in such a way that he does not have to see the thing.

"I worked for Jim once," Carter tells the woman. "Painting."

She nods. "I know who you are. Jim and I got to send a hundred twenty-five dollars to your sister every month of our lives."

Heavy footsteps sound at the other end of the duplex, and then a large figure blocks the light from the kitchen.

"That you, Clay?"

Jim Miner limps down the hall. Once heartbreakingly handsome, Jim is sensitive about the fact that he has gained sixty pounds since high school; to make matters worse, his gout is acting up after a recent tryst with summer sausage and burgundy. In no humor to be hospitable, he regards Carter's shaved head with a look that says: bad joke.

It is Jim's own bad joke that he sends Carter to look for Cheryl Lynn Clay at the house of Del Kelly, the arc welder in whose bed Jim found Cheryl Lynn some years ago.

From the Kelly porch, Carter can see into a kitchen lit by only the weak fluorescent light from the hood above the electric stove. At a small table, a man and a teenage boy, and a woman who is clearly *not* Carter's sister, eat bowls of some sort of gray food. All three members of the little family look as if dawn itself leaves them discouraged, and Carter is grateful that none of them chance to look up and see him on the porch before he sneaks away.

▪ ▪ ▪

"I'm not going to explain everything just yet." So Carter tells Cheryl Lynn from the pay telephone at the Tip Top Laundry where he has found her listing in the Fort Powden telephone directory. He wants to tell Cheryl Lynn he is born again—or maybe he should say "I've found the Lord"?—but he fears the words would sound phony to her, and he settles on a simple, "You can trust me, Cheryl Lynn."

Trust me. Always alarming words in Cheryl Lynn's book. But this is her baby brother, Carter, and Cheryl Lynn is almost sick with happiness at the sound of his voice. Carter. After he hangs up, she stubs out her cigarette and rouses her handsome boys, ages six and ten, from their bed: "*Alfred! James! Your uncle's coming! Your uncle's coming!*"

The bare-chested boys reluctantly shuffle from their bedroom to the little front room and there lie down to watch early-morning cartoons on the television. Should they care about the arrival of their uncle? James does not recall him. Alfred has never met the man. Their mother wails over the state of the house, a small wooden rental not so different from the rental in which she and Carter grew up (two bedrooms, rusty screens, roof with shingles sticking up like so many cowlicks, pervasive mildew scent that Cheryl Lynn does her best to conceal with a collection of aerosol sprays).

If Cheryl Lynn had known Carter was coming—well, she could not have done anything about the carpet, which always makes her think of a dirty ace bandage, or about the fact that the walls of the front room are lined with boxes of the boys' toys, but maybe she could have figured out a way to conceal the wads of yellow insulation tucked in around the frame of the front room's sliding glass door—a nice thing to have, that glass door, but it does look as if someone with an itch for more light simply *rammed* the unit into the wall with a forklift.

Cheryl Lynn sneaks a glance at herself in the mirror over the bathroom sink. Should she tuck in her shirt? No, that would only emphasize her hips, and she bought the shirt to cover her hips. Cheryl Lynn is bigger than she would like—taller, wider—though size is useful to her when she mans the bar at Rex's Bowladrome. She sets her hands on her hips and gives her reflection a tough look: want to make something of it? Then laughs and heads for the kitchen. She wants to call the Bowladrome, to tell Rex and Maggie Fishbeck her good news, but even before she finishes dialing, she sees a large, bald-headed man disappearing around the side of a rusty van parked in front of her house.

Carter?

Both shy and eager, Cheryl Lynn bangs out the screen door and sets off down the walk. *Trust me*. Why would Carter say "Trust me"?

Someone—a stone-faced woman—sits in the van's front passenger seat, and, automatically, Cheryl Lynn lifts her hand in greeting.

The woman—a hitchhiker?—does not respond, but her gaze follows Cheryl Lynn's passage around the front of the van, as if Cheryl Lynn might be a fish, just swimming past.

The cargo door of the van stands open, but Carter is not in sight. The woman in the passenger seat, however, turns as Cheryl Lynn sticks her head through the open door, and the woman says something Cheryl Lynn does not understand—

"Oh!" Cheryl Lynn cries out at the sight of the wheelchair-bound girl in the back of the van; then she laughs and presses her hand to her chest. "Excuse me!"

"Cheryl Lynn?" From the rear of the van, there emerges a big bald head. "Hey!" Carter ducks forward to grab her hand, give her an awkward hug.

Cheryl Lynn's eyes fill with tears. "I'm his sister!" she says to the girl in the wheelchair, who smiles and nods, but also looks a little sick.

While Carter sets about hauling out a ramp for the wheelchair, he rattles on: how he met the stone-faced woman—*That's Katherine, up front, and this is Jersey*, and the Lord this, the Lord that, and he and Katherine decided to tie the knot, and now they're all three going on a kind of camping honeymoon—

Cheryl Lynn nods. Though years and years of bar work have dredged her deep enough that she can accommodate most situations, *this* one spins her for a loop. Not so much the pale little girl and her wheelchair, but the woman—Cheryl Lynn cannot help but hope that maybe this Katherine seems like a zombie because she's whacked out on one of the heavy-duty drugs Carter liked to pop, now and then.

Cheryl Lynn teases Carter about his Yul Brynner look while he gets the woman out on the sidewalk, and the girl and her chair down the ramp. She bites her tongue about the scar on his forehead. Instead, she sets a hand on the girl's shoulder and says, "I bet you're hungry, Jersey! Listening to Carter always made me hungry."

The girl appears to try to smile. She stretches her eyes wide open, as if to force herself awake.

"How about you, Katherine?" Cheryl Lynn asks. "D'you ever feel like you burn up calories just being in the company of Carter's jaw?"

Carter laughs, but Katherine drops her head back and stares up. "Ni' trees," she says to no one in particular.

Once Carter has hoisted Jersey's chair up the three steps to the screened porch, Cheryl Lynn introduces Alfred and James.

"Handsome, ain't they?" she says to Carter—she cannot help herself—and he nods and smiles.

"You bet."

A pleasant moment, but then the group clusters and swells and breaks apart in a nervous effort to clear a path for Jersey, who has begun to slowly wheel herself toward—"Cheryl Lynn? I'd like to use your rest room," she whispers.

"Oh! Sure!" Cheryl Lynn gestures toward the bungalow's inner hall. "Do you need—"

"Let me go ahead," Carter interrupts. "To see about her chair—"

The little hall that leads to the bathroom is dark enough that Jersey feels she can whisper to Carter, "Would you ask your sister—does she know a doctor? It's—there's something happening. And could you ask if she's got a hand mirror?"

Carter pats the girl on the head. "I got an idea about all that. I been—well, I'll tell you later."

After he leaves, Jersey stares out the bathroom window. In several spots the screen has rusted away. Beyond the screen lie clear sky and grass, and she tries not to think about her strange sore; to think, instead, only of that rusted screen, and how in one of Joe's favorite movies, *The Incredible Shrinking Man*, mere window screen imprisoned the shrinking hero—until he grew so minuscule that he could step right through one of the tiny squares formed by the threads of the screen.

"Jersey," Cheryl Lynn calls from outside the door, "there's a little mirror in my compact? Would that work?"

"Never mind," Jersey says.

Really, just now, she is not so sure she wants to see.

▪ ▪ ▪

At Cheryl Lynn's house, breakfast is coffee and a marshmallow-packed novelty cereal that the old Katherine did not allow in her house, but that the new Katherine devours enthusiastically. Jersey, slumped in her wheelchair, stares at the vinyl cloth covering the kitchen table (roosters and hens and chicks worn to ghosts by years of elbows and plates). At her side, pretty little blond-haired Alfred whispers, "I save the marshmallows out for last," and touched by his attention, his sweet blue eyes, Jersey whispers back, "Good idea."

On her other side, Carter says, "Looks like you got an admirer there, Jersey."

"Hoop Tate's his dad," Cheryl Lynn tells Carter, and leans over the table to rumple Alfred's fair hair before continuing. "Was. He dumped me for some *boy*, I swear to God, a kid who played football at St. Jude, and I hope to hell we never lay eyes on the son of a bitch again."

When Carter's face grows somber, Cheryl Lynn gives a wave of her hand in his direction. "The Lord is not *my* shepherd, and I got *plenty* of wants." She rises from the table and begins to push things noisily about in one of the cabinets. "Actually, Carter, about once a week people come by pushing *Watchtower* or some other damn thing, and I'm such a heathen I don't even let them in the door!"

"Well, then"—with his finger, Carter follows the outline of one of the tablecloth's little chicks—"I guess it's lucky I'm just here to visit my sister."

Cheryl Lynn hesitates, then grins and raps her brother's shiny head with her knuckles. "You're right."

▪ ▪ ▪

While Carter sits on the boys' bed to pull off his boots, Cheryl Lynn sits in the director's chair that serves as the family clothes hamper. She inclines her head toward the door, through which it is possible to see Jersey and Katherine and the boys watching television. "Can I shut the door a minute?" she whispers.

Carter stares wearily at the boot he works from one foot with the toe of the other boot. "They'll know you're talking about them if you shut the door, Cheryl Lynn."

"Well." She takes a deep breath. She is nervous. "Are you going to tell me about—what you're up to?"

Carter eases onto the mattress and lies down. "Things with Jersey and Katherine"—he twists his neck back and forth on the pillow in a way that makes Cheryl Lynn nervous; didn't their mother used to do that same thing when she was upset?—"they was in a bad accident. Katherine hurt her head, but she's getting better, and Jersey—I got some ideas from this place I used to work on how to help her walk again. Plus prayer, of course. Faith. The pastor from the church we went to in Florida—he told how the disciples did miracles, too. Through the power of Jesus, of course. And you remember that guy, Carter McKay, that Mom used to watch? Hell—well, if you believed it, he was curing people right and left. Through faith, Cheryl Lynn. Pure and simple."

Cheryl Lynn gives her head a shake made up of equal parts of admiration and embarrassed skepticism. She is only too happy to use the slamming of the porch door as an excuse to jump from her chair and stick her head out into the front room where James is now handing the girl a canvas knapsack.

"What's going on, James?" Cheryl Lynn asks the boy.

"I just got her something from the van."

Cheryl Lynn nods, then returns to the bedroom. Carter has rolled onto his side, facing away from her, and she steps close to him, pokes him in the back.

"You know, there's plenty I'd like to ask you, Carter—like, where you been?"

He shakes his head without turning her way. "Long story."

She separates the dirty clothes from the director's chair into lights and dark, and waits for Carter to begin, but he never does, and, eventually, she asks, "You going to visit Dad?"

"I hope to, sure."

"The bastard. Still, that's good. He's getting old and all. But, hey, you need to sleep, don't you?"

"Cheryl Lynn"—Carter rolls over to face her—"listen, don't let them go off on their own anywhere." He hesitates. "Seriously. Because Jersey might try to run off, or something."

"*She's* going to run off?" Cheryl Lynn can hardly help but laugh at the idea. "Why?"

"Well"—he closes his eyes—"she don't like me very much, Cheryl Lynn."

The idea of any person not liking her brother makes Cheryl Lynn angry, but when Carter lifts his hand—very slow—and gestures for her to draw near, she feels a chill. She does not want to hear what Carter has to say, and so she does a funny little dancing movement toward the door, and in a voice as light as she can make it, almost teasing, she calls, "Okay, Okay! I'll watch her! You sleep!"

The girl looks up from the book in her lap when Cheryl Lynn steps out into the front room. Cheryl Lynn tries to smile as she goes to her—this girl who doesn't like Carter. "Now what kind of coloring book is that, Jersey?"

A friendly question, but it leads to a scene in which Alfred tries to yank the coloring book away from Jersey, and then receives a swat on the bottom from Cheryl Lynn that starts him off on a tantrum. Cheryl Lynn—swearing—tears through the various cardboard boxes and ruined laundry baskets that sit here and there in the front room, and yells, "Why you guys can't never put a damn thing back, I don't know! Here! Here's a coloring book, Alf, now shut up!" With her free hand, Cheryl Lynn hoists the weeping boy from the floor and onto a shoulder, from which he glares spitefully down upon Jersey.

Cheryl Lynn herself gives a testy glance in Jersey's direction. "I'm sure," she says, as she plunks Alfred down beside the wheelchair, "your cousin won't mind sharing her pencils."

Cousin. Jersey stares in amazement as the damp-lashed Alfred rattles through her pencils with his delicate, grubby fingers. She does not know whether to be delighted or horrified. She has never had a cousin. Cousins have always been something other people had and that you did not necessarily want—like red hair or a British accent.

Alfred sniffles and takes up a vermilion pencil. After a quick peek at Jersey, he strums the pencil lightly across the spokes of the near wheel of her chair. "My book's 'Teenage Mutant Ninja Turtles,'" he says.

Jersey nods. She feels a slight vibration from the boy's strumming. "That's—who's your favorite turtle?" she asks.

"Knock that off, Alf!" says Cheryl Lynn, and when the boy obeys, she turns to Katherine to ask, "So—you met Carter at church, huh? Carter didn't used to be much for church."

Jersey glances at her mother, then back to her coloring book. Her pencils make an insectlike noise as the heavy paper gnaws bits of color from the leads. When Katherine continues to sit silent, Jersey says, "Our family was in an accident. My grandma didn't think she could take care of my mom. After my mom got out of the hospital. My dad"—she blinks at the sliding glass door, waiting to catch her breath, and, automatically, Cheryl Lynn turns and looks in the same direction.

"—well, my dad was killed. In the accident."

"Oh!" Cheryl Lynn turns back to the girl. "I'm sorry!"

"I only mention it," Jersey says, "because—my mom and Carter knew each other from when my mom was at Fair Oaks, too." She hesitates, then adds a soft, "Where Carter worked? In Bradenton?"

Cheryl Lynn is grateful for the girl's tactful way of dispensing information.

"There Sam!"

Jersey and Cheryl Lynn turn to Katherine. Throughout the brouhaha over the coloring book, Katherine sat quiet, but now she is animated, pointing at the television, where, sure enough, there *is* her brother-in-law, Sam Alitz. In tails and a belly and a big white mustache and some gizmo that covers his hair so that he appears as bald as Carter Clay—or perhaps Sam's head, too, has been shaved. An advertisement: Sam playing the millionaire icon of a famous board game.

"Who's Sam?" asks Cheryl Lynn.

"My uncle," says Jersey. "Sam Alitz."

"Peekaboo!" cries Sam-the-millionaire, and several beautiful young women squeal and chase after him.

"Yuck," says Katherine, and makes a face of disapproval that piques Jersey's interest. What was that all about?

"Your uncle?" Cheryl Lynn rests a palm on top of James's head. "Did you hear that, kids? That guy's your cousin's uncle!"

Dark and scowling, James ducks out from under his mother's hand, then asks, "So is he our uncle too?"

"Sort of!" Cheryl Lynn says gaily. "Wouldn't that be right?" She turns to Katherine, then remembers Katherine is not up to such questions, and turns back to Jersey. "Has he been in other ads?"

Jersey is both embarrassed and pleased by this attention, and, for a moment, she draws a blank. "Well, he's an actor. He was on *American Theater Playhouse*. And if you ever saw the soap opera *Texas Oilmen*—he was a guy who had an affair for a while with the wife of the main character on *Texas Oilmen*."

"Pete?" Cheryl Lynn drops down next to James on the couch. "I loved Pete!" Cheryl Lynn continues to stare at the television, although the board-game ad is finished and a sports star is now promoting breakfast cereal. "I got to call Maggie and tell her I can't come in! We got to do something special, you know?" She glances at Katherine, then back at Jersey. "I could take you two to the alley. I work at the bowling alley. Do you guys bowl?" She glances at Jersey's chair. "Oh, but—we'd have to leave Carter if we did that. You like videos? We could get a video."

"*Teenage Mutant Ninjas!*" Alfred cries. "*Teenage Mutant Ninjas!*"

"I could make chili," Cheryl Lynn says. "You like chili, Katherine?"

Katherine nods.

"Jesus!" Cheryl Lynn sticks her hands into the back pockets of her jeans, and rocks onto her heels. "You remember Pete, James! He always wore a white hat and his hair was sort of silvery but he didn't look old or nothing."

James shrugs. "Maybe."

"I could go to the store," says Jersey. "If you need anything. I could take my mom. She's supposed to take walks."

"Wha' about Car-er?" Katherine asks.

Cheryl Lynn gives Jersey one of the various winks she has perfected at the Bowladrome's bar: the you-know-and-I-know-that-you've-had-enough-to-drink wink. "James'll go," she says. "Put on a shirt, James. And get us a six of Bud. I'll call ahead."

Jersey stares out at the mossy rooftops and trees—the green light of Washington—and finds it hard to breathe. She is being submerged in the world of Carter Clay.

Submerge is a word that first entered Jersey's vocabulary when she was a tiny girl and her parents bought a metal box trap for the riot of mice they found in a cabin they rented near a dig in Montana. After the trap filled, Joe and Jersey drove several miles in order to release the creatures far from the cabin, only to discover that the trap had no release. In seeking an alternative to those neck-snappers that so upset his wife and child, Joe had missed the instructions pressed into the box trap's metal base: "When trap is full, submerge in water."

It made a good story. Members of the family told it now and then; and, sometimes, when someone missed an essential point, one Alitz/Milhause would whisper to another, "When trap is full . . . ."

▪ ▪ ▪

After Cheryl Lynn finishes calling the grocery store, she steps out on the porch and latches a high hook on the screen door. When she returns to the kitchen, she tells Jersey, "Carter told me to keep you from going outside alone."

If Jersey were less smart, she might respond to this; instead, she reaches into her sidepack, pulls out her journal, and says, "Would you like to call my uncle? I have his number."

"Call *Pete*?" Cheryl Lynn slaps her hands to her cheeks. "But we probably better wait till Carter gets up—hadn't we?"

Without looking up from the journal through which she pages, Jersey says, "I'll call collect. If you're worried about costs."

"Collect!" Cheryl Lynn just has to laugh at the idea of making a collect call to the actor who played Pete.

▪ ▪ ▪

Before leaving for England for two weeks, Sam Alitz changed the message on his machine to something in a mobster mood: "This is Sam, see. Your message or your life, see?" But all that Jersey hears is the operator informing her that there is currently no one at that number to accept a call.

"Well," she says, trying to sound oh-so-casual, "we could call regular long distance, Cheryl Lynn. Leave a message. You could leave the message, if you liked."

Cheryl Lynn reaches behind herself to the counter where she knows her pack of cigarettes sits. *Time out*, she thinks. *Time out, Cheryl Lynn*. She has been suckered by enough guys over the years to recognize a potential trick. "Let's wait till Carter wakes up," she says.

Without argument, Jersey returns to the front room, leaving Cheryl Lynn to call the bowling alley:

Carter is home! Yes, really!

Will Rex and Maggie be okay if she doesn't come in?

They are a couple of sweeties!

Sure, of course she means to bring him and his family by.

After the call to the bowling alley, Cheryl Lynn calls Brent's Rooms for Duncan Clay—who is disappointed to find that the caller is his daughter. Duncan was hoping he had won a sweepstakes or that the caller was one of the radio shows that gave you money if you knew their slogan:

Today's best music mix.

Big band sounds for the nineties.

All the news, all the time.

In order to take the telephone call, Duncan had to leave his Cup of Noodles in the microwave, and there is a possibility that someone may steal it.

"Carter's here, Dad!" says Cheryl Lynn. "He's got his new wife and daughter with him. I'm making chili for supper. Want me to come get you?"

Duncan breathes heavily into the phone. Driving her back. Her and Carter and their mother—they were like a radio you could never turn low enough to keep your sanity. "I told them I'd be here for supper," he says. "You got to tell them the night before if you're going to be away."

"Just this once couldn't hurt! Don't you even want to see your own son?"

"He'll come see me if he's interested. I got to go eat my noodles."

Cheryl Lynn lights up a cigarette and looks out the kitchen window that opens onto the porch. Sometimes, she focuses on the trees and pretends she lives out in the country: no streets, no sidewalks, no cars. Just now, she doesn't mind seeing Carter's van, of course, because she is happy to see Carter, and his van reminds her of the days of hippies. Cheryl Lynn would have liked to have been a hippie, but that would have required her to reinvent herself. Hippies did not go to beauty school or support the war in Vietnam, and Cheryl Lynn had her heart set on beauty school, and she did not know how she could oppose a war while her brother fought in it. Still, she was almost a hippie once; all she would have needed was a push. That was in 1970. She was pregnant with the baby of a mill worker named Ray Cole. It was Christmastime. Everyone was doing a lot of drugs and some people had moved onto farms, but the thing that really convinced Cheryl Lynn that she could be a hippie was the arrival in Fort Powden of a girl in an old VW van. Cream, this girl called herself, and boldly informed everyone that she was a Gypsy. A Gypsy! Cheryl Lynn, who felt wise in her pregnancy when she did not feel like a fool, wanted both to laugh at Cream and to be her. It embarrassed her that the boys in Fort Powden were fascinated by Cream, whose heavy makeup did not hide the fact that she had snaggleteeth and a chin swallowed up by her neck. Cream was the name of a rock group that was popular at the time, and another group, just then, had a hit song called "Gypsy Woman." The man in the Gypsy-woman song loved the Gypsy woman; he and all the other men were entranced by her dancing and her hypnotic cat eyes. Ray Cole—who had cooled toward Cheryl Lynn as soon as she told him she was pregnant—Ray danced with Cream at the Christmas party he had gone to with Cheryl Lynn. Cheryl Lynn went outside to cry. Cream's van was parked alongside the party house, and Cheryl Lynn crawled into the back of the van and, there, put on Cream's clothes and Cream's makeup. Amazing! Her skin looked tanned, her outlined eyes in the van's rearview mirror were huge. She put on one of Cream's long skirts and draped one of Cream's scarves about her neck.

The people at the party howled when Cheryl Lynn came in. They thought she meant to be funny, so she played it funny. *I'm a Gypsy! Let me tell your fortune!* Ray Cole was not there, however. He and Cream had left the party, and Cheryl Lynn ended up in bed with his best friend, and a few days later—despite pleading with the doctors to help her, help—she miscarried Ray Cole's baby at Fort Powden General.

▪ ▪ ▪

The Incredible Shrinking Man is Jersey's lunchtime video selection. Roundly opposed by James and Alfred ("Black-and-white!") and enforced by Cheryl Lynn ("I got you Cheetos and Kool-Aid, so no more complaints").

"Hey, Mom," Jersey says, "remember how Dad started doing pull-ups after we watched this?" She glances over at Katherine, but, because the boys have pulled the curtains on the day, she cannot tell whether Katherine's eyes are open or not, and she turns to Cheryl Lynn as she continues, "Because the hero gets out of so many jams by being strong, see?"

Her eyes on the screen—where the diminutive hero now battles a rat—Cheryl Lynn says, "Pull-ups. Sure. Good for upper body strength."

"Cheryl Lynn," Carter calls from the bedroom, "what time is it?"

"You don't have to get up." Cheryl Lynn goes to the bedroom door. "We're all fine. I called in to work. I'm making chili. Remember how you liked my chili?"

"Sure. Hey, have you seen Neff?" Carter pushes himself into a semi-upright position, his shoulders against the wall at the head of the boys' bed. "I thought maybe he'd let us camp at the Boulders till I get a job."

"Carter"—Cheryl Lynn wants to warn her brother against trying to camp with a girl in a wheelchair, but she senses this is not the time, and so she continues—"Neff's fine. Same old same old. He still comes in the alley now and then to say hi."

"I'm going to call him." Carter scootches down on the mattress, closes his eyes. "Just give me a few more minutes."

"Sure," Cheryl Lynn says, but she is too hungry for the sight of her baby brother to leave the room, and so she stays, tidying things, sneaking glimpses of that scar on his forehead. Her brother. Carter Clay.

Katherine looks up when Cheryl Lynn finally steps out of the bedroom. "How you doing?" Cheryl Lynn asks, so surprised by the loopy smile that Katherine offers her that she misses the fact that Jersey and her chair no longer sit in the living room's dark back corner. It is sheer luck that Cheryl Lynn returns to the kitchen in time to hear an odd noise by the screen door, and to find that Jersey—using the tip of Cheryl Lynn's broom handle to spring the hook on the screen door—has managed to slide out of her chair and haul it and herself down the three steps from the porch to the sidewalk.

. . .

"Your brother should not be married to my mom!" So Jersey shouts once she is back in the kitchen. Tears spill down her cheeks, but her voice is full of fury. "He should leave us alone. I don't know why he won't leave us alone!"

"What the hell are you talking about? You ought to be grateful—"

"We have a house in Arizona. He was driving us there so I could go to a special clinic in Phoenix. But all of a sudden he's married to my mom and we're not going to Phoenix after all, we're going here!"

"Well—"

"Don't you see?" Jersey whispers. "It doesn't make sense. Why did he marry my mom? Why won't he take me to a doctor?"

Cheryl Lynn shakes her head. "He'll take you to a doctor if you need one, Jersey. There's good doctors here."

"My mom"—Jersey pulls her journal from her carryall—"I have a picture of my mom before the accident. From the cover of a book she wrote. You want to see?"

Cheryl Lynn shrugs, noncommittal, but Jersey hands over the photo anyway.

"She's a paleontologist."

Cheryl Lynn shies at the long word. "That's—what's wrong with her?"

"That's what she *did*. Before the accident. She and my dad. They studied fossils?"

"I see."

"That's our house, behind her."

"In Arizona."

"Right."

Though she has not quite admitted to herself why this should be so, Cheryl Lynn feels a glimmer of hope at the fact that the girl's family is from Arizona. "So—you got hurt in Arizona, and your grandma moved you to Florida to take care of you?"

Jersey shakes her head. "The accident was in Florida. We were there, visiting my grandma."

At a noise in the doorway behind them, the two turn: Carter, in his stocking feet, blinking against the bright lights of the kitchen. "Cheryl Lynn," Carter says, "did you give Katherine beer?"

Cheryl Lynn rolls her eyes. "One beer. Is that a problem?"

"She ain't supposed to drink alcohol."

"Well, *I* didn't know that! And she"—Cheryl Lynn points at Jersey—"she tried to run off!"

Carter gives Jersey a long, injured stare. "I suppose we better be taking off," he says.

"What are you talking about?" Cheryl Lynn hurries to the pot on the stove and begins to stir. "I'm making supper for tonight! Chili, remember?"

All of a sudden, Jersey herself is afraid of leaving, and she says, "I was just going to call M.B., Mr. Clay. Is that so awful? I thought we should let her know where we are. She might be worried."

Carter takes a seat at the wobbly kitchen table. He sets his big head in his hands. *Dear Lord, help me not be angry*, he prays. *Let me do your will.*

■ ■ ■

In the front room, where Cheryl Lynn takes Jersey so that Carter can make his call to Neff Morgan in private, the boys and Katherine now watched the TV ("St-op ther'!" Katherine commanded when the remote control brought up the black-and-white *Moby Dick*, and the boys were too intimidated by their odd guest to disobey).

Gregory Peck in the role of Captain Ahab.

"How you doing, Mom?" Jersey asks, and while Katherine appears to consider a response, Cheryl Lynn says, "That Gregory Peck's handsome, but in that funny way. Like, you can't say why he's handsome. Like with Kevin McCarthy. Remember him, Katherine? I could never quite say if Kevin McCarthy was handsome *because* his chin was so big, or in spite of it being so big."

Katherine leans into the light and smiles and nods. "Ab-aham Lin-con."

"Right," says Cheryl Lynn. "I always thought there was something sexy about Lincoln, too."

At first, James and Alfred want to change the channel, but by movie's end they are converts of a sort. They are so happy to see Captain Ahab lose that they cheer the final image: Ahab bound in his own harpoon lines to the side of the great white whale.

Jersey understands why Cheryl Lynn shushes her sons—"Boys, that's not nice!"—but Jersey, too, prefers the whale to the captain. The whale, after all, did not ask for the fight.

33

When the van finally pulls away from Cheryl Lynn's street, the sky is growing dark. Jersey does not mean to fall asleep, but the woman on Carter Clay's Bible cassettes invests her voice with such singsong awe that even when she tells of Saul's jealousy of David—

> Saul has slain his thousands,
> And David his ten thousands!

—against her will, Jersey's eyes grow heavy.

So it is that when she first awakens in the dark of the van, in the check-in area of the Boulders Campground, she does not understand what she sees. Half-asleep, she interprets the cone of lavender light in which the van sits as extraterrestrial: something emitted from the belly of a flying saucer rather than a mercury lamp. Its bright chinking all aglow, a nearby log cabin appears a skeleton of a cabin that might get up and dance a jig. Moonlight renders scattered camping paraphernalia alien, menacing, until a heavenly turquoise cube reveals itself to be a tent in which a family of campers have set their lantern burning as they prepare for bed.

"Mom?" Jersey says. "Where are we? Where's Carter?"

Katherine sits slumped in the passenger's seat, her cheek at rest on the rubber rim of her rolled-down window. She raises her head and points toward the log cabin, as Carter—followed by a man holding a large thermal mug—now proceeds out the door.

The man is Neff Morgan—a short, bearded fellow who, except for his cardigan sweater, looks remarkably like Ulysses S. Grant. Neff Morgan calls, "Hello, ladies," as Carter opens the side door of the van. Though Jersey has closed her eyes, intending to feign sleep, the moment Neff Morgan is aboard the van, he begins to chat. "Guess I'm going to travel back here with you, Jersey, right?" He leans forward to give Carter directions perfumed with whiskey and a fruity chewing gum.

"Just head down to the dead end, Carter. Yup"—Neff pats the back of Carter's headrest, then grins at Jersey—"Carter and me are old buddies."

"Neff's got a place for us to stay," Carter says.

A cabin that he's hoping to fix up, Neff explains. "Just turn right at the gravel road, then we got a half-mile drive. There's no electricity yet, but it's got a gas oven I could get you a cartridge for, and a wood stove and water. And a toilet! And, hey, there's even a little chicken coop out back! You want to raise chickens, Carter?"

Jersey tries to shut out Neff Morgan's chatter. After Carter turns the van onto the gravel road, the headlights catch a bright yellow DEAD END sign. Then they leave the world behind and, together, the dense woods and the headlights make a soft yellow tunnel.

Could it be only a half-mile? She tries to note some sort of details beyond the tunnel, but her position in the van and the night conspire against her, and then Neff Morgan—who also watched *Moby Dick* that afternoon—cries out, "Thar she blows," and the woods on one side of the road suddenly stand open to brush and moonlight. "Turn in here, Carter."

For Jersey, the rough little cabin conjures up a memory of a shanty she remembers from a certain ride at Disneyland—a shanty that appeared always to be in the process of burning down. "Do I get out, Car-ter?" Katherine asks.

Carter pats her knee. "You two just stay put for now," he says, then turns to Jersey and smiles. "Let me and Neff set up a little."

"Sure!" says Neff Morgan—who is so happy to be helping his pal, albeit a bit confused by the makeup of this new family. Neff pops the handle on the side door and climbs down. "You all understand, it's in progress, right?"

Like a kid, Katherine climbs up on her knees to talk to Jersey over the seat back. "I don-t like this place!" she whispers.

"So tell him."

Katherine's eyes widen. "No way!" she says, and drops back in her seat.

Inside the cabin, a flashlight beam skips here and there, now and then offering a view of Carter Clay in the dark: Carter looking at a big piece of metal tubing that must be the chimney for the woodstove. Carter outlined by flashlight as he heaves open one of the double-hung windows.

When Carter returns to the van, Jersey closes her eyes and pretends to sleep. "Oh," Carter says, then instructs Katherine to climb out so that he can hand Jersey down to her. "So's we don't have to get out the ramp," he whispers, and Jersey is more than grateful to snuggle into what could almost pass for a motherly embrace.

"This way," Carter says.

The small sounds of their entry to the cabin—Carter's whispers to Katherine and Neff Morgan, the adults' footsteps on the wooden floors—strike Jersey as highly theatrical, exaggerated, like sound effects from a radio drama.

"I got you two's sleeping bags and pads laid out here in the bedroom," Carter whispers to Katherine. "I'll use the main room."

Jersey opens her eyes to slits once he has zipped her inside her bag and explained to Katherine that he means to run Neff to the campground: "I'll be back in a flash."

It is possible to make out that the walls of the little bedroom are uncovered insulation, the yellow fiberglass faintly green in the light from the window. A mostly empty room. The only object she can make out is a bag of concrete with an all-too-human aspect: its upper half slumped over the lower, like a fat man napping.

Along with the cabin's odors of mice and old wood and new, Jersey smells the familiar odor of her own sleeping bag. She lays her tongue on the silky cloth covering of the bag, and even before she tastes it, she remembers its flavor: both bitter and pleasantly milky, like the hair ribbons she sometimes chewed upon when she was little.

"Mom?" she whispers when she can no longer hear the van's motor. She raises herself up on her elbow to look at Katherine. With eyes closed, Katherine looks more like her old self, doesn't she? That is, more like her old self, asleep?

"Mom?"

When she receives no answer, Jersey raises her voice to a volume that would surely waken anyone. "*Mom*?"

A depressing moment, that: when she realizes that her mother, too, can pretend to sleep.

▪ ▪ ▪

And Carter: Carter feels half nuts as he removes Jersey's wheelchair from the van and carries it up the steps of Neff Morgan's cabin. What is he doing? All the way to the campgrounds, he has had to listen to himself ramble on about his faith in God's power to heal Jersey, and he is now at the point where he would as soon jump out of his own skin and run down the road before he heard another word. Still, he cannot stop.

"See, Neff"—he sets the wheelchair against one of the walls of the little screened porch—"it's, like, up here we'll have a kind of retreat, where I can build up her faith."

The doubt on Neff Morgan's face is not pleasant to see, but Carter can bear it, and he plunges on, hoping there is some coolness or relief ahead, "Remember the Last Supper, Neff?"

Neff shrugs, and looks off into the woods.

"At the Last Supper, how Jesus told His disciples they could ask things in His name and He'd do what they asked?"

“To tell you the truth, Carter, I’m not much of a student of the Bible. But I don’t see how leaving her chair here—”

“‘Whatever you ask the Father in My name He will give to you.’ That’s what He said, and you can see it all over the place. There’s a lame beggar, and Peter says to him, ‘*Silver and gold, I have none; but what I have, that I give thee. In the name of Jesus Christ of Nazareth, arise and walk,*’ and the guy walks. Because of faith, pure and simple.”

“Uh-huh,” says Neff, though without much enthusiasm—a little uncomfortable even, Carter can tell, and to change the subject, Carter stretches his arms high, and turns in a circle under the campground’s mercury lamp. “Neff,” he says, “I love being back here!” He sniffs the air. “The pine needles—can you still smell them?”

“That’s why I live out here, buddy. You sure you won’t have a nightcap? Help you unwind?”

“Not me.” Carter laughs. “I’m Mr. Natural, these days.”

Still, after Carter returns from the campground, he finds that he is, indeed, too wound up to even consider sleep. Too wound up to even go inside.

Boom, boom, boom.

It comes back to him, and he sits on the wooden step leading up to the cabin’s front door and he squeezes his hands together and he prays. *I turn my life over to you, God. I cast the burden of Finis upon you, Lord. Thy will be done. Thy will be done*, he prays, then he heads around the cabin and retrieves M.B.’s bottle of wine from the black plastic bag he earlier placed inside the cabin’s back door. Eventually, he thinks, he will get rid of the wine. He will. But right now it feels like insurance, and—casually, slinging the bottle between two fingers—he carries the bottle back to the chicken coop.

A cute little place, really, like a kid’s playhouse with its peaked roof and white paint.

There is no padlock on the door’s hasp, only a nail thrust through the latch and swivel eye, and he slips out the nail and lets himself inside.

For a moment, that close, dusty space, the highest spot of its peaked roof not much taller than he is—it makes him nervous and he almost backs out again; still, the coop does seem the perfect spot to stash the bottle, and so he stays put and lets his eyes adjust. Two windows. The one beside the door casts a square of fluffy light on the floor. At the back, and to the right, are the nesting boxes, and he tucks the bottle of wine behind one of them. Maybe Jersey would like to use the coop as a playhouse? Maybe then she would not be so angry when she finds out about not having her chair? Stooping to avoid the ceiling and its cobwebs, Carter sweeps the coop with a broom he finds in the corner, and murmurs a rehearsal of his speech.

Yeah, I gave it to Neff for just while we're here. For—collateral. Is that the word he wants? *Collateral*?

Yeah. It's cool, Jersey, don't worry. Your chair? Yeah, Neff's got it—

Yeah, I left it at Neff's as collateral on the cabin. Just for a little while. Hey, why don't you use the time to build up some strength and practice walking? I'll build you some parallel bars if you'll work on building faith in your recovery.

ACTS: Adoration, Confession, Testimony, and Supplication. The four things Pastor Bitner said were essential to a Christian.

Yeah, Neff's got your chair for now, Jersey, so this morning why don't we practice having you stand?

Why not? Why not combine practice and prayer? It's not as if she is likely to get so good she can run away. And if she does have a miracle, then she'll be grateful, and not even want to run off, right?

As dawn comes on, more awake than ever, Carter uses his pocket knife to clear the berry brambles away from the coop. Though the air is cool, he sweats—not merely an effect of his work, but also of his worry.

Huh-huh-huh-huh! he puffs. Huh-huh-huh-huh! He slashes at the brambles in time with this little worker's chant until the sky is blue enough that he can force himself to make a mad dash at the cabin, pop open the door with his shoulder, and call in a noisy voice, "How about some breakfast, you two?"

His show of good cheer does not, however, prevent Jersey from calling back, "Where's my chair?"

"Your chair." Carter stands stock-still in the main room. Its furnishings consist of a peeling picnic table, a squat woodstove connected to a metal chimney, and a couch and a cane chair that look as if they came from the dump. But it is a beautiful day, damn it! Beautiful. This is the day that the Lord hath made, let us rejoice and be glad in it, and Carter makes himself laugh, though his heart beats hard before he asks—"Are you girls decent?"

From Jersey, a glum, "We're decent."

"Okay!" Carter smiles as he sticks his head through the bedroom door. "Neff's got your chair, just now, Jersey. For collateral. For the cabin. But I'll get it back when I get a job. And we can work on your walking in the meantime, you know?"

Dumbfounded. That's what she is, all right. She stares at him, not saying a word, while Katherine clambers from her sleeping bag and shuffles across the room to look out the curtainless windows. "I hear birs," Katherine says.

Carter nods, glad of the distraction. "Sure. And you got to see the chicken coop! I swept it out." He turns toward Jersey. "I thought you might like to have it as a place to play—"

"You used my *chair*?"

"Only till I get a job. And, hey, you may not even need it! By then, with the help of the Lord, you may be walking again—"

"Mr. Clay, we *have* money!" the girl says. "My mom's got credit cards! She could get money at a bank!"

He shakes his head. "Nope, she couldn't, Jersey. I left those things back at the house in Seca. They ain't nothing but trouble."

"Mom? Is it true? You let him take your cards?"

Katherine turns from the window. The frown on her forehead looks fake, applied like a postage stamp. "Di' you take my car's, Car-er?" she asks.

Both panicky and proud, Carter nods and says, "I'm going to take care of you two. I don't want no cards in the way of that. And I'll haul you anywhere you want, Jersey. Hey, we're rich in God's love and prayers, ain't we? After we're settled in, I'll take you two to town again. You didn't really see much of it. It's pretty. The courthouse's like a castle out of a fairy tale, and we got this famous tree—a Tree of Heaven that a China emperor gave to the town a long time ago. The flowers stink—if you step on them—but they're pretty."

To escape the girl's wobbling eyes, Carter goes down on his knees where he stands. "Katherine? Jersey? Can we say a prayer now? Start the morning right in our new home?"

▪ ▪ ▪

While Katherine steps to Carter Clay's side and joins him in kneeling, Jersey lies back in her sleeping bag. The ceiling above is made of sheets of unpainted drywall, marked here and there by footprints: prints from two different pairs of boots, and prints from a dog, and then, across the corner of one sheet, prints from something very tiny—a mouse? a squirrel?

While Carter Clay and Katherine say their prayers, Jersey stares up at that patterned ceiling, and does her best to have faith in its message that those who were here before her, in one way or another, managed to escape.

34

These are the items on Finis Pruitt's current list of wants:

A. He wants Clay dead.
B. He wants to be Rear End again.
C. He wants Clay alive so that Clay can be blackmailed.
D. He wants to destroy the girl's and her mother's idea of Clay; to let them know that Clay is the one who hit them and killed their father and husband.

While it is true that (D) is not strictly necessary, Finis Pruitt cannot quite resist the idea of fouling Clay's image, and D would have to be before A, and C before D. So: C, D, A?

Has Clay shown Finis Pruitt that he can never be safe with B again? Perhaps. But perhaps there are other possibilities for Finis.

"Hey"—he turns to the driver of the big rig that stopped for him in El Paso—"you ever see *The Wizard of Oz* when you were a kid?" Without waiting for the trucker to answer, Finis produces an imitation of Margaret Hamilton's Wicked Witch that makes the trucker laugh: "These things must be done delicately. Delicately!"

As the day progresses, the driver—Donny Espinoza of Sacramento—reveals that he sympathizes completely with his anonymous passenger's membership in the Militia. Hell, he wishes he could be part of the movement himself! But the wife—

"I understand, man," says his passenger. "I walk with God one way, you walk with Him another, but we're both serving."

How thrilling for Donny Espinoza, then, when his passenger asks him to handle his telephone call to another Militia member. This occurs at the pay telephone in the Seca loading yard where Donny Espinoza is making his drop.

"You get an answer, you ask for Jersey, then hand it to me."

Donny is almost misty-eyed when he turns to Finis to report: no answer. "What does it mean?" Donny asks.

"I don't know yet," Finis says, "but I thank you for your help to the cause."

▪ ▪ ▪

What a disappointment Finis finds the neighborhood in which the Alitz/Milhause home sits! On his way there, he passed through a section of big, creamy places so exquisitely appointed and manicured and contained that even the lawns appeared to grow in pots.

Finis considers himself a connoisseur of such sights, one who knows how to appreciate, simultaneously, both their perfection and their absurdity.

The family's neighborhood, on the other hand, is a typical aging southwestern subdivision with neither curbs nor lawns. Various colors of gravel—one yard has been spray-painted turquoise—spill out of front lots and mix with the crumbling asphalt edges of the road. The outstanding feature on most of the properties is a monster eucalyptus or aleppo pine that has survived since the subdivision's birth and now dwarfs the modest home below.

"From Bauhaus to Our House," Finis sneers as he presses his nose to the glass block of the front entry, but when he ventures around back, he cannot help applauding the choice of floor-to-ceiling windows, one of which is broken and eliminates the necessity of any arduous entry.

"Hello?" he calls through the hole, then edges his way past a few nasty shards of glass and into the living room, where a set of silvery tracks on the floor lead to a dead mallard, head beneath some sort of sideboard.

"Carter? Dr. Milhause? It's Finis! Just an old friend come to call!"

Conflicting signs: the hum in the kitchen signals electrical current, yet he finds nothing in the refrigerator but a leftover piece of steak that smells a little funky, and a cucumber that shows the beginnings of a coat of delicate blue fur.

Again: "Hello!"

Unlike Carter, Finis recognizes the charms—and pretensions—of the house. Dark wood. Old rugs. Middle Ages, Finis thinks. A bit of ye old monastery tempered by the row of Mexican masks on the dining room wall (man with a lizard clamped to his face, etc.). Many bookcases filled with fossils and rocks and, of course, books. Books, books, books.

Could he have enjoyed talking to these people?

He runs the back of his nails along the spines—tick, tick, tick—as he reads aloud: "*The Birth of Tragedy. Cult Movies. Psychology and Religion. Wonderful Life. The Evolution of Consciousness. The Writings and Drawings of Bob Dylan. Coming of Age in Samoa. Texas Crude. The Man Who Mistook His Wife for a Hat. The Encyclopedia of Philosophy. Ever Since Darwin. Cruden's Complete Concordance. Zen Mind, Beginner Mind. The Sacred and the Profane*—"

To be suspicious of a thing because it comes easily—that is unreasonable, and Finis knows it. Thus: after he sees that his hand is covered with the prickly pear stickers that he picked up as he made his way around the outside of the house; and he steps to the kitchen to look through the drawers for something to remove the stickers; and he finds a number of keys and a small deck of credit cards—several still unexpired—well, he is not entirely skeptical. He *does,* however, start when the Scout parked in the attached garage leaps to life with the first key that he tries.

So: back to the kitchen, where he folds himself into the window seat. During his days at the mission in Oneco, he perfected a blank look—something like stupidity—and that is the look he wears now. But his brain works.

Could Clay somehow be forcing a car upon him? Could this be a trap? In all of his years as Rear End, Finis never allowed himself the weight of a car, a credit card. Does the great gloved hand of his life's story mean to reach down and tempt him with ease in his hunt for Clay?

Or is this a gift bestowed by an appreciative audience?

There is nothing to sooth his nerves in the family's bathroom medicine cabinet—a true pharmacological wasteland—but, for the sake of certain aches and pains, he swallows several aspirins, then lays himself down for an afternoon nap.

▪ ▪ ▪

In the daughter's room, as it turns out. Finis eyes the mural of the *Archaeopteryx*, the copy of *Six Easy Pieces* on the bed stand, a photo of two girls, one of whom is Jersey Alitz.

The bedroom of Goldilocks.

He is going to sleep in Goldilocks's bed.

The idea of himself as one of the avenging bears makes Finis smile.

Several hours later, when the front doorbell rings, he does not come completely awake, but the noise arouses him sufficiently that when he hears footsteps in the hall, he sits bolt upright, and then—precisely as Jersey could *not* do several days before—slides over and down the side of the bed and onto the floor.

"Kitty? Jersey?" A woman's voice. Older. Loud, but tentative. "Carter?"

With a flick of his wrists, Finis removes a screen from a curtained bedroom window, pushes the thing out ahead of himself, slips into the backyard and behind a toolshed.

"Do you know you've got a dead duck in your back room, there?"

M.B., just arrived from the airport. Though she is still favoring last week's sprained ankle, she hopes her voice sounds strong. Full of confident amusement. A little like the voice of Patsy

Glickman, who has been giving M.B. much-needed pep talks ever since the morning she came to M.B.'s rescue in the master bath.

You can do it! She's your daughter! You gotta be strong for her and then you'll respect yourself and you won't feel like you have to hide out like an old fool!

M.B. has never in her life ever traveled anywhere on her own, let alone flown on an airplane. The experience has left her feeling—all at once—plucky and tired and spooked.

A peculiar experience for M.B.: to walk through the home of her child for the first time. A child who is no longer a child, or even the adult who lived in the home. In a way, the house is a museum, isn't it? With its tile and concrete floors, white walls, and old furniture, doesn't it look like one of those places M.B. and Lorne sometimes visited? A pioneer homestead, say, or an old schoolhouse? M.B. finds herself stopping at the doorway to each room as if a velvet rope blocks her entrance. In the narrow hallways with their shelves full of books and fossils, she holds her arms tight to her sides, afraid she may cause breakage or leave evidence that could be used against her.

God is in M.B.'s heaven, yes; still, she worries that He might not realize that she is not responsible for the slovenly housekeeping around her, and so she runs a hand along a dusty window ledge and asks, *sotto voce*, "Is this what I pay six-fifty an hour for, Mrs. Hinkey?"

Initially, the refrigerator door resists her pull—FLASH: NEWS STORIES OF BODY PARTS ON ICE!—but then the door pops open, and it offers evidence far less horrific but not entirely reassuring (spoiled meat, fuzzy cucumber).

The important thing, of course—M.B. reminds herself of this as she dials the housekeeper's telephone number—the important thing is not to criticize Mrs. Hinkey, but to learn whether or not the woman has seen Katherine and Jersey.

Mrs. Hinkey takes several whistling breaths before she says, "Let's see. I got my team doing that house. I'd have to ask my team about that one, ma'am."

M.B. sniffs, then cannot stop herself from muttering, "*Not* doing it would be a better description!"

"What's that?"

"It's filthy! There's—a dead duck in the living room!"

"I thought you said your daughter'd been there, ma'am."

"I don't know if she was here or not. That's what I'm trying to find out."

Rather sharply, Mrs. Hinkey informs M.B. that if there were a dead duck in her living room, she would not wait for somebody else to come by to clean it up.

"Kid," says M.B., "if you keep your house the way you keep my daughter's place, I suspect you'd miss a cow if it died in your living room."

This testy conversation derails M.B.'s original panic somewhat, and after she hangs up the telephone, she uses a thick pad of newspapers to pick up the duck—albeit with shivers and shudders—and to set it in the kitchen trash basket, which she then sets outside the front door.

She could call the university, maybe. Or that couple that came to visit Katherine at Fair Oaks. What was their name? She could speak to the neighbors?

Damp hay. That is the taste of the herbal tea—Silk Road?—that M.B. finds in the cupboard. *Sugar, sugar*, she mutters aloud, opening and closing cupboards, poking her head here, there, pursing and unpursing her lips.

How mortified she would be if anyone could detect the upbeat of her heart when she opens the door to a cupboard holding a large bag of pinto beans, cans of chicken broth, and an assortment of bottles of liquor: rum, Kahlua, vodka, sherry—

Immediately, she slams the door shut. Carries her cup of Silk Road into the dining room where she stands erect at the window and watches for Carter's van to appear. A watchdog. So she sees herself. The watchdog guarding the house. In Wyoming, when she was a girl, her family had a dog. Big tan and black Dolly sat on the front lawn, erect and proud, tail lifted high when she barreled down upon intruders. A shepherd. Loyal and true. Of course, it was M.B. and Dicky whom Dolly most staunchly defended. Her flock.

M.B. shivers. Perhaps she is just the old fool guard dog, the one who woke to defend the pasture only after the sheep were already lost.

From room to room, she wanders. How can it be that every view in her daughter's house contains a sunset?

Back at the dining room window, she watches several neighbors come and go: a man parks in the drive across the street and, suit jacket hanging from one finger, begins to water a tree. He reminds M.B. of the boss from *The Mary Tyler Moore Show*—what was his name? When a little red car pulls up in the driveway next door, a second man trots over from across the street to talk at some length with the woman who emerges from the red car. M.B. supposes the woman must be about Kitty's age. A friend of Kitty's? Probably not. This woman has professionally styled and streaked hair. She wears nylon stockings and cobalt-blue high heels and a matching suit that M.B. herself would not mind owning. Trim. Organized. While she unloads a number of brightly colored file boxes from her little car, she chats animatedly with the man from across the street. A friendly person. Still, how could M.B. step out and say, "Excuse me, miss, but I seem to have lost my daughter. Would you happen to know where she's gone?"

Dusk falls early and fast in this city ringed by mountains. Boom. M.B. marks the change by chucking the rotten food in the refrigerator. Locating the switches for the "swamp cooler," and setting the thing to blowing its bit of damp air through the house. While she brews herself a second cup of tea, she carries the bottles of liquor out to the trash can that already holds the dead duck. Then, failing to find a deck of cards anywhere at all, she takes a seat on the living room couch with a copy of *Rethinking the Evolution of Birds*.

When the book was first published, Kitty gave M.B. a copy. M.B.'s experience of trying to read *Rethinking the Evolution of Birds* was very much like Carter's; not only did she find the book difficult, she did not see the point of it. This evening, however, the book makes M.B.'s heart twist in her chest. Though she still does not understand the contents of the thing, its sheer weight in her lap—all of those words, page after page!—the black-and-white plates of fossils; well, she feels how they make up something like the house in which she now sits, a testament of a life.

For Jersey and Joe,
who make my life worthwhile.

So reads the book's dedication.

"Oh, Lorne!" M.B. cries but finds only her own spooky reflection on the floor-to-ceiling windows, and she rises from the couch and—heavyhearted—goes for her purse so she can look up her new voice mail number and call for any possible messages that may have come in at #335.

▪ ▪ ▪

Golden, enchanted—that is how the Alitz/Milhause living room appears from the backyard, but Finis Pruitt knows that if he were inside, the light would become common, sullied with life's ordinary mess. (He has already witnessed M.B. Milhause's dragging of a piece of cardboard into the living room, her loony bandaging of the cardboard to the broken window with the same roll of duct tape that he earlier used to remove the prickly pear stickers from his hand.) No, Finis does not care too much about the fact that he is outside. Really, he is quite comfortable on the chaise cushion he has dragged behind a hedge of boxwood, and amused by the sight of the grandmother framed in the enormous drape-free windows. Clearly, she assumes that it is her imagination that makes her feel watched, and—ho!—it gives Finis a kick to see her jump and twitch when he throws the occasional twig at a window screen or up on the roof.

▪ ▪ ▪

Perhaps Finis trains M.B. to not trust her senses in that house?

However it happens, that night, when M.B. wakes in the big bed her daughter used to share with Joe Alitz, and M.B. hears over the little storm of the swamp cooler a noise like the starting of a car, she assumes that this is just one more instance of the unfamiliar sounds the house of her daughter is capable of generating, and she rolls over and goes back to sleep.

35

On the morning of the day that M.B. arrives in Seca, Carter carries Jersey out to the chicken coop and shows her what he has been working on for most of the two days since they have been at the cabin: parallel bars, built from lumber donated from Neff Morgan's remodeling piles.

"They're real sturdy," he says. In demonstration, he bumps his hip up against one side of the bars. "And I sanded them smooth."

"Take me to a doctor. Then I'll try them."

Carter stares over the top of the girl's head at the windowless back of the chicken coop, the row of empty nesting boxes. Always an awkward thing: to talk to the girl when he carries her in his arms. He can feel how she stiffens her neck and back to keep from touching any more of him than is necessary.

"But you can *try* walking now," he says.

"I need to see a doctor. I need my chair." She is so close to him he can hear her breath whistle from her nose.

Lighthearted, but not mean; that is the tone Carter strives for, but what comes out is just sad, tired. "You think God don't know more than doctors, Jersey? If you ask God to help you walk, He might just do for you the next great thing He's going to show the doctors!"

A little shudder passes through the girl, and she says in a quaking voice, "Please, don't make me try, Mr. Clay. I've already got a sore. If I fall again—"

He would give her a hug but he fears it might scare rather than reassure her, and so instead he says, "You know I wouldn't do anything to hurt you, don't you? You're not afraid of me, are you?"

When she does not answer, he feels bitter, and, quick, he carries her back to the cabin and sets her on the battered little couch in the main room.

"Why do you keep us here like prisoners?" she asks.

Carter slams out the back door without answering, but the question disconcerts him. Partly because he is certain he has heard it before. In a movie, he thinks. Some quaking woman asks some crazed lunatic, *Why do you keep us here like prisoners*? Some nut who could not have explained his actions even if he wanted to.

But Carter is not a nut. As he passes by the window at the side of the house, he can see the girl crying on the couch, and he feels sorry, and he thinks, hard, of the words he needs to use to justify himself to God. *Dear God, I am heartily sorry for what I done. Please, God, make Jersey walk. If you make her walk, then it will be as if the accident never happened.*

Almost.

Or, really, it will be almost better, God. Because then she'll have faith in you. She'll be a Christian. And I want to bring her and Katherine to you, Lord, because you forgave what I done. But if her and Katherine find out about me, that may screw up their believing in you, so please don't let them find out. And, please, forgive me, Lord, for being afraid maybe you don't forgive me or that you won't cure Jersey.

He finds Katherine sitting on the cabin's front steps, and fits himself next to her. He squeezes his hands together tight. Forget about the possibility that Finis is out there. Now that Carter has put his faith in God curing the girl, he can't take her to the doctors, right? He can't act as if he don't believe God has the power to do it, right?

He sighs, then says to Katherine, "You think about old Abraham"—lately he often finds himself talking to her almost as he would talk to himself—"when God told Abraham to sacrifice Isaac, Abraham had to show he was willing to do it before God would say, 'Hold it.' And Jesus—Jesus said you could ask for anything. All you have to do is believe."

Katherine does not give Carter any indication that she hears or does not hear, but he continues, "It's hard to know if you believe enough, unless God tells you so. I guess if God come down and said you didn't believe enough—well, you'd believe enough after that!" He laughs, then taps on Katherine's knee and she turns his way. "I just want to show God I'm faithful, you know? Believing Jersey can get well—that's a way to show I'm faithful." He puts his head in his hands. He stares at the creases in the toes of his boots. "Or maybe I just want God to show Jersey what He can do. Like Jesus turning the stones into bread, you know?"

Katherine gives him a quick sideways glance, as if he is a stranger who has taken a seat beside her on a park bench, then says, "He din't do tha', though."

"What?"

"Stone in'o brea-*d*."

"Sure, he did. It's even in that Willie Nelson song."

Katherine shrugs a shoulder, and stands. "He wrong. Jesus tol' the De-vil, no. 'Ma' shall no-*t* live by brea-d 'lone.' 'Member?"

Carter is so unnerved by this string of words from Katherine that he has failed to answer her question by the time that she rises and moves off around the side of the house, but when he is alone on the steps, he pleads, *God, tell me what do*.

No answer comes, and when the light rain that has fallen off and on all day finally turns into a genuine downpour, Carter gives up on his solitary vigil and steps back inside the cabin.

Mother and daughter sit on the little couch. Neither looks up to take notice of his soggy presence. Is this good? Bad? Should he go for dry clothes, or make a statement out of his wetness? Undecided, he stands by the double-hung window, staring out. The rain makes a sweet frying-pan sizzle that he remembers from high school camp-outs with Neff. "Breathe," say the electric-green leaves and grass and the dark brown of the tree trunks. Though Carter does not realize that such sights restore him to himself, he does eventually recognize his toes in his boots, the cool tip of his nose, and then he turns to face the inhabitants of the room once again. Jersey. Katherine. He makes three cups of instant cocoa and sets them down on the floor in front of the couch.

"What's going on, guys?" he asks.

"She draw me maze," Katherine says.

"Can I see?"

Jersey tilts the pad of paper in her hand his way.

Instantly sweaty, almost nauseated, Carter asks, "Why'd you write *FINIS* in the middle, there, Jersey?"

"*Finis*—it means 'the end,'" she says, without looking up. "I put it where the end of the maze is."

"'The end'?" Carter shakes his head. "I never heard that before."

"It's Latin."

Latin? Why would she know Latin? Then again, why would she lie? He, after all, is the liar. But suppose she lies because she knows Carter lies. Suppose Finis got to her somehow and told her and now she has her own game running? God on Carter's side, the Devil on hers?

To calm himself, Carter goes to the picnic table and sits and consults the list of readings in the front of his Bible: "HELP IN TIME OF NEED." Shall he turn to selections pertaining to "The Way of Salvation" (Acts 16:31 or Romans 10:9)? "Comfort in Time of Loneliness"? "Strength in Time of Temptation"?

He supposes it does not matter which one he reads. Everything applies.

▪ ▪ ▪

The rest of that rainy day, and then on into the night, guided by the bright moth of flame that flies inside the lantern on the picnic table, Jersey watches Carter Clay out of the corner of her eye.

Unnerving: her sense that he watches her in like manner.

HELP—THIS IS NO JOKE! I AM BEING HELD IN A CABIN ABOUT HALF A MILE BEYOND THE BOULDERS CAMPGROUND. I NEED A DOCTOR! DON'T KNOW PRECISE LOCATION BUT THERE'S A HUGE ROCK IN FRONT YARD! PLEASE CALL POLICE AND MY GRANDMOTHER, MARYBELLE MILHAUSE IN BRADENTON, FLORIDA, 1–941–794–1111.

So read the underside of the paper plate that Jersey persuaded Katherine to put outside that morning. ("Here, Mom, give the birds the rest of my bread.") The entire time that Carter Clay sat out on the porch, Jersey was terrified that he might come upon the plate.

An unnecessary worry. The plate had immediately blown across the yard and tucked itself under an edge of that big boulder Jersey hoped might serve to mark the spot for her rescuers. In the rain, the plate is already turning to pulp; the words on the back are indecipherable. But Jersey continues to imagine the thing blowing against one of Carter Clay's big boots. He picks it up and reads her words and knows she views him not as just some poor substitute for her real father but as a threat to her existence.

. . .

That night, however, after he has set her down in her sleeping bag beside Katherine, Carter Clay stands and begins to whistle "Down Yonder Green Valley," and, for a moment, he becomes actually Joe, her *dad*, and her dad says—or maybe it is the rain falling outside, through the trees and on the thin roof of the cabin—*The guy may mean well, Jersey, but if you have to kill him to save your life, you do it. You hear me?*

Dad?

Near tears, she wants to call out to the figure to come closer, let her see his face, but she understands somehow that this is not allowed, and so she only whispers, "I hear you," and when the figure takes a step forward and into the light coming through the window, it is Carter Clay, his shaved head a blue moon, who asks, "One of you say something?"

"Jers," Katherine says.

Jersey makes no reply. She waits to hear more from Joe, but all that comes is the hiss of the rain, then Carter's low whistling and the sound of his footfalls as he crosses the wooden floor to the main room.

Such a different sound comes from the wooden floors of the cabin than from the concrete floors with which Jersey grew up! The crawl space beneath the cabin forms an echo chamber, while in the Seca house, with its heavy plaster walls and concrete floors, a person in socks or bare feet might appear behind you without your ever having heard anyone enter the room.

36

M.B. does not sense that the Seca house might conceal important sounds from her; nor does she even remember, upon waking the next morning in Katherine and Joe's bed, that she heard a noise like an engine starting the night before.

Really, M.B. is too deeply filled with dread to think clearly about much of anything. The swamp cooler's blast of air has grown bitter-cold overnight; she covers her head with the Indian rug her daughter apparently used as a bedspread, and she shivers and moans.

Waking up in Katherine's bed puts M.B. in mind of waking up that morning beside the stiffened body of Lorne. And the days in the hospital after the accident.

She rolls onto her side, pulls her knees up to her chest, and stares at a carved wooden mask on Joe and Katherine's wall—a red thing, with eyes as big as chicken eggs, horns, and long strands of white hemp spouting out of its head for hair.

A very particular memory returns to her: an awful moment when she lost three-year-old Kitty in Carson Pirie Scott. It was Christmastime. The store was full of shoppers and loud carols. M.B. was looking for a gift for her mother—a robe—and all of a sudden Kitty was gone. After several minutes of calling and rushing up and down aisles—scared to death and so ashamed, too, because a mother was *responsible* for the safety of her child, and suppose Kitty turned up with her head chopped off, M.B. had read of such things, nightmare things done to innocent children—M.B. cried out to another woman shopper and a clerk, *Help me, my little girl's lost*!

For the half-hour that Kitty could not be found, M.B. vowed that she would kill herself if harm had come to Kitty—who eventually turned up inside a rack of housecoats close by the spot where M.B. had stood when she first noticed her missing. Kitty was pale, gripping the chrome racks. She had been, it seemed, too frightened by M.B.'s fear to make herself known. When a man helping in the search reached into the rack to take Kitty out, she fainted dead away.

Who can M.B. possibly ask for help in finding Kitty? She knows that Carter has family in Washington. A father, a sister.

M.B. forces herself to push her feet out from under the covers and onto the cold concrete.

She tells herself: start somewhere.

■ ■ ■

"This is the day that the Lord hath made. Let us rejoice and be glad in it." So reads the piece of folded cardboard that Carter has propped on the picnic table that serves for both meals and school; just now, however, the cardboard catches the late afternoon's golden light, and thus burnished, its message is temporarily obliterated.

Carter—not rejoicing himself—peels potatoes in the cabin's dark little kitchen. A week has passed since their arrival in Washington, but he is not sure whether a greater number of days without news of Finis Pruitt signals safety ahead or danger's hulking advance. Also, Jersey has yet to try the parallel bars; and though he has spent the last four days looking for work in the little towns around Fort Powden, Carter has had nothing even close to a bite.

He puts his head into the cabin's main room to check on things. There, at the head of the picnic table, Jersey—in a rattan chair so ancient it wheezes—Jersey pretends to be Katherine's student. Recites for Katherine what Carter knows perfectly well is the lesson she means to *teach* Katherine: some gobbledygook about how knowing the way in which cartilage is replaced by bone can help a paleontologist ("Such as yourself, Mom") to determine the maturity of a fossil specimen.

"So, how's school going?" Carter asks. Depressingly tinny, his voice in the little wooden cabin. He steps out to the picnic table, to bring self and voice closer to the pair, but, in response to his question, the official teacher merely sighs and moistens her thumb with spittle. Holds her thumb against Carter's cardboard sign, forming a faint bond between the two. Sighs again. She is easily distracted. Petulant. Messy. Disorganized. On top of this, she is now angry. She flicks a finger at Carter's piece of cardboard. Tick. Tick. Tick.

Katherine and Carter have a deal: if Katherine does not wander out of the cabin while Carter job-hunts, and if she carries Jersey—when asked—to the little closet that holds the cabin's toilet, then she is allowed to listen to the Bible tapes in the afternoon. Today, Carter was to buy batteries for the tape player, and he forgot.

Which was understandable. That morning, after job-hunting in Bain, he decided to drive through Fort Powden while he ate his lunch, and, of course, there were the red brick buildings of his life, and people going in and out of them. The changes he saw upset him (Fuller Drug was now a kite shop called Play It by Air, and the Ben Franklin was selling sporting goods). Still, the office supply store remained. Lillian's Card and Party. Secondhand Rose. He longed to go into Secondhand Rose to see if Teddy would look up from organizing his boxes of jigsaw puzzles and old Avon bottles and say, "Hey, you played football for Fort Powden!"

But Carter drove on to Marpool, one of the little towns where he believed he was less likely to run into anyone he knew. In Marpool, he filled out applications at a dry cleaner and a place not unlike the Accordion Cafe. Afterward, when the van would not start up, he pretended not to notice—a little trick he had used on the van several times before. He just climbed right out of the van, as if he did not really want to leave Marpool then, anyway. Whistled a little "Down Yonder Green Valley" as he walked off.

Maybe while he went for a cup of coffee the engine would cool off a bit, or the wires would get a rest, whatever. But, no, forget the coffee, he decided. A return to the café might be unwise. You didn't want a potential boss speculating about you maybe having vehicle trouble.

He walked down Marpool's little main street. Looked at the offerings in the shopwindows. A hobby shop. An extermination service displaying a lot of boxes and cans of bug and slug killers. He stopped to consider a layout of fishing supplies in the window of a sporting goods place. Someone had taken care with the display, making it appear to be a spot to which a fisherman would soon return, perhaps to have a drink from the thermos that stood between the camp stool and the bait box, and Carter stared at all of this, and thought that there might never again be a thing he wanted. Or else he would want everything—all of the bright and tiny flies, and the fat lures painted bold as totem poles, and the jars of coral-colored bait, and you name it. Then he saw himself reflected in the store window, and before he even had a chance to absorb himself—so big and faded—behind him a Native American woman with waist-length black hair hopped out of a UPS truck with a package.

Bonnie Drabnek.

Carter had spun around and even yelled her name before it dawned on him that the startled young woman who turned his way was probably the age of those babies of Bonnie's whom he had known twenty-some years before.

"Sorry," Carter called. "Sorry, miss."

The whole incident upset him, though, and so he forgot the batteries.

And now Katherine is upset.

In an effort to cheer Katherine, Carter says, "Jersey's a good student, ain't she, Katherine?"

Katherine looks up from fiddling with the cardboard homily on the picnic table, and demands, "Wha-*t abou' me,* Car-er?"

"Well, hey"—he smiles—"you're the teacher, Katherine!"

Somewhat absently, Jersey says, "My dad called me Biblio sometimes. Short for Bibliophile."

Carter nods and continues to smile. He always does his best to smile when the girl mentions her father. Which is not always easy. Because, sometimes, Carter envies the girl's love for the dead man; and he forgets—yes, it's true—he forgets that he caused the death that caused the circumstances that make him wish the girl loved him, too.

"So, what's that biblio-thing?" he asks.

The glance she casts his way is almost suspicious—as if he has joined in on her conversation with someone else. "A book lover. It's—like, from Greek. *Bible*, 'book.' *Phile*, 'lover.'"

"So the Greeks got their word for book from the Bible?" Carter nods and smiles to convey interest and enthusiasm. "That's neat, isn't it?"

The girl gives him a blank stare, then reaches for Katherine's hand on the table and squeezes it, and he retreats to the kitchen and his potatoes.

In the moment between his striking of the match and the catch, the smell from the stove always makes Carter think of the time his mother tried to gas herself. The little *whomph* that sounds as the parrot-blue flames leap to life: it makes his heart clench.

Today, in the want ads, the best-paying of those jobs for which Carter qualified was live-in aide to a handicapped person (seven dollars an hour). But how could he be a live-in aide and take care of Jersey and Katherine? Each time he left the pair alone while he went on his job-hunts, he felt uncertain about who was watching whom. He could, and did, apply for jobs in Bain as a cook, server, or busser at five dollars an hour. Kennel cleaner. Pest control worker. Lumberyard driver.

He liked the lumberyard—the smell, the cutting sounds, and the way it seemed the men in the yard had time both alone and together. The manager of the yard, however, was no more than a kid. A little guy with a big class ring on his finger. Maybe the boss's son?

"There's some years on there that might not look so good, but since I become a Christian, I been real responsible on the job," Carter explained.

The manager tapped his pencil against his teeth. Good straight teeth. Braces, Carter guessed. "How long's that been?" the manager asked.

"A year now. And I was straightened out even before—a year before that. I got on track. I'm on track now."

With the eraser of his pencil, the manager rubbed at a spot on his desk top. "That's good," he said. Then he stood. "We'll be looking over applications starting next week." He nodded and held out his hand to Carter.

"I got a wife and daughter," Carter said. "I need the job."

"Hm-mm," the manager said.

"My daughter's handicapped."

"I'm sorry," the manager said. He sounded as if he meant it, but Carter still knew he would not get the job.

▪ ▪ ▪

"So, Jersey"—Carter covers the pot and turns up the gas under the potatoes before he steps back into the main room—"Jersey." He taps on the illustration of mammal and reptile bones that Jersey now traces for Katherine—"how about you leave off that and we do our Bible reading and then have prayers?"

Without lifting her eyes from her work, Jersey shakes her head. "It's still schooltime."

Carter crouches to poke through the scant remains of the boxes of groceries he packed up at the Seca house. A sixty-four-ounce can of tomato juice, a tiny tin of mandarin oranges. He bounces the tin of oranges in his hand and tries to look casual. "Did you read that section I told you?"

"I read it."

"You like it?"

"Sure."

"So, you think we should forgive everyone so we're forgiven, too?"

She leans forward in the creaking chair to rifle through the books spread out upon the picnic table, then lays her hands upon the Bible from the Turquoise Motel. The book is now well feathered with her own as well as Carter's page markers (scraps of paper bags, bits of the margins of Jersey's journal pages, gum wrappers). "You mean, should I forgive Hitler? Should I forgive the guy who hit us?"

She looks Carter right in the eye, as if he ought to answer (a sickening moment; his right knee begins to jiggle), but then she continues, "Do you feel like you're forgiven by God for—well, in the war, even if *you* didn't actually kill anyone, you were part of killing people, right?"

Carter lifts the edge of the Geisha label on the tin of oranges and carefully peels it back. "That's right." He senses that the girl continues to look at him out of some sort of politeness; as if she wants to let him know that she does not consider him an outcast because he killed people.

"Maybe God can forgive people because we seem so *small*," she says. "Maybe I could forgive the person who hit us if he were really, really far away. Like a star in the sky. If all I see is this tiny twinkle—"

In a choking rush, Carter interrupts, "As far as the war goes, though—well, you got to defend yourself and your buddies when the enemy's shooting at you. And there's your duty, too. Honor. And duty. Plus, don't forget, Jesus *did* say he come as a sword."

Jersey nods. "But he didn't really mean—I think he meant more, like, he was going to change things. Anyway, I don't believe he said *everything* they say he did, do you?"

At that moment, Carter senses that the single frown line stitched above Jersey's right eyebrow as she waits for his response—that tiny line is the needlework of her intelligence and her earnestness, and he appreciates it. He nods, then says a guarded, "That part in Revelations where the ones with the mark on their foreheads are damned, I asked Pastor Bitner about that, 'cause, you know"—Carter points to his scar—"and he told me not to worry. And you know that place where Jesus's mom and brothers come for him, and he says they aren't his family? I never liked that. I always wondered if that was true."

"Yeah"—Jersey takes up the book and, again, flips through the pages—"but there, I figure he's just trying to say you shouldn't let certain people have greater claims on you just because they're your blood relatives."

Carter folds the can label in half. Irons the fold between index finger and thumb. "So, I guess, according to Jesus, you and I can be close as you and your dad, then?"

"Well"—as if the room has suddenly become too bright, Jersey looks out from under a raised hand as she replies—"it's an ideal, of course."

Tsk, tsk, tsk. Both Jersey and Carter glance toward the window, where Katherine now makes one of the noises she uses to draw curious birds into the open. *Tsk, tsk.*

Oh, Lord, Carter prays, *give Jersey a sign, Lord.* He closes his eyes. *Please, Lord, give her a sign to help her believe in you. Anything. Make her walk, Lord, please. Change water to blood, a stick to a snake—*

"Ah!" cries Katherine, and then a creak sounds from Jersey's rattan chair, and Carter smiles and opens his eyes. But there is no river of blood rushing across the floor. There is no burning bush, no miraculous cloud—only the girl, still seated, and now staring at him somewhat suspiciously. "So, Mr. Clay," she asks, "when am I going to get my wheelchair back?"

To hide his disappointment at his prayer's failure, Carter goes to stand beside Katherine at the window.

"See, Car-er." Katherine points happily to a rufous-sided towhee that flings leaves here and there in its search for bugs.

Of course, the miracle stories have always reminded Carter too much of Superman comics. Even when Carter was a kid, it occurred to him that while Superman fought and defeated one bad guy, there were still all kinds of other bad guys doing bad deeds in other places. And with Jesus—you had to wonder why Jesus didn't just heal everybody all at once, once and for all.

"Mr. Clay?" says Jersey, and Katherine, "Robin Hoods!"—her response to a pair of cardinals that shoot through the rough undergrowth at the side of the clearing.

"You want to keep an open mind, Jersey—about walking," Carter says.

"I want my chair, is what I want!" Forget the pleasantries of a minute ago. Now the girl howls. "I've got a pressure sore. You've got to get me my chair and take me to a doctor."

Carter stares at Jersey—her thin little face, the long hair straggly from not being washed. She reminds him of a newborn chick. A poor little newborn chick whose head is too big for it to hold, and he cries, "Oh, Lord," and he goes down on his knees right where he stands, in the middle of the room, but then he cannot tell whether he is truly with God or making a show of himself, and he opens his eyes when Katherine says a sharp: "Wai-t!" Katherine's expression of concentration—the lift of her chin—makes her appear unfamiliar to Carter. For a moment, she looks a little like the woman on the jacket of *Rethinking the Evolution of Birds*. "Car-er," she cries, and then, "some-ing's burning!"

The potatoes. He forgot to add water.

When Carter returns from putting the burnt pot to sizzle on the grass outside the back door, he gives Jersey a look meant to suggest—though he knows this is goofy—that Jersey burned the food. "That was supper," he says.

Jersey sighs. "I'm not hungry, anyway, but I'll make you two peanut butter sandwiches, if you bring me the stuff."

"With honey," says Katherine.

Carter hesitates. He suspects that Jersey means to shame him, to suggest that he has taken away her appetite; still, he goes to the kitchen for the peanut butter and honey and bread and brings it back to the table.

"Just for Katherine," he says. "I ain't hungry neither."

"You sure?"

"Yes, I'm sure! You ain't the only one who can be not hungry," he says. Then takes the Bible from the table and carries it out to the front steps.

A dictionary is what he needs. This noon, while he drove through Fort Powden, he had the idea of stopping at Cheryl Lynn's house. He thought he might ask if Cheryl Lynn had a dictionary, so he could look up *Finis* and that *biblio* word, but when he turned down Cheryl Lynn's street, he saw that a little man stood on the steps to her porch, talking through the screen door.

Black trousers, white shirt, Bible in hand. Jehovah's Witness, Carter thought, and not wanting to interrupt any possible conversion of his sister or her children, he drove on by.

▪ ▪ ▪

Had he stopped, Carter would have discovered that the fellow on Cheryl Lynn's porch was, in fact, Finis Pruitt—whose delight in that day's persona did give him an air of kooky religiosity.

Had he stopped, Carter would have found that it was James who spoke to Finis. Cheryl Lynn was in the kitchen, talking on the telephone, trying to reassure M.B. Milhause—just then calling from Arizona—that Carter and Katherine would probably give M.B. a ring any day. Yes, yes, they had stopped at her place for chili before starting on their camping trip. They were probably just having so much fun they'd forgotten to call! But sure, sure, Cheryl Lynn would have them get in touch with M.B. the moment they came back from the woods!

37

"Anatomical Evidence for Evolution: Conservativism: Mammalian Ear Bones" reads the chapter heading of *The Human Evolution Coloring Book* Jersey holds open on the couch. Katherine sits in the rattan chair while, lying on her left side—her good side—head propped up by hand and crooked elbow, Jersey explains, as best she can, how the gill structures of the jawless hagfish of the Devonian era evolved over time into the human jaw and the tiny bones that make hearing possible.

So they are occupied when Carter Clay arrives home from his latest job-hunt. "I decided to fast," he announces. He hangs his key ring on a nail by the door, then gives it a flick, and watches it spin on the nail. "The idea come to me after me and Jersey skipped supper last night. Why not see if I can go without breakfast, too? And then I skipped lunch, and I asked myself, why not go whole hog? The whole forty days?" He steps over to the couch to look down at the coloring book, then continues, "Maybe we need an extra boost to bring Jesus closer to us, you know? Maybe this'll help with your walking, Jersey."

In much the way she would say to a large and frightening dog, "Nice puppy!" Jersey does her best to smile and nod and say, "Forty days!" Just before Carter Clay's return, however, she wrote the following page in her journal:

> Dear MB—I could probably tear this out and mail it to you but I doubt I will. And how could I mail it when Mr. Clay's holding us prisoner? But maybe you'll get it someday, anyway. Who knows? Maybe I'll die here. It's possible. I've got a pressure sore and Mr. Clay won't take me to the doctor. Maybe I'll be dead when you read this. I *do* have a fever. Can you believe that, M.B.?
>
> At first, after I found out you'd agreed to our going to Arizona, I wished you were dead, but now I don't have to because—you *are* dead. To me. I used to *want* to kill the guy who hit us. I used to think about it all the time—like I was hungry for it. But that was just an idea. I don't ever think about him/her anymore. At least *he* didn't make us into his prisoners. He didn't ask us to love him. We don't have to look at him or hear what he thinks. He's not arranging every day of our lives.
>
> I'm pretty sure I'm sick because of this sore. You'd be grossed out by it, no doubt—

She broke off her writing at the sound of the van pulling into the drive.

Now, Carter Clay watching, she taps the coloring book's illustrations with her finger, and says to Katherine, "In us, the gills are only present when we're embryos, see? Then, as the fetus develops, the first arch—see this?—it becomes, over here, in the newborn's ear, the malleus, the incus, and the tympanic ring?"

Katherine bends forward to look at the illustration more closely. "I'll un-er-stan this someday, *righ*?" she says. "I use to, righ?"

Jersey reaches out to pat her mother's hand. "Yup, and we'll go over it as many times as you like."

Carter Clay takes up the Bible from the picnic table and he says, "Pastor Bitner always told us, the way to shut up an evolution guy is to ask which came first, the chicken or the egg? You want to explain *that* to your mom, Jersey?"

Jersey smooths her hand back and forth across the slick cover of the coloring book that was a present from her parents. "My dad always told me only people who didn't understand evolution asked that question. Anyway, we're studying now."

With a thump, Carter Clay drops the Bible on top of the picnic table. The cabin vibrates as he crosses the room and snatches the ring of keys from the nail. "Oh, shit," he mutters. He hangs up the ring again. "I'm going to Neff's. Don't wait up for me."

After the back door slams, Katherine hurries to the kitchen. Through the window, there, she watches Carter Clay pass by the chicken coop at the rear of the property, then move off into the thicket of trees. Almost immediately he is erased by a great swag of foliage.

"Oh!" Katherine cries, and then, "There he is!" Still, his big frame grows smaller and smaller. The denim jacket loses color and finally disappears altogether.

"But he di-n't make din-ner!" Katherine protests. She returns to the main room, eyes wide with indignation.

Jersey nods, but her attention is elsewhere: on the van keys, which hang on the nail by the door.

"I'm *hung-ry,*" Katherine says and, like a bored adolescent, drops down on the couch. "I wish I ha' some pie."

Nothing too big, nothing likely to set off alarms—that is how Jersey thinks of the smile she conjures before she responds, "Well, there's no reason we can't have pie. Mr. Clay left you the keys and the van. We'll just drive into town. They have great pie in town."

Katherine frowns and casts a sideways glance down the couch to her daughter. "Where?"

"Great pie," Jersey repeats dully, but then her glance falls on the cover of coloring book, and the name of its author. Adrienne Zihlman. "At Zihlman's," Jersey says. "Strawberry. Chocolate. Lemon meringue. Open twenty-four hours a day. Every day." When Katherine wrinkles up her nose, as if she means to reject the idea, Jersey almost gives in to tears, but she holds on, she regroups, and then manages to ask, "What's your favorite kind of pie, Mom?"

"Rhu-bar."

"Zihlman's has excellent rhubarb pie."

"But Car-*er* shou' have coo-k din-*ner!*" Slowly, petulantly, Katherine unfolds herself from the couch and ambles across the room. Takes the keys from the nail. Inspects them as if learning their nature. "Okay. I be back," she says, and lifts a hand in farewell.

"But, Mom, you need me to show you how to get there."

Katherine bounces the keys in her hands. "Jus' *tell* me."

"It's—tricky. Zihlman's—they're sort of set back off the main road. I don't think you'd find it alone. Come on, Mom. You carry me out to the van and I'll give directions. I'd like some pie, too, you know. I'm hungry, too." She hesitates, then cannot resist adding, "I'm your daughter, you know."

Katherine nods wearily. "I know. I know."

▪ ▪ ▪

At the Boulders Campground, the children walk back and forth on the logs of the fireless campfire ring while, over by the tents, their parents sit on lawn chairs and drink beer. The children make a happy group. Two boys, two girls, their feet and ankles powdered a fine gray by the ash of the campfire ring. One of the girls has a pretty white cockatiel on her shoulder, and after a time, she and the others approach the office steps where Carter sits whistling. What's Carter doing there, the children want to know? What's that song?

Waiting for Neff Morgan to return, Carter says to the first question; and to the second, "A Whiter Shade of Pale."

"This is Mr. Clown," the children say of the orange-cheeked bird. One of them—a dusty little boy—leans familiarly into Carter.

Why couldn't Jersey like him like that?

"You got to make him think your finger's a branch," says the little boy, "if you want him to climb on," and the girl who seems to be the bird's master shows Carter how to take the bird on his index finger by lightly pressing the finger against the bird's breast.

Yea! say the children, and they chatter at Carter as if he is just perfectly normal and fine.

"How come it don't fly off?" Carter asks, but then Neff Morgan is driving into the campground, and Carter gives the bird back to the girl so that he can help unload the big packages of toilet paper and paper towels from the rear of the Boulders station wagon.

"Listen, Carter"—Neff looks a little twitchy, itchy—"I ran into Hammerholt, man, and he said some guy was asking about you at Kirby's. Some little religious guy?"

"What do you mean, religious?"

"I don't know. Ted thought the guy was maybe a Jehovah's Witness." As he sets one of the thirty-six-packs of toilet paper on the cabin porch, Neff calls a greeting to the circle of adults by the tents, then lowers his voice again. "I had the impression you weren't all that eager for visitors, so I told Ted I hadn't seen you. Was that the right thing to do?"

Neff waits eagerly for Carter's response to this question. Neff's own life is small. Made small by himself. Kept on a high and dusty shelf for safekeeping.

Which does not mean that Neff has no interest in the idea of more, bigger, wilder. Neff loves to hear the particulars of the lives of the campers who come through. For details of the lives of celebrities, he drives over to Marpool to buy the tabloids he would be embarrassed to buy in Fort Powden. Hence, when Carter only nods, yes, thanks, and does not explain who might be looking for him, Neff is disappointed. Still, he does not hesitate to offer complete privacy to his old friend when Carter asks if he might use the telephone in Neff's office. And, a few minutes later, when Carter comes into the kitchen to see if he can borrow Neff's station wagon for a quick run to Fort Powden, Neff says an immediate yes.

"I been having trouble with my van. I don't know that I can trust it all the way to town."

"No problem. But how's your—wife? And your new daughter? How's she doing with your parallel bars and all?"

"Jersey?" With a jerk of his head, Carter looks down the hall, as if he has just heard someone come in. A device like that—it hurts Neff even more than Carter's unwillingness to explain whether or not he is, indeed, laying low.

"—well, Jersey's stubborn, Neff. I made her those parallel bar things I told you about but she won't use them."

"So, you want her chair back?"

Carter shakes his head. "No. I put the matter in the hands of the Lord, Neff. But, hey, how about the key to your wagon?"

▪ ▪ ▪

Although it has been almost ten years since he last visited Brent's Rooms, Carter has been there often enough in dreams that there is no question in his mind of where to turn to find his father's room.

You still got that old Colt? That is all he will say. *Can I borrow that old Colt of yours?*

Is he afraid of his father still?

A little, but Duncan Clay—with a shiny red pimple of a nose, and false teeth that give his skinny skull a graveyard look—Duncan is far worse for wear than Carter imagined he would be.

Stooped, wattled, Duncan lifts a thumb to signal Carter inside. The little room smells stale, but it sits up in the trees and holds the soft green light of the end of the day, and, for a moment, Carter confuses that lovely glow with the reunion with his father, and reaches for his hand—

"So, what'd you call for?" Duncan steps away. His gaze fixed on a silent but active television set, he backs into a vinyl chair, puts his feet up on a hassock fan. "Better not be money 'cause I ain't got a nickel to lend."

Carter nods. He did not remember the room's being so small, but perhaps it is just more crowded—TV trays laden with bottles of pills and boxes of dried soup, jars of instant coffee and jelly and peanut butter. "I wondered if you still had that old Colt from the war?"

"I suppose it's the drugs." Duncan Clay stares at his son's shaved head. "That's what the hairdo's about, too, ain't it? You one of them neo-Nazis?"

Because Carter cannot bear the thought of having to repeat his story twice, he tries to be clear from the start. "There's a guy in Florida. He was a vet—that's what he told me. But that was a lie, I guess." He stares at a lamp shade that glows just beyond his father's shoulder. It features a rough but golden sea, a red sailing ship pitching on blue-green waters. *Why didn't you use my gun*? That was what his father shouted at his mother. Cheryl Lynn told Carter. She had been at the hospital, sitting with Betty, who was just then recovering from carbon monoxide poisoning. Cheryl Lynn had heard Duncan's shouts. *You wouldn't be whining around if you ever thought to use something that'd get the job done!*

It is hard for Carter to imagine telling Duncan about Katherine and Jersey, but he goes on, "In Florida—I got stabbed. They put me in the VA."

Duncan turns from the television. "Fucking VA? Your sister tell you I was in a couple years ago? They said I was going to die! I showed them!" Duncan laughs, then slowly rises from his chair. He makes his way to the closet against the far wall, and, there, he takes out a bottle. Four Roses. Over by the closet is a little sink, and a medicine cabinet where he fiddles about while Carter continues:

"The guy who wasn't really a vet—a bunch of people think he's the one who stabbed me. And another time—for sure—he pulled a gun on me. But I didn't know then"—Carter waves his hands in the air, dismissing the story's complications—"anyway, it looks like he followed me up here. I think he wants to kill me, Dad."

Duncan turns from the sink, and he holds out to Carter what, to judge by the residue in its bottom, would appear to be Duncan's toothbrush glass, or maybe the glass in which he soaks his dentures. The glass holds several inches of the Four Roses.

"Why'd he want to kill you?"

"I don't know. He wanted people to think he was a vet and some people found out he wasn't? But that was after the stabbing, so I don't know."

Duncan shakes his head. "You understand you disgust me, right?"

Carter nods. "I just want to borrow your gun. I ain't asking you to like me."

Duncan sets the cloudy glass of scotch on the TV tray beside his chair, then pours from his bottle into a coffee cup on the tray.

"This is mine," he says. "The glass's for you. What you waiting for? A goddamned toast?"

"You going to give me the gun?"

Duncan shrugs. "What do I care if you take the gun?"

"Fine, then," Carter says, and he picks up the glass and drinks the contents down.

■ ■ ■

Imagine Carter—maybe six ounces of alcohol circulating in his veins. Imagine him reaching under the seat of Neff's station wagon to tap his fingers against the Colt stashed there. Imagine Carter imagining himself fleeing to Canada, alone, in Neff's station wagon. Imagine Carter imagining himself inserting the Colt into his own mouth in woods so far off that no one would find him before he was more than clean bones. You can make what Carter imagines almost as real as this next scene, which does not feature Carter at all.

Jersey, safety-belted into the van's front passenger seat.

Her sweaty reschooling of Katherine in the basics of driving.

On one of Katherine's first attempts at starting the engine, the van—which should be in reverse—leaps forward and actually *bumps* against a corner of the cabin just before the engine dies.

"I can't do this!" Katherine wails, but Jersey's desire for escape and her now percolating terror of Carter Clay become her inspiration, and she produces grand laughter, and reassures Katherine with pats on the knee, and makes merry sound effects (chug a chug a choo choo). Repeats on a crescendo I-think-I-can-I-Think-I-Can-I-THINK-I-CAN-*I-THINK-I-CAN*.

■ ■ ■

Dusk has fallen by the time that they finally have the van turned around and are able to start down the road without Katherine killing the engine. The green of the trees and brush is almost swallowed by the deepening day. The van dies on a shift, and Jersey giggles and says, *I think I'm going to have the lemon meringue. Two pieces. Or maybe one piece of the lemon meringue and one piece of the rhubarb. I'm not sure I ever had rhubarb.*

Her mouth is dry, her face wet. She imagines Carter Clay in every boulder and bush and tree that lines the road.

And if he should be there—a very real possibility—could Jersey persuade Katherine to drive by him without stopping? And if Katherine would not drive by him, could Jersey turn the wheel so they drove *over* him?

The pair inch along the gravel road until, finally, they come to the stop sign—*Stop!* Jersey commands—and they turn left onto the asphalt road and, oh, they are actually moving past the Boulders Campground, and no one is stopping them; soon they will reach a highway that will carry them to one town or another, and surely, somehow she will find help. She will go on TV! Plead for help! HELP!

Maybe, then, M.B. would be shamed into coming through—

"I li-*ke* to dri'?" Katherine asks. She grips the steering wheel as if it is a snake she cannot release or it will bite her. Her face is contorted with tension, but Jersey answers her with a cheer: "Sure! And, really, you can go quite a bit faster. Really, you don't have to go this slow."

At this point, however, before Katherine can even begin to accelerate, the van begins to buck and lurch.

"No!" Jersey protests.

"Wha'?" Katherine removes her foot from the gas, her hands from the steering wheel—as if now she fears the way in which the engine rebels against her guidance.

On the side of the road, the van sputters to a stop.

"Okay, Mom," Jersey says, "Okay, there's a car coming, but don't worry. Just get started again. You were doing fine."

"No." Katherine clutches her fists to her chest. "I *don't* like dri-ing!"

"Mom!"

"Look!" Katherine cries. "Tha' car stopping! They take us to tow'!"

A white station wagon. Out of the driver's door lumbers Frankenstein's monster. Jason. Mr. Body Snatcher. One of the Living Dead. Carter Clay. Who yanks open Katherine's door and shouts, "What's going on?"

Katherine tilts away from Carter and toward Jersey. "May-be we run ou' a gas?"

Carter Clay shoves his big head into the van to shout at Jersey, "Why you want to ruin everything?"

"You smell like al-col," Katherine says. "An' you're shou'ing. I don't like shou'ing."

Carter Clay shouts, "Get out of the van, Katherine!" After she does so, he tries without success to start the engine, then steps around to the passenger side and yanks off Jersey's seatbelt and lifts her from the van. "Get in the station wagon, Katherine. We're going home."

"Bu' I ne'er go-t pie," Katherine whimpers, and Jersey—squashed against Carter Clay's chest, in a cloud of boozy breaths—Jersey says, "Mr. Clay, I know you mean to help—"

"*Shut up and shut up and shut up!*" he yells.

He climbs behind the wheel after he has set Jersey in the backseat of the wagon. She eases herself down on the vinyl upholstery, rests her cheek on her hand, stares into the pale back of the seat before her. In front, her mother is crying. Jersey herself does not begin to cry, however, until the wagon stops in the cabin's yard.

"Mr. Clay," she says when he throws open the wagon's rear door, "can I stay here, please?"

He does not answer, but grimly pulls her toward him—"Careful! Please!"

"Sorry," he mumbles, but after he has started toward the front door, he hesitates, then moves off around the cabin and toward the chicken coop.

"Car-er!" Katherine calls. She runs alongside the pair. "Where you going? Are you go-ing spang her? Don't spang her, Car-er! Please!"

He gives his head a rough shake. "You just stay put, Katherine. This is between her and me."

Jersey struggles against the coop's door and Carter Clay's chest while he removes the nail from the hasp. "You're not going to hurt me, are you?" she yelps. "I'm sick! Please, don't hurt me!"

"I ain't hurting you. I'm teaching you a lesson, is all. I ain't no monster."

. . .

So Carter replies, but even in his own ears his voice sounds strange, as if it has been shaken up like soda, and released in a fizzy spray.

"Car-er," Katherine cries from the yard. "Don't hur' her!"

"I'm not hurting her! Go in the house!"

He sets the girl on the floor, then backs off a step. "You got to learn. You'll stay here till you learn."

"Mom! If you let him do this, you aren't my mother anymore! Do you understand that? My mother would never let this happen to me!"

"You be quiet," Carter says. "What do you mean, talking like that to your mother?"

In the dark, he can feel the girl's stare. He can hear her jagged breath, and how she works to gain control over it before she says in a rattling, grief-stricken voice, "The accident changed her, and you're nuts if you think she's okay! Maybe it's because she's scared or something, but I can tell you, before she got hurt, my mom would have shot you for treating me like this!" Then she lays her head on her arms and begins to sob.

Carter feels grateful for the booze in his veins, and he makes a face for his own benefit—a kind of trial run of a monster's grimace. How's that? Mouth stretched wide and long? After he relaxes the face, he steps over to the nesting boxes, yanks M.B. Milhause's bottle of wine from its spot, and steps with it out into the yard.

Where, to his surprise, Katherine is waiting for him.

"Car-er," she begins, but Jersey starts up again:

"Mom! Help! Please, don't leave me here! Mom! Help me!"

With his free hand, Carter sets the nail back in the hasp on the coop's door. "Come on," he whispers to Katherine. "Let's get you set up with some tapes, and—I'll get her out when I come back from taking Neff his car. It's for her own good, right? You know what's good and bad, don't you?"

Katherine sighs. Her eyes look odd in the hollow light of the backyard—like olives or stones. Their suggestion of blindness frightens him a little, but she nods, yes.

"Well, all right! We got to help her to—*stay* here, so's she can learn to walk again! She's got to believe and be obedient before our prayers are going to work. Right?"

"Righ'."

"Right!"

▪ ▪ ▪

From her spot on the coop floor, Jersey can hear the opening and closing of the cabin's backdoor and, shortly thereafter, the sound of the station wagon starting up and driving away.

Could they have left her? The only noise is the wind, a rustle of leaves. But her mother would be inside surely.

(Yes. Tucked in her sleeping bag. Staring at the sheetrock ceiling overhead. Feeling scared, and grateful that the man—her husband—put the Walkman on her head; that she can listen to Old Testament stories and not Jersey's cries. Joshua and the battle of Jericho. Samson and Delilah. Joseph and his brothers.)

I must calm down. If I'm calm and call to her maybe she'll take me in. So Jersey thinks for a time. But then the panic in her rises again, and she calls *"Help, please, somebody!"* And then, *"I'm sorry, Mr. Clay! Mom! Help me, Mom!"*

▪ ▪ ▪

As soon as Carter is out of sight of the cabin, he pulls off on a little fork of road that leads back to someone else's cabin, and he unscrews the cap on M.B.'s bottle of wine. Because Neff Morgan never quite understood the way that Carter drank. Also, though Carter feels sure that Neff would laugh at Carter's drinking such swill, Carter does not want to risk the chance that Neff might expect Carter to share.

▪ ▪ ▪

When Jersey understands that no one means to rescue her—do the three cars that pass in the night simply choose not to stop, or do they truly not hear?—she stops crying and tries to remember her mother's story of the man on his way to the execution. Tries very hard to experience each blue moment in the coop. The sharp, peppery smell left behind by the chickens. The way the worn surface of the floorboards feels almost like cloth. The squares of blue light in the window. By paying attention to such things, it is possible—sometimes it is possible—to avoid giving all of her attention to her fear, and her body's demands, its feverish tingle, the pain that radiates up her spine and into her skull and her shoulders.

Breathe in deep. Expel the breath. She hears her mother's voice tell her: *In through the nose, out through the mouth*. Maybe it is not right to pretend that she and her mother lie on the twin beds in Jersey's room. Maybe she should not allow herself to go there, but it is so reassuring. Her mother, an arm's length away, trying to help Jersey fall asleep, offering Jersey some technique or other that she has read about. Mostly, of course, what Jersey likes is the presence of her mother, her voice taking Jersey through things called Progressive Muscle Relaxation or Mindfulness Meditation or whatever. *Breathe into your belly. Hold it. Now let all of the air come out until you've totally expelled every bit of breath, and you feel your stomach touch the back of your spine*. She can hear her mother's voice say this, and it helps. Just as the voice helps, later in the night, when Jersey must move her bowels:

The ones who survived the concentration camps were the ones who exercised as much control over their own lives as possible, her mother says, and so Jersey drags herself to one corner of the coop, hikes her skirt, and lowers her underpants—an action that does not keep her entirely clean, no, but makes her feel relatively sane.

It is important to feel sane in a night without sleep.

The first light of morning comes through the small high window on the eastern side of the chicken coop's door, but a good deal of time passes before the sunrise smokes the dusty glass and tints with gold the rotten wood of the frame.

Jersey has a plan for what she will do when Carter Clay comes to the coop. If he comes. She will not allow herself to think about the fact that he might not come, that both he and Katherine might be gone.

So: when he comes, she will hit him with a brick—heavy, whitened with old chicken shit—that someone perhaps used as the coop's doorstop, once upon a time.

Suppose she fails to kill him with the brick? Suppose she cannot bring herself to hit a person with a brick—

It is hard for her, even while planning a murder, and feeling feverish—it is hard to ignore the fact that she has begun to smell. Like a pack of hamburger forgotten at the back of the fridge.

She thinks about her father's favorite movie, *A Man Escaped*. The Resistance hero's patient destruction of the cell door with his spoon. Such a thing might be necessary if the brick fails. If Carter Clay does not return.

There are nails in the wooden nesting boxes, and though she could never pull a nail from its wooden bed, surely, with the brick, she could smash up one of the boards enough that, over time, she could shred the wood, work out a nail. Use that nail as some sort of tool of destruction.

In her father's movie, the enemy fed the prisoners of war. Maybe not much food, but even so, the food did keep up the prisoners' strength, and strength was needed for escape. Funny to think of feeding your enemy. Funny to think that human beings could make up rules for the way they killed each other. Actually held conventions to discuss such things.

She smashes the brick into the edge of one of the nesting boxes. Again. Again. But the effort of several blows leaves her weary. Which will not do. She must save her energy for dealing with Carter Clay. She must balance on a square of hip that has, perhaps, not born her weight too much.

Listen: some kind of woodpecker or flicker laughs in flight. A cardinal calls. *Pur-ty*. And there is something that sounds like the house finches that fly all over Seca. And blue jays.

Footsteps rustle through the brambles and grasses that grow behind the coop. Always an ominous sound, those rustles, unless transformed by visuals into the background noise of, say, a fall hike.

She takes a deep breath and raises herself onto an elbow and picks up the brick. Her heart beats hard. Ready, she thinks, but at the sound of the nail being removed from the latch, she cries out, "Don't come in, if that's Mr. Clay!" And then: "I want my mom!"

There is a sound of shoes shifting on the piece of old board that serves as the coop's front step; then Carter Clay speaks through the door, his voice strained and exhausted, his breath coming hard as if he has been running:

"Jersey. I'm going to let you out. But you got to promise something—hey, I meant to come right back last night! I didn't mean to leave you out here! It's just—I started talking to Neff and I fell asleep. No. That's not the truth. The truth is: I passed out. Because I was drinking. And I promise you—I make a solemn vow—I will never have another drink so long as—"

"Where's my mom? I need my mom! I'm sick!"

"I ain't finished! I was saying you got to promise not to pull anything like what *you* did, too, Jersey."

Carefully, Jersey lowers her hot cheek onto the pillow of her fingers. She stares at the nesting box before her. A piece of broom straw pokes out from between two of the box's boards, and part of the straw is broken and hanging at an angle.

"Jersey?"

The bit of straw swings back and forth in time with the girl's breath, in and out, and if there is any reason in the world for her speak to Carter Clay, she cannot think what it might be.

"Jersey?" Almost as if he does a dance, Carter Clay's boot heels rattle on the board outside the door. "You got to listen to this, okay? It's a prayer I found in the Bible, okay? '*Silver and gold, I have none; but what I have, that I give thee. In the name of Jesus Christ of Nazareth, arise and walk.*'"

Jersey sighs. Eyes fixed on her piece of straw, she makes an effort to bend a knee, wiggle her toes. "No good," she calls. "Unless the spell needs time to cook or something."

"Don't make jokes!"

"It's no joke. I'm sick. I need a doctor. Anyway, Mr. Clay, remember how, before he was crucified, Jesus prayed three times that God would make it so he wouldn't have to die? Even in the Bible—even if you're Jesus—you don't always get what you pray for."

When she hears the nail scrape in the hasp, and then the creak of the door, her fear disperses the other words that she needs to say. She tries to call them in from various locations, and sweep them up into a little pile—

"You ready to go inside now?" Carter Clay says.

"Can't I have my chair, though? Please? I can't lift myself without my chair—"

He draws a little closer. "Neff's going to pay me to do some work for him at the campground till I find something else. But getting back your chair—see, you have to *believe* God'll make you walk, Jersey. Otherwise, you won't be able to."

Jersey tries to consider this, but the thought slips away from her. It is a cartoon thought in a cartoon balloon. She closes her eyes. To herself, she mutters a begrudging, "I believe," but the words remind her of the wrong thing:

How, in the play *Peter Pan*, to save the life of Tinkerbell, Peter Pan begs the members of the audience to declare that they believe in fairies. Jersey went to *Peter Pan* with her mother and one of her mother's friends, and everyone in the audience seemed willing to say "I believe." Katherine and her friend—grown-up women with tears in their eyes—chanted right along.

But, of course, they did not believe in fairies. It simply felt good to them to say "I believe," to pretend to be little children for the two hours until the curtains closed and they all got clobbered by the daylight of the parking lot.

"I told Neff about my fasting idea," says Carter Clay. "He thought maybe you shouldn't do it, so I guess it'll just be me for now."

Jersey stares at a large, oddly familiar bulge in the pocket of Carter Clay's jacket. "Is—that a gun?"

Carter Clay glances down at the pocket as if embarrassed. "It's—yeah, a gun. 'Cause—well, Neff says somebody's been asking about us in town."

"Somebody's asking about us?" The girl starts to cry. "Oh, please, Mr. Clay. Suppose it's my uncle or my grandma! Can't we try to find out? Please? They could take me to a doctor—"

"It ain't—" He breaks off at the sound of voices. Yanks the gun from his pocket—ripping the jacket slightly in the process.

. . .

Out in the yard, the children he met at the campground the night before stand in a circle around Katherine. Katherine joins them when they begin to call up into the trees, "Mr. Clown! Mr. Clown, where are you?"

"HELP!"

Jersey. In that split second before he registers the madness in his movement, he has spun and pointed the Colt her way.

A nightmare moment. "I didn't mean it," he whispers. He starts to lower the gun, then stops because the girl's eyes are filled with not just terror, but careful watchfulness. She is studying him. His every move.

"Jersey," he says, and crouches low, "I only got this gun to protect us from *other* people. You got to be quiet, though. People might misunderstand. Or you might give us away, here."

She turns her face away and stares at the ceiling. "I'm sick," she says. "Maybe they would've helped me."

"Hey, *I'm* going to help you, Jersey." Carter reaches out the thumb of his free hand to wipe away the tear that runs from the girl's eye into the hair at her temple. It is true, her face is warm. Which worries him. And also relieves him a little; at least when she said she felt sick, she did not lie.

She pulls back from his touch and raises herself up on an elbow. She listens, then says a mournful, "They're leaving. They didn't hear me."

"God damn it, Jersey." Carter springs to his feet. He jams the gun back into his pocket. The weight of the thing continually surprises him, wearies him. "I guess—till you change your attitude," he declares, "you can just stay out here."

But—hey, he does not *want* to be a tyrant, and he makes himself stop before he goes out the door. He grabs hold of the parallel bars, tries to soften his voice. "I'll send Katherine out. To give you some breakfast. Maybe you and her could try and work on the bars. Or you and me can do it when I get home."

"Wait." Her voice is flat. She lowers herself to the floor, then says, not looking at him, but still sounding a little scary, "I heard what you said to my mom the other day, Mr. Clay. About Abraham and Isaac. Just remember, though: you don't have a right to sacrifice me. The point with Abraham was—he *loved* Isaac. You may want to love me, but you don't." She pauses to cough. "My parents loved me. I know the difference."

■ ■ ■

Maybe if she were not so sick and tired, she could pretend to go along with him. But she *is* sick and tired, and so she is glad to see him go. She has begun to suspect correctly that the hospital filmstrip that her grandmother found so grisly did not explain everything about the decubitus ulcer to its audience. The filmstrip did not detail how, if unchecked, the destruction of tissue begins to affect the patient's entire system. The body begins to fall to sepsis, to circulate toxins. The condition has stages beyond what is visible at the site of the sore. If the toxins are not stopped, they begin to damage the blood vessels, organs, and cells. If the damage continues, the cells become unable to extract sufficient oxygen from the hemoglobin in the blood. In time, all of the vital organs begin to fail. Such failure leads to the buildup of even more poisons in the body. The lining of the stomach and intestines are destroyed. Gastrointestinal bleeding follows and, eventually, death.

Better to know? Not to know?

After Carter Clay has been gone for a time, Jersey hears Katherine step out the backdoor of the cabin and into the yard, where she begins to call to the birds. *Tsk. Tsk.*

"Mom"—Jersey raises her voice, does her best to sound full of authority—"you've got to get me to a doctor, Mom."

Nothing, then a bleating, "I can-'*t*!"

"Come on, Mom!" She hesitates, then adds a stern, "You would have done it before, Mom."

"Don-'t talk!" Katherine's frightened face appears in the window by the coop door. "'Less you nee-d a go toi-let!"

"Mom! Please! At least sit with me!"

Katherine wags her head from side to side, but she remains at the window, staring in.

"Hey, Mom? Remember how you used to wonder what it would be like to be in prison or a concentration camp? You wondered how you would stand it, and you told me a story about a man who was going to be executed. You remember that? How it made you feel better?"

When Katherine neither nods nor shakes her head nor makes any sign that she has heard, Jersey goes on: "That's what I did last night. I mean, I told myself that story, and I tried to do what the man did, to pay attention to things. I used to do it at the hospital, too."

The face disappears from the window, but Jersey continues. She closes her eyes, and she says, "Sometimes, I do different stuff. I go through the Desert Museum, or the house in Seca. Like, I pretend I'm in the kitchen and I run my hands along the tile on the counter. Remember where the grout's missing by the sink? I see that. I take a banana out of the fruit bowl. A really nice banana. With the little freckles on it. This one has freckles. Because it's perfectly ripe, the top doesn't snap when I bend it back, but opens a little mouth—you know what I mean? It sort of dents the top of the fruit inside, but it's not serious or anything, and that's where I start peeling it." She shivers, and makes a little noise of revulsion. "There's a string thing on the fruit, and I have to pull that off, but then it's okay. I always hesitate a little before I bite into fruit. The first bite. It always feels like a little test, you know? Then my teeth slide into the banana. There aren't very many foods that feel quite like this—cheesecake? The banana feels a little like cheesecake, but of course it's—"

Katherine's return to the window is announced by her forehead's knock against the glass. "You don-*'t* have banana!" she says with some indignation. "You mak-*ing* it up!"

Jersey takes a breath. "That's okay, though, Mom." Again, she closes her eyes. She says, "Sometimes I go through the linen closet, too. I press my face into the towels. The old ones Grandma Ann gave us—the green ones we use for the pool, and the blue ones. They smell like wood. Sort of pulpy? The sheets—are different. More like dry grass."

"We're not *home*," Katherine says.

But Jersey shuts the door to the linen closet and steps out of the hall and into the living room. Her feet are bare, and the concrete floor is cool on their soles. She runs her fingers along the books in the bookcase on her left and this makes a small drumming sound. There is a book by the singer Bob Dylan and it has a cracked spine of some pink and glossy material, and long, long ago someone taped that crack. With cellophane tape. Three rows. Yellowed. The edges grown sharp with age. To the right of the books, a small brass frog in a short red jacket holds a tiny barbell over his head. Jersey used to play with that frog, and now she lifts it in her hand and feels its cool weight, and the spot on the back of the jacket where the enamel is chipped—

And what else? What else?

Agitated—how hot she feels!—she says, "We could sing, Mom." The hollow sound of her voice insists to her that she is in the chicken coop, but she forces herself back into the Seca living room, where the second bookshelf holds alphabetized record albums and CDs. Some of her father's record albums come from the fifties—how can her father be dead?—but it is her mother's albums from the sixties that have spines worn to an unreadable fuzz.

"Smokey Robinson?" Jersey whispers. It helps to whisper, to not jar the world too much. "'Ooo, Baby, Baby'?" She pulls the record from the bookcase while her mother sits behind her on the love seat and whispers a response that Jersey cannot hear—though it must certainly be yes.

You know what the trouble with you is? You're too much fun. So her mother used to say, laughing, when Jersey distracted her from her work.

Remove the album from its jacket. Set it on the turntable. Place the needle. After the first thrilling notes, there is a not unattractive skip that Jersey—who has heard only this scratched recording—thinks of as part of the song.

Jersey has always loved to sing—even now, feeling sick and in pain and a little crazy, she is glad to sing, glad, glad, and, after the first few lines, Katherine joins in:

"What a price to pa-ay-ay-ay-ay! I'm crying!"

Is it better to feel that she sings at home—even if that is only imagination—or to know that she sings in the chicken coop while her mother, the guard, sings outside?

Irrelevant, because the next words she says aloud—"How about 'Tracks of My Tears,' Mom?"—they let in too much light, and Katherine shouts, "Qui-*et*! Now!" and then she is gone, the backdoor to the cabin slamming.

Rain.

A sweet sound on the little coop's roof. If Jersey were well, and she and Katherine and Joe were all together, and the coop were clean and had a little braided rug on the floor and curtains—it would be a nice place to sit and read, wouldn't it?

Even if it were only her mother and herself—

Though Jersey supposes she would need someone to help her with her mother. And then she thinks, *really, it would be easier on my own*.

A guilty thought, that. The sort of thought, she supposes, that must have driven her grandmother to let Carter Clay take them away.

M.B., she hums. *Come in, M.B.*

At some point, she must have fallen asleep, for now the rain has stopped and Katherine is hoisting Jersey in her arms, carrying her to the cabin. "Here," Katherine says, and sets the girl down in the cubicle that houses the cabin's toilet.

"But, Mom," Jersey calls through the plywood door, "listen to me, Mom. I'm cold out there. I'm sick."

"Hur-ry! Hur-ry!"

"Mom"—as Katherine steps back into the cubicle, Jersey grabs Katherine's hand and presses it to her forehead.

"See?" she demands.

Katherine's eyes open wide. "You sick!" she says. "You—you' eyes loo' yellow, Jers'!"

Jersey was not aware of this fact but she nods since it has seemed to her that the skin on her hands has begun to look slightly orange.

"I tell Car-er," Katherine says, and she hoists Jersey and starts for the door.

“Mom. Just—put me on the couch now, and go out to the road and get somebody to take me to a doctor.”

Katherine’s eyes fill with tears. “No way! Car-er says there’s a ba-d guy ou’ there! And las’ nigh-t, Car-er was *mad*. At us! He ne’er came home! I was s’care!”

“Mom. At least you can keep me in here, can’t you? You can explain to Carter that I’m sick.”

Katherine hesitates, then carries Jersey to the little couch and sets her down. “Oh! I forgo’. I wa’ bring-ing you foo’!” In demonstration, she pats the lumpy pockets of Joe Alitz’s barn coat. “Here.” From one of the coat’s great pockets, she removes two woebegone slices of bread and an apple. From another, she extracts a peanut butter jar full of milk. From a third, comes the gun that Carter Clay pulled on Jersey that morning. Quite casually, Katherine sets the gun on the couch, its snout resting on one of the slices of bread.

Jersey glances away, uncertain that she wants her mother to know that she has seen the thing. Katherine, however, makes a point of picking the gun up and pointing it toward the ceiling. “Car-er gay me thi-s, but don’t wor-ry. Tha’”—she points to the safety mechanism—“you have to move tha’ to shoo’.”

She returns the gun to the coat pocket, then unscrews the lid of the peanut butter jar of milk. “Car-er says it’s to protec’ us. It was his da’s gun, in a war.” She widens her eyes for Jersey’s benefit. “He say it’a chop dow-n a tree!”

While Jersey drinks from the jar of milk, she wonders: *What would happen if she were to try to take that gun away from Katherine? Would Katherine hurt her?*

To Jersey, guns are so foreign and full of menace that she thinks of them as almost make-believe, something like witches or ghosts, monsters; this despite the fact that the former Katherine told Jersey more than once that a person—“a person” being Katherine’s nonthreatening way of saying Jersey—“a person” should always do her best to run away if a stranger tried to get her into his car, *especially if he threatened her with a gun*, because statistics showed that "a person" almost always ended up dead if forced into the car of a stranger with a gun.

Run away.

All that intimidating, well-thought-out advice that the old Katherine gave: no help at all for *this* Jersey in dealing with *this* stranger.

38

More rain falls in the late afternoon. The rain and general humidity have swollen the wood of the cabin, eliminated the gaps that gave the floors and walls the creaks and squeaks of drier weather; the acoustics of the place have changed now. The rooms feel almost padded, and this sensation adds to Katherine's panic.

Back and forth she circles, from feverish Jersey on the couch to the front window, again and again. Carter has told Katherine that there are bad men out there; people upon whom she might need to use the gun that knocks against her leg at every move—but Katherine can hardly think about the bad people since that moment when Jersey insisted Katherine look at the sore that Jersey says is making her sick.

A volcano. That is what Katherine thought of. A red hole surrounded by black, with black wisps coming off it, and something else Katherine knew she should not see: the glisten of bone.

Katherine begins to cry as soon as she hears the campground station wagon pull up in front of the cabin: Neff Morgan, driving Carter home. She pushes on the swollen front door several times before she finally forces it open.

"Car!" She rushes out into the rain and grabs at the front of his jacket as he turns from the wagon. "Jers' needs a do-tor! She *hot*! She has some-pin! You never! Like she sai'*d*."

From his window, Neff Morgan calls, "Anything wrong?"

"Is Jers'! She's sick!" Katherine cries, but Carter waves Neff Morgan off, *Go on, I'll take care of it*, as he starts to the cabin.

On Carter's heels, Katherine protests, "I tol' her we get a doc-er! I promise! And—I her moth-*er*, Car-er!"

He squeezes Katherine's hand as they step inside the cabin. "You're her mother, and I'm her father, now, too, ain't I? Ain't I the one fasting to try to make her walk? I gone forty-eight hours so far—"

"There." Katherine points to the little couch, where Jersey lies curled on her side, eyes closed. "I brough' her in."

Carter nods, though this independent act on the part of Katherine makes him a little nervous. Suppose she has undone whatever good came from last night's discipline? But, then, he could not be certain much good came of last night, anyway.

"So, hey, Jersey." He seats himself on one arm of the couch. "Your mom says you don't feel so good. The thing is"—he makes a production of rubbing his boots on the floor, letting the wood soak up a little of the wet—"what neither you understand—"

"Fee' her forehea'!" Katherine commands. "An' look a' her so-re! There' bone!"

"You awake, Jersey?" A queer smell comes off the girl and he does his best to ignore it. Perhaps she has soiled her pants? He gives a little whistle, a kind of *yoo-hoo*, then says, "I'm going to feel your forehead, Jersey. Your mom thinks you got a fever."

Though his fingers are cold from his lack of food and the cool drive from the campground, Carter knows, instantly, that the girl's forehead is much hotter than it was this morning. Hot like a glass of tea that you took without understanding that you could not hold it, and so it slid through your fingers, and crashed to the floor.

He starts when he realizes that the girl now considers him with open eyes.

"Wait," she says. Wanly, she begins to tug at the fabric of her skirt, drawing up the hem. "Look."

A wad of damp and dirty cloth sticks out from the elastic of her underpants, and he must fight down a shiver of nausea to ask, "So, you want us to clean you up? We can do that. No problem."

"No." She makes a movement with her head that is so small, it seems large. "I want you to see."

He takes a gulp of air, then glances up at Katherine, who gives him a decisive nod, yes.

"All right, then." Gingerly, he lowers the elastic waist of the briefs over the soiled cloths. Lifts the cloths.

In the war, Carter learned how to conceal from another soldier the fact the soldier's limb was now little more than rags, or that the larger part of the man's face lay on the ground by his head. That, however, was over twenty years ago. Today, Carter is not prepared for anything but some level of embarrassment; and so Jersey spies the horror that passes over his face, and she cries out in alarm one split second after he does.

The world convulses as Carter leaps to his feet. Berry-bright explosions fill his head, and he reels backward against the picnic table. Which shrieks as it advances across the bare floor.

"Jersey." He does not understand. The skin surrounding the gaping wound appears dark with gunpowder, as if she has been shot. "What happened?"

"What I told you." She has covered her face with her hands in order to hide from the look in his eyes. "A pressure sore."

"God." Carter kneels beside the couch. "God," he murmurs, "is there something more you want from me? You want me to offer her up without complaint? Well, I won't! I won't!"

With her right eye—her topside eye—Jersey can see the weeping Carter Clay. Opals form where her left eye presses into the fingers she now cups beneath her cheek. She gasps for the execution story. She reaches for it with a breath so jagged that Carter himself feels torn, but the execution story is not there today, and Jersey pleads, "Don't let me die, Mr. Clay."

"No." He adjusts her briefs and skirt over the sore. "I'm going to get Neff's wagon and take you to the hospital."

39

The BA is how many of the Fort Powden locals refer to Rex's Bowladrome. A modest alley. Cement block outside and in. Curiously, though the building was constructed to house the Bowladrome, the place has always looked makeshift, as if alley and grill and bar were cobbled on as afterthoughts. Fifteen years ago, at Cheryl Lynn Clay's suggestion, Rex and Maggie Fishbeck changed the interior paint from pale green to pale yellow, but otherwise the place looks the same as it has looked for the last thirty years.

On slow nights, like tonight, when no one feels like coming out in the rain, Cheryl Lynn can tend both the bar and the alley, and the Fishbecks can get off their feet and sit in booth #1 and maybe even do the books in between making up the occasional order at the grill.

Cheryl Lynn will never leave the bowling alley. It is by working at the alley that she has learned a large part of the good things she knows about how to be a mother and a friend. Also—as if it were a boy she fell in love with thirty years before—the alley's particular aroma has never entirely ceased to remind Cheryl Lynn of how happy she felt that first time she stepped inside the Bowladrome, and saw the dark and romantic bar juxtaposed so enticingly with the clean blond beauty of the lanes, and heard the crisp *pockpockpock* of pins falling while Freddy Scott sang "Hey,

Girl" on the jukebox. Cheryl Lynn received her first kiss in #2 of the grill's five booths. Bought her first package of cigarettes from the machine in the foyer. She feels tender toward the aging of the place, the way she feels toward Rex and Maggie, and tries to feel, now, toward her own face in the mirror over the bar.

How did she get so old? When was it her skin started to drape around her chin like that—like a spread hanging over the edge of a bed and pouching out a little above the spot where it hits the floor?

Undeniably, some of Cheryl Lynn's gloom this evening has to do with the fact that she received another call from M.B. Milhause earlier in the day.

"Any news?" M.B. asked. M.B. sounded perky until Cheryl Lynn said no. Then she began to cry. "I'm flying up there tonight!" she said. "Them disappearing like this—and did you know they never went to that clinic they were supposed to go to? You know about that? For Jersey? I called the clinic and checked and they never went there, Cheryl Lynn."

Cheryl Lynn, M.B. Milhause said. As if they were friends, or even relatives, and in this together.

Well?

Cheryl Lynn is happy to be distracted from the thought of Carter's mother-in-law arriving in Fort Powden by the entry into the alley of a little cowboy. "Ma'am," he says, and tips his hat her way as he approaches the bar.

You would recognize that cowboy but Cheryl Lynn does not. You would also notice that the costume he wears (ten-gallon hat, jeans, cowboy boots, snap-button shirt) is remarkably like the one that Carter Clay adopted for himself after the accident. Perhaps this is ironic, perhaps not, given how many boys once wanted to grow up to be cowboys.

Today, at any rate, Finis Pruitt would not be amused to discover that he wears the same brand and style of cowboy shirt that Carter Clay himself picked out for Sundays at Vineyard Christian. Finis Pruitt is in a foul mood. None of the people to whom Finis has spoken about Carter Clay have seen him—no, not in years!—but each has a little tale to share about that former citizen of Fort Powden.

Remember how he drove Neff's car into the mud at the fairgrounds? That was when he was in love with the Indian girl, and he brought her and her kids to town to meet his dad? Drunk as a skunk, and he's trying to fish these little kids out of the mud, and the girlfriend's lost her high heels, and then Carter falls in—

Oh, yes, that story made the people at the bar snort and laugh with their eyes all crinkled up and their gums exposed—so ugly Finis would have imitated them, then and there, if to do so would not have spoiled any chance of learning something useful.

Someone else offered: *Remember when he poured sugar in that Pattschull girl's gas tank*?

Which meant Finis had to listen to people debate just how rotten and despicable Becky Pattschull was for breaking Carter Clay's heart. Becky Pattschull—Finis could not believe it! A person named Becky Pattschull existed. And these people remembered that Clay had loved her twenty-five years before!

At the grocery store where he stopped on the pretext of buying a six-pack of beer, an old lady—her sweatshirt reading ONE LIFE'S ENOUGH IF YOU DO IT RIGHT—lowered her voice to say that she had taken the Clay kids in for a couple of weeks when they were little. *The dad was on a rip, and it was after one of the times the mom tried to kill herself*.

The geezer bagging Finis's beer shook his head. *A suicide spoils a house*, he said. *Even if it don't take, it spoils it*.

And the hag in the sweatshirt: *He was a good-looking kid. Of course, everybody wanted to fight him 'cause he was big, you know*?

Another woman, a customer eavesdropping from the candy rack, edged closer to the checkout to say, *He was a pretty good fella, 'cept for the booze. That was the war. Everybody says he was never the same after he came back*.

Oh, hell! said the bagger. *Two purple hearts, he got. At least. I'd say he did fine in the war*.

Finis produced a simpering smile as he took his bag and sent a mental telegram to the gathering: *Yes, yes, and he killed a little girl's daddy and crippled her and turned her clever mom into a ghoul*.

Needless to say, when Finis slides onto a stool at the bowling alley bar, it is not his intention to ask Cheryl Lynn Clay about her baby brother. Finis is ready to rock and roll. Give me the map, Jack. Let's go to the show, Joe.

The nervous jitter of cowboy heels against bar stool: Cheryl Lynn picks up on that. Slimy little dude, she has decided, and feels glad to see Neff Morgan come through the door, and shake the rain from his hair, and stomp the rain from his shoes, and flap the wings of his rain poncho. After M.B. Milhause's phone call, Cheryl Lynn thought of calling Neff, but was embarrassed at having to admit that, once again, she did not know where her own brother had got to.

"Hey, Neffer! I been thinking about you!"

Neff grins and calls out, "Well, all right! Hope it was something flattering." The rain poncho—transparent, blue—rustles and gives off a gassy chemical odor as Neff scoots himself up to the bar. "But listen"—he bends close, suddenly serious—"have you seen Carter lately?"

She shakes her head. "That's why I was going to call you—"

Neff interrupts her with a raised hand, but then he does not speak, just looks down at the bar top, where he begins to work his fingernail into a pair of initials carved into the wood. *A.D.*

"Neff?"

Still not looking up, Neff asks, "Did you know he took away the wheelchair from the little girl? 'Cause he's thinks his faith'll make her walk?"

A cold cloak of horror and shame settles on Cheryl Lynn's shoulders, moves on down her spine, then gets serious, and gives her a shake: *I told you so*. "Hey"—her voice breaks as she calls down the bar, "cowboy, you okay there?"

"Just fine, ma'am."

"Cheryl Lynn?" Neff says.

"Jesus, Neff." She fumbles for the pack of cigarettes in her shirt pocket. "I thought he'd gotten a little weird with that stuff—"

"I don't want you worrying, but I got him doing some odd jobs for me, and this afternoon—his van's out so I drove him back to the cabin—well, have you been out where they're staying?"

No.

"It's out by me. Just this little cabin I'm fixing over in bits and pieces. I said they could stay there a while, and—anyways, today I dropped him off and his wife comes running out. She says the girl's sick and needs a doctor, and Carter's, like, 'I'll take care of it, Neff.'" Neff goes back to digging at the initials in the bar, now with the help of a toothpick. Cheryl Lynn watches until the toothpick breaks, and he looks up again, and asks, "So what do you think, Cheryl Lynn?"

Cheryl Lynn stubs out her cigarette. She thinks of Jersey, possibly sick, and then of her own boys at home with their not entirely wonderful baby-sitter, a fifteen-year-old by the name of Marissa McPhale. She would like to call the boys, right now, and make sure they are okay, nobody is burning down the house or smoking cigarettes or watching dirty movies while Marissa gabs on the telephone; but, of course, Neff Morgan is waiting for her to answer. Lacking words of her own, she echoes his. "What do *you* think?"

"I think you should ask him what's up, Cheryl Lynn. He came by last night, drunk. He didn't talk much but he was upset about something. He slept on my porch. I don't know. I think he trusts you."

"Not enough to let me know where he's living! And that Katherine's mother—she's flying up here, Neff! Maybe even tonight—she's all flipped-out 'cause Carter was supposed to take Katherine and Jersey to Arizona so's Jersey could go to some doctor there, or something, and he never did."

"Geez, I got my own private sauna here," Neff says, and plucks the rain poncho away from his torso, lets it fall. "At least Carter can't run off, though. We hauled his van into Hansen's this morning, and he can't afford to get it fixed."

"Okay. Okay." Cheryl Lynn squeezes the rim of the bar. "You headed back to the campground?"

Neff nods.

"OK. Give me a minute. I'll see you out there. You can show me how to get to their place and—I'll run the wheelchair over and—"

Is that cowboy listening in? Cheryl Lynn gives the man a cool stare. To which he tips his hat before stepping away from the bar to consider the brightly lit song titles listed under the glass front of the jukebox.

▪ ▪ ▪

Finis Pruitt reaches Joe Alitz and Katherine Milhause's Scout just after Neff Morgan—real estate flyer tented over his head—climbs inside the Boulders station wagon.

To follow the white station wagon through Fort Powden's rainy streets is relatively easy. Once the wagon heads out of town, however, Finis feels more visible. He must hang back a bit, and, then, the downpour becomes more of a hindrance. Also, the outskirts of Fort Powden dip in and out; on several occasions, just when Finis believes the station wagon has left town for good, up comes another clump of houses, grocery store, gas station—all seeming like ghosts of themselves in the rainy night.

As he drives—to soothe himself, agitate himself—Finis recites:

> Is it thy will thy image should keep open
> My heavy eyelids to the weary night?
> Dost thou desire my slumbers should be broken,
> While shadows like to thee do mock my sight?
> Is it thy spirit that thou send'st from thee
> So far from home into my deeds to pry,
> To find out shames and idle hours in me,
> The scope and tenour of thy jealousy?

Would you expect Neff Morgan to signal as he reaches the campground? He does not signal, and, thus, Finis misses a chance to stop further back on the road, and, instead, must drive beyond the entrance.

There, on the narrow shoulder, with a curse, Finis flicks off the Scout's headlights and parks.

Ah, but what a sight greets him when he turns in his seat! For who should hurry out from the campground office but Carter

Clay himself? Instantly, Clay commandeers the campground station wagon, backs it up, and swings out of the lot, sizzling the gravel as he drives by Finis, now ducked low in the Scout.

> Oh, no! thy love, though much, is not so great:
> It is my love that keeps mine eye awake;
> Mine own true love that doth my rest defeat,
> To play the watchman ever for thy sake:
> For thee watch I whilst thou dost wake elsewhere,
> From me far off, with others all too near.

Steady, Finis tells himself as he rises in the seat. *Steady*.

Lights off, he follows that white wagon down the rainy road.

▪ ▪ ▪

Wet, shivering, teeth rattling as he drives up the sloppy road—Carter feels like a wet dog. *Let me die and let Jersey live*. His prayer. And, *Forgive me for not waiting for you to cure her, Lord, but I can't tell anymore if I haven't taken her to the doctor because of faith in you or fear of Finis*.

Then he wonders: if you do not eat, but drink alcohol, does that still count as fasting? He is beyond hunger now but does feel light-headed.

Also: Would it be best to lower the station wagon's backseat? Make the rear into a kind of bed for the girl? He plays this out in his head. How he will do it. How he will whip the seat down, then run through the rain to the cabin, scoop Jersey up and run her out to the station wagon. Settle her in back on a sleeping bag. So: lay out a sleeping bag before carrying her to the car. Then drive, oh, so gently, to town. But quickly, too. Quickly.

His chest should have doors to throw open so that he could show his heart to Jersey and Katherine. Then surely they would see that he has always meant well.

The cabin is a jack-o'-lantern shining in the rainy evening. It looks cozy from the road, but Carter knows it is bare inside. Bare and cold. A box full of misery, not a home at all. That is what he offered Jersey and Katherine. Was that the best he could do?

Put the wagon in park in front of the door. Make sure the thin red line is set at P.

He steps out into the rain, then opens one of the wagon's backdoors so he can feel around for the hinge that will release the backseat into the cargo position. There. His fingers catch on the thing while he lowers the seat. The skin tears, but he scarcely notices either the bleeding or the rain as he hurries toward the cabin and the stairs to the front door.

The door sticks. Carter yanks on it, hard. It is his enemy, that door. He yanks again, feeling—in his despair—that species of hot panic he felt in the months following his return from Vietnam, when his sleeve snagged on a piece of furniture or a nail sticking out of a piece of wood, and he feared he had caught a trip wire.

This sensation is replaced, however, by a chill pressure that fits itself against his backbone at the moment the door gives, and, surely, under the circumstances, it is not entirely preposterous for Carter to suppose that pressure might be the finger of God?

"That's a gun," says the voice behind him, and, of course, it belongs to Finis Pruitt, who whispers, when Carter turns his head ever so slightly to look over his shoulder, "Yup, it's me, man. Now, be cool and step inside."

"Katherine," Carter calls ahead of himself, but Finis Pruitt raps the gun against Carter's spine and says, "No! You—stay where you are, dear, and be quiet till I tell you to talk."

Katherine is seated at the picnic table, making herself a peanut butter and honey sandwich. The honey on top of the peanut butter is thick and beautiful, a golden lens that magnifies the swirls and bumps beneath it, but Katherine looks up from her sandwich, and she leans backward on her bench to peek at Finis Pruitt and ask, "Who you?"

Finis Pruitt flicks the rain from his cowboy hat. "Friend of the family."

From her own spot on the sofa, Jersey does not know what to make of the little man behind Carter. A man in a cowboy hat? Jersey has noticed a number of suspect things lately—lately being this time in which, now and then, the cabin walls slide up and down like the lid on her father's old wooden pencil box. Behind the walls' sliding pieces, sometimes she spies rows of grinning sheep. That can't be right, so is the man in the cowboy hat really real? Or a cutout delivered by her fever? So hot! So hot!

She takes a chance that the man is real—his face seems somewhat familiar; perhaps he has come with Carter Clay from the hospital—and she raises herself on her elbow to ask, "Can you help me?"

When the man laughs—a mocking, blue-jay laugh—she shuts her eyes against him. *Not real,* she tells herself, and, immediately, she finds that she is in a blizzard, lost, like one of those prairie girls she used to love to read about—or was it M.B.? Wasn't M.B. lost in a blizzard once, in Wyoming? Stuck in somebody's old Ford? But, no, this blizzard is merely the effect of Jersey's having closed her eyes, and she makes herself open them, and she finds herself still inside the damp and dusty cabin, and she says, her voice throwing off odd sparks in her ears, "I need to go to the hospital."

The elbow that she has been using to hold herself up begins to flop back and forth, like a jib sail, and she must lie down, then, go away, and so she does not see Finis Pruitt draw near to the couch or hear Carter Clay cry, "Don't hurt her!" or her mother's "Car-er! He go' your gu-*n*!"

"Your gun?" Finis Pruitt gives Carter a quick frisk. "Frisk, frisk, frisk!" he says, his voice both giddy and sullen, as if he might suddenly announce that this was all a joke, or shoot every one of them without further ado.

Using the Colt from Post Road as a pointer, Finis Pruitt signals for Carter to take a seat at the picnic table. "Clay, man," he says while Carter backs toward the bench, "man, the whole scene is so classic! And none of you can even appreciate it! Like, you're trying to hide from me so I won't tell these people the bad news, and, in the process, you do in the kid!"

"I was taking her to the hospital, R.E. Let me take her, and then—after, you can do what you want with me. But let me take her now. You can drive along. I can get you money—"

Finis Pruitt laughs. "So you take people to the hospital these days, hm?"

From the picnic table, Katherine protests, "It's no' funny! Jers's sick!"

Pruitt nods. "Most people wouldn't think it was funny. I know that. I can also see by looking at you that you wouldn't think it was funny if a man hit you and your family on the side of a road. Would you?"

"Qui-et," Katherine says.

"You might think a man who did that was even more of a bastard if—instead of helping you, or at least calling an ambulance—he just drove off?"

Katherine moans. "Qui-et."

Katherine does not want to listen to the words of the wicked man. She needs to concentrate on Carter's gun, which is *not* the gun in the little man's hand. She has remembered. *She* has Carter's gun. Carter's father's gun. It was in the pocket of Joe's barn coat, and now it lies in her lap, and makes her knees twitch.

"Am I right?" the little man asks. "I mean, assuming some timely first aid might have made your injuries less—grievous, and maybe even saved your husband's life? How long did you have to wait for somebody to come along? Twenty minutes? Thirty? Of course, you weren't in any condition to know, were you?"

Katherine reaches a hand across the table to Carter Clay. "Tha' what happen 'a us!" she cries.

The way Carter Clay holds his head in his big hands as he sits at the picnic table, you might think that head no longer belongs to him at all, it is a burden he cannot support. "Don't do this, R.E.," he murmurs. "Please."

In a blizzard, Jersey remembers, what you must do is hold onto the rope that goes between the chicken coop and the house. That is how M.B. survived the blizzard. Or was it Laura Ingalls Wilder? Or some other girl who went out to collect the eggs and was almost lost in the storm? At any rate, there is a rope. There must be a rope to guide you back, and you must not drop hold of it. If you keep hold of the rope and keep moving forward, you will eventually be safe—

But when Jersey takes a step, she finds there is no ground beneath her, and she tumbles forward, and the air fills with so much electricity that it crackles and rips with shocks.

"Do'-n't hur' Jerse!" That is her mother's shriek, and then someone else shouts, *"Open your eyes, little girl!"*

She opens her eyes.

There are legs in front of her. Blue jeans. The delirious back and forth and up and down of woven cloth. "What?" she says to the cold that presses against her temple, and she turns toward it, and her eyes travel up to the man above her who is saying—his voice a kind of brass gong—"Your friend Mr. Clay has got something to tell you." When the man sweeps his cowboy hat toward Carter Clay, he leaves beautiful ribbons in the air. Turquoise. Pink. Yellow. He is one big Fourth of July sparkler.

There is silence. Then the voice of Carter Clay, very small, saying, "Please, don't hurt her, R.E. Jersey. Katherine. I'm the one who hit you guys. The driver."

The gun barrel at Jersey's temple shakes. It skates off into her hair, snags there, then is pulled back to her temple, and the voice at the other end of it says, "That's a start, Clay, but you left out the part about leaving them to die!"

Carter Clay's big shoulders bob up and down. He rides in a tiny boat on a choppy sea. He wants to explain that things are so much more complicated than what R.E. says, and yet—what R.E. says is true.

"You're quite an actor, aren't you, Clay? Playing the good Samaritan when you're really the thief. Stand up and take a bow, man."

Carter Clay shudders. "Please, R.E."

Finis Pruitt cocks the gun.

From a very great distance, Jersey watches Carter Clay stand. And her mother cry. The strange man says, "Don't die on me, little girl. I need to know you understand your stepdad here's the one who hit you and left you to die. You got that?"

She does her best to nod; then asks, "Can I go to the hospital now?"

"No!" The little man moves over to the picnic table, where he jabs Katherine with the gun. "Do *you* hear what I'm saying? Do you get it? Clay's the one who hit you!"

Katherine shakes her head. "Tha's not true," she whispers, but Carter whispers back, "It is. I wanted to tell you. I was just scared you wouldn't let me help if you knew."

"Oh, Clay." The little man moves back toward Jersey. "Clay, when these people were all mangled up on the road and maybe the dad still had a chance to live—you think they were in any shape to turn down your help?"

"Not then, R.E., but *after*—if they'd known, they wouldn't have been able to forgive me."

▪ ▪ ▪

"Oh, after." With a hey, and a hi, and a ho, Finis dances a jig in front of the girl on the couch. A jig. He does not recall ever learning to dance a jig, but he feels the need to do *something* to demonstrate that he receives a transfer of power from Clay—though he is disappointed that Clay has such a very little to offer: not even an audience.

"So"—after a neat pivot, Finis spins himself back toward Clay—"tell them how we drove away and left them there!"

"We did that," Clay whispers.

"Blood all over the place!" Finis bends at the waist. "Oh, sick! And you"—he points to the woman, now staring at him wide-eyed, but weeping—"your fucking head all smashed!"

"Go 'way!" she screams. "Go 'way!"

"Me?" Finis hoots in return. "Are you crazy? Doesn't anybody get this?" Gun trained on Carter Clay, he moves to the closer of the cabin's two front windows, and sees that his guess is correct: that blossoming of the cabin's walls and ceilings means a car approaches the house.

"A better audience," he murmurs. "Your sister, Clay. And the campground guy. God bless their souls." He laughs. "Let them in, Clay, but don't do anything goofy, you dig?"

▪ ▪ ▪

When Finis Pruitt starts toward the back of the cabin once more, he does not give much thought to dull Katherine Milhause as he passes by the picnic table. Katherine, however, watches Finis with all the power that she possesses. Like a driver who waits at a busy intersection until she knows exactly how much time she requires to cross, Katherine has readied herself for this moment, and when she lifts Duncan Clay's gun from her lap, she does so with a sure sense that she cannot miss.

▪ ▪ ▪

Who screams at the firing of the gun?

Cheryl Lynn. Who drops the wheelchair she was removing from the trunk of her car, and now runs through the rain to the cabin.

Where Finis Pruitt chokes on blood and bits of shattered bone.

Carter and Katherine stare as Finis Pruitt crashes into the length of aluminum chimney that makes a crooked connection between woodstove and ceiling, and the chimney collapses, and Pruitt crashes to the floor.

Unmediated surprise: the look on his face. Perhaps the noises he makes contain a message; if so, it is rendered nonsense by the swift spin of death and a mouthful of blood.

"Carter!" Cheryl Lynn is yanking on the door. "Are you okay?"

"I di-n't shoo' *Car-er!*" Katherine protests. She scrambles out from the picnic table and waves the gun toward Finis Pruitt as Cheryl Lynn and Neff Morgan step inside and look about themselves. "I sho' the ba-d guy! But, Car-er"—Katherine points at Carter, who snivels into his hands as he makes his way toward Jersey on the couch—"Car-er's a bad guy, too!"

Cheryl Lynn is too distressed by the scene to recognize the man on the floor as the cowboy from the bowling alley bar. It is all that she can do not to gag as she steps around the dark mess that spreads out from the body and across the pine boards, but Neff Morgan prudently takes the gun from Katherine, and asks, "Who is he?"

Katherine shakes her head. "He tole us Car-er hi' us! It's true! Car-er hi' us! An' lef' us a die." She rushes at Carter then, and begins to pummel him on the back. "Car'er's the one!"

"It's true," Carter keens from beneath Katherine's rain of blows, "but, right now, Jersey needs a doctor, Cheryl Lynn."

Cheryl Lynn's teeth chatter as she steps to the sofa. Her brother looks up at her from where he kneels beside the girl. "See what I done," he moans. "I'm a monster, ain't I?"

Cheryl Lynn gasps at the sight of the child, the rotting smell. That neck under which Cheryl Lynn immediately slips her arm—Cheryl Lynn wants to cry out at that skinny neck, its heat, but she says only, "We're going to get you fixed up, honey. I got your chair for when you want it, and nobody'll ever take it away again, okay? Right now, though, I'm going to get you to a doctor, okay? 'Cause I know you're not feeling good."

Whether Jersey merely stirs or actually nods, Cheryl Lynn is not certain, but as she rises with the girl in her arms, Cheryl Lynn says, "Did you see her nod, Carter? She knows we're going to get her help. Did you see?"

When Carter does not respond, Katherine leaves off cuffing Carter's back to say a passionate, "*I* saw."

"Me, too," says Neff Morgan, and steps briskly to the front of the cabin to hold open the screen door for Cheryl Lynn. "She knows we're getting her help, Carter."

"I ha' a shoo' him," Katherine says as she follows the others to the door. "He wa' ba-d."

"You should've shot me, too," Carter says, but Cheryl Lynn hushes him, and, Jersey in her arms, she and Neff Morgan and Katherine move out into the rain, and toward the station wagon—still running in anticipation of the trip to the hospital.

"I'll just leave my car for now," Cheryl Lynn tells Neff Morgan. "I can ride back here with Jersey, and Katherine and Carter can ride up front with you."

Neff Morgan nods. "Come on, Carter," he calls toward the open door of the cabin.

All three adults turn to watch for Carter to come to the door. They imagine him there even before he arrives: a silhouette outlined by the cabin's light. They do not anticipate, however, that the silhouette will raise a hand and say, "You go on," then pull the door closed.

▪ ▪ ▪

Carter! Come out of there! Come on! What're you doing?

Crouching beside the body on the floor. Fishing Finis Pruitt's gun from that sad, rank puddle.

R.E.

"Carter!" It is Cheryl Lynn who calls from under the front window.

"Cheryl Lynn," he calls back, "take Jersey to the hospital and go."

▪ ▪ ▪

"Don't you dare hurt yourself!" Cheryl Lynn yells. She gives a little jounce to the limp bundle in her arms. "Jersey." She presses her face close to Jersey's face. She pleads, "Help me, Jersey! Katherine! Tell him not to hurt himself!"

And, voice warbling, Katherine calls, "Car-er! Do-n't hur' yourself! Come ou'!" and Neff Morgan, at the back of the house, "Don't do something crazy, man."

Really, Carter does not want to talk anymore, but he sits back on his haunches, and he looks away from Pruitt, and wets his lips, and calls, "You forgive me, Jersey?"

Jersey? Jersey is lost in the blizzard, her ears so full of snow and high winds that she cannot hear even the shrieks of Cheryl Lynn: "He's going to shoot himself, Jersey! Wake up! Please!" Cheryl Lynn kicks at the cabin door. "She can't hear you, Carter! It's not that she's saying no! It's just she's—asleep!"

"Carter? It was an accident, right?" Neff Morgan calls. "And you believe God forgives all your sins, right?"

Carter looks down at Finis Pruitt, and he nods. That's right. God forgives him. God *has* to forgive him. Like what Jersey told him Katherine had said years before: If there is a God, he *has* to forgive you because He knows He didn't make you or the world quite right.

The cabin's one closet sits off the kitchen, and that is where Carter takes himself, to hide and contain the mess. His foot rustles against a plastic garbage bag when he steps inside, but he kicks the bag further back into the closet as he closes the door, and then there is only the dark, pure dark, and the dark extends out from him, infinite black emptiness, as if there are no walls eight inches or so to either side of him, nothing contains him, he can join that black nothing, pierce the balloon of his brain, let out dark into dark.

He is quite right in believing his mother felt something similar when she set the Colt in her mouth in 1970. The same juddering passed through her. The same taste of saliva reacting to metal. But the gun in Carter's mouth is not the gun Betty Clay used. The gun that Betty Clay used is the one that Neff Morgan now lifts to break the glass at the cabin's back door, while Carter employs the gun that he took away from Finis Pruitt back on Post Road and, later, returned.

Epilogue

There is a world in which, after the dust settles from the above sequence of events, you see a young blond-haired woman—fifteen years old? sixteen?—hard to say as you only see her from behind. At any rate, you see her walking up the stairs of a building that you recognize as Earth Sciences at Arizona University. The young woman has a slight hitch to her step, but this does not prevent her from topping the stairs and heading into the building, proceeding down a dark hall that you also remember: yes, those fish-scale glass doors that transmit a bit of milky light from the offices they conceal. The young woman stops at one of the doors. Knocks. A female voice within says, "Come in," and the young woman opens the door. In the now-exposed office, a woman—hair drawn into a graying bun at the nape of her neck—sits bent over a desk. She turns, however, and she smiles and she is Professor Katherine Milhause, who stands to say, "Oh, honey! It's you!"

. . .

That is not this world. In this world, two women—one middle-aged, one a generation older—sit in molded plastic chairs with metal legs and stare at a hospital bed that holds a girl who is decidedly frail, adolescent.

Katherine. M.B. Jersey.

Sometimes, Cheryl Lynn Clay and Neff Morgan come to sit in the molded plastic chairs, too, and, once, Cheryl Lynn was allowed to bring James and Alfred. Alfred carried a gift for Jersey: a sugar-fogged plastic bag that contained all of the marshmallows he could find in a box of Lucky Charms.

On Jersey's fourth day in the hospital—another wet day—while Jersey is transferred to a gurney and wheeled to a debridement session, Cheryl Lynn and Neff Morgan and the boys drive through the rain to Hendrick's Mortuary.

Many townspeople show up at the mustard-yellow mansion that houses the mortuary. Though most have come to pay honest respects, a few are curiosity seekers, and as such they are disappointed by the simple service—until Duncan Clay arrives, swearing, incoherent, pants unzipped. It is Neff Morgan and Rex Fishbeck who escort Duncan to the wet curbing in front of the funeral parlor and keep him there while he babbles on about Carter and Betty and how he'd like to get a dog—just a little one—but Brent's Rooms don't allow pets.

Eventually—with the rain still coming down—the mourners begin to emerge from the mortuary, and Duncan looks up to ask, "Is it over now?" Then Rex and Maggie escort him to Brent's Rooms, and Cheryl Lynn and the others drive to the cemetery.

After the debridement session, an aide wheels Jersey back to her room. "Your mom and grandma went to the cafeteria," calls a passing nurse. "They'll be back in a bit."

Jersey nods. She is exhausted from the debridement session and dull with pain medication. After the aide finally leaves, Jersey stares out the window at the rain. Her room in little Fort Powden General—ground floor, sliding windows, print curtains—it reminds her a bit of Katherine's room at Fair Oaks, but the green light that comes through the rain and the trees outside is like the light that came through the windows of the cabin.

Which was a beautiful light, despite the rest.

■ ■ ■

"I need to get home as soon as I can," Jersey tells the doctor when she comes by that evening, and the doctor knows enough of

Jersey's story to say, sure, and she can help make arrangements with the airlines, and so on. "But Jersey"—the doctor strokes Jersey's hair from her forehead in the loveliest, loveliest way—"you have to understand, Jersey: even there, you're going to need at least six weeks more in the hospital."

M.B., Katherine, and Cheryl Lynn are in the room, and, impulsively, Cheryl Lynn asks, "So why not stay in Fort Powden till you're out for good, Jersey?" and M.B., picking dead blooms off a cyclamen she brought the girl, looks up to pipe, "Or go back to Florida? We got good hospitals in Florida."

Jersey does not scream at M.B., but the look on her face makes M.B. say an immediate, "Okay, okay, we're going to Arizona," and Cheryl Lynn adds, "Right, 'cause she wants to get home."

Cheryl Lynn is all for promoting harmony between M.B. and Jersey and Katherine, and when M.B. steps out into the hall with the doctor, Cheryl Lynn draws close to Jersey's bed to whisper, "Your grandma—she cried and cried when she found out you were sick and Carter had you and your mom in that awful place. She feels so bad about things."

In the corner of the room, Katherine looks up from reading a tattered lady's magazine she found somewhere or other. "I sor-ry, too, Jers," she says.

"I know, Mom." Jersey smiles at Cheryl Lynn. She understands that part of the reason that Cheryl Lynn wants to promote peace among M.B. and Katherine and Jersey is that Cheryl Lynn also wants Jersey to forgive her brother.

"I gla' we go-ing Ar-zona," Katherine says. She comes up on the side of the bed opposite Cheryl Lynn, and she pats Jersey's foot. "And you ge' we-ll there, o-kay?"

Jersey squeezes Katherine's hand. Then she squeezes Cheryl Lynn's hand, too, because Cheryl Lynn has just lost her brother, after all, and surely the way Cheryl Lynn felt about that little brother is a bit like the way that Jersey herself felt about the pre-accident Katherine: for so long, it seemed to Jersey as if the pre-accident Katherine were inside, waiting to get out. Now she understands that *this* is the mom she has, and even if this mom does keep getting better, she will never actually be the old mom again. She will be this mom, getting a little better.

You can hope, but not too much.

▪ ▪ ▪

On the day that Carter Clay is buried, the body of Finis Pruitt remains in the hospital morgue, unidentified. Perhaps Finis Pruitt would have been happy to know that he remained anonymous after death as well as before. For a time, the police thought—on the basis of credit cards found on his body—that they dealt with a man named either Alitz or Milhause. This error, however, was cleared up soon enough.

Once upon a time, there was a person who would have been sad to know that Finis Pruitt—in the guise of R.E.—was dead, but that person was Carter Clay. No one at all will mourn Finis Pruitt. In the years that she will live beyond Finis's death, his mother—never knowing what became of her son—will occasionally point to his photo among the many on her walls. She will tell visitors that she cannot remember the name of the profession of that brainy, long-absent boy, but will readily agree to sibilant suggestions ranging from statistician to therapist, when what she really seeks is the word Finis himself once gave to her, and pronounced with a parody of swishy delight: *thespian*.

Mother, I want to be a thespian!

▪ ▪ ▪

The paradox of Finis's ambition to play the role of Everyman: he believed himself superior to every audience.

And what is the difference between ambition and hope?

How much hope does a person need to stay in his own skin in the world? What's the deadline for its arrival when you are suffering?

If you agree that Carter Clay *deserved* to suffer for his actions, could he hope to be redeemed by such suffering? Especially when—in his suffering—he made Jersey's undeserved suffering so much greater. Does her suffering, then, cancel out his possible redemption? And does Jersey, as an innocent party, earn something beyond redemption?

What would that be? Glory?

Jersey certainly does not think so. But then Jersey does not think in these terms at all.

The truth is, Jersey likes Carter Clay *more* once she knows that he was the driver. Which is not to say she would have welcomed him into her life had she known before. But it is as she told Carter once; at a distance, the driver is bearable, and, as it turns out, even pitiable. Also—she feels grateful that she now knows how she and her mother fit into Carter Clay's story, and how he fit into theirs.

It is true, any person who looks at Jersey might guess that she has a more complicated story than average simply by virtue of the fact that Jersey rides while most of us walk. Jersey, however, is and will remain a private person. Unlike M.B., with her story of the Ferris wheel, Jersey will tell the story of Carter Clay to only a few people (a college roommate, two lovers, her own children when they are grown). After all, she tells herself, there are many events and thoughts that have shaped her life, and she has no intention of letting Carter Clay be the defining one.

Enough that he continues to take an occasional role in her dreams. Enough that he now exists in that world of possible ghosts that can be attached to a laugh in a hallway or a whistle outside a window that makes her raise her head, and listen for the tune.